ALSO BY CHRIS GLATTE

Tark's Ticks Series

Tark's Ticks

Valor's Ghost

Gauntlet

Valor Bound

Dark Valley

War Point

A Time to Serve Series

A Time to Serve

The Gathering Storm

The Scars of Battle

164th Regiment Series

The Long Patrol

Bloody Bougainville

Bleeding the Sun

Operation Cakewalk (Novella)

Standalone Novel

Across the Channel

To find out more about Chris Glatte and his books, visit

severnriverbooks.com/authors/chris-glatte

TARK'S TICKS VALOR BOUND

A WWII NOVEL

CHRIS GLATTE

SEVERN RIVER

PUBLISHING

Severn River Publishing
www.SevernRiverBooks.com

ISBN: 978-1-64875-566-8 (Paperback)

1

Staff Sergeant Tarkington opened his eyes after a solid eight hours of sleep and for the first time in a long time, felt normal. The fan directly overhead shifted the air just enough to create a slight breeze. He stretched his arms and legs, then threw off the thin layer of bedding. He marveled at the day's warmth and wondered if he'd slept through the morning and into the afternoon, then remembered that October in Australia was mid-spring. The days were warming steadily here in the northeastern city of Brisbane.

Out of habit, he pulled his olive drab T-shirt up and poked and prodded the ugly, puckered scar on his belly. He felt the familiar tingle—not so much pain, but more of an annoying reminder. He swung his bare feet to the wood floor, the coolness seeping into his arches. He stretched his neck, massaging the knots.

An outside breeze shifted the feathery curtains, blowing them inward. He stood and walked to the window, pulling them aside and gazing out over the perfectly manicured lawn and garden. He marveled at the place. For months he'd been in a hospital full of soldiers, sailors, and marines. Australians and Americans mostly, but there were also Filipinos and even a few Africans.

For much of that time, he'd been in and out of delirium as infection gripped his body. He remembered little—only fleeting visions of concerned doctors and nurses hovering over him like white apparitions. He learned later that they'd decided to reopen his wound to find whatever part of his gut was causing the infection, but his fever broke on the scheduled surgery day and he'd improved every day since. His squad-mates had never left his side. He remembered seeing them alongside the doctors and nurses, probably driving them crazy.

Now, two months later, there was no sign of infection. He felt better than he had in a long time. Attributed—no doubt—to his stalwart regimen of physical exercise. At first, he'd been as weak as a kitten and needed help every step of the way. Nurse Gallup stayed with him, helping him stand, then walk, and finally run. He'd taken every opportunity to get himself back into fighting shape as quickly as possible.

There was a light knock on the door. He turned from the window, knowing who it would be. "Come in, Sergeant Gallup."

The door opened and he smelled the faint hint of her perfume, fresh and alive. Her thick brown hair was pinned up tightly and her eyes sparkled behind her thick lashes. "Good morning, Staff Sergeant Tarkington," she smiled, showing off slightly crooked teeth. Tarkington thought the gap between her two front teeth was the most alluring part of her. She wasn't as drop-dead beautiful as many other women he'd seen on this island. She was sturdily built and nearly as tall as he was, but her smile, disposition, and complete commitment to his welfare made her astoundingly beautiful in his eyes. He smiled back at her, "Good morning, Sergeant Gallup. Any word from my men?" he asked hopefully.

She shook her head, the smile fading from her full lips. Tarkington hadn't seen or heard from them in weeks and worried they'd been split up and sent to other units. It made him physically ill to think of it, but every attempt to find their whereabouts was met with a brick wall of silence. It was almost as if they'd never existed.

Though he stood in his skivvies and T-shirt, he didn't cover up. She'd seen every bit of him by now, and his relationship with her was as a patient and a nurse. She'd made it clear from the start that she had a "beau," as she called him. There'd be no romance between them; she was merely doing her job and the fact that they got along well meant nothing beyond that.

Tarkington had taken that at face value, concentrating on using her skills to advance his health, but he noticed as the days and weeks passed that she put more effort into her appearance. It was subtle and sometimes he thought he might be imagining it, but when she'd first been helping him, she didn't wear makeup or perfume.

She handed him two letters, "More mail for you. One's from the States."

He took the two letters eagerly, reading the handwritten return address first, "My kid brother, Robert." His grin faded when he read the more official-looking piece, written on a typewriter. "And something from Colonel Bradshaw's office?"

"Colonel Bradshaw? I've heard of him. He works for MacArthur, I think. What's he want with you?"

He shrugged and threw the official letter onto the bed, then tore into the letter from his brother. Since arriving in Brisbane, there'd been a smattering of mail from him. The army had sent word to his family that he was alive and well after being rescued from the Japanese-held Philippines, but didn't give them specifics. Tarkington wrote them when he'd recovered enough to do so, telling them he'd been wounded but was healing and feeling better every day. He doubted his family had received that letter yet, or if they ever would. Sending mail from across the world in peacetime took a long time and the war only compounded the problem.

The first letter he'd gotten from Robert, written about the time Bataan and Corregidor fell, caught up to him in Brisbane months later. Tarkington angered when he read his brother had dropped out of college and joined the marines of all things. His reasoning being he'd be assured of fighting the Japanese and avenge his killed or captured brother.

Tarkington had immediately written a long letter urging him to reconsider—urging him to stay out of the war at any cost, to stay in school and become something he himself would never have the chance to become. He'd reread what he'd written, then crumpled the six-page scrawl in his fist, soaking it with the sweat of frustration.

He read the date and shook his head, "This one was sent before he knew I was alive." He skimmed it quickly, shaking his head.

"I take it he's still bound for the marines?" Tarkington nodded and pursed his lips. She touched his arm, "He'll be okay, Tark. The marines are the best."

He swallowed the bitter acid rising in his throat, "He's probably already halfway through training." He shrugged, "Maybe already deployed."

"Any word from your parents? They must know where he's headed. Perhaps he'll get stationed here. Wouldn't that be wonderful?"

Anger flashed in his eyes and she pulled back slightly. She'd seen it before, like some evil demon lived in the darkest depths of his soul and only came out when provoked. It disappeared as quickly as it emerged and he shook his head, "If he's here, he'll be going into . . ." His voice broke. "He'll be in the thick of things."

"You don't know that. Maybe he'll get a staff job, or something in supply."

He shook his head, the bright airy room suddenly losing its warmth. "He'll volunteer for combat duty. He said it himself, he wants to avenge me."

She touched his arm and he felt the heat of her hand on his bare skin. "Now that he knows you're alive and well, he'll reconsider. Have you written him? Told him how you feel?"

He bit his lower lip. "I wrote him," he said, nodding. "Laid it all out for him. Six pages of pleading drivel."

"Well, good. He'll . . ."

He pulled away from her touch, turning back toward the window, interrupting her, "I tore it up and threw it away." He leaned against the windowsill, the sinewy muscles of his back snaking beneath his shirt as he gripped the sill. "I can't tell him how to live his life, dammit. He's a grown man. Besides, he's stubborn as hell. Tell him to do one thing and he'll do the other just out of spite." His voice went low and he rubbed his neck, "God, I'd give anything to see him. Warn him." He glanced at Sergeant Gallup who tilted her head and he continued, "Tell him not to be a hero. Don't stick your neck out."

A long silence followed, but she was used to that. It unsettled her knowing that they felt so comfortable in each other's company, no amount of silence was awkward. Did she have that with Johann? She shook the thought from her mind. "What about the other letter from the colonel. Aren't you going to open it?"

He shrugged, tossing Robert's letter onto the bed and picking up the other. He tore it open quickly and read silently. He grunted, "From a staffer. I've got an appointment apparently."

"Whatever could that be about?" she asked nervously.

"Maybe I'll finally get some answers."

"About what?"

"Why the hell they worked so hard getting me and the rest of the squad off Luzon."

A few days later, Staff Sergeant Tarkington was standing at attention in front of Colonel Bradshaw's desk. He'd traveled north from Brisbane, covering over 800 miles aboard an Australian sea plane, which continually dove and jinked whenever the pilots thought they spotted a Japanese Zero. He'd been happy to leave the plane and crew behind.

Tarkington could feel the sweat dripping from his scalp, past his temple to his chin. It wasn't the heat—the colonel's office was an ideal temperature —but being in the presence of a colonel he knew next to nothing about.

Colonel Bradshaw looked about as comfortable behind the mahogany desk as Tarkington felt standing at stiff attention, wondering what the next few minutes would reveal. While Bradshaw finished reading and signing a paper, Tarkington stole glances, noticing the officer's tanned skin and the deep crow's feet at the corners of his brown eyes. He surmised this was an officer used to being outside, not a desk jockey.

Bradshaw set the pen down and stood, revealing broad shoulders, which pressed against the seams of his uniform. He was of average height, but Tarkington felt the power of the man. It emanated from him like the ample sweat rings around his armpits. He was in the presence of a tough leader.

Bradshaw looked him up and down, finally stepping around the desk and extending a weathered, calloused hand. "Staff Sergeant Tarkington, it's an honor to finally meet you face to face."

Startled, Tarkington took the colonel's hand and tried to match his firm grip. "Uh, thank you, sir."

Bradshaw leaned against the desk and crossed his arms across his thick chest. "Relax, Staff Sergeant." Tarkington relaxed his stiff pose slightly. "How do you feel? Any residuals from your wound?" He pointed at Tarkington's gut.

"No, sir. I feel good. Better than I've felt in a long time."

Bradshaw grinned mischievously. "Those Brisbane nurses taking good care of you?"

Nurse Gallup's visage filled his mind and a momentary flash of anger passed at the officer's leering tone, but he quickly squashed it, knowing the colonel wasn't being specific. He answered in deadpan, "Yes, sir. Quite efficient and professional. I can't say enough good things about them, sir."

Bradshaw nodded, slight disappointment showing through. "Well, I'll get right to the point. You know a General Krueger?"

"The name rings a bell, sir."

"Mac personally requested him to lead the new Sixth Army down here. He'll be arriving soon, probably early January. I'm a part of the advance party, so to speak. He's tasked me—with Mac's assent—to form a new unit." He lifted his square chin and Tarkington noticed the hint of a scar on the underside. He figured it was probably from some long-ago street fight; he looked like the type. "A special unit," he finished.

Tarkington refocused. "A special unit, sir?" he repeated.

"Yes. You see, this war down here's a sideshow at the moment. We're tasked with keeping the Japanese from advancing farther, holding them until we have the resources we need to take the fight to them." Tarkington scowled and Bradshaw grinned, "You don't agree with that strategy, Sergeant?"

Tarkington stared straight ahead. "Not my place to agree or disagree, sir."

Bradshaw nodded, "True, true, but I can read your expression. A defensive posture only makes the enemy stronger, allows them time to build their forces. Mac and most of the other brass down here don't enjoy sitting on their hands waiting for the other boot to fall. Mac wants to take the fight to the enemy. That's why he's bringing in General Krueger. He's an old warhorse. Hell, he joined up to fight in the Spanish-American War and he's been in every campaign since. He's a little long in the tooth, but he's a fighter who's never lost."

Tarkington fidgeted, wondering what any of this had to do with him. After a long pause, Bradshaw continued, "Krueger has tasked me, along with my Australian counterpart, to put together a crack unit whose sole function will be reconnaissance. As you well know, these damned islands are just too damned thick with jungle for proper aerial recon. We need boots on the ground. Men who can get in and out without the Japs being the wiser."

Bradshaw looked him straight in the eye and Tarkington asked, "So, what's this got to do with me, sir?"

"Well, you and your squad have already been doing this sort of thing. Not by choice, of course, but you survived where so many have perished. Mac got wind of your exploits and he wants you and your men to be a part of this new unit."

Tarkington nodded his understanding, "So you want us to train these men, sir?"

"Initially, yes. But Mac and Krueger have other ideas beyond just training." He straightened from the desk, unfolding his beefy arms and facing Tarkington. "You and your men are uniquely qualified to take this one step beyond mere reconnaissance. You've proven yourselves as . . ." He shrugged. "Well, there's no nice way to say this—you've proven yourselves as killers. Your unit will be tasked with more direct-action missions."

"Direct action, sir?"

"You struck fear into the Nips on Luzon, and by all accounts gave them more than just bloody noses. Hell, even Colonel Fertig on Mindanao can't stop singing your praises. Whether or not you like it, your unit's good at killing and even better at intimidation. Tark's Ticks? Playing cards?" Tarkington felt his ears getting hot with embarrassment. "We heard about that all the way down here. A captured Jap on New Guinea spoke of it, hundreds of miles south of Luzon." He pointed at Tarkington, "You and your men will go through the training first. I've set it up. It's a six-week course. You'll be the guinea pigs. If we can improve it through your suggestions, we'll do it. Strictly volunteer." He licked his lips and refolded his arms. "What do you think, Staff Sergeant?"

"I haven't seen my squad mates for weeks. Have you passed it by them yet?"

Bradshaw gave him a sideways grin. "That's my fault. I pulled them kicking and screaming from your bedside. They're already here, getting things ironed out a little."

Tarkington grinned, happy to hear his men hadn't been split up and sent to the far corners of the world. He nodded, "I think you've got yourself a squad then, sir."

2

The unmistakable drawl of PFC Henry emanated from the depths of the barracks, "Well, well, well. Look who's here."

Staff Sergeant Tarkington grinned, taking a moment at the threshold to allow his eyes to adjust to the dark barracks. There was scuffling movement and excited voices as men sprang from their bunks and moved toward him. "What died in here?" Tarkington asked, holding his nose.

Sergeant Winkleman's grinning face emerged beside him and he pointed a thumb back over his shoulder, "That's just Stolly. He's been eating a lot of cheese."

PFC Stollman punched Winkleman's shoulder, making him wince and pull away. "Screw you, Wink."

Soon he was surrounded by his squad mates, all slapping his back and talking over one another. It felt good to be back among them. His men. He didn't realize how isolated he'd felt until now. He enjoyed Nurse Gallup's company immensely, but this was where he belonged. These were his brothers in a way even Robert could never be. They'd been through hell together. Fought beside one another against huge odds. They'd watched friends die together—too many to count. These were men he could rely upon under any circumstances.

After the hubbub died down a little, Tarkington asked, "Where's Sergeant Gonzalez?"

Winkleman answered, "Back with G2. Haven't seen him since they forced us out of your hospital room."

It made sense. He'd never been a part of the squad, although he'd earned their respect. Tarkington put his gear on an empty bunk. "So, what's this all about? I heard they're training you to be some kind of commandos."

PFC Stollman nodded, "Mostly just making us do a whole lotta P.T. I haven't run this much since Vick's pa caught me with his mom."

Vick slugged him hard. "What the hell's the matter with you, Stolly? Sorry about him, Tark. He's got an inflated sense of himself. Can't get enough of hearing his own voice." He shook his head, "He's right though. They've been putting us through the ringer. It's like they're training us to be Jesse Owens or something."

Henry drawled, "I'm assuming you're joining us, Tark?"

Tarkington nodded, "That's the idea. I got it straight from Colonel Bradshaw. He's the one behind all this. Well, him and General Krueger. They want to hone our skills and turn us into more efficient killers," he mocked.

Winkleman reared back at the notion. "That's what he said?"

Tarkington nodded, "Pretty much. Apparently, we're the guinea pigs for a brand-new unit. Krueger's from Texas, so he's calling it Alamo Scouts. By the way, we're in the Sixth Army now."

"Alamo Scouts?" PFC Raker tested the phrase. "Sounds like we're a part of the Cub Scouts or something. We gonna earn badges for how many Japs we kill?"

Tarkington shrugged, "You're not far off. Apparently, the program's primary purpose is to form small reconnaissance units that can operate behind Jap lines for days on end without a lot of support." The others nodded and Tarkington continued, "But we'll be a little different."

"Different how?" asked Raker.

"Bradshaw called it 'direct action.' He wants us to do all that, but instead of just observing and reporting back, he wants us to hit targets. Keep the Japs off balance by killing them where they think they're the safest."

Winkleman tilted his head and squinted. "So, we're assassins," he stated matter-of-factly.

Tarkington nodded, "For all intents and purposes . . . yes." He looked at each man. "Anyone have a problem with that? Colonel Bradshaw wanted me to assure you this whole thing is strictly volunteer. Anyone can opt out. Every one of you has already done more than was ever expected of you. No one will think lesser of you."

A long silence ensued as the men considered. Winkleman finally said, "And what about you, Tark?"

Tarkington scowled, looking at his sergeant with hard eyes. "What about me? I'm in. The Japs have a lot to answer for and I'm . . ."

Winkleman interrupted, "No, no, I mean look at you. Been languishing in Brisbane eating nurse pussy while we've been out here getting strong." He flexed an arm muscle and grinned. "I'll bet I could kick your ass right about now."

Tarkington laughed, "Well, you've obviously been drinking too much Aussie beer, Wink. You've got delusions of grandeur." He lunged, taking Winkleman's head into the crook of his arm, attempting to give him a noogie. They all joined in and soon they were on the floor in a pile of sweating, grunting, wrestling bodies. Tarkington couldn't stop laughing. He didn't remember when he'd felt this good.

The barracks door burst open and filling the space was a diminutive man standing with his hands on his hips. A stout stick hung from his wrist by a cord of leather. Another soldier was behind him, holding a clipboard. In a loud, crisp English accent, he barked, "Well, would you look at that, Danny boy. Americans in their natural habitat! Piled on like stacked shite!"

The sudden entrance of the two British noncoms didn't have an immediate effect upon the GIs. The British sergeant grasped his stick and slammed it solidly against the metal of the closest bunk frame. The sound was like a rifle shot and all frivolity ceased.

The GIs untangled themselves, grinning and poking fun as they dusted themselves off. Since the newcomers didn't outrank Staff Sergeant Tarkington, there wasn't a tremendous rush.

The sergeant didn't wait for them to pull themselves together. He stepped forward and faced Tarkington stiffly, the stick now firmly held under his armpit, his hand still grasping it with white knuckles.

Tarkington glanced at Winkleman who shrugged slightly. He'd never seen the British sergeant before. Tarkington grinned, "Sorry about that, Sergeant. We just haven't seen each other in a ..."

The sergeant spoke as though Tarkington didn't exist, or was a bug on the floor, something to be ignored. "I am Sergeant Clive, your new training officer, and this is Corporal Millcutty, my assistant." He focused his glare on Tarkington. "You outrank me, Sergeant. However, over the next six weeks," he lowered his voice, "that rank means nothing. Indeed, you can consider yourselves buck privates ... all of you. You will call me and Corporal Millcutty 'Instructor.' We will rotate experts through occasionally and they will also be referred to as 'Instructor.'" He raised his voice, "Clear?"

As one, the GIs answered, "Clear, Instructor."

Sergeant Clive smiled, showing off a mouthful of crooked teeth. "Excellent. I want you out front in five minutes." He did a perfect about-face, stomped his shiny boots on the wood floor, and strode out.

When they were gone, Henry asked, "What the hell was that all about?"

Tarkington shrugged, "Guess we'll find out in about six minutes."

The men scrambled to make themselves somewhat presentable, but by the time they emerged and lined up under the blistering sun, they looked like a ragtag group of thugs.

Clive, with Millcutty right behind, clipboard ready, strode in front of them and stopped. He looked them over with barely concealed disdain. "Now that Cadet Tarkington is back among you, we can finally get to the business at hand." Tarkington bristled at his new rank, but didn't react outwardly. "Over the coming weeks, we will focus on five things. We will not stop until each of you has perfected each of them. If you fail to perfect them, you'll be dropped from the program." He paused, and the GIs glanced at one another from the corners of their eyes. "Number one: physical fitness. You will be pushed to your limits physically—every day building your stamina. Many of you have already been training, but this will be more difficult, I can assure you. Number two: navigation. Both on land and in small rubber boats, which will be your primary insertion method. Number three: hand-to-hand combat. We'll have instructors teaching you new and interesting ways to kill the enemy." He smiled grimly. "Believe me, there are more than you can imagine. Number four: weapons. I will require you to know every weapon in our arsenal, as well as the

Japanese. And finally, number five: explosives. Everyone will be required to know how to make and set off a bomb. Two of you shall become experts in the field."

He paced, the stick still stuffed tightly into his armpit. The sun beat down upon them and the GIs dripped sweat. They were used to it, but the heat seemed to have no effect on Clive, whose spotless uniform somehow still had crisp creases. He stopped and faced them again, continuing, "I know you men have already seen more combat than most will ever see. You're a tight-knit group who've been through a lot together. We understand that." He looked them over, resting his blue eyes upon each man. "This program won't be perfect. A work in progress, as it were. It will require concentration and immense effort to get through successfully. You're paving the way for an entirely new type of unit." He looked down, kicking a stone away. He changed to a more amicable tone, "You might wonder why a bloody Brit's in charge." There was a smattering of snickering. "Colonel Bradshaw asked us to help since your newly-formed Sixth Army isn't all here yet. We've some experience in this type of training, mostly airborne units, parachutists and whatnot." He lifted his chin, looking down his misaligned nose. "At the end of the six weeks, I expect you'll be highly-trained killers. I know you're already accomplished at such things, but we'll add to your bag of dirty tricks." More snickering. He raised his voice, "We start in the morning—0400 hours. Questions?"

Stollman raised his hand and Vick, standing beside him, rolled his eyes, wanting to pull it down. Clive pointed and Stollman asked, "Are we going to eat during the six weeks . . . Instructor?" He almost forgot that last bit. The GIs guffawed, shaking their heads. Tarkington felt the urge to step in, but he was just a cadet now.

Clive gave Stollman a sideways smile. "Cadet Stollman, correct?" Stollman nodded, grinning. Clive answered, "You'll be fed quite well. You'll be burning calories, and food deprivation isn't part of the training. Tomorrow, breakfast will be at 0530, after a nice brisk run." There was grumbling and Clive growled, "Dismissed."

Back in the barracks, Tarkington was unloading the rest of his sparse belongings into the footlocker at the foot of his bunk. He looked at the five soldiers lazing around reading dime-store novels and old *Life* magazines. They'd been to hell and back with one another, and being back among them was like coming home again. He glanced at each man.

Beside him, his rangy assistant squad leader, Sergeant Winkleman, cleaned his fingernails with the tip of his knife. He hailed from the northern California coast. He'd led an austere life, being raised mostly by his uncle. He'd spent much of his youth exploring the damp woods and endlessly wild coastline. His exploration hadn't ended with the land either, venturing into the untamed ocean to spear fish and pry abalone off the bottom with old rusty knives.

Beyond him, PFC Raker read a novel, the spine folded in half, assuring it would most likely fall apart soon. He was his 2nd Scout. He'd grown up in a western city but took every opportunity to venture into the wilds to hunt and fish. His average frame belied a strong, unbendable character. He'd accomplish any task, no matter how impossible, or die trying. His devilishly good looks got him in trouble sometimes, but nothing his charm couldn't mend.

Beside him, snoring softly, was PFC Stollman, his heavy weapons man. His dark red hair grew faster than any military decorum mandate could keep up with. Even though it'd been recently shorn, his hair was already curling over his ears. His light complexion wasn't optimum for living and fighting in the blistering hot tropics and he joked that he didn't tan so much as turn deeper and deeper shades of red. He was as a solid soldier, solidly built. He loved big guns and was happiest when looking over the sights of his cherished Browning Automatic Rifle. He was also a bit of a hothead, but his best friend and loader, PFC Vick, kept him in line—or at least did the best he could.

The trials and tribulations of the past year had turned PFC Vick from a timid loader and assistant gunner to a soldier of all trades. He'd been severely wounded on Luzon and only survived with the help of native Filipino healers. Watching his comrades having to fight while he convalesced speeded his recovery. Somewhere along the way, he'd discovered he was a natural in knife work. Having to kill face to face had changed his features from boyish to hard and deadly. He'd also become the de facto medic of the squad, simply because he was used to carrying more supplies than everyone else, including bandages.

Henry was beside him, chewing on a piece of short grass, staring at the ceiling. They'd gone through boot camp together and been instant friends. He was a man of few words, but when he spoke, it was worth listening to. He was the squad's lead scout. He'd grown up in the Louisiana Bayou and was Cajun through and through. His great grandmother, whose age was a mystery, still rocked on her rocking chair with a .22 caliber rifle over her lap, occasionally shooting and rarely missing various rodents. Her roots and Henry's, too, were steeped in Voodoo.

At an early age, PFC Henry, whose actual name was too long and foreign for the army and had been shortened, hunted and fished with his kin and knew the mysterious bayou waterways like the back of his hand. His clan was extensive, their survival depending on their ability to put food on the table through subsistence living. More than once, Henry's sixth sense had saved them from bumbling into Japanese ambushes.

Henry sat up and spit out the piece of grass. "Feels like we're back in boot camp. Don't it?" he asked in his drawl.

Tarkington nodded, "It's uncanny." Despite the no-ranks mandate, the others gave their squad leader space. They'd been there for weeks already and were used to the demotion to cadets, which predated Sergeant Clive, but Tarkington was still fresh to the idea. "How are the men handling it? Are they resentful?"

Henry shrugged, "Not really. Although the guys before Clive didn't dwell on it as much. It's horseshit, far as I'm concerned."

Tarkington nodded his agreement, "Colonel Bradshaw told me he wants feedback on the whole thing. Wants to make it better for the next batch of soldiers. First thing I'm gonna tell him is to ditch the whole cadet thing. It's one thing to be treated as equals, quite another to lose your rank. It starts things off the wrong way." He put his last pair of folded socks into the locker and closed the olive drab lid. "From what he told me, they're only taking prime candidates, men who already excel at soldiering. The cream of the crop. That being the case, they should treat us as professionals. We've already been through bootcamp. No need to rehash that crap." Henry nodded slowly. Tarkington asked, "So no open rebellion?"

"Nah. Might be if they cut one of us out though."

Tarkington rubbed the scar on his side and nodded. "Yeah, I didn't like that part either. It makes sense for guys who haven't been through it already, but we're a team."

"Think they'll stick us with an officer?"

"I don't think so. Bradshaw told me officers will lead the regular teams, but he didn't say that about us. He woulda told me something like that. I think it's just us."

"So, you trust this Colonel Bradshaw," he stated.

"I do. He's not your typical officer, that's for sure. I could tell he hates all this admin stuff. I got the feeling he wanted to join us for the training. He's the guy that put the whole regimen together. He's built like a brick shithouse too. He's older, but I think he can probably run circles around us."

The squad made their way to the door. Stollman asked, "You two coming? I hear they brought in proper cooks for us, so we don't have to eat that crap we've been suffering through up till now."

"Was it bad?" Tarkington asked.

Vick answered for him, "Let's just say it won't be hard to improve upon."

3

As promised, they were up and standing at attention a few minutes past 0400 hours. None of them slept well anyway. Sleeping lightly was how they'd functioned and survived so long in the jungle. It wasn't an easy habit to break. So, unlike raw recruits, the griping didn't last long and mostly centered on friendly ribbing back and forth.

Sergeant Clive and Corporal Millcutty were in front, and when all were present and accounted for, Clive barked, "Cadets. We'll start with a brisk, six-mile run. No packs or weapons and drop your canteens." He turned, ran a few paces and barked, "Follow me. Keep it tight."

Tarkington had been running and exercising every day he'd been able to at the infirmary, and he thanked God for that, because the pace was faster here and the terrain full of hills. Winkleman's comment the day before about him being out of shape wasn't totally accurate, but he was certainly not in the kind of shape the rest of the squad was in. But he'd be damned if he let it show. He gritted his teeth, swallowed his pain, and pushed through it, relying heavily on will power. He wouldn't allow himself to show weakness in front of the men. He was the leader of Tark's Ticks, for crying out loud.

It was still dark when they finished the six-mile run. The GIs were barely breathing more heavily than normal. Tarkington did everything he could, but his labored breathing was obvious. Sergeant Clive was hardly sweating. He spoke as though he'd just arisen from a nap, "Right. Let's get some breakfast but keep it light. We meet back here for calisthenics in half an hour. Dismissed."

The food was fabulous. They had brought cooks in from the very best in the US Army, at least the ones in-theater. The evening before, they'd crooned over the multiple taste sensations offered. This morning was no exception. The coffee was hot and rich, the eggs fluffy and laced with real cheddar cheese, and the sausage cooked to perfection. But since they only had 20 minutes, they wolfed it down, slamming coffee and orange juice, hoping they wouldn't pay the price later.

They were at the parade ground five minutes early, which meant they were late. The Brits were none too happy and punished them for the next hour with pushups, situps, burpies, lunges, and planks. With each exercise, Tarkington thought he'd lose his breakfast, but he held on, refusing to give anyone the satisfaction. Winkleman kept glancing his way, seeing his discomfort. At one point, he leaned in and whispered, "Look a little peaked, Tark."

Tarkington bit back, "Fuck off, Wink."

The session ended none too soon and they moved off to the next adventure: boating. The black rubber boat was halfway deflated, making it difficult to carry and even harder to paddle through the crashing surf. Since this was mostly new to them, Clive lectured them on proper seating, paddle strokes, rudder work, and cadence. They'd gotten a crash course in paddling months before while fleeing a sinking submarine, but it was a good review.

Winkleman had the most water experience, having spent most of his summers along the Northern California coast with his uncle. Like their time paddling the rubber boat off the doomed Eel, he directed them once they were in the water. As a result, they made their way past the breakers without getting flipped, much to Sergeant Clive's surprise. However, on the way back in, a sneaker wave caught them by surprise and flipped the boat violently. By this time, they were all exhausted—none more so than Tarkington—and it took a long time to right the boat and get everyone back inside.

They broke one of the paddles, which was completely unacceptable in Clive's eyes, leading to another run before lunch. This time on the sand in wet boots.

After lunch, which was grilled cheese sandwiches and delicious home-made tomato soup, they were allowed an hour before reporting to the firing range. Tarkington excused himself from the table after devouring the food, went to an out-of-the-way shade tree, laid down, and immediately fell asleep.

What seemed like seconds later, but was actually 25 minutes, Henry nudged him with his boot. "Come on, Tark. Time to get back to it."

Tarkington was instantly awake and on his feet. He tried not to grimace at the stiffness overtaking his body, but failed. "I'm ready. Lead the way."

Henry nodded, and as they walked said, "No need to push yourself so hard, Tark. We've been doing this crap for weeks. You don't have to prove anything to us. Wink's just yanking your chain."

Tarkington nodded, "I know. I just can't fail and let the squad down. Particularly in front of a couple Brits."

"Just pace yourself. Let your body ease into it."

"I'm gonna be sore as shit tomorrow."

Henry shook his head, "I don't think you'll have time to be sore, Tark."

By the fourth week of training, Staff Sergeant Tarkington felt as though he could keep up with his men and the instructors, even bypassing some of them occasionally on the longer and longer runs.

There was a noticeable shift in the daily regimen. Physical fitness was still a daily occurrence; however, more emphasis was placed upon hand-to-hand combat and explosives.

One predawn morning, after a beach run and before breakfast, Sergeant Clive mentioned the change. "Training from here on will focus more on what you men are specifically being trained for . . . killing the enemy. This is where the program diverges from what Colonel Bradshaw has in mind for the regular scouts."

Once they inhaled breakfast, which continued being top-notch, they went to the parade ground area and seated themselves in front of a long table, upon which were various devices. Another instructor was present. He towered over Sergeant Clive both vertically and—if stood on edge—horizontally. His US Army uniform was bursting at the shoulders, barely containing powerful muscles gained through hard work. Stubble darkened his face, even after presumably shaving only hours before. His blue eyes had a steel coldness to them, and the deep crow's feet at the corners added to their intensity.

Sergeant Clive introduced him jauntily, "This is Sergeant Dwayne Bulkort. A countryman of yours, attached to the Army Corps of Engineers. Before the war, he worked extensively in drilling and mining. His expertise is in demolitions. I can assure you, he's forgotten more about making things go boom than any of you will ever learn."

Clive gestured toward the big man and he stepped forward, giving them a goofy sideways grin, which didn't match his impressive size. His baritone voice boomed deep, "Hello, men." He waved his plate-sized right hand. "You've been introduced to the basics of demolition already, and it's my job to hone your skills. When I'm done with you, you'll be intimately familiar with new and interesting ways to blow things up." He grinned, expanding his arms to the table. "These are the contents of a box our friends in Britain put together. These little treasures are sent across the Channel to saboteurs to use against the Nazis." He pronounced the "a" as in apple. He looked around as though someone might eavesdrop. He put his massive hand beside his mouth as though lip readers were in the woods. "This is a secret, but a few of these boxes were captured by them Krauts and modified."

Stollman leaned toward Vick and whispered, "This guy's a piece of work." Vick elbowed him in the side to shut him up.

"Ingenious, really," the big man continued. "The most important thing we found is this stuff." He lifted a coiled bit of what looked like parachute cord, but stiffer. He unwrapped the black tape holding it together. "This is detonation cord. It's highly explosive—burns at a rate of 29,000 feet a second." He looked around at the faces. Everyone was paying attention, but he was clearly disappointed at their lack of enthusiasm. He scowled and continued, "You set it off the same way you set off any of the other stuff, with a blasting cap or short-cord detonator."

Stollman raised his hand and Sgt. Bulkort lifted his square jaw, "Yes? Question?"

Stollman asked, "You telling me that entire roll of cord's a bomb?"

Bulkort's face brightened, "Yes, exactly. The concept's been around a long time, but the Germans seem to have perfected it." He picked up the cord, bent it, and smacked it against the table. Everyone flinched. "It won't blow unless triggered by a detonator, similar to composition bombs and plastic explosives."

Stollman nodded, clearly interested. "So instead of putting a detonator on each chunk of TNT, you could just wrap that stuff around it and trigger the det cord stuff and it'll blow the TNT all at the same time?"

Sergeant Bulkort's smile and suddenly shining eyes looked as though he were falling in love. He spluttered, "Yes! Yes, exactly right. What's your name, soldier?"

Stollman looked around, suddenly embarrassed. "PFC . . ." he shook his head, correcting himself, "I mean, *Cadet* Stollman."

Bulkort nodded, his grin spreading even wider. "It's easy to carry and has countless applications. Hell, you can use it to cut a thick tree in half, block a road or something."

Stollman's excitement was growing too, "Stuff it into a metal canister for a makeshift grenade."

Bulkort's eyes lit up and he nodded, pointing at Stollman, "Yes! Or how about wrapping it around a grenade and turning it into a huge grenade?"

Vick was shaking his head and the others were grinning at the spectacle. Tarkington chuckled and said to Winkleman, "I think we found the squad's explosives expert."

Stollman stood and approached the table with all the other explosives, blasting caps, and charges. He touched a flexible plastic tube, capped at one end with a black cover. It was about 15 inches long and had a black cord connecting each end. "What's this one do?"

Sergeant Bulkort held the piece up for the rest of the group to see. "This is one of my favorites." He flexed and unflexed the plastic tube, bending it well past 90 degrees. "This is for blowing up airplanes after they've left the ground. It's like a timer bomb, but there's not an actual timer." He looked at it as though he were an art lover being given a private tour of the Mona

Lisa. "The saboteur stuffs the bomb into a hatch on an airplane, or maybe inside the cockpit under the pilot seat. There are batteries at both ends, separated by a light spring. When the plane climbs, the air thins and the tube expands, connecting the battery charges, and completing a circuit which ignites the detonator and explodes the bomb. It's small but would devastate a light aircraft, or any aircraft really."

Tarkington gave a low whistle, "That's ingenious."

Winkleman nodded and added, "And downright dirty."

Sergeant Bulkort took them through various other designs, all equally brutal and diabolically simple to use.

They spent the next several hours learning how the bombs worked and then set them off, placing them beneath old rusted farm equipment. They were even allowed to blow up a dilapidated wood building, which was about to fall over on its own anyway. The explosion of TNT blocks connected by detonation cord did a wonderful job of obliterating the structure.

Tarkington and the others were having fun, but nothing like Stollman and Sgt. Bulkort. They were like kids on Christmas morning showing off their new toys to each other. Their enthusiasm was contagious, and the day flew by.

For Stollman, it ended all too soon. Bulkort drove away in his borrowed lorry, promising to see them tomorrow for more demolitions. It was time to head back to camp for chow, which was only a short four-mile run away. The entire run, Stollman kept regaling Vick and anyone close enough to hear, replaying all the explosions repeatedly as though recounting a book he'd read. Vick finally stopped it, "Christ's sake, Stolly. You should just ask him out. I'm sure he'd say yes. You two could raise a wonderful brood of kids and blow them all to kingdom come."

Raker chimed in, "After you blow him, of course."

All the GIs, except Stollman, burst into laughter. Even Sergeant Clive and Corporal Millcutty couldn't help themselves.

Stollman shook his head, murmuring, "Fuck off." He was quiet the rest of the run.

The rest of the six weeks passed quickly. Tarkington felt they could take on the entire Japanese Army without breaking a sweat. Their already refined patrolling skills were honed to an even sharper edge. Even Henry, who grew up hunting for his family's very survival, learned new things. Where they made leaps and bounds was in hand-to-hand combat and demolitions.

The hand-to-hand combat trainers showed them a mixture of deadly techniques to quickly and viciously kill the enemy. The methods didn't include bowing or different-colored belts, just brutal efficiency. They trained hard, practicing on one another, leaving one another battered and bruised.

The trainers stressed the need for continual training, lamenting that even weeks of daily workouts only scratched the surface. But they only had six weeks. They were already proven soldiers, and the extra training made them truly deadly.

No one realized when the six weeks were up. On their supposed graduation day, they stood at attention on the parade ground while the sun poked over the eastern horizon. Colonel Bradshaw stood beside Sergeant Clive. His blocky, square jaw jutted as he lifted his head and looked the men over. "At ease," he started. "You may not realize it, but today is the last scheduled day of training." Murmurs of surprise swept through them. He gave them a slight smile. "From everything I've observed personally and," he indicated Clive, "the words of the other trainers, you've all performed wonderfully." He held up a patch, which was too small for the men to make out from afar. "This is the unit patch. You'll get one soon enough." The patch portrayed a side view of a Native American with the words Alamo Scout. "You'll notice a lightning strike superimposed over the Indian's head. The normal scout patch won't have the lightning strike. That's just for this unit and any follow-ons like it." He smiled, "Congratulations, men, and well done!"

The GIs looked at one another, then back to the colonel. It was an accomplishment, but none of them had ever doubted getting through, so it muted the effect. There was some back slapping and smiles, but the course —though intense—was business as usual for them.

Colonel Bradshaw nodded, held up a hand to get their attention again, and said, "You've got the rest of the day off but don't get too comfortable. You're shipping out tomorrow for Milne Bay."

Tarkington exchanged a glance with Sergeant Winkleman. They hadn't had a lot of time to keep up on current events; the news was sporadic and sometimes full of conjecture and propaganda, but they had heard about a recent battle at Milne Bay. Tarkington asked, "Didn't the Japs try to take that from the Aussies in September?"

Bradshaw nodded, "Yes, and the Aussies kicked their yellow butts right out of there. We're building airstrips on the extreme eastern tip, but it's boggy and wet. It's tough going. The Japs bomb it, along with Port Moresby, nearly every day, sometimes twice." He lifted his chin and waved the squad to approach. He went to a knee and in the blazing Australian sun, the squad formed a tight circle around him, matching his crouch. Sergeant Clive stayed back, watching for any looky-loos. Bradshaw continued, "I won't go into specifics—I wasn't planning on telling you any of this yet—but I'll give you the gist. In three days, you men will help secure Milne Bay from further attacks."

He drew a long shape in the dirt, "This is Milne Bay." He drew another smaller circle northeast, "And this is Goodenough Island. When the Japs lost at Milne Bay, they left troops here. Without support, they're not much of a threat, but their proximity to our bases and any," he cleared his throat, "upcoming operations, which may or may not be happening, is unacceptable. They need to be cleared out of there. The Aussies are going to lead the mission, but have asked for a better assessment of what they'll be facing." He nodded while looking the men over. "I figured it would be a good shakedown mission for you. Go in under cover of darkness, most likely from a PT boat, assess enemy strength, and report back."

Tarkington asked, "Do we have good maps of the area?"

Bradshaw nodded, "You'll get all that when you get to Milne Bay and have the official briefing. I wasn't planning on telling you any of this," he shrugged, "but what the hell? Cat's out of the bag now." Bradshaw stood, and the others followed suit, shaking the stiffness from their legs.

Tarkington brushed his boot over the drawing and nodded, "Thanks, Colonel. Sounds pretty straightforward, and I agree, it'll be a good shakedown mission."

Bradshaw extended his beefy, calloused hand to each man, "Good luck to you all." When he got to Tarkington, he reminded him, "Before you leave, I want a detailed report on anything you think we could improve upon with the scout training."

Tarkington released his hand, stepped back, and snapped off a crisp salute, "Yes, sir. It'll be on your desk first thing in the morning."

Bradshaw shook his head, "I want it done now, Sergeant." His tone was harsh and Tarkington nodded, stunned by his sudden change in demeanor. Bradshaw smiled, "That way you'll have plenty of time to enjoy the festivities that've been arranged in honor of your graduation." Bradshaw yelled, "Corporal Millcutty!"

From the barracks, Millcutty and a few Australian soldiers walked out carrying multiple kegs of beer between them. The GIs' faces lit up. Most hadn't enjoyed a drink in months. A cheer went up, but before they could charge off, Bradshaw barked, "The party starts at 1600 hours and not before! Meantime, they will transform the mess hall into a ballroom. Some local ladies and a band'll be on hand too. Tarkington can get his report done and the rest of you I'm *ordering* to rack out. Understood?"

The cheering died down, focused instead on a rousing, "Yes, Sir!"

4

Tarkington entered the mess hall as the sounds of music and raucous laughter rolled over him. He'd finished his report, handed it off to Colonel Bradshaw's aide, and gone straight to his bunk. He'd awoken to the sounds of the party kicking off.

He made his way to the party. His eyes took a moment to adjust to the mess tent, dazzled by the bare-bulb lights strung up like Christmas strands. A makeshift stage was in the corner and a four-person civilian band played. The lead singer was an Australian beauty whose voice wasn't nearly as nice as her ass.

The smells of grilled meat turned his attention toward the near side where a hearty buffet of food was stacked. They'd been eating well, but this was something else altogether. They pinned the sides of the tent up, creating airflow, but the food and packed humanity made the inside stifling. It didn't matter though; the area in front of the band was filled with men and women, both civilian and military, grooving to the fast-paced music.

He saw Raker and Stollman out on the dance floor, but none of the others. Then he heard the unmistakable drawl of PFC Henry. On the other side of the tent, five beer kegs perched on a table. Henry, along with everyone else from the squad, crowded around them, drinking and laughing.

He stepped their way but before he got there, a woman in a US Army uniform stepped in front of him, stopping him cold. "Hello, Sergeant Tarkington."

He broke into a wide smile and felt a twinge of desire. "Sergeant Gallup. What're you doing way up here?"

She laid her hand on his chest and her cherry-red lips parted seductively. "I heard one of my patients needed urgent medical care."

He looked down at her hand, her long fingers bare of the engagement ring he remembered seeing back in Brisbane. He grinned down at her, "Is that right?" She nodded and smiled, showing off the small gap between her teeth. He touched her bare ring finger, "Perhaps you're breaking hearts already."

She gave him her best puppy-dog eyes, "I couldn't get you out of my head. He's a lovely man, but—well—I gave him back his ring and here I am."

He looked into her eyes, not having to look away this time. She stared back, smiling coyly. The moment shattered when Winkleman stumbled up to him with two steins of beer. "Tark," he bellowed. "There you are, you son of a bitch. I thought you'd never get . . ." He stopped when he saw Nurse Gallup. "Oh, excuse me," he stammered. He swayed on his feet, a goofy grin on his face.

Nurse Gallup stepped aside slightly and Tarkington reached for the extra stein of beer. "Gimme that before you spill it all over yourself . . . or us." He took a long pull and let out a satisfied "ahh." He wiped his mouth with the back of his hand. "This is Sergeant Gallup. She nursed me back to health down in Brisbane. This is Sergeant Winkleman, my assistant squad leader."

She extended her hand, "You can call me Nancy, Sergeant. It's wonderful to meet you."

Tarkington heard the other squad members laughing raucously and he recognized the tail end of a filthy joke being told. Nurse Gallup's ears colored before she laughed at his uncomfortableness. She tilted the stein to his lips for him, "Drink up, Sergeant Tarkington. This lady wants to dance!"

He upended the stein, handed it to the stunned Winkleman, and joined Raker and Stollman, who greeted him heartily and exchanged sly looks, seeing how closely Tarkington held onto the sergeant from the nursing corps.

The next morning, the squad was aboard a DC3, traveling from Cairns to the newly-built tarmac at Milne Bay. They were all hungover, some still outwardly drunk. The uncomfortable seat, a plank of metal folded from the wall, didn't help. Tarkington, despite a pounding head, felt good. Thoughts of Nurse Nancy Gallup kept him occupied. It was a night neither of them would soon forget. She'd made the war seem far away, but he knew it was only a brief respite. After making love several times, she'd laid in his arms, their sweat mixing. The fan overhead had moved the air, keeping the room tolerable. They talked and sobered up quickly.

Tarkington told her that this whole thing was probably a bad idea. The war promised to be a long one and he doubted he'd survive, and if he did, he'd likely be a broken man, someone incapable of love. But before he could finish, she seemed to sense it, beating him to the punch.

He replayed her words over in his head: "I want you to put me out of your mind, Sergeant. Concentrate on surviving. That's it. Get yourself and your men through this. Tonight is a refuge, an oasis. Go to it when you need to." She'd given him a sad smile. "And look me up when it's over, Sergeant Tarkington." They'd fallen asleep, the best couple hours of sleep he ever remembered having.

His throbbing head brought him back to the present. He looked down the aisle of seated men. Their gear was stacked in the center. The dual engines were loud, making his headache worse by a magnitude of ten. The jarring ride as the plane traversed the ups and downs of turbulence didn't help matters, and the pungent smell of vomit permeated the space. They looked like shit, but they were his men, *Tark's Ticks,* and by God, he'd do his damnest to get them through this war.

He took a deep breath, blew it out slowly, and shoved the image of

Nurse Gallup's naked body deep into the recesses of his mind. He replaced it with the upcoming mission. One mission at a time—one day, one hour, one minute at a time.

He was pulled from his revelry by a sudden and violent turn to the right. They were held to their seats by a thin safety belt. It was wholly inadequate for the job, made worse because each man had the belt as loose as it would go for the sake of comfort.

Tarkington clutched the side of the plane, latching onto a metal strut. He felt himself slipping from the seat. The right side of the plane, now effectively the floor, would not provide a soft landing. Just before losing his grip and rolling out of the seat, the plane banked the other way, smashing his back into the wall behind him. Raker, across from him, slipped from the seat and seemed to float toward him. A sudden flattening, followed immediately with a violent pull upward, sent him crashing to the floor.

"Hold on to something!" yelled Tarkington.

The plane's nose was rising, the centrifugal force pulling Raker towards the rear. He rolled head over heels. Henry reached out from his seat and snagged him just before he slammed into the back bulkhead. Henry held on and finally shoved Raker to an empty seat when the plane flattened. "Buckle up, dammit," he cursed him.

Raker's nose was bleeding and his eyes were wide with dizziness and confusion, but he managed to strap in and pull the belt as tightly as it would go. Suddenly, just over their heads, the thin skin of the plane filled with gaping holes. The ripping sound was deafening over the increasing din of the twin engines.

The cabin filled with streams of light, reflecting dust and bits of debris. The plane suddenly dove, making them all lighter. Loose items rose as though held by ghosts. Tarkington winced as the belt cut into his hips and legs. He held onto the bottom of the metal seat, doubting he'd be able to hold himself there if the belt broke.

The roar of a nearby aircraft made him glance out the small round side window. He glimpsed a green painted aircraft with a red "meatball" on the wing flash past. He gasped, "Zero."

From beside him, Stollman yelled, "No shit!"

The plane's descent abruptly ended and the floating objects fell to the floor and Tarkington slammed into the seat. He wondered how much stress the flimsy metal slab could take. The hinges must be near their weight limit. The pitch of the engines changed, settling into a less intense whine. The plane's wings leveled and besides the gaping holes in the roof, everything seemed to return to normal. Winkleman, who looked like he was about to vomit, exploded, "What the fuck's going on?"

The copilot leaned from his seat, his dark glasses somewhat askew. He pushed them up his nose and yelled, "Jap Zero nearly punched our ticket, but help arrived." He pointed out the windscreen.

Tarkington unbuckled and walked forward, careful to keep a hand on the wall. He poked his head into the cockpit and the copilot grinned, pointing, "A P-40's giving him the business. Saved our bacon."

Tarkington squinted, finally seeing a smoking dot in the distance. "Is that the Zero?" he asked.

The pilot pulled one side of his headphones off and nodded, "The P-40 came from above and nailed him. See the black smoke? That's an oil leak."

Tarkington nodded, "Where's the P-40?"

The pilot shrugged, "Probably above him somewhere looking for more. The Zero can out-turn any of our planes, so the strategy is to come in fast, hit 'em hard, and run right past him. Altitude equals speed."

"Will he finish him off?"

"Only if he can get away with it. They've got more planes, so our flyboys don't take unnecessary risks." The pilot turned to look at him, "Everyone okay back there? It happened rather suddenly, didn't have time to warn you."

Tarkington glanced back at the men. They were still wide-eyed, but besides Raker's bloody nose, uninjured. "They're okay, but you took some damage."

The copilot unbuckled and pushed past Tarkington, surveying the new ventilation system the Japanese had installed. He gave a low whistle,

"Another foot lower and you'd all be dead." The GIs stared back at him, shooting daggers. The copilot took the hint. They weren't in the mood, and he returned to his seat. "Riddled us pretty good, but no engine damage, that's the most important thing."

The pilot glanced left, "Our boys are coming alongside." The pilot grinned and gave the fighter jock a thumbs up.

Tarkington leaned in, seeing the insignia of the RAAF on the wing. The pilot lifted his flight goggles, smiled, and waved. He keyed his throat mic and Tarkington saw the pilots touch their headphones, listening. The pilot responded, "Roger. Thanks for the help, thought that bugger had us." More talk and the DC3 pilot nodded and said, "Roger, see you on the ground. Out." The pilot looked back at Tarkington, "He said that he and a mate will give us cover the rest of the way."

Tarkington nodded his head, "Tell him the yanks on board'll buy them a round of whatever they're drinking in Milne Bay." He walked back to his seat, hearing the copilot relaying the message. He strapped back in, making sure the belt was good and tight. Winkleman was rubbing his hand through his sweat-soaked hair, the others looking at him expectantly. Tarkington raised his voice over the engine, "Fighters ran the Zero off. They'll be escorting us the rest of the way."

Winkleman breathed a sigh of relief and tilted his head back, resting it on the vibrating wall for a moment before adjusting himself in the seat and staring Tarkington in the eye. He yelled, "That was some scary shit. I'd take being surrounded by a thousand Japs in the jungle than go through that again. Least out there we've got a chance." Everyone nodded their agreement.

Twenty minutes later, the DC3's wheels bounced on the nearly-flooded tarmac of Milne Bay. Great sprays of water accompanied the touchdown. The disconcerting feeling of skidding made the GIs grasp their seats with white knuckles. When the plane finally taxied into a parking place, and the engines shut down, the GIs unbuckled and shouldered their packs and duffels, eager to get onto firm ground. The copilot unbuckled and opened the side door, letting in the smells of Milne Bay.

Tarkington scrunched his nose. The combination of swamp and rotting jungle wasn't a pleasant combination. A hot wind hit him in the face as he descended the short flight of stairs. His shirt was already half wet and streaked with salt from the plane ride. The humidity of Milne Bay immediately opened his pores and sweat poured off him. He waded through water that came up to his ankles. Metal grating was the only thing keeping them and the parked planes from sinking into the mud. Mosquitos buzzed around his head. He ignored them as best as he could, knowing they were a fact of life in this region of the world, but he wasn't sure he'd ever seen them as thick. Luzon during the rainy season was bad, but this was far worse.

The squad's scowls told him no one was pleased with their new digs. He shook his head, *they'll adapt . . . they always do.*

Through the haze of mosquitos and mist, he saw someone standing in the doorway to a Quonset hut, waving at him. He hitched his pack and veered that way. A corporal stiffened as he approached. Tarkington nodded and the stocky soldier said with a heavy Australian accent, "I'm Corporal Nutchenko. Welcome to Milne Bay." He stepped aside, pushing the door open, "Come on in. Fewer mosquitos inside."

The squad stepped inside. The thin metal structure was one or two degrees cooler, and as promised, had fewer mosquitos. From outside, he heard aircraft landing and wondered if it were the P-40s.

A soldier sat behind a desk at the far end, and upon closer inspection, Tarkington saw it was an Australian officer. The men braced and saluted as the officer noticed them and stood. He pulled a hand across his dark hair and smiled, returning the salute, "At ease, men. You must be the Yanks we've been expecting. Welcome."

Tarkington relaxed and nodded, "Yes, sir. Just landed." He indicated his duffel bag and pack.

"Ah, yes. We'll get you settled soon enough. How was the flight? Heard you had some trouble with a couple Jap Zeros." He said it as though it were no more of a nuisance than ants at a picnic.

Tarkington thought how close the entire squad had come to dying, but took on the same nonchalant attitude, "Yes. Luckily, the P-40s showed up and ran them off."

"Yeah, Lieutenant Spaulding got a confirmed kill out of it." He indicated the corporal standing behind them, "Nutchenko will show you where you'll be staying, although you won't be there long. I'm Captain Leeds with the 7th Infantry Brigade." He said it in passing, as though it were an unimportant sidenote. "Once you're settled in, Nutchenko will show you around and get you fed, then we'll meet back here for a briefing at 1700 hours."

Tarkington nodded, surprised things were moving so fast, "Yes, sir."

Leeds lifted his chin, "We're on a bit of tight schedule on this one. The mission's for tomorrow night."

"Yes, sir." He was about to follow Nutchenko but held up a finger, remembering, "I'd like to repay those P-40 pilots. We owe 'em a drink."

Leeds looked embarrassed, "Sorry, it'll have to wait. We still don't have alcohol, despite being here a month. Very unlike us, but we've been quite harried."

Tarkington looked at Stollman. He never went anywhere without bringing a bottle. Stollman grinned and nodded. "I think I can help with that."

The Aussie licked his lips, "Give it to me, I'll pass it along to them. They're still on patrol."

Stollman looked sideways at him and Tarkington interjected, "Nah, we'd rather thank 'em ourselves, sir."

Leeds reared back, offended. "What? You don't trust me? I'm an officer and a gentleman, I can assure you." Stollman glanced at Tarkington, but before things escalated, Leeds grinned, leaned in, and winked, "I wouldn't trust an Aussie with alcohol either, 'specially one as parched as I am." He clapped his hands together, "See you at 1700, Yanks."

The P-40s landed an hour later; the roar of the Allison engines was unmistakable. The squad was settled into their cramped, leaking barracks tent. The adrenaline from the near-death experience on the transport was still coursing through their veins, so Tarkington said, "Stolly, bring the booze. Let's thank those guys properly."

Stolly pulled one of two bottles from his duffel and kissed it lovingly. "I suppose they earned it. Only leaves us with one, though."

They all walked from the barracks, making their way around puddles and mud to the airstrip labeled Number 3. It was shorter than the one they'd landed on.

They watched the two P-40 Kittyhawks deftly bounce along the freshly-laid Marston Matting—interconnected perforated steel plates—and park in revetments made from cut and stacked coconut trees. Flight mechanics and crews waited to push the planes into place after the pilots exited. The nearest pilot jumped from the wing, obviously excited, and trotted over to the other pilot who was taking things more slowly.

The exuberant pilot put his arm over the other pilot's shoulder and shook him, "You got him, Spall! You got him. I saw him go down."

The other pilot nodded, pushed the man away, and jokingly said, "Get off me! You gone soft or something?"

"That's number four. You're nearly an ace!"

"Let's get with our chiefs and meet after for an iced tea."

Tarkington hefted the bottle of whiskey and shook the brown liquid. It caught the light seductively. "I think we can do better than iced tea, sirs."

Both pilots stopped and stared at the new arrivals. "Who're you?"

Tarkington introduced himself and the others, "We were on that transport. You two saved our bacon."

The less exuberant pilot grinned, "Aha. Glad we could help. I'm Flight Lieutenant Spaulding and this ugly one's Flight Lieutenant Riggins." He pointed at the bottle and licked his lips, "You mentioned bacon, but I'm more inclined toward that at the moment." He took the proffered bottle and whistled, "Whiskey? Where the hell'd you get this?"

Tarkington pointed his thumb at Stollman, "PFC Stollman can pull this stuff from thin air, or so he leads us to believe. But I think it's more likely that there's a supply clerk back in Brisbane scratching his head and wondering where his stash disappeared to."

Spaulding handed the bottle back, "We've a debrief and we're still on duty till 1900 hours. But we'd fancy a drink after that."

Riggins nodded, not able to take his eyes from the golden liquid, "Aye, we would."

Tarkington nodded, "We've got a briefing around that time too. Where should we look for you?"

Spaulding pointed beyond the airstrip to an elongated thatch hut a couple hundred yards off, "In there. The blokes'll appreciate that."

Tarkington held up the bottle, "See you then."

5

Despite the heat and humidity, the GIs wore long sleeves and tucked in their pant legs to combat the millions of voracious mosquitos. None of them had seen anything like it and were told it was because of the 200 inches of annual rainfall, which meant there was standing water everywhere. Perfect breeding grounds for the annoying bloodsuckers.

They spent as little time outside tents and huts as possible, hustling across open mud-pits where they sunk to their shins with nearly every step. Even Henry, who'd grown up in similar circumstances, shook his head and stated, "The less time we spend in this hellhole, the better."

They'd slogged their way to the mess hall, ate the cold gruel, and reported to the briefing early, wanting to get this whole thing over with as quickly as possible.

Captain Leeds was sitting behind the desk and when they came in, he glanced at his watch, "You Yanks are early. I don't mind, but the others aren't here yet."

Tarkington said, "We don't mind. Just didn't want to slog our way across the grounds again."

Leeds nodded his understanding, "I don't blame you. It's even worse a few miles inland where the ground dips. This area's actually fairly dry, comparatively. Port Moresby's a veritable paradise in comparison, of course, but we don't want the Japs to have this bay, so here we are."

Tarkington got the impression that the officer was more interested in talking than filling out whatever paperwork he'd been working on. "The mountain range to the northwest's impressive," Tarkington stated.

Leeds put his pen down and nodded, "Yes, it is, isn't it? The Owen Stanley Range. You can't see most of it from here, but the range reaches over 13,000 feet in places."

"Tough terrain."

Leeds nodded sagely, "The worst. The Nips have been pushing from Buna along the only track leading through them to Port Moresby. It's called the Kokoda Trail. It runs some 55 miles and it's used by the locals." He shook his head, "From everything I've heard, it's brutal beyond measure." He sighed heavily, "Suspect we'll be having to fight the buggers there soon enough."

Captain Leeds's eyes lit up when he saw the door to the Quonset hut open as men dressed in Aussie Army uniforms entered, "Ah, here come the rest of the lads."

Despite the sauna-level heat, clouds of mosquitos, and wet conditions they lived in, the Aussies were all smiles. Most of them wore shorts, their bare legs tanned and cratered with countless mosquito bites. They greeted the six Yanks heartily, making introductions all around. It seemed more like a social event than a briefing on an upcoming mission. Tarkington decided he liked these soldiers. Cheery even in the face of misery. He settled back into the folding chair facing the captain's desk.

Captain Leeds's face turned serious and he began the briefing. He motioned toward a map focused on the southeastern tip of Papua New Guinea, "We are here, at the lovely Milne Bay. A few weeks ago, the Nips launched an attack against us, which we were fortunate enough to fight off. Enemy naval units—their version of marines--were dropped at Goodenough Island," he pointed to a small island 10 miles from Milne Bay, "here. They lost their rides home when our air forces discovered their beached barges and destroyed them. The marines are stranded. Their navy has already tried to rescue them but were unsuccessful. We believe they'll try again any day now.

"Something big is brewing. An Allied push. MacArthur doesn't want to leave them there on our flank, nor let them escape. So, our boys are going to land and destroy them, but command wants to know what they'll be facing." He lowered the pointer stick, "That's where you come in. Over-flights show perhaps a hundred men in the southeast corner, near Galaiwa Bay." He extended the pointer again. "The PT will drop you off on the west coast, here, at Taleba Bay. Depending on where you land, it's only less than two miles to where the Japs were spotted."

Tarkington had his elbows leaning on his knees, concentrating on the small map. He asked, "So just a look-see then?"

"Right, we'll do the heavy lifting once we know what we're facing. Insertion will be by rubber boat launched from the PT boat." He smacked the pointer in his hand, "You'll have the rest of today and tomorrow to prepare. It's a short boat ride. Insertion time is 2300 tomorrow night."

Tarkington nodded, then stood and approached the map. "Looks like a mountainous island like the others around here."

"Yes, quite right. The northern range is over 8,000 feet in spots. We had men stationed there before the Jap marines arrived, mostly engineers and stranded pilots who'd ditched their planes. They left soon after the marines arrived but they say the northern reaches are mostly kunai grass, while the area you'll be working in is jungle. Line of sight communication should work well as long as you can make it to higher ground."

Tarkington didn't like relying on their radios, as they tended not to work after minimal exposure to the tropical conditions, but he nodded his head. "Okay. Looks pretty straightforward."

After the briefing, they postponed getting ready for the upcoming mission, deciding to properly thank the Australian pilots instead. They slogged their way across the base, made their way to the Number 3 airstrip, and entered the dilapidated building on the eastern edge.

They were greeted by smiling faces and invited inside. It felt odd at first to be among officers, but they were immediately welcomed. The promise of alcohol greased the way and soon there were dirty glasses half-filled with the amber whisky.

Tarkington raised his glass, "To you airmen. We would've been feeding the fish if not for you."

The officers not on duty slugged the first one down heartily. The bottle was down by half and Stollman left it on the table for the Australians to dispense among themselves.

Once the alcohol had them feeling all right, Tarkington asked, "So how is it flying one of those machines?"

Lieutenant Riggins's eyes turned glassy, and he gazed at the ceiling as though thinking of something beautiful, "There's nothing like it, mate. Freedom. Of course, it would be a lot more enjoyable without the damned Japs."

Flight Lieutenant Spaulding shook his head. He was much less outspoken than his younger wingman. Tarkington asked him, "You don't agree?"

"I agree about the Japs, sure. But freedom? Hell, I barely have time to enjoy it between the constant engine tweaks and watching for impending engine failure."

Tarkington looked surprised, "Are the planes failing?"

Spaulding shrugged, "The mechanics are miracle workers, but if we weren't in a combat situation, there's no way we'd be flying. Everyone of 'em is several hundred flight hours past mandatory engine rebuilds. It's just a matter of time before they seize up." He gestured at Riggins, "Riggins had to do a dead stick landing just the other day. Engine quit on the downwind. He barely cleared the palms."

Winkleman asked, "How do they match up to the Zeros?"

Riggins answered, "Not well. The Japs can outturn anything we've got. Our only chance is to stay above them, dive, take a shot, then run like hell. They can't take a hit like we can though. That's why they're so damned maneuverable. They don't have any armor weighing them down. That means we can knock them out with just a few hits. But we've learned not to get into a turning fight with them. We'll lose every time."

Spaulding added, "Their pilots are top-notch too." That got a few guffaws and gaffs from the others, but Spaulding waved them off, "It's true.

They've been flying in combat for nearly ten years by now." He grinned, "But like young Riggins said: We've learned a lot." His grin disappeared, "We've had to."

As the squad pushed off from the PT boat, Tarkington couldn't explain the nervous energy he felt. They'd been in nearly constant combat since December of last year. He'd faced the enemy countless times, yet this somehow felt different. Alamo Scout training had honed their skills to a razor sharpness, and they'd all learned new tricks. He knew they were a better trained, more deadly force than they'd been a month and a half earlier, but he couldn't shake the feeling that he was entering combat again for the first time. He pushed the feeling aside, chalking it up to his long absence from the frontline, and concentrated on the mission.

He sat in the back of the rubber boat acting as the rudder man. They'd trained with the small boats endlessly, so there were no surprises. The other five men sat on the tubes, taking smooth, powerful strokes. The boat moved well, the only sound the dripping and swirl of the paddles. They wore dark mottled camouflage, their faces streaked with dark green and black face paint. Some wore nothing on their heads, others—like Tark-ington—preferred the soft baseball bill-style hats. Anything to help cover exposed skin from the vicious mosquitos.

Goodenough Island loomed large like a black shadow against the night sky, blotting out the stars near the horizon. Tarkington glanced back, seeing the PT boat slipping into the blackness. The muffled engine noise was barely noticeable.

They'd be on their own for at least the next 24 hours. This was no different than training; in fact, it would probably be easier since there'd likely be fewer surprises than what the instructors normally threw at them. Their packs were stacked in the center of the boat, easily accessed if they needed to exit quickly. Their M1 carbines were tightly slung across their backs. The carbines were much lighter and shorter than the more widely available M1 Garands, making them a perfect weapon for their missions. Each man had qualified expert with the carbines and preferred them. Hopefully—if all went as planned—they wouldn't have to fire a shot.

The slight sea swell died as they entered the natural protection of Taleba Bay. The night took on an unnatural quietness, making the paddlers slow without being told, making as little noise as possible. The boat continued straight, Tarkington making slight adjustments.

There were no lights on shore. They'd been told there were few inhabitants and the ones that were there would most likely be hiding from the Japanese. Taleba Bay was mostly undeveloped, although there was a rickety docking area they'd seen when going over naval reconnaissance photos. There'd been no sign of boats, but they'd be avoiding anything which might lead to their being discovered.

As they neared the shore, they stopped paddling and listened. The lapping of tiny waves hitting the beach was the only sound. Raker and Henry, sitting in front, stowed their paddles and unslung their carbines. They lay on the front tubes with their muzzles aiming toward the beach, scanning for targets.

After a minute, Tarkington signaled and the paddlers continued stroking slowly to shore. Seconds before the boat beached, the others stowed paddles and readied themselves. Raker and Henry hopped off the side, moved forward, and crouched 20 yards ahead, looking for trouble. The other four jumped out, grabbed the carry handles alongside the boat, and hefted it up the beach. It was tough going. The weight of the boat sank them into the sand, but their heart rates barely elevated.

Once they reached the jungle line, they lowered the boat and unslung their carbines. Raker and Henry continued into the jungle, making sure there was no one nearby. The night was quiet, only the buzzing and clicking of insects and the occasional night animal.

Raker appeared from the jungle. He looked deadly, like the grim reaper come to collect souls. He signaled, then helped lift the raft into the first few yards of jungle. There was a depression, something most likely left over from a storm surge. Tarkington signaled them to hide the boat there. The squad dropped the raft into the depression, then after a silent count of three, opened the air valves. The sudden gush of air was loud but short-lived. They deflated it halfway, the rubber form fitting into the depression nicely. They removed packs and gear and covered the boat with large jungle leaves and draping vines.

The starlight shining down from clear skies helped illuminate their surroundings. The squad's natural night vision made the beach look almost like dusk or early dawn. Tarkington wondered—not for the first time—if night vision improved the more often you used it. He supposed if that were true, Tark's Ticks would be at the top of the pyramid.

He motioned to Winkleman, who passed it along, and soon Henry led them carefully along the edge of the jungle toward the enemy. The nervous tension Tarkington had felt on the boat ride vanished, replaced with the confidence of business as usual. They were Tark's Ticks *and* Alamo Scouts.

Henry and Raker stayed in front, keeping fifteen yards between them. Tarkington and the rest followed at ten-yard intervals, watching the darkness for anything unusual. So far, they'd seen nothing but bugs, snakes, and stinking jungle. Tarkington grinned to himself. It was still a far sight better than Milne Bay.

When they got to the southern end of Taleba Bay, they were forced to climb a steep band of hills. The jungle gave way to kunai grass, and Tarkington was glad to have sleeves and pants to avoid the grass's sharp, cutting edges. They wove through the waist-high grass, moving upward steadily. Finally, after he estimated they'd gained 1,000 feet, they crested, and Raker and Henry stopped. The effort had them all sweating buckets, but their breathing was slow and steady.

The squad spread out without a sound. More bands of hills and cliffs spread before them, although the one they were on looked to be the tallest. It wouldn't be easy going, however. The water of Ward Hunt Strait separating Goodenough Island from mainland Papua New Guinea spread out like a blanket of blackness to their right. Somewhere out there, their ride home lingered. Tarkington whispered to Henry, "Be hard pressed to finish this mission tonight."

Henry pointed toward the waterline, "We could go lower, avoid these ups and downs, but it's probably marshland."

Tarkington shook his head, the movement lost in the darkness. "We'll continue this way. We'll have a good overlook position once the sun comes up."

Raker and Henry pushed over the ridge and descended the far side. The kunai grass continued, making the walking relatively easy. They traversed three more hills, each steeper than the last. They slowed as they fatigued.

Finally, what Tarkington thought must be Malaiwa Bay, spread out before them. The slope toward the bay was gradual, not nearly as steep as what they'd trudged up. Instead of kunai grass, low jungle spread out below them, stretching nearly to the water's edge. Tarkington checked his watch; they'd come two and a half miles and it had taken them nearly three hours. Not bad for steep terrain at night, but with the sunrise only an hour away, they'd need to hustle to get close enough to see anything useful.

He signaled a brief break and the squad quickly and quietly drank water and ate dried fruit and jerky. They were on the move ten minutes later, moving through the much more ominous jungle.

They'd gone half a quarter mile when Henry and Raker simultaneously stopped and lowered themselves slowly. Everyone froze and mimicked their move until they were all lying flat. A cough from somewhere nearby, followed with an indistinct murmur, made them all hold their breath.

Tarkington crawled forward, inch by slow inch, until he was beside Henry. He heard moans and coughing and smelled something foul. Movement caught his eye. Twenty yards away, someone went into a crouch. *Have they seen us?* He shunned the thought, knowing they may as well have been invisible behind the darkness and camouflage.

More moaning and again the shape of someone standing, then moving and crouching. Henry leaned into him, "Hospital."

Tarkington nodded. It made sense. The Japanese naval troops had been stranded for weeks and would be running low on supplies. Perhaps they were suffering from malaria, dengue fever, foot rot, or any of the other myriad ailments this part of the world held. Half the US troops, and the better adjusted Australians and New Zealanders, suffered from the same ailments. *The diseases are the only ones winning this war,* he thought bitterly.

He touched Henry's arm, signaling him to retrace steps and go around the hospital. Tarkington made a mental note of the location, not wanting to run into it if forced to leave in a hurry.

An hour later—the hospital at their back—they held up where the jungle met the sea. In the predawn light, they saw manmade structures dotting the area. There were no lights burning, but it was obvious the place was occupied. Even in the darkness, it was apparent the buildings were in good upkeep and there were dug-out canoes pulled up on the short beach.

The GIs dug themselves into the jungle, making themselves as invisible and comfortable as possible. There was no telling how long they'd need to stay in place, and taking small steps toward comfort now would go a long way in the coming day when adjusting position could get you killed. With excellent views of the bay, dry ground beneath them, weapons, and rations at the ready, they watched the sun come up.

They'd been counting enemy naval personnel for hours. As was normally the case, the reconnaissance overflights had underestimated the Japanese by half. So far, they'd counted upwards of 500 men packing the bay.

A nearby trail led from the beach back toward the makeshift hospital in the jungle. Tarkington thought it odd not to use the buildings dotting the shoreline for the purpose, but perhaps the Japanese feared an air attack from Milne Bay or Port Moresby. From his experience, the Japanese had no problems hitting well-marked and obvious Red Cross symbols with strafing runs, so the Japanese probably assumed the Allies were the same.

He decided they'd count the patients in the hospital area on their way out. It would mean little, since those sailors were most likely out of the fight anyway, but he wanted to be thorough, it being the Scout's first mission.

Tarkington flexed his feet, tightened his buttocks muscles, and moved various other body parts in an effort to keep blood from pooling and making his joints stiffen. Although none of the micro-movements would be noticed even if an enemy soldier were inches away, he still did them slowly. Sitting in one place without moving for an entire day was hard on a body, so the micro-movements were necessary, especially if they needed to move out in a hurry. Adrenaline helped in emergency cases, but having to move when an entire limb was numb was nearly impossible.

Although the other Scouts were within yards, Tarkington barely noticed them. When he glanced their way, he had to concentrate to find them, even though he knew their approximate positions.

Henry was to his right. Tarkington moved his head slowly until he saw just the faint outline of his head. He may as well have been a rock or a bush. Tarkington startled when he realized Henry was staring back at him, just the whites of his eyes giving him away. Henry pointed to his darkened ear.

Tarkington listened, concentrating on what Henry was hearing. Finally, just the hint of something. An engine. It was coming from the sea.

Tarkington shifted his eyes toward the bay. Japanese naval personnel had been walking back and forth along the small dock all morning, but now they were standing still, gazing out to sea. One of them gestured quickly, sending another sailor running back toward the buildings. Tarkington had a good idea of the command structure. Picking out officers from enlisted men was easy, but the sailor who'd sent the man was probably an NCO. He catalogued the information for later.

Sailors streamed out from the jungle, some carrying men on stretchers, others helping comrades along acting as a crutch. Finally, a handcart pulled by two struggling, shirtless sailors emerged. The back of the cart was stacked with bodies. The entire entourage ended at the docks, as though expecting rescue. The engine noise increased, and around the northeastern corner, a small ship emerged.

Tarkington had a decision to make. There was definitely a rescue in process. His mission was to assess the enemy so the Australians could destroy them before they escaped. MacArthur didn't simply want them gone, he wanted them dead. Beside him in his pack was the radio. Radio silence until pickup time was the order, but he could call the PT boat who could transfer the information to Milne Bay, and within minutes, there'd either be air support or shipping moving to intercept. If he called them now, they'd be here in a few hours.

A coldness crept through him. Calling in an attack against wounded would make him like those Japanese pilots he'd seen strafing hospital ships in Manila Bay. He remembered the impotent rage they'd all felt back then, vowing revenge. Perhaps one of those wounded men he was watching had taken part. Their navy certainly wasn't above atrocities. Perhaps one of those men had killed innocent civilians, or sat idly by while others had. *Was that any better?*

An image of his brother Robert flashed into his mind. He pictured him charging up a nameless beach somewhere against an enemy machine gun nest. That sealed it for him. *The more Japs I kill, the better chance that Robert survives.*

6

Moving from concealment was too risky, so Tarkington moved glacially. It took a full ten minutes before he had the radio out of his pack and another ten before he felt comfortable enough to transmit. He didn't worry about the Japanese picking up his broadcast and triangulating his position. He doubted the ragtag, stranded sailors had such technology at their disposal, but he did worry about the squelch and static being heard by the sailor sitting on the porch only ten yards away.

He waited for the right moment to transmit. If he didn't do it in the next twenty minutes, it would probably be too late. The enemy ship had anchored and sent in a couple skiffs to gather the wounded. They were already on their second trip, and it would probably be their last. He assumed they'd collect the healthy sailors next. The entire operation wouldn't take more than two hours.

Finally, an NCO approached the lounging sailor on the porch and barked harsh orders at him. The enlisted man jumped to his feet and trotted after the NCO, who continued berating him.

Tarkington pressed the side of the SCR-536 radio, "Trapdoor One. This is Tango Two. Do you read? Over." Low static met his effort and he pushed himself as low into the jungle floor as possible, hoping the sound wasn't carrying. He tried three more times. The last time there was something—a ghostly voice—but he doubted it was the PT boat crew. He cursed to himself. He had a good line of sight. He could nearly see the entire bay stretching toward Papua New Guinea. Why the hell weren't they answering?

He tried different frequencies, secondary options for just such occasions, but still nothing but static. *Dammit,* he cursed. If he wanted to get this done, they'd have to abandon their spots and move to the hills for better reception. He gave up on the radio, stuffing it back inside the pack carefully, wanting to thrash it against a rock.

The rescue operation was in full swing. Now would be the best time to leave—while they were distracted. He signaled Henry, who nodded slowly and passed the order along. Tarkington found Raker's eyes watching him from the left. He signaled and Raker passed it to Winkleman and Vick.

It was excruciatingly slow going, but they were finally far enough back from the bay to gather and discuss. Tarkington told them his plan. No one questioned it, and they moved diagonally away from the emptied hospital area toward the nearest hill. Tarkington's muscles were stiff despite his best efforts. He grimaced as the pins and needles coursed through his extremities.

Suddenly—from his right—a Japanese marine appeared. He was midway through strapping his belt buckle. For an instant, they stared at one another in disbelief. Tarkington's training took over and he reacted first. He stepped into him and broke his jaw with a quick swing of the carbine's stock. The enemy marine staggered backward, his fall arrested by a thick tree trunk. Tarkington followed with an equally brutal thrust into the marine's face. The butt-stock drove into his nose. His head snapped back and slammed against the tree with a sickening crunch. Blood splattered Tarkington's face. He ignored it as the marine slumped and slid down the trunk, his legs spasming unnaturally.

The squad crouched, watching the jungle for alerted enemy. The noise from the grisly killing sounded like rifle shots to them after being silent so long. A full minute passed before Tarkington hissed, "Move out." He dragged the body farther into the jungle, dumping him among ferns and foliage.

Stollman covered him. "Where the hell'd he come from?" he whispered.

Tarkington shrugged, "Beats the hell outta me. Must've just finished shitting."

They left the area quickly and quietly. The ground sloped up and they followed a winding game trail. They finally stopped when they reached an open area with commanding views of the bay.

As Tarkington pulled off his pack and fished out the radio, Winkleman said, "That Jap came outta nowhere. Hopefully he won't be missed."

Tarkington nodded. The squad spread out to cover him while he tried to raise the PT boat on the radio. This time he made contact on the first try. The signal was strong and clear, and within minutes he'd passed the information along and was told to standby for more instructions.

The view of the bay from their new vantage point was better than the previous spot. Although not as close, they could still see the dock and skiffs ferrying men to the ship. After thirty minutes, the ship pulled anchor and moved off around the jut of land, out of sight. Most of the Japanese sailors and marines were still down there, and they surmised the ship wasn't big enough to take more than the wounded and dead.

An hour passed before the radio crackled, making Tarkington jump. He kept his voice as low as possible, and after a few minutes of back and forth, signed off. The squad looked on with curiosity. He waved them closer, "So here's the deal: P-40s from Milne Bay are on the way. I told them the ship already left, but it shouldn't be hard to find. They want us to hold here and report on any more targets. Pickup time is 2100 out of Taleba Bay."

There were nods all around and Winkleman asked, "Are they gonna strafe the bay here?"

Tarkington shrugged as he stuffed the radio into his pack, "I dunno. Maybe."

A half hour after the radio call, they heard the faint buzzing of aircraft approaching. Henry was the first to spot them. He pointed, "There."

Tarkington strained and finally saw four tiny black dots against the white clouds. Rain squalls were all around the area, dark columns of water beating down unpredictably. The sky directly overhead was scattered with white and gray clouds, but none of the squalls looked as though they'd hit their area.

The dots grew until they appeared to be more than just globs. They flashed overhead at 3,000 feet, their throaty engines momentarily blotting out any other sounds. The Japanese below scattered like cockroaches when someone flicks on a kitchen light. The planes passed out of sight in seconds. The engine's hum faded until it was only a memory.

Henry whispered, "Japs are up to something."

Tarkington crawled forward until he was beside his lead scout. Sure enough, fifteen Japanese with slung rifles were moving toward the jungle, spread out in a long line. Even from their perch 400 feet above, they could hear them calling out, as though searching for a lost dog . . . or comrade.

"Shit," cursed Tarkington. "Must be looking for their lost man." Henry nodded and Tarkington wondered if he'd hidden the body well enough. It wouldn't be easy to find, but . . . "They'll find him—and when they do—they'll hunt us." He looked around at the squad's camouflaged faces and raised his voice slightly. "We've gotta find better cover, wait 'em out till extraction time. I'd say we've got about a half hour before they find the body." He took in the terrain. The hills toward Taleba Bay were covered in kunai grasses and wouldn't provide enough cover. He pointed up the hill, "We'll get into the jungle up there, find a good viewpoint, and disappear."

They moved fast, being careful not to leave signs of their passing. The ground was relatively spongy, but they stayed off game trails and minimized their boot-prints as much as possible. Pursuit up these hills would be taxing, even for healthy troops. The Japanese they'd observed were mostly malnourished and sickly. Tarkington was confident they could avoid detection. If he were wrong? More Japanese would die. His mission was reconnaissance only, but his men were willing and able to take the fight to the enemy if it came to that.

Henry and Raker found a suitable spot to lie another 200 feet up the hill and one ridge northeast. The bay was still visible through the trees, but now they could also see around the cape and into the Solomon Sea where the Japanese ship had gone. It was nowhere in sight, nor were the RAAF planes.

The GIs buried themselves in the undergrowth until the only way they'd be discovered was if they were stepped on. The day passed into afternoon. Bugs and worms crisscrossed their backs, unaware of their presence. The GIs itched but ignored the urge to scratch. Once you gave in to that urge, it was a slippery slope.

They hadn't heard from the Japanese since they'd left their previous spot. Whether or not they'd find the body was soon answered when they heard a panicked, shrill yell. More distant yelling answered, then silence. Tarkington checked the time. They'd remain in place until dark, then start the long trek back to Taleba Bay. Just a few more hours.

Tarkington stopped breathing when he heard someone slip and curse in Japanese. He froze, listening and searching for the source. More sounds of scraping and climbing mixed with indistinct murmurs. They were coming from below. He couldn't see them, but they seemed to come directly up the slope. It wasn't excessively steep, and there were animal tracks coursing through the area like chaotic spider webs. Tarkington was surprised the emaciated marines had gotten this far up the hill.

Movement from the right. He didn't look, but kept his head perfectly still, relying on his peripheral vision. Two Japanese marines labored their way up the hill. Each held an Arisaka Type 38 rifle. He was intimately familiar with the weapon. He'd been forced to use one on Luzon and Mindanao when they'd run low on ammunition for their army-issued Springfields.

No other enemy appeared, and Tarkington thought they must have split off from the main group to cover more ground. They moved slowly, their breathing deep and labored. They were following the slight crest of the hill, and if they kept their current course, they'd pass within feet of their position.

They passed behind them—close but out of sight. Tarkington suppressed his breathing and his heart rate, concentrating on listening to their footfalls, ready to react at the slightest hint of discovery. The marines stopped and exchanged low words. He heard one of them unscrewing the cap to a canteen and glugging loudly. They sat down and Tarkington thought they were only feet from where he lay hidden. Even if they stepped on his position, they probably wouldn't notice anything out of the ordinary.

Long minutes passed. The marines talked in low murmurs and—not for the first time—Tarkington wished he knew more Japanese. They'd studied some basic phrases in Alamo Scout training, but not enough to understand what they were talking about. In fact, it had been one of his suggestions to Colonel Bradshaw: full immersion language school.

After fifteen minutes, Tarkington wondered if they'd ever leave. The day was waning toward evening, and if he wished to make their rendezvous, they'd need to leave right at dusk.

The two enemy marines had been quiet for a few minutes, and Tarkington wondered if they were napping. One spoke suddenly, his voice sharp and full of concern. The other spoke and was hushed by the first, as though listening for something. Tarkington heard it a second later: the dull hum of airplane engines.

He heard the two marines get to their feet, their voices excited. He imagined them trying to get a better view of the sky as he heard their feet rustling. One stepped forward and he felt pressure on his right foot. He tensed, but the marines continued babbling back and forth.

The engine noise changed pitch, increasing, and the marines' voices went up an octave. The planes sounded close, like they were making a run on the bay. He refocused his attention that way, not daring to move his head. He couldn't see the planes, but he could see the dock and some buildings. The hammering of heavy machine guns accompanied the scream of the diving aircraft. Through the trees, he saw huge geysers of water and sand erupt. The marines were yelling. Tarkington thought now was as good a time as any to take them out, but as he steeled himself to make the move, the two marines took off running back the way they'd come.

Tarkington allowed himself to breathe again. He moved his head, looking the way the marines had gone. They were out of sight, but he could hear them pushing through branches and vines on their way back to the beach. He shifted his body, letting the dirt sift off him. The others did the same, and soon they were exposed. Tarkington grinned, thinking they looked like zombies from a comic book rising from graves. The feeling of pressure on his right foot remained like a ghost, reminding him how close the enemy soldiers had been.

The roaring of aircraft and their hammering guns continued raking the beach and bay. Tarkington brushed himself off and ordered, "Let's get the hell outta here before those sons-a-bitches come back."

The squad made it back to Milne Bay without incident. They'd been awake for the better part of twenty-four hours, and their drooping eyes and dragging asses showed it. Tarkington sent the men off to shower, eat, and sleep. He and Winkleman scrubbed the grease paint off their faces as best they could before reporting to the same Quonset hut where they'd been briefed a few days before. They'd been ordered to report for debrief ASAP.

It was early morning. The sun had peaked over the eastern horizon less than an hour before. There was a guard posted outside the hut, causing them to exchange curious glances. The guard looked serious, although his Australian infantryman's hat—pinned up on one side—made him look downright jaunty. He blocked their way until they told him who they were, then he stepped aside and stiffened as they passed.

Winkleman whispered, "Who's in here? MacArthur?"

The row of windows along the curved walls were wide open, but it was still dim inside. They remembered to take off their grimy soft caps as their eyes adjusted from the bright sun to the gloomy interior. They both stiffened upon seeing a row of officers sitting at a rickety table at the front of the room.

Beside a nervous-looking Captain Leeds, the Australian officer who'd briefed them, sat Colonel Bradshaw and an older officer whom neither of them recognized. The three gleaming stars on his collar told them everything they needed to know, however, and they snapped off crisp salutes.

The general grinned and in a voice that made them want to clear their throats, said, "At ease."

Tarkington and Winkleman relaxed a little, and now that their eyes adjusted to the light, they could better see who they were facing. The general was a short, older man with steel in his eyes. The three officers stood and approached them, the general leading the way. He extended his hand, first to Tarkington, then Winkleman, and said with a Texas drawl tinged with something slightly foreign, "Welcome back, men. I'm Lieutenant General Krueger. I've been wanting to meet you and your team for quite a while now."

A light went off in Tarkington's head. Bradshaw had mentioned Krueger as being his boss and the brains behind the Alamo Scouts. *Holy shit, he leads Sixth Army!* "It's an honor to meet you, sir." He looked them up and down. Their uniforms were filthy and Tarkington was sure he'd probably stained the general's hand with dirt and grease camouflage paint. "Sorry for our appearance, sir. We were told to report immediately."

He waved the comment away, "A successful first mission, Sergeant?"

Tarkington nodded, "Yes, sir. We have a good understanding of the enemy forces on Goodenough Island, sir."

Krueger clasped his hands behind his back and raised his chin, looking down his crooked nose. Despite his short stature, Tarkington felt he was facing a giant. "You broke radio silence protocol, Sergeant. Care to explain?"

"Yes, sir. It was my decision. Our mission parameters were to gather intelligence on the enemy forces on the island. Captain Leeds and Lieutenant Trebain informed us it was the intention of senior command to destroy the forces on the island. When I saw them escaping, I broke radio silence to inform command that their quarry was escaping, sir."

Krueger nodded and glanced at Colonel Bradshaw, "Good. We want our scouts to think on their feet." He continued, "Turns out the ship slipped away, unfortunately. The RAAF flyboys couldn't find her, but they spent their munitions on Japanese marines on the beach." He grinned, "Must've been quite a show."

Tarkington nodded and couldn't keep the grin from his face, "Yes, sir. Although at the time, there were two Jap marines within spitting distance, so we couldn't do much celebrating."

The general shook his head, "I'd love to hear about that over a beer sometime, Sergeant." He glanced at Bradshaw, the corners of his mouth lowering, "I'd like to stay for the debrief, but I've gotta get back to Port Moresby. Besides, that part of the operation's for our Australian friends." He extended his hand again and they shook, "Good job. If I were twenty," he grinned, correcting himself, "thirty years younger . . ."

They stiffened and saluted as he walked toward the door. He returned the salute and before leaving said, "By the way, I got your recommendations about the training. Very interesting and informative."

"Thank you, sir. It was an honor to be the first soldiers through the training."

Krueger glanced at Bradshaw, "Yes. I don't think we'll do a lot of advertising about that sort. It's best to keep this whole thing under wraps." He eyed them both, "Understood?"

Both Tarkington and Winkleman stiffened and barked simultaneously, "Understood, sir."

"You and your men'll be busy over the coming months. Hope you're ready."

Tarkington answered, "Yes, sir. We're ready!"

7

"How long we gonna have to stay in this hellhole, Tark?" asked Stollman. They'd been back from the Goodenough Island mission for three days, sitting on their hands in Milne Bay.

"You think they tell me anything, Stolly? You know as much as I do, probably more."

Raker chimed in, "I'm about ready to try out one of the local women if we stay much longer."

Winkleman shook his head, "You know they're off limits. Besides, you've got as much in common with these women as a turd and a pineapple."

Raker reared back, shaking his head, "What the hell does that even mean, Wink? I'm male; they're female. End of story." He leaned in and lowered his voice, "Well, there's more, but I don't wanna make you blush."

They were spread out on a shady and semi-dry area overlooking Milne Bay and the jetty at Gili-Gili. Tarkington was putting his carbine back together after a cleaning. The others were doing the same, the weapon parts spread upon dirty white cloths.

Henry grinned at the exchange. The banter between the two occurred like clockwork if they were near each other for more than a few seconds. He pointed, "Maybe he'll know more." Captain Leeds was approaching.

Tarkington replaced the magazine into his carbine, the final step after he'd cleaned the weapon. He looked up, seeing the officer striding their way. He wore khaki shorts, and a shirt with the sleeves pinned up smartly. Tarkington moved to get to his feet, but Leeds held up a hand, "No need to get up, Sergeant."

Tarkington gave him a sideways grin, squinting through the sun, "You here to give us a new mission, sir?"

Leeds looked around. There was no one nearby. He sat beside the men and enjoyed the view overlooking the green waters of Milne Bay. He pointed, "You know the Japs landed a couple miles from here. Somewhere up there."

Tarkington asked, "Were you here, sir?"

He nodded, "That I was. Happened in August. If they'd landed right here, or even just over there," he pointed east, "they might've kicked us out of here. But for some reason, they chose the worst spot in the whole bay. They had to trek through the swamps and grasses, giving us time to whittle 'em down and set up a proper defense." He thumbed over his head, "Back there at Number 3 strip—that's where we set up. Japs could only come from one direction; the other routes are mud and swamp. It was a bloody massacre." He shook his head, remembering the day. "But they just kept coming and coming. For a while, we thought we might run out of ammo." He paused and flicked a mosquito off his arm. "A couple of your Army Air Corps A-20s out of Moresby hit their ship trying to offload. Destroyed most of their supplies. They were on the ropes the whole time. They never really had a chance."

"Sounds rough, sir."

"It was touch and go for a while, but the outcome was never really in doubt, especially once we destroyed their supplies." Tarkington exchanged a glance with Winkleman, who lifted his eyebrows. *Where is this going?* "Anyway, the Japs failed, obviously. They would've used this bay to launch against Moresby, but instead were forced to land on the north coast at Gona and Buna and use the Kokoda Trail over the Owen Stanleys."

Tarkington nodded, "Yes, we've been briefed on the situation around here, sir. Sounds like terrible fighting up there."

Leeds shook his head, sadly, "I've a mate in the 25th Infantry. Told me stories. It's a bloody mess. Beyond all reason, I hear. Those boys in the 39th

Militia had no idea what they were getting into. The Militia's mostly conscripts, they get a bad rap from us AIF troops, but they proved themselves from everything I've heard . . . except from the official news outlets."

Tarkington nodded, knowing firsthand the difficulties of fighting in close jungle terrain. The scuttlebutt said that MacArthur wasn't impressed with the Australians' efforts. If true, Tarkington had no doubt Mac would change his tune if he had to pick up a rifle and trudge over the Owen Stanleys himself—all while being hunted by ruthless Japanese.

He'd only been on Papua New Guinea a week and had seen very little of the island, but already had the sense that the place was a quagmire. "Sounds like they're doing their jobs and then some, sir. The Japs are being pushed back toward the coast."

Leeds nodded, "Yes, yes. Which is where you blokes are being sent." The entire squad leaned in, their interest piqued. "I'll give you a proper briefing back at base, but I can give you the gist of things since I've got you all together." He looked around again, "And this area looks secure enough."

Tarkington nodded, "Yes, sir. Don't see any spies around."

"Quite. Well—like you said—our blokes have pushed the Nips back toward Kokoda village. They're dug in tight and fight for every foot. Allied command wants the job done so they can get onto other things without worrying about the airfields at Buna. The Japs are finished—malnourished—" he shook his head, "You should see some of the prisoners—like skeletons with skin. But you know how they are, they won't surrender even with their backs against the sea and starving."

Tarkington nodded sagely, knowing exactly what he meant. "So, more reconnaissance?"

Captain Leeds shook his head, "Not this time." He looked around the group of hard men, "Sabotage."

Stollman lit up and clapped his hands, "Hot damn! 'Bout time!"

Two hours later, the squad gathered inside the same Quonset hut they'd been in before. Captain Leeds, along with a tall, thin American officer, stood in front, and when they were all gathered, Leeds introduced him,

"This is Lieutenant Hurst from the 128th Infantry Regiment of the 32nd Division, logistics. I'll let him brief you."

Lieutenant Hurst nodded and looked the men over. He scowled and addressed Captain Leeds, "Is this it?" Leeds nodded and Hurst shook his head and mumbled something under his breath. He stepped to a map of the northeastern coast of New Guinea, which extended all the way up to Buna and Gona beyond. He shook his head slightly, as though the briefing was a total waste of time. He sighed heavily and carried on, "Buna," he smacked the map with a pointer, "is here. There're an estimated 1,000 Japanese troops trapped there. Our troops, along with our Australian allies, have been pursuing them down the Kokoda Trail for the past several weeks. They've dug in, making things difficult. So, we're bringing in more troops so we can put pressure on their flanks." He paused and chugged water from a glass, his Adam's apple rising and falling as he gulped. He smacked the glass down and continued, "Over the next week, we'll fly the 128th into Wanigela," he circled an area on the map, "from Port Moresby and soon after, we'll move up the north coast. Some will move by boat around Cape Nelson, and some elements will move overland to Gobe, a town on the north shore of the cape." He smacked an area on the map. "Command wants to send you men in advance to Gobe. Reconnaissance flights have shown a possible Japanese stronghold there. It's an ammo dump or heavy weapons. They want you to destroy them in place before the main force arrives."

Tarkington raised his hand and Hurst's face reddened, but he pointed to him to proceed. "Why not just hit them with an airstrike or have the Navy pound them from the sea?"

Hurst looked at Captain Leeds as though he wanted help with a dense child. Leeds's face remained impassive. Hurst answered testily, "Well, Sergeant—I only know half the answer. The sea's uncharted. There're reefs and shallows everywhere. Ships can't risk going in there. I don't know about air strikes. I'm not one to question orders. I'm just here to relay your mission brief as they gave it to me."

Tarkington raised his hand again and Hurst extended his chin and shook his head quickly, then nodded for him to speak. Tarkington asked, "Can we see the reconnaissance photos, sir?"

Hurst tucked his chin into his neck as though smelling something repulsive. "No. They're classified, I suspect. Regardless, I don't have them."

Tarkington nodded, keeping his tone even, "Yes, sir."

Silence pervaded the area and finally Hurst put the pointer down, crossed his arms, and shook his head. "I came all the way out here from Moresby to brief two sergeants and—and four PFCs," he spluttered. He dropped his arms and paced, "A six-man squad? This isn't worth my time. You're being sent to your deaths, or more likely capture. That'll put the 128th's lives in danger."

He was about to say more but Tarkington raised his hand again and Hurst's face went from red to purple. He nearly yelled, "Speak, Sergeant. What?"

"Can you tell us how we're getting there and when we leave, sir?" Captain Leeds kept a stoic face but Hurst's eyes shot daggers his way. Vick had to pinch Stollman who was desperately trying to keep from laughing out loud.

Hurst's eyes darted around the room, knowing he was being played the fool. He was about to burst, he'd put every man here on report, but then he remembered the orders that sent him here. Captain Lentworthy had passed them along to him. The orders and the mission brief had been prepared by a Colonel Bradshaw, and upon inquiry, he learned that Bradshaw was a part of the newly-formed Sixth Army. It was highly unusual having orders given this way, but a colonel was a colonel and his signature certainly seemed to grease the wheels well. He hopped a flight without any trouble and was at Milne Bay the same day.

He bit back the anger rising in his craw. He opened a folder and read it in a clipped tone. "You'll fly to Wanigela tomorrow evening. You're to take enough rations for ten days. A barge will take you around the cape and insert you near Gobe. After completing your mission, you'll await the 128th, which will have more orders for you." He shut the mission folder with a snap and asked, "Any more questions?"

Tarkington nodded, "When is the 128th expected to arrive in Gobe, sir?"

Hurst had to open the folder again to find the information. He finally did, "Sometime around the 16th of October."

Tarkington nodded, "Thank you, sir."

Although Tarkington's tone was even and without a hint of malice, Hurst bit back, "I'm not sure why command thinks you're so special." He sat on the rickety table and looked the men over, "A six-man force is worthless. Actually dangerous. You'll most likely give up our plans to the Japanese when they cut on you."

Tarkington knew the young officer was trying to get a rise out of him, to give him an excuse to write him up, but he couldn't keep from smiling and saying in a low grumble, "I'll be sure to tell them all about you, Lieutenant."

Hurst's mouth went into a thin line and he was about to retort when Captain Leeds put his hand on the lieutenant's shoulder, "Thank you, Lieutenant. That'll be all." Hurst spluttered and started to say something, but Leeds raised his voice, "You're dismissed, Lieutenant. Soon as the C-47's offloaded, you can head back to Moresby and count bullets, or whatever it is you quartermaster folks do."

Hurst looked ready to explode but saluted and stormed out past the grinning GIs. Winkleman called after him, "Thanks for the briefing, Lieutenant. Have a safe flight."

Hurst stormed out the door, slamming it behind him. They heard him yelling for his driver, who'd probably catch hell the entire ride to the airfield. The GIs shook their heads and laughed, but Leeds put an end to it. "That'll be all, men," he said, grinning.

The squad stood as Leeds left out the back door. When they were alone, Henry drawled, "You're a cruel son of a bitch, Tark."

Tarkington raised his hands as if to say, "Who, me?" and said, "I was the epitome of politeness and decorum."

Winkleman guffawed, "When you raised your hand the second time, I thought his head was going to explode."

Raker laughed, "I've never seen that shade of purple."

When the laughter died down, Tarkington got serious. "We could be out there longer than ten days—you know how these things go—so bring extra rations. We've got the rest of today and tomorrow to prepare, but there may not be enough on hand around here, especially ammunition, so start scrounging."

Stollman proclaimed, "We've got plenty of bombs. We could take out an entire regiment of tanks with what we've got."

"Pare it down, if you need to, and disperse it. Remember, this weather runs havoc on those blasting caps."

The next day, two P-40s took off early in the morning. The squad was outside doing calisthenics, trying to keep up their fitness levels. Tarkington waved at the pilots, recognizing Flight Lieutenant Spaulding in the lead plane.

After sharing drinks with the Australian pilots who'd run off the Japanese Zero on their flight to Milne Bay, they continued to meet in the thatch hut alongside the airstrip whenever possible. Even after the booze ran out, they continued spending time together. The Australian Imperial Forces, or AIF, were pleasant enough, but the one night of drinking with the pilots had cemented their friendship and the GIs enjoyed hearing flight stories almost as much as the pilots enjoyed hearing the ground-pounders' war stories. Respect grew between them, despite the GIs thinking all pilots were a bunch of pansies and vice versa.

After PT, the squad spent the next few hours preparing their gear for the upcoming mission. They laid everything out, taking stock of exactly what they had and what they still needed. It was plainly obvious they were low on rations. They'd see what the AIF had, and if they were stingy, Stollman and Vick would find a way to supplement their food. If it came to that, Tarkington made it clear he didn't want to know about it.

A piercing sound like a high, loud whistle brought them to their feet. *Air raid.* It wouldn't be the first time the Japanese bombed Milne Bay; the enemy planes coming from airfields in Buna or Rabaul hit them regularly. The sound of a stuttering engine pulled their eyes to the sky. A smoking, listing P-40 Kittyhawk came over the hill. Normally, the pilots circled once or twice, reducing speed, evaluating wind, and lining up on the runway, but this pilot wasn't doing any of that. He was in trouble and coming straight in.

An old truck trundled from around an aircraft revetment and parked alongside the runway. Men scrambled from the cab and entered the back, manning metal barrels with hoses stuck out the top. Tarkington and the others ran to the side of the truck. Two pilots burst from their tents, shielding their eyes from the glaring sun. They ran to the truck and gave curt nods to the GIs.

Winkleman asked, "Who is it? Can you tell?"

Flight Lieutenant Yuncy answered, "It's either Spaulding or Riggins." From behind the struggling plane, another Kittyhawk appeared, this one healthy. It zoomed past the runway and arced up after passing. Yuncy pointed, "That's Riggins. It's Spaulding in the other."

Everyone watched the struggling plane. It seemed to inch its way forward. To Tarkington, it looked as though it would simply fall out of the sky. "Is he gonna land short?" he asked.

Yuncy shrugged, "I think he'll make the field, but look at his gear, it's only halfway down, and the right one's missing the wheel. He needs to bring the gear up, or it'll be ugly."

"Land without gear?"

Yuncy nodded, "Better that way. It's easier to pancake in than to land with half the gear down. The tower will tell him to raise it, I hope."

"Does he have enough time? He's close."

Yuncy pointed, "See? He's raising it by hand. Must have a hydraulic leak."

Sure enough, Tarkington saw the gear reversing back into the wings, agonizingly slowly. "He'll be down before the gear's up."

"It'll be close," said Flight Lieutenant Willingham. He shook his head, "Bringing in a damaged plane, keeping up speed, watching the stall, engine smoked and hand cranking the gear—he's busy."

The truck driver put the vehicle into gear and started moving down the runway, trying to gauge where Spaulding's stricken plane would end up. The two mechanics held onto the water barrels, never taking their eyes from the plane.

The P-40's engine spluttered and coughed, sending great gouts of black smoke trailing behind. The engine suddenly stopped, the propeller seized and stopped spinning. The plane nosed down as Spaulding pushed the stick forward to keep from stalling.

"Shit," hissed Willingham. "You've got it, Spalls. Put her down easy."

Tarkington thought the plane would crash nose first, but at the very last instant, the nose rose and the plane belly-flopped the last few yards onto the metal Marston Matting. The sound of metal on metal was deafening. The landing gear was ripped off the fuselage and careened to either side, sending metal chunks in all directions. Orange and white sparks mixed with choking black smoke as the plane ground to a messy halt. The truck raced across the tarmac and pulled up close beside it. The men in back pumped the barrels and sprayed the engine cowling with weak streams of water. The two men in the cab leaped out and ran to the plane, straight into the smoke, tinged with the orange of fire.

The GIs and other pilots sprinted to the scene, arriving as Flight Lieutenant Spaulding, draped between the two mechanics, emerged from the smoke. His face was pale white, and he hacked raspy coughs. He finally fell to his knees and vomited violently, his body spasming uncontrollably.

Another trolley trundled up and they lay Spaulding onto a stretcher, quickly whisking him away to the makeshift infirmary farther down the road. The P-40 hissed and the black smoke turned to white steam as the water crew finally got the better of the flames. The cowling was blackened and charred, the green paint peeled and bubbled. The cockpit glass was blackened and streaked with dirty oil. Tarkington shook his head, wondering how Spaulding had managed to land at all.

Yuncy and Willingham were near the back, inspecting the elevator and rudder. "Japs chewed him up. Half the rudder's gone and the elevator's holed too."

Raker put his finger into a ragged bullet hole in the side and whistled, then said, "This one's going to the scrap yard."

One of the mechanics, still spraying water, shook his head, "We'll see about that. The engine seized, but we may be able to salvage her."

The second P-40 flew over the wreckage and landed with a soft bounce, the gear struts flexed and absorbed the plane's weight. Riggins braked quickly, then parked in an empty revetment. He quickly dismounted and joined them.

Yuncy and Willingham surrounded him, and Riggins asked, "Is he okay?"

Yuncy nodded, "Think so. They took him to the infirmary, but he was walking and awake. Shaken up a bit, I'll wager." Riggins nodded; relief flooded his face.

Willingham asked, "What happened?"

Riggins sighed, "We dove on a couple of Jakes but got jumped by four Zeros. Never saw 'em coming. We were evasive the whole time. Spalls told me to dive away while he took a turn with 'em. I don't know how he broke away; Japs must've been low on fuel or something."

Tarkington asked, "What's a Jake?"

Riggins answered, "Jap floatplane. It's a reconnaissance plane but they can drop bombs too."

"Out of Buna?" asked Willingham.

Riggins nodded, "Probably. Love to do something about that damned airbase."

8

The trip onboard the C-47 Dakota from Milne Bay to Wanigela Airfield was terrifying, especially considering what they'd seen the day before on the Milne Bay Airfield.

The plane was full, occupied not only with the Alamo Scouts but also with engineers and anti-aircraft crews, along with one of their disassembled weapons. Before taking off, the pilots informed them that to avoid enemy fighters, they'd be flying at night and low, timing their arrival to the airfield at dawn. None of that made the GIs feel better. Whether they died by enemy aircraft or by running into the side of a mountain was merely a difference in levels of terror. At least if the pilots plowed into a mountaintop, they wouldn't know it beforehand. They'd simply cease to exist.

The flight was just over one hundred miles, so it was over quickly. The constant up and down as they avoided hills and mountains kept anyone from sleeping. It ended with a sharp banking turn and steep descent, followed with a harsh bounce and a sudden braking stop.

The side door opened and the GIs jumped down, their legs threatening to buckle beneath the weight of their packs. The eastern horizon was aglow with the coming dawn. They were immediately surrounded by scantily-clad, smiling natives. Their skin was coal black and their hair rose straight up from their foreheads, the varying heights an indicator of their age.

They offered to relieve them of their packs but the GIs shook their heads and moved away, allowing them to offload the other supplies.

A familiar face greeted them and the big man waved. Sergeant Winkleman nudged Stollman in the gut, "Well, would you look at that. It's your butt buddy, Sergeant Bulkort."

Stollman glared, but otherwise ignored him. Sergeant Bulkort's booming voice cut through the Dakota's engines, "Hello again. Welcome to Wanigela." He said it as though introducing a tropical paradise. It was drier than Milne Bay, but hardly a destination resort.

Tarkington shook Bulkort's hand, "What're you doing here, Sergeant? You weren't mentioned in the briefing."

"No?" His mouth turned down at the corners, "An oversight. I've been assigned to your squad for the mission."

Tarkington exchanged a glance with Winkleman, then addressed the powerfully-built sergeant, "In what capacity?"

He grinned and lifted his chin toward Stollman, who tried to keep the smile from his face. Bulkort said, "The blowing up kind. Gonna help with the demolitions."

Tarkington liked the gregarious sergeant but didn't know him beyond his skills with everything explosive. "We'll be in the bush over a week, Sergeant. We'd be glad to have your skill set. But have you ever been on a mission like this?"

Bulkort's face turned serious, "I've spent time in the field, but nothing like you guys. I'll stay out of your way, Sergeant."

"You seen any combat?"

Bulkort looked at his boots and shook his head, "No, Sergeant."

"Who authorized this, Sergeant?"

Bulkort stiffened, pulled out a sheet of paper, and handed it to Tarkington, "Colonel Bradshaw."

Tarkington read the orders, noting the scrawled signature. "Well, okay then. I don't mean nothing by it, but we're a tight-knit squad. Adding a relatively unknown . . . well, it's not optimal."

"I understand your apprehension. Like I said, I'll stay out of the way. You won't even know I'm here."

Tarkington shook his head, "You're not an easy guy to miss, Sergeant."

Bulkort didn't answer, just stood rigidly, looking straight ahead. "Stollman." Stollman stepped closer. "He's your responsibility. Got it?"

Stollman nodded, "Sure thing, Tark." Vick whistled as though a pretty woman had walked past and Stollman glared at him while the others laughed.

Wanigela Airfield was rough, and the men who'd arrived on the C-47 with them got to work on cutting back the kunai grass threatening to overgrow it and smoothing out the dirt landing strip. The anti-aircraft crew got busy assembling their weapon. It would be the first of many. Wanigela was a jumping-off point. In the coming weeks, the airfield would have to accommodate an entire regiment from the 32nd Infantry Division, and an Australian regiment from Milne Bay.

The squad didn't linger in Wanigela. An ungainly barge was nudged up to the beach waiting to take them around Cape Nelson to Gobe. It was a far cry from the sleek lines of a PT boat, but the Australians running the craft assured them it was reliable. The Japanese they'd acquired it from had kept it in good working condition, and although it had taken fire from Allied strafing runs and shrapnel from nearby bomb hits, the engine was undamaged. The Australians had fashioned a canvas cover to provide some relief from the incessant beatdown of the sun and the frequent torrential downpours common to the area this time of year.

They boarded the barge at noon after rounding out any supplies they still needed from the meager stores in Wanigela. The natives helped them with their packs and waved and ran along the beach as though sending off a cruise ship.

Henry shook his head, "Not sure what they're so excited about."

Raker, peaking over the wooden edge beside him, answered, "I don't think they get a lot of visitors. Must be the most excitement they've seen." He shook his head, "And look at those flapping titties." He waved at the running, topless native women.

Henry shook his head and spit over the side, "Rather not if it's all the same to you."

Winkleman overheard them and punched Raker in the ribs, "Your mind's always in the gutter."

Raker turned, pretending to throw a punch, and grinned, "That's where the good stuff is, Wink. Stick with me, Sergeant. Next time we get any R and R, I'll show you how to get laid."

"R and R? You getting laid?" Winkleman shook his head in bewilderment, "I'm not sure which is more unbelievable."

Despite the boxy shape and the overall look of disrepair, the barge made good time. The dual outboard motors purred steadily. The Australian crew of three were obviously proud of their captured craft. Tarkington noticed that the gunner, seated behind a mounted Bren light machine gun, scanned the skies dutifully. The gunner saw him looking and smiled, "Swapped out the Jap Nambu. Nifty weapon, but we ran out of ammo for it." Tarkington nodded and turned away, trying not to look interested. The young sailor wanted to talk, so he spoke to the back of Tarkington's head, "This little beauty's just as good, although it doesn't hold as much ammo." He tapped the stack of spare magazines beside him. "I'm good at swapping them out fast though," he smiled proudly.

The Australian seaman steering the boat shook his head, "Shut up, Barney. The sergeant's not interested in your malarkey. Keep your eyes peeled for Zeros."

The gunner looked exasperated, "I *am*."

Tarkington leaned closer to the driver, "See a lot of Zeros out here?"

The driver nodded, "Mostly in the distance, going somewhere else usually. Bombers out of Rabaul too."

"Ever been attacked?"

The sailor equivocated, moving his head side to side, "The Japs see a barge and assume it's one of theirs." He rolled his eyes and pointed his thumb at the gunner. "Barney shot at one that passed close, though. Nip would've gone right on by, but after being shot at, he took a keen interest. Came around, gave us a close look, and Barney fired again, so he came around and strafed us. Either he ran out of ammo or his guns jammed, cause after a short burst he flew on by."

Tarkington looked at the gunner whose jaw was rippling, obviously trying hard not to add his own two cents' worth. "Did he hit anything?"

The driver's mouth turned down at the corners and he slowly shook his head. "Missed by a mile."

The gunner could take no more and burst out, "Not true! I hit his wing. Lonny saw it." He pointed at the other sailor who was doing his best to keep out of the conversation, "Tell him." Lonny, a deeply tanned sailor with a perpetually bored look, just shrugged and continued scanning the surface for enemy boats. Barney shook his head, mumbling as he resumed watching the skies, "We're out here to kill Japs."

They stayed close to shore, having to detour around shallow shoals occasionally. Cape Nelson was fenestrated with countless inlets and bays. The water was sometimes dark blue, sometimes translucent green, and every combination in between. Inland, the land sloped up toward a lofty peak, shrouded in white puffy clouds. From the sea, Tarkington thought the greenery covering the land resembled a perfectly-manicured lawn. Though it looked inviting, he surmised the reality of having to traverse it would be far different. The views were breathtaking, and like he'd thought many times before, would be a paradise if not for the war.

He'd studied maps of the area. None of them were comprehensive, but he remembered seeing a named town and inquired, "Is Tufi nearby?"

Singlet shrugged and pointed, "There're hundreds of inlets, Tufi's in one of them, but I'll be damned if I'd be able to find it given a hundred years to do so. The natives sometimes come out in their outrigger canoes to greet us, but that's the only way of knowing. Of course, we don't come out here a lot either."

Tarkington nodded, "How long till we're around the cape?"

"Not long. The sea gets a little rougher and the wind kicks up a notch or two near the tip, but nothing drastic. We'll be near the drop point around dusk."

As they rounded Cape Nelson, the day grew darker with storm clouds and soon the tarp over the barge used for sun protection took on the secondary role of rain protection. The rain came down in sheets, and if not for the tarp, they would've been forced to use the buckets along the sides to bail water.

It forced Singlet to slow and bring the barge closer to shore as visibility deteriorated to less than thirty yards. With night descending quickly, Singlet had to yell to be heard over the drumming of the rain on the tarp. "I've gotta find cover and anchor or we're bound to run aground."

"How far from Gobe are we?" Tarkington asked.

"Maybe three miles." He pulled out a wet, drooping map and showed him in the fading light. "Figure we're about here."

Tarkington nodded, "Rain can't last forever. Find us some cover."

Singlet cut the motor to half speed, just enough to maintain steerage, and turned inland, hoping to tuck into a protected bay. Having abandoned the Bren gun, Barney and Lonny, along with the GIs, propped themselves along the front edge of the boat, searching for signs of land or shallow reefs and shoals. With each passing moment, the task grew more difficult. It didn't seem possible, but the rain intensified, coming down in a nearly solid sheet.

Lonny called out first, "Stop! Stop!" but it was too late. Even over the hammering rain, the crunching of the wooden boat's bottom against the reef was deafening. Their slow speed didn't keep them from falling into one another, and they crushed up against the bow.

The barge tipped upward, and even with full reverse, it didn't budge an inch. "Shite!" yelled Singlet. "She's stuck. Are we taking on water?"

After pulling himself off the floor, Lonny yelled, "No way to know with all this rain. There's water, but mostly from the rain, I think."

Tarkington added, "I don't see anything poking through the hull."

Lonny shook his head, "You wouldn't necessarily see that. This boat has a double hull. If the outer hull's punctured, water would fill it and come in through the seams and joints."

Tarkington nodded and searched for the shore, but couldn't see it. He couldn't tell how close or far they were from dry land. There was nothing they could do until the rain stopped. Getting out and trying to walk or swim would be a great way to get separated and probably killed. "This rain won't last all night. Once it stops, hopefully the clouds will clear a bit. There's a quarter moon that'll help."

Singlet struggled to open a sealed container. He fumbled inside, finally finding what he was looking for. He turned on a red-lensed flashlight, holding it in his mouth as he turned pages of a small booklet. He addressed the men, "We're at low tide moving toward high. Another six hours or so. It usually swings two feet—more sometimes. We should float off of this thing in a couple of hours."

Tarkington ordered the men to fill canteens from the water coming off the tarp and have a final meal. The natives had supplied the food at Wanigela, so they didn't have to disturb their tightly-packed packs. They tore at strips of dry, salted fish, and stringy mystery meat.

Two hours later, the rain stopped the same way it started: as though a valve had been closed. One second it was pouring, the next it wasn't. The blackness lifted as the massive rain squall passed them by, leaving partially overcast skies. The quarter moon was low on the horizon, but it put off enough light to make the sea surface sparkle, and also illuminate the shoreline. The stern of the tilted barge had standing water up to Singlet's ankles. It had rained hard enough and long enough to have such an effect; however, he suspected they had breached the hull—not catastrophically, but enough to be noticeable.

The GIs stood on the ledges, looking out over the surreal scape. They figured they were 200 yards from shore, propped on the tip of a reef. Despite their predicament, the scene was beautiful.

The Aussies carefully lowered themselves into the water, trying to evaluate the damage. The sea had already risen, floating the boat higher and decreasing the harsh upward angle of the bow. It looked as though it would be free-floating in another hour or two. Singlet swam as far as he dared beneath the hull and poked and prodded, trying to feel the damage. The boat definitely had a hole in it. The water continued to rise inside despite the end of the rain.

The GIs helped haul the Aussies back on board. The squad was eager to get off the boat and into the jungle. Tarkington asked, "So, how's it look?"

"Outer hull's definitely punctured. We won't get back to Wanigela without a repair."

Tarkington raised an eyebrow, "You have a way to repair it?"

Singlet shrugged, "We've got some patching material, yeah, but getting to the hole will be tough."

Tarkington grabbed Singlet's arm and pulled him toward the engines, away from the others. "Look, we've got a mission to run. We've gotta get to shore soon. We can't be out here when the sun comes up. Hell, it's bright enough now that a passing enemy boat or plane would see us."

Singlet nodded his understanding, "Another half hour should raise the tide enough for me to back us off the reef. Then we'll find a place to hide the barge until we can fix it. We don't need you to stick around for us, Sergeant."

They waited a full hour, when the tide was still two hours from the peak. Singlet started the single gasoline-powered engine. All the men were near the stern, taking their added weight off the bow. He put the gears into reverse and added power. The boat moved an inch, then stopped. He added more power until he was at three quarters full. It slid another inch, jolting and grinding. He pushed the throttles to full power and the 60 hp engine screamed. Finally, with a sickening rending of wood and metal plating, the barge broke free and lurched backwards, sending everyone to the floor, which was quickly filling with seawater.

"Shite," growled Lonny. "Now she's holed for sure."

Singlet yelled, "Grab the buckets and bail! I'll move inland along this bay and beach her before she wallows. Barney, get up front and watch for more reefs."

Singlet swung the barge to deeper water, traveling along the bay toward the main island. Barney pointed where to steer while the GIs frantically bailed, trying to stem the rising water. Lonny was stuffing life jackets and anything else he could think of into the now-gaping hole in the bottom. He knew it was useless, since the outer hull was punctured and water would come in from other places, but he managed to stem the main fountain of water.

Finally, Barney pointed, "Beach! Over there. The way's clear all the way in."

By now the bailers were up to their knees in seawater and the barge was sitting noticeably lower and moving slower despite the screaming engines.

Singlet turned into the beach, not bothering to slow down. Just before impact, he yelled, "Brace yourselves!"

The GIs stopped bailing and grabbed for whatever was close, but most of them ended up in the bottom, coming from the bilge water spluttering and cursing. The barge slid up the beach ten yards before finally stopping. The bow was again angled upward. The sudden stop sent the water cascading forward, sending up a large splash, then quickly shifted to the stern. The mini-tsunami swept over Singlet's head and sloshed over the hissing engines. He cut the gas and the engines coughed and stopped. The only sound was the water sloshing and the men cursing as they pulled themselves together.

The sudden grounding had launched Barney from the bow like a cannonball onto the beach. He rolled a few times, finally coming to a stop near the edge of the jungle. He shook himself, getting to his feet slowly. When he determined he wasn't injured, he started laughing hysterically, the adrenaline and fear finding an outlet. A flash and a rifle shot from the darkness ended his maniacal laughter. He dropped like a popped balloon, a gaping hole where his face used to be.

9

The GIs were already leaping from the boat when Barney's laughter was interrupted by the gunshot. Tarkington rolled over the boat's edge and fell the ten feet to the sand, landing on his stomach. He stayed down and quickly pulled his carbine off his back, aiming into the night. Henry, Raker, and Winkleman were already out too, but no one fired, waiting for a target.

From the blackness another shattering muzzle flash and the loud thump as the bullet smacked into the bow of the barge. Henry and Raker returned fire, each firing the semi-automatics as quickly as they could pull the trigger. Another muzzle flash to the left of the first. Tarkington adjusted aim, noting the bullet passing over their heads and slamming into the sea beyond. He fired three times, Winkleman adding his own fire.

Stollman and Vick launched from the other side of the barge, and Stollman yelled, "Going right!" Tarkington and the others fired into the darkness. Stollman and Vick dashed into the jungle but there was no return fire. *Are they dead or waiting?* He hissed, "Move up left." Henry and Raker rose as one and moved left, then darted forward to the tree line. Still no firing.

Stollman emerged a minute later and went to his haunches. In the dim moonlight, Tarkington thought he resembled a gargoyle statue he'd once seen on a government building back home. He got to his feet with

Winkleman doing the same, and they trotted forward. Tarkington hissed as they passed Barney, "Check on him."

Winkleman stopped and crouched, feeling for a pulse, but it was obvious the young sailor was dead.

Tarkington met Stollman and Vick at the edge of the beach. "Found one dead Jap. The first guy I think."

Tarkington nodded, "Henry and Raker are on the left flank. If the second guy's out there, they'll find him." He licked his dry lips, suddenly thirsty. "You two help Bull with the gear and get those sailors helping too. Keep 'em quiet. We've gotta get off this beach in a hurry." Vick and Stollman sprinted to the barge.

Winkleman sidled up beside him and shook his head, "He's dead, Tark."

"Figured," he growled. "We'll wait here for Henry and Raker, then we gotta move."

Winkleman nodded and pointed, "Here they come now."

In the pale moonlight, Raker and Henry looked grim, their camouflaged faces like something from a horror novel. Raker whispered, "No sign of the second Jap. It's as dark as the inside of a coal miner's asshole in there though, so we might've missed a blood trail."

Tarkington shook his head, "We gotta assume the son of a bitch made it out unscathed and is on his way to tell his buddies all about us." The grunts of men hauling packs and gear from the barge made him turn. "Keep watch, Raker. Rest of us'll get the gear."

Sergeant Bulkort was suddenly next to him, depositing three packs besides his own. They quickly donned the packs. The rest of the gear was offloaded. The shaken Aussie sailors crouched, breathing hard. Singlet asked, "Is—is Barney . . . ?"

Tarkington nodded, "Dead. Yeah. Jap shot him through the head."

Singlet's voice was weak and airy, "Poor sod. He—he was a good man—kid, really."

Tarkington turned, bringing his face within centimeters, and hissed, "You've gotta put it past you. You can mourn later. Focus—both of you." He nodded towards Lonny and continued, "We're trained for this. Do exactly what we say; keep your shit together and you'll live to tell your grandkids.

Understand?" Singlet gulped against a dry throat, nodding quickly. Lonny simply nodded once, his eyes settled and his expression calm.

Tarkington thought Lonny would do fine out here but Singlet would need to be watched closely. He focused on Lonny, "Get the Bren and all the ammo." He smacked Stollman's shoulder, "You and Bull rig the boat with explosives. I wanna leave the Nips with something to remember us by. And make sure the engine doesn't survive."

As Bulkort, Stollman, and Lonny went back to the boat, Singlet looked panicked. "You can't destroy the boat. It's our only way out of here. We can patch it and be off by noon, evening at the latest."

Tarkington took a fistful of his shirt, "One of those Japs got away. They could be back in two minutes or two hours, but they'll be back long before you could patch her up." He released him and seethed, "You've used up your 'get out of jail free' card." Singlet looked confused. "That's the last time you question my orders. Understand?" Singlet nodded.

While Stollman and Bulkort rigged the boat, Barney's body was carried into the jungle. Tarkington gestured to a thicket, "Put him over there. No time to bury him." Singlet protested, but clammed up seeing Tarkington's warning glance. Tarkington was sympathetic but whispered, "We'll get back to him when we can." Singlet nodded, not liking it but accepting it. Once the body was rolled into the bush and covered, Tarkington whispered to Henry, "When the boat's done, take us inland." Henry nodded. Tarkington found Raker, "Stay with our Aussie friends. Keep 'em quiet."

Raker shook his head, "That won't be easy."

Tarkington slapped his back, "I know."

Minutes later, Stollman and Bulkort trotted up the beach. Stollman gave Tarkington a thumbs up, "Done. They'll get a big surprise."

Tarkington hissed to Stollman, "Stay with Bull. Keep him quiet." Bulkort wanted to tell him he didn't need babysitting, but thought better of it and kept his mouth shut. "Move out." Henry disappeared into the bush and the squad followed.

They moved slower than normal. Henry understood the need for stealth, but having men unused to moving in the jungle tagging along made that nearly impossible. The slower he went, the less noise they'd make—at least he hoped so.

Tarkington remembered how terrified he was the first time he patrolled at night in the jungle. The Australian sailors would see enemy soldiers everywhere. Nothing would be familiar and everything would be trying to kill them. That was why he'd told them to keep their sidearms holstered. They'd looked stunned, but he explained that Raker would be with them and if they needed their weapons, he'd tell them. One panicked shot or accidental discharge would give away their position. He was already fuming that their landing hadn't gone unnoticed. He didn't want to compound their problems. His plan was to take the Aussies somewhere relatively safe —perhaps a friendly village—and leave them there so they could continue their mission.

After relatively easy walking, the terrain sloped steeply upward. The ground was slick from the recent downpour and they struggled to keep their footing. The last ten feet, they had to form a human chain to get up the cliff side.

Once beyond the cliff, the jungle gave way to a plateau of kunai grass. A breeze blew the sharp-edged grasses, which shimmered in the dim glow of the quarter moon. They drank water from their canteens and watched the dense swaying grasses for any human activity. Satisfied they were alone, Tarkington waved them forward and they moved along in single file. The grass was shoulder high and they alternated the lead to stave off exhaustion.

From behind, a dull rumbling made them all stop and turn. A faint glow from the beach told them that the unaccounted-for Japanese had indeed escaped and brought reinforcements back to the barge. Stollman held up a finger, "Wait for it . . ." A second rumbling added to the first and the glow increased. Stollman and Bulkort were grinning, their white teeth shining against their camouflaged faces. "That second one was the engines going up. Doused 'em with gasoline."

Tarkington grinned at the giddiness in Stollman's voice. "Let's keep moving, Stolly."

They were soon at the far edge of the grass plateau. A dark chasm stretched off to the right and the sound of rushing water cutting through the bottom wafted up through the trees and vines. The terrain sloped upward into another section of jungle. Tarkington pointed uphill, "Another hour, then find us a spot to bivouac." Henry nodded and moved off again.

The jungle wasn't as thick as it was near the coast. The trees were bigger and older; the roots snaking along the ground looked like huge black boa constrictors. Some were so large, they had to straddle them to pass. The slope was gradual and Henry stopped near an enormous tree with spine-like roots. The chasm to the right wasn't deep here. The creek had half the water it did toward the coast and would be easy to access to refill canteens.

With what little light that shone through the jungle canopy, it looked like a good place to settle for the night. Assuming any Japanese had survived the rigged barge, they'd have difficulty following their path at night. If they somehow managed, there was a small clearing they'd be forced to cross and the GIs would see and hear them long before they could get close. The thick roots would be perfect defensive walls if it came down to that.

Tarkington turned to Winkleman, "We'll stop here." Winkleman nodded and passed the news along. Tarkington heard Singlet say too loudly, "Thank Christ. I didn't think . . ."

He was cut off by Raker hissing, "Shut the fuck up, mate." There was no more talking, just the sounds of scraping cloth and boot-falls as the men settled in.

The night passed without incident, although Singlet and Lonny had to be nudged occasionally to keep their snoring down. Tarkington didn't put them into the guard rotation. They were obviously exhausted and he didn't trust they'd stay awake. Besides that, they weren't trained for such things.

Bulkort took a turn, although Tarkington made sure Stollman stayed awake with him. Normally, Stollman would've complained, but he didn't raise a fuss. Tarkington wondered if there were any growing animosity from Vick. He and Stollman were best friends, and Bulkort and Stollman obviously got along well. Tarkington shook his head, *I sound like a high school counselor.*

The mosquitos were nowhere near as obnoxious as they were in Milne Bay, and Tarkington got a few hours of sleep. His shits were still somewhat solid and on schedule. The influence of New Guinea hadn't hit any of them yet. During their time in the tropics, they'd all had bouts of the screaming shits and would no doubt have them again, but they'd been in this region of the world for years—long before the Japanese invaded—and their systems were used to the micro-organisms which wreaked so much havoc among newly-arrived soldiers and sailors. During their short time in Milne Bay, they'd seen many men struggling with the various ailments. Luckily, Singlet and Lonny had been spared so far.

As the sun rose, they ate cold K-rats and drank cool water from the creek. The view was spectacular. Through the trees, they could look down the green slopes all the way to the sparkling sea. The different shades of blue, green, and aqua were breathtaking. The only thing reminding them of the war was the slight smudge of wispy smoke rising from the barge, miles away.

Tarkington moved over, making room for Winkleman. The roots were perfect backrests. "What are we gonna do with the Aussies?" Winkleman asked.

"Gotta find a safe place for them to hole up. They can't stay with us. Hell, their uniforms may as well have beacons on 'em. Whose idea was it to send men into jungle combat dressed in white?"

Winkleman grinned, "Started off khaki maybe, but the sun bleached 'em quick."

"We could send 'em toward Tufi and hope they find it," Tarkington suggested. Winkleman was silent and Tarkington continued, "But I doubt they could find their way back to the barge, let alone going cross-country. Probably be a death warrant for 'em. We need to find a village, or barring that, somewhere we could find them again once the mission's complete."

"They'd likely run out of food. We don't have much to spare."

Tarkington shook his head, "Which leads us back to finding a village. We can only spare a day at the most for this horseshit. We've gotta hit Gobe before the 128th gets there." He stood and stretched his back, swaying side to side. "We leave in five minutes."

"On it, Sarge."

After crossing the small canyon and creek, they continued moving in the general direction of Gobe. Every couple of hundred yards, another canyon, usually with a creek at the bottom, had to be crossed. Since seeing the Japanese at the beach, there'd been no more signs of them. There were trails snaking throughout the area, some obviously frequented by humans, but the distinctive notched toe of the Japanese infantryman was absent.

They'd passed over the trails, not wanting to follow them toward the sea and give up their altitude advantage. Raker was in the lead, Henry taking a much-deserved break from running point. After ascending from the bottom of a ravine and cresting on the next spine of land, Raker stopped and motioned Tarkington forward.

Raker pointed. "This one looks bigger," he whispered.

The trail in front of Tarkington was bigger and better used than any they'd found yet. Unlike the others they'd come across, this one looked to be leading inland. Tarkington motioned Raker, "We'll follow it inland."

Raker nodded and pivoted to follow the trail. The rest of the squad moved without a sound, although Singlet mumbled something about having to move uphill again. Henry had taken over watching them and simply glared at him until he got his ass in gear.

They spent the rest of the morning following the trail. It followed the ever-narrowing ridge of land snaking toward the tallest peak in the area. Finally, it turned north and looked to be heading toward an area of cleared jungle.

Tarkington gathered the squad, giving them a minute to drink water. He whispered, "Looks like a village ahead." He pointed at Raker, then Henry, "You two check it out. We'll wait here."

Henry tapped the Aussies' shoulders as he passed and gave them a slight grin, placing his finger against his lips for quiet. Lonny and Singlet nodded, although Singlet's red face made him look as though he'd drop at any moment. Henry and Raker disappeared into the scrub, their dirty, mottled camouflage uniforms blending perfectly.

Tarkington waved the two sailors forward and when they crouched, asked, "You guys okay?" Lonny shrugged, his facial expression stoic and accepting despite carrying the heavy Bren gun. Singlet looked ready to reply but Tarkington didn't give him a chance. "I'm guessing there's a village ahead. The natives are generally friendly toward us, but we'll check it out first. If it checks out, we'll leave you two in their care."

Lonny's face didn't change but Singlet looked panicked. "You can't just leave us there."

Tarkington shook his head, "You'll be fine. They'll keep you out of Jap hands and feed and take care of you until we can arrange to have you sent back to your lines."

Lonny nodded, "We'll be fine, Sergeant."

Singlet shook his head and guffawed, "Yeah, just like poor old Barney."

Tarkington's voice went an octave lower and his eyes narrowed as he addressed Singlet, "People die in war. It's a fact. The sooner you get past his death, the better. To survive out here, you need to focus or you'll end up just like him." Singlet swallowed against a dry throat and Tarkington added, "Your mission was to get us here. Mission accomplished. *Our* mission is to hit Gobe and we can't do that with two sailors tagging along. Got it?"

Before Singlet could respond, Raker and Henry emerged and slithered to Tarkington's side. Henry drawled, "It's a village all right, but there's a problem."

Raker finished for him, "Japs."

10

Lonny and Singlet stayed behind while the rest of the squad moved toward the village outskirts. Sergeant Bulkort had shown he was a skilled patroller. For a big man, he moved surprisingly well, and the squad quietly accepted him into the fold, at least for now.

Tarkington pulled himself to the edge of the clearing. At the far end, he saw a cart being filled with supplies. Japanese soldiers holding long rifles stood facing the villagers, who leaned on their spears or against the struts of their huts, watching.

Even from this distance, Tarkington could tell the Japanese were thin and emaciated. He'd seen some prisoners—mere skeletons—they'd pulled from the Kokoda Trail, and he wondered if perhaps these soldiers had been a part of that failed attack. They watched them fill the small cart with as much food as they could find. Tarkington doubted they'd find even a quarter of it. If these locals were anything like the men and women he'd encountered on other South Pacific islands, they'd have a well-hidden stockpile somewhere. That didn't make the robbery any less galling, however.

The Japanese finally finished filling the cart and backed away from the villagers, keeping their rifles leveled. The villagers watched them go, their faces slack and emotionless. The soldiers pushed the cart northeast along a track leading out of the village. Tarkington figured it probably led straight to Gobe.

They waited another thirty minutes. The villagers milled about, most entering their huts while children played games around the struts supporting the buildings. Tarkington turned to Vick, "Bring up the Aussies." Vick nodded and silently slipped away.

Once they rejoined, Tarkington stood and stepped into the open field. The kunai grass was short here, only coming to their waists. The villagers immediately noticed them, obviously assuming they were seeing another group of Japanese. But when they saw their painted faces, different uniforms, and weapons, they smiled and called for the entire village to greet them. They spoke in Pidgin and Tagalog, both of which the squad recognized.

Tarkington greeted them the way he'd learned on Luzon, by lightly shaking their hands and smiling and nodding. "Magandang hapon," he said.

The greeting was returned by many but soon only one native was talking, "Maligayang pagdating."

Every squad member, besides Sergeant Bulkort, had a good working knowledge of Tagalog and Pidgin English, and soon Tarkington was in a discussion with the village elder, whose deep creases indicated a life lived outside.

They talked and the rest of the squad listened intently, nodding occasionally, driving Bulkort and the Aussie sailors crazy.

With much gesticulating, smiling, and back-slapping, the conversation ended and Tarkington filled them in. "This is the village elder. Tavist is his name. He welcomes us and will allow you two to stay as long as you need to. They say that's the first time the Japanese have been to their village, but doubts it'll be the last. He wanted to attack them and take back their supplies, but I think I talked him out of that." He grinned, "They seem similar to other natives we've come across: fearless and deadly fighters. The Japanese would've certainly died, but I convinced him they would be dead soon enough. They're willing to help any way they can."

Singlet looked around the tiny mountain village. The huts were thatch and wood and looked stout and well-built. The grounds were clean, but it wasn't an Australian town by any stretch of the imagination, and Singlet scowled. "We're staying here?" Tarkington scowled back and turned away, ignoring him.

Winkleman leaned in and whispered loud enough for the rest of the natives to hear, "Kumakain tao," gesturing toward the hapless sailors. The native's foreheads crinkled with concern, then they smiled and laughed uproariously.

Singlet, knowing he was being made fun of, stammered, "Wh—what the hell'er they going on about?"

Winkleman wiped his eyes, "I told them you're worried that they might eat you."

Singlet shook his head, "I never thought that . . ." His voice trailed off, renewing the GIs' laughter. Singlet finally smiled, "Well, it might have crossed my mind."

Winkleman put his arm around Singlet's shoulder and shook him, "There you go, sailor. It's always good to laugh at yourself."

The village elder directed nearby women to show the soldiers where they could stay for the night. There was still plenty of daylight left, but Tavist insisted they stay for a feast and a good night's sleep. In the morning, he promised his best hunters would show him the way to Gobe. Resisting his hospitality would be folly bordering on insult, so Tarkington nodded, smiled, and allowed the topless females to lead him. He noticed Raker ogling them and barked, "Don't even think about it, Raker."

Raker shook his head and spoke through a sideways grin, "Too late, Tark."

The villagers killed a huge wild boar and as it cooked over a glowing bed of coals, the GIs talked and laughed with them. Singlet was sitting beside Tarkington watching the GIs' interactions. He shook his head and mumbled something Tarkington couldn't quite hear, but the derogatory tone was obvious.

Tarkington leaned close to him and said, "You think these people are savages or simple. Is that right?"

Singlet startled, not realizing his voice had carried, and stammered, "Well—well, they aren't exactly civilized."

"Why? Cause they don't dress like you? Because they're dark? Speak a different language?"

Singlet's mouth turned downward, "We have Aboriginals in Australia—Bushmen, they're called. Some have embraced the modern world and adapted. I don't suppose that's an option out here."

Tarkington shrugged, "Doubt your Bushmen are much different than these people, and I *know* they look at us with similar disdain. Everyone thinks their way is the best way." His tone softened slightly, "We've been living among natives for a long time. My respect for their bravery and sheer tenacity has grown. Sure, there's the occasional outlier," the image of the traitorous young village elder on Luzon crossed his mind. "But nine times out of ten, I'd choose a native warrior over a western soldier for sheer guts." He grinned, looking his hardened GIs over, "Not including my men." He focused his glare at Singlet.

The firelight reflected in his eyes, making Singlet shift and look away. Tarkington said, "You're their guest. They'll bend over backwards for you, but only as long as they respect you. Treat them like savages and they'll return the favor. Understand?"

Singlet nodded, poking the embers with a long stick, "Understood, Sergeant."

When the boar was deemed cooked, they passed enormous slabs of dripping meat around, accompanied by cooked roots and other village delicacies. The GIs dug in with vigor. The fire was stoked, and in the flickering firelight the GIs looked like otherworldly creatures with their camouflaged faces and hard eyes. Topless women weaved between them, serving food and filling cups and bowls with water infused with some kind of fruit flavor. Children of all ages darted in and out of the firelight, playing a game only they knew the rules to.

Some indigenous people had perfected the distilling process, but apparently not here. His men were professionals and wouldn't drink on a mission, but they were human, and could be tempted. It was a nonissue tonight, but it didn't keep Tarkington from pining for a tall pint of Australian beer to wash down the succulent boar meat.

With full bellies, the GIs and sailors didn't last long. Tavist assured them they had nothing to fear from the Japanese. He had men watching the roads and paths leading to the village who would give them ample warning if they returned.

The GIs sprawled out, sleeping where they'd eaten; they would've been happy like that, but the women would have none of it and tucked woven strips of thatch beneath them. Soon the entire camp was quiet, the only sounds coming from the incessant buzzing of insects and the calls of nocturnal beasts.

Tarkington slept lightly. He never slept deeply out here. His night was a series of short half-hour naps followed by an hour watching the stars. His mind was trained to operate that way, and he doubted he'd ever change, even if he survived the war. The stars were bright. The village was mostly under the jungle canopy, but the firepit was in the open field and he had an unobstructed view of the sky.

During one of his hour-long up-times, he saw someone stand and stretch. He recognized the diminutive frame of the engineer, Lonny. Tarkington sat up and Lonny noticed him across the glowing firepit and waved. Tarkington lifted his chin and Lonny slowly stepped around sleeping GIs until he was beside him. He sat and looked up at the stars, "Beautiful night."

Tarkington nodded his agreement, "Yep." He wasn't looking for company. He was approaching the hour mark and his eyes were growing heavy. Even though Lonny had gained some respect for his lack of complaining, getting to know the Aussie sailor wasn't a priority and would most likely be a liability. People died out here and the less he got to know someone, the less the loss would affect him.

Lonny continued, "Looks about the same in my hometown." Tarkington looked at him questioningly, and Lonny explained, "I mean the sky. The stars are the same. Must be different where you're from. Aye?"

Tarkington rubbed the back of his neck, feeling the tension there. *Is this kid lonely, scared, or just talkative?* He sighed and nodded, "Yeah, it's different."

There was a long silence and Tarkington was just about to lean back for another catnap, when Lonny said, "Singlet's a pain in the arse, but he's okay. I think Barney's death really shook him."

Tarkington sighed. He could shut the kid down, but he didn't seem the talkative type and maybe he just needed some conversation to ease his mind. "Not you?"

Lonny didn't take his eyes from the heavens. He shrugged, "He was a mate, but he's gone. Dwelling on it won't change anything. Like you said: gotta get past it." Another long silence. Tarkington tried to lie down again, but Lonny foiled him once more, "I'd like to go with you guys to Gobe." Tarkington shook his head, but Lonny continued, "I'm an engineer for a reason. Machines make sense to me. I can fix anything with moving parts. That might come in handy for you out there."

Tarkington sighed, "Look, Lonny. You're not bad in the field, I'll give you that. You haven't complained, even though I know all this trekking is hard on you, but you're not one of us. You're not trained for this."

"But I could . . ."

Tarkington cut him off, "It's not up for debate." He laid down and shut his eyes, ending all conversation.

The squad left the village before dawn, leaving behind Lonny and Singlet. They watched them go like lost puppies. Tarkington told Winkleman about his midnight conversation with Lonny, and Winkleman surmised he might seek revenge for Barney's death. Regardless of Lonny's motivations, Winkleman agreed the Aussies were far better off waiting in the village.

Tavist sent three of his best hunters to guide the GIs to Gobe. It wasn't difficult. The track, which was a couple feet wider than what could be called a trail, wound its way downhill, leading directly to Gobe.

By mid-morning, they'd traveled the six miles and were now hidden on a hillock overlooking the town. Gobe was tiny and Tarkington wondered how it even registered on a map. The few buildings he could see were ragged, some having obvious holes in the roofs, and others tilted as though sinking into the mud. The only part the Allies were interested in was the docking facilities. They looked okay, usable anyway, but Tarkington wondered why they'd chosen such a dilapidated area. No matter, his mission was to clear out any heavy artillery or Jap armor they might find.

He dug into his pack and pulled out the set of small binoculars they had issued him. Compared to most sets he'd seen, this pair was half the size and weight. They were nowhere near as good as the set he remembered using onboard The Eel, the submarine which had been shot out from beneath them, but they enlarged the scene enough for him to realize the intelligence report which sent them on this mission was either completely misinterpreted or the Japanese had moved on.

He shook his head and handed the binoculars to Winkleman. "This looks like a dry hole. All I'm seeing is run-down shacks and a few half-starved Japs."

Winkleman scanned the area and came to the same conclusion moments later. "Well, shit," he hissed.

Tarkington passed the information to the rest of the men. Stollman looked dejected, as a kid who'd been told they canceled Christmas. "You mean to tell me, we come all this way and there's nothing for me to blow up?"

Vick shook his head, "Relax, Stolly. You can still blow Bull."

Sergeant Bulkort stiffened. He'd heard them joke about their friendship and hadn't felt comfortable enough to put an end to it, but he'd reached his limit. "Hey Vick, how about I squeeze your neck till your head blows off?"

Tarkington shook his head, *this is why fresh blood's not a good idea.* "Can it. Both of you," he glared at Bulkort. He'd been briefed prior to the mission: as long as he was assigned to them, his rank meant nothing. But old habits die hard, especially for NCOs.

Vick lifted his chin and smiled at Bulkort, but there was no mirth in it. The message was clear: try it, asshole.

Tarkington broke the tension, "Our mission is to take out any Japs in Gobe and I see a couple Japs down there. So let's get a closer look, and if there's nothing to blow up, we'll take them out and occupy the town till the calvary comes sailing around the corner."

It was child's play for the squad to move through the kunai grass to the edge of town. There were very few villagers, and the ones they could see didn't look like they were there voluntarily.

The cart they'd seen the day before was empty, the contents most likely inside the hut they parked it in front of. It seemed to be the only hut occupied by the Japanese. There wasn't much activity, but the few soldiers they saw were near that hut. The roof was sagging and didn't look up to keeping out the torrential rains that plagued the area. An old poncho was draped over part of it, but looked as holey as the roof.

It was midday by the time they'd reconnoitered the entire town and decided there was nothing there beyond the few enemy soldiers. There were no signs of tanks, ammo dumps, or even much in the way of weapons. Unless the Japanese had them expertly hidden or they'd been moved, the information was false.

Tarkington pulled the men back from the village to discuss strategy. He kept his voice low, "Doesn't look like much. Those Japs look ready to topple over if we breathe on 'em heavy." Most of them grinned and nodded agreement, but Henry scowled and Tarkington knew him too well not to notice. Tarkington nodded, "I know. I know." He held up his hands, "It's never a good idea to underestimate 'em; they've surprised us before." Henry spit the piece of grass he was chewing on and adjusted his stance. It was as much of an acknowledgement as Tarkington was likely to get from the Cajun. "There's only five of 'em. I don't wanna just go in with knives slashing. They're used up. I wanna take a few alive and ask 'em some questions."

Winkleman nodded, "I didn't see any officers. One might be an NCO but hard to tell with their raggedy-ass uniforms."

Tarkington nodded, "Even better. The officers won't talk, but the enlisted guys have nothing to lose. They might not know much, but they'll sing like canaries. We'll wait until they have their dinner. After raiding the villagers, they'll be focused on finally getting a good meal; that's when we'll hit 'em."

Vick asked, "So we take 'em all alive?"

Tarkington glanced at the native guides; they'd been quiet all day, only speaking when asked a direct question. "I promised Tavist we'd avenge him for the robbery. A few dying might loosen the others' tongues up." Every member of the team except Bulkort had killed with knives. It was deeply personal and highly disturbing to kill someone that close. Smelling someone, hearing them breathe, their tiny mouth noises as they got close, then striking and ending their lives with a vicious, ancient killing tool—it wasn't for the faint of heart.

His men weren't sadistic killers and he hoped he wasn't either. *How would I know?* They were killers before the Alamo Scout training, but now they were as sharp as the blades they carried. It was still a hard thing to ask someone to do. "I'll do it," Tarkington said flatly. *What's a few more faces for the nightly parade?*

Henry lifted his chin and drawled, "I'll do one, too." Henry's voice was ice and broken glass, and Bulkort shuddered and gulped loudly. Henry turned his cold eyes on him, "Unless you want to, Bull."

Bulkort lowered his eyes and shook his head, "I—I will—but I've never done it."

Henry's grin held no mirth, "Not much to it, really."

Tarkington shook his head, "You stay back, Bulkort. We'll deal with the Japs." His face brightened, "Maybe they'll show us something you can blow up."

11

It wasn't long before the Japanese started preparing their stolen meal. All five of them stood around a small stove. It was old, rusted, and looked as though it might fall apart with the slightest touch, but soon the large pot of rice atop it was cooked. The Japanese held bowls and formed a line, queueing up to the server who wore a rotting cap atop his longish black hair.

Tarkington had seen a lot of Japanese soldiers, but these were the first he'd seen that looked beaten. Things in this part of the world were changing for the Japanese. More and more shipping was being sunk or damaged by the deadly presence of Gato-class submarines, making life miserable for men this far from their supply lines. He wondered how long they'd been here. Tavist said yesterday was the first time they'd raided his village, but they looked like they'd been here awhile.

The soldiers had leaned their rifles against a fallen log to free up their hands for the food bowls. They were shifting from foot to foot, laughing and joking—clearly excited for the coming meal.

Tarkington glanced at Henry, who shook his head as though scolding a child: this would be easier than they thought. They were concealed only yards away from the queue. Tarkington gave Henry a nod and they stood and stepped from the jungle with their rifles leveled. At first, there was no reaction. The enemy soldiers were so focused on getting fed, the GIs were almost upon them before their eyes finally widened.

The soldier serving the rice stopped mid-scoop, his mouth dropping open in utter incomprehension. Then he lunged for his sidearm, fumbling with the holster flap. Henry quickly closed the distance and swung the stock of his carbine, crushing the man's jaw with a meaty smack. The Japanese toppled backwards, a stream of blood and tooth fragments spraying the rice. He was out cold. The others didn't move, just stared with their mouths agape.

Tarkington barked, "Kofuku, kofuku." The soldiers didn't move. He stepped forward, reversed his carbine, and slammed the stock into the bridge of the nearest soldier's nose. Blood sprayed and the soldier's head snapped back, but he kept his feet, dropping his bowl and clutching his broken nose. "Kofuku!" Tarkington yelled.

They got the hint and raised their hands over their heads in surrender. Even the fear of being killed didn't make them drop their bowls, however, and Tarkington thought their gnawing hunger must be overwhelming.

The rest of the squad stepped from the jungle and spread themselves out. Soon the few natives joined them and the guides from Tavist's village spoke with them excitedly. One of them—a young woman—went straight to the stacked rifles. Before anyone could react, she chambered a round, placed the barrel against a Japanese soldier's head, and fired. The sudden rifle crack, along with the shock of sudden violence, made the GIs hunker.

The young woman watched her victim crumple. Her face dripped with his blood and brains, but she ignored it and quickly tried to chamber another round. The bolt action jammed. It was the only thing that saved the next soldier's life.

As she tried to free the jam, Raker stepped forward and placed his hand on the hot barrel. "Easy now. Easy," he said and gently pulled on the rifle. She held tight but looked into his eyes, and he smiled and nodded. "It's okay now. You're free." She didn't understand the words but understood the tone and she released her grip. Her hands shook and tears clouded her eyes. Despite the gore dripping from her face and hair, Raker thought she might be the most beautiful islander he'd ever seen.

The Japanese soldiers swayed on their feet, shocked into silence. The dead man looked small, almost unidentifiable as human. The front of his face was gone, replaced with a smoking crater of red and gray wetness.

Tarkington said, "Well, I guess now that she put the fear of God in 'em, let's ask 'em some questions."

With the GIs' limited Japanese language skills, interrogation was difficult. But their combined efforts provided them some useful information. The Japanese were from the 144th Infantry and had been fighting the Australians on the Kokoda Trail. They withdrew for much needed rest, and after a few days, their commanding officer ordered their company to search the countryside for villages to plunder. Their decimated platoon had been sent here. Their officer had split them into squads, but they hadn't heard from the other squads in days. Their plan had been to haul what they'd confiscated back to Buna tomorrow.

After the interrogation, Winkleman sat beside Tarkington. "You were right about those guys spilling the beans. Once they got to talking, we could hardly shut 'em up."

Tarkington nodded, "Yeah, too bad our Nip is so spotty. They'd probably give up Hirohito at this point."

The three surviving Japanese were sitting cross-legged on the ground. Their faces were lowered and Tarkington thought they looked more like beaten dogs than feared soldiers of the empire. The one with the broken nose had swollen cheeks, making it hard for him to see past them. Dried blood caked his face like peeling paint. The one Henry had clobbered was still unconscious and might never wake up.

Winkleman pointed at him, "His pulse is weak and ragged. I didn't think Henry hit him that hard, but . . ."

Tarkington said, "They're weak. Starving. Their bodies can't take the abuse they normally could."

"Wonder if the Japs in Buna and Gona are in as bad of shape as these guys. If so—should be a pushover."

Tarkington shook his head, "Don't count on it. Even if they're all half-starved, it doesn't take much energy to pull a trigger. Besides, they've had a lot of time to build defenses. It'll be a tough nut to crack no matter what."

Winkleman asked, "So what now? What do we do with them?" He nodded toward the silent soldiers.

"Well, half the 128th is coming overland and the rest will come around the cape in a day or two. We'll wait here and hand them over to the G2 guys."

Winkleman shook his head, "Seems like an awful waste, coming all this way for nothing."

Tarkington nodded, "I know, Wink. Kind of a letdown after all the buildup." He considered, "We'll give the prisoners to the islanders. That'll appease Tavist and keep him from eating the Aussies." Winkleman laughed and Tarkington continued, "We'll push up the beach and do some reconnaissance for the troops. There's a good-sized river, the Musa, not far from here. We'll check it out while we're waiting."

"Might as well sign the Jap's death warrants. Doubt Tavist will be merciful," Winkleman noted.

Tarkington shrugged, "We'll ask him to be nice, but seeing the hatred in that island girl's eyes . . ." He shook his head sadly, "They mistreated her no doubt—so they've got it coming."

He expected Winkleman to protest, it was how he would've reacted a year ago, but instead Winkleman said bitterly, "Raker's trying to console her, I'm sure."

"Jesus, Winkleman. The girl's been raped. The last thing she wants is another man's hands on her." Winkleman looked embarrassed. Tarkington continued, "I thought you were going to argue about the prisoners' fates, not be jealous of Raker."

Winkleman sighed and took a long moment before replying, "Guess I'm not as soft-hearted as I used to be, Tark."

Tarkington nodded his understanding but felt a little hollow with the loss of Winkleman's innocence, no matter how misguided he'd thought it was. "War will do that."

They stayed in Gobe the rest of the day. The two guides from Tavist's village left, towing the Japanese prisoners behind them like oxen. The Japanese soldiers looked terrified and Tarkington couldn't blame them. He'd tried to tell the islanders they were prisoners of war and should be handed over to the Allies when they arrived. The guides smiled and nodded, but Tarkington doubted the soldiers would see another sunrise.

After a buggy, sweat-soaked night of tossing and turning, they had a light breakfast of leftover rice and dried fruit from a J-ration, then moved north. It would've been easier to move along the beach; however—if the prisoners were to be believed—there were still stray patrols out and about, so they moved up to the jungle and kunai grasses overlooking the beaches.

The sunrise was beautiful, as the rays lit up the cloudy horizon with pink, orange, and red. The sweltering heat turned their camouflage clothing dark with sweat after only a few steps. Their faces dripped sweat, streaking face paint, and making them look more like a race of striped zebras than soldiers.

Henry was on point, moving silently. This part of the cape wasn't as fenestrated with bays and inlets. They crossed a few creeks, but nothing like the deep canyons they'd had to deal with before. They saw no signs of anything human. The little game trails snaking every which way were small and obviously not used by humans.

Tarkington tried to keep track of their progress with the dilapidated map he referenced occasionally, but most of the features they came across weren't on the map. For a while, he tried updating the map with his own scrawling; however, the paper was rotting, both from the humidity and his own sweat, so he stuffed it into his pocket along with the pencil nub.

They finally crossed a field of thick kunai grass and stopped when the grasses ran out and they were greeted with a vista overlooking a large river estuary emptying into the Pacific.

Henry spit out the blade of grass he'd been chewing on, "Guess'n that's the Musa River."

The entire squad stood on the impressive precipice. After the confines of the jungle and the grasses, the sudden expansiveness gave them all pause.

Winkleman gave a low whistle, "You can see for miles and miles."

The river was dirty and the silt-line extended into the sea all the way to the horizon. Upstream a few miles, the river was still one massive cohesive unit, but as it snaked closer to the coast, countless fingers split off finding their own way to the sea. The estuary stretched for miles. It would take a lifetime to explore each finger of water.

"We sure as hell ain't crossing that," muttered Stollman.

Tarkington agreed, "No." He looked over the edge: it was straight down 200 feet to the southern-most finger of water. "We're at the end of the line. Must be a bridge somewhere upstream though."

Winkleman shrugged, "Maybe, but maybe not. From what I've seen, we're not exactly in a booming metropolis."

"True, but the Japs got across somehow and I doubt they swam. The river's too wide and the estuary could eat an entire division." Tarkington chewed his bottom lip, then decided, "We'll rest here for twenty minutes, then move upstream along this ridge. See what we can see."

Within seconds, the squad had their packs off and were lazing around on the precipice, some hanging their legs over the edge. Winkleman was as far back as he could get without actually being in the kunai grasses.

"Hey Wink. You sure you don't wanna come join us over here?" asked Stollman.

Winkleman gave him a sideways grin and lifted his middle finger. Alarm and panic crossed his face suddenly, "Where the hell's Bulkort, Stolly?"

Stollman looked startled as he glanced side to side, "Shit. I dunno. He was here a second ago." He leaned over as far as he dared, gaping into the chasm beneath his feet. "I—I don't see him down there," he said with relief.

Winkleman got back onto his feet, clutching his carbine. The others did too, each man suddenly alert and ready.

Tarkington looked back the way they'd come. The kunai grass was thick, the tops swaying lazily in the light breeze. "Was he with us here? Did he come out of the grass?"

Stollman concentrated, trying to remember, and finally shook his head and lowered his voice, "I don't think so."

Tarkington nodded and said, "Stay close enough to see one another. We'll sweep our way back through. He's probably taking a shit, but who knows. Be careful." Tarkington would be more alarmed if it were one of the core squad missing; they knew better. As he stepped into the grass, he thought of all the ways he was going to punish Sergeant Bulkort.

They left their packs and stepped back into the grass. It was miserable stuff; the edges were sharp as razors and having to re-enter it wasn't on their wish list. This particular patch was thicker and older, making their progress slow and arduous. It hadn't been bad the first time through, but now they were moving slower and it seemed hotter somehow. Stifling.

They stayed six feet apart. Any more and they'd lose sight of one another. They tried to follow their original path, but it was as though their passing only minutes before hadn't happened. Tarkington stifled the urge to call out. If the big man was taking a shit, he'd respond: mystery solved. But of course, he wasn't about to do that.

They'd nearly crossed the 300 yards of grass before Henry, on the left flank, held up a hand and crouched. Vick, to his right, did the same, and soon the entire squad was crouched and silently scanning.

Henry stayed in a crouch and moved forward slowly. Vick followed and soon they were all creeping forward, their carbines ready. Tarkington's hands looked as though he'd shoved them into a vat of razor blades. The countless cuts from the kunai grass itched and stung as sweat ran into them, but he ignored it.

Henry went fifteen yards and stopped again. Tarkington heard him hiss, "Bulkort. What're you doing?"

Tarkington scowled and moved toward Henry's voice. The others spread out, creating a tight perimeter. Tarkington saw Bulkort on his belly only yards away. He was white as a sheet, beads of sweat on his forehead and his eyes wide with fear. He was frozen in place. Tarkington whispered to Henry, "What the fuck's wrong with him?" He raised his voice, "Bull!"

Sergeant Bulkort's wide eyes never left the ground but he stammered, "S—snake. Big fucking snake. One of them adders." Henry shook his head and strode towards him, drawing his hunting knife at the same time. "D— don't piss him off. Don't do it," stammered Bulkort.

Henry didn't respond but sheathed his knife and approached the back of the huge six-foot-long snake's tail. He hesitated for a moment, rubbing his hands together, then quickly darted in. His hands were a blur as he gripped the back of the snake, whipped it over his head, then flung it forward and snapped it back again like a whip. The whipcrack of the adder's head snapping off sounded like a rifle shot. He threw the writhing but now harmless snake's body at Bulkort. It landed on his back and the sergeant writhed and contorted and finally flung it off, darting to Henry's side. "Damn! Damn! Damn!" he exclaimed.

Henry shook his head slowly, "You had us all worried sick, Bull. What a pussy."

Bulkort stammered, "Death adder. That's what they call 'em. They're—they're deadly. Six hours is all it takes." He shook as though trying to rid himself of the heebie-jeebies. "I—I really hate snakes."

Henry grinned, "No shit? I couldn't tell. Thought maybe you were gonna make love to it or something."

The squad laughed and ribbed him mercilessly until Tarkington finally put an end to it, "If you're all done snake charming, I'd like to continue the patrol. Is that alright with you, Sergeant?"

Bulkort, fully cowed, nodded, "Of course, Sergeant. Of course. I'm—well, I'm sorry. It's just that . . ."

Tarkington interrupted, "Yeah, we get it. You're afraid of snakes. Got news for you: this part of the world's chock full of 'em and most of 'em are deadly. Now shut the hell up and don't let that crap happen again. Understood?"

Bulkort nodded quickly and brushed the dirt from his fatigues, "Understood."

12

It didn't take long to realize that moving upstream along the Musa River wasn't a viable proposition. The terrain got steeper, the jungle thicker until it would've required machetes and hours upon hours of back-breaking work to move even a half mile. So they turned around and headed back to Gobe. If they had time, they'd send word for someone to ask the Japanese prisoners how they'd gotten to Gobe from Buna. If it were an overland route, that information might be valuable to the Allies.

Without the Japanese presence, there were more native islanders in Gobe than there had been when they'd left the morning before. One of the native men spoke with Tarkington, telling him there was a sizable force of American soldiers coming their way along a trail which passed just north of the towering highlands jutting up from Cape Nelson.

Tarkington passed the information to the squad, "From what he said, they should be here this evening. Right on time. The boats should come around the cape soon too."

"What happens then, Tark?" asked Vick.

"I'm expecting they'll have new orders for us. I expect we'll either head back along the route the 128th came over and catch a ride back to Moresby or Milne Bay, or join the main force as a reconnaissance unit."

Winkleman shook his head, "You really think they'll have orders for us? I'm amazed they're actually on time in the first place."

"You've become quite the cynic, Wink. We'll know soon enough. For now, we'll wait for the cavalry to show up."

They passed the time cleaning weapons, napping, and eating. More and more natives showed up. They came from all around to greet the Americans. If the 128th meant to keep their arrival a secret, they'd failed. By the time the first elements arrived from the jungles, the once-deserted town was hopping with activity. The GIs reportedly were right outside the town and would be there in minutes.

Tarkington and Winkleman stood in the middle of the town awkwardly waiting to talk with the first senior officer they came across. Tarkington had the order signed by General Krueger in his pocket. He hoped he wouldn't need it.

The first elements of GIs filtered into town cautiously. Tarkington was aghast at their condition. Their uniforms were hanging off their frames, black with sweat and mud. Their faces and exposed arms were covered with the red welts of insect bites. Fat, blood-infused leeches hung from some men's necks and arms, as though the soldiers had simply given up trying to rid themselves of them. These men hadn't even met the Japanese, and they already looked defeated.

A dark-complected sergeant noticed the squad. He halted, looking them up and down with outright suspicion. He was in better shape than some others, but he still wobbled on his feet as though suffering from extreme exertion and heat.

Tarkington realized how they must look to an outsider. They were dressed in filthy, mottled camouflage. Every exposed piece of skin was covered with black and green paint, which was streaked with stripes of sweat. They had M1 carbines slung over their shoulders, weapons which weren't available in great numbers yet in theater. The sergeant continued looking them up and down trying to process who the hell they were. Tarkington wished he'd taken the time to clean up.

Tarkington smiled and stepped toward him with his hand extended. "Hello, Sergeant. I'm Staff Sergeant Tarkington." The sergeant didn't extend his hand to shake, so Tarkington withdrew it. "We're Alamo Scouts sent here by Colonel Bradshaw."

The sergeant sneered, "Where's your rank? Your unit insignia?"

Tarkington brushed his shoulders and chest, exposing the dim outlines of their Indian head unit insignia and the three stripes over the rocker. The sergeant leaned forward, trying to get a better look at the Indian head. "Never heard of your unit, Sergeant."

"We're newly formed. Consider us a reconnaissance squad."

The sergeant looked dubious, "Just a squad? Where's the rest of your platoon?"

Tarkington was losing interest in the twenty-questions game, "Look, Sergeant," he leaned forward reading the man's nametape, "Pavel."

The sergeant brushed his own filthy nametape, "Ravel."

Tarkington continued, "Sergeant Ravel. Who's your commanding officer? I'd like to speak with him." Ravel pursed his lips and hesitated, weighing whether he should believe him. Tarkington's patience vanished, "I haven't got all day, *Sergeant.*"

Ravel stiffened and thumbed back over his shoulder. "We're spread for miles back there. Captain Grunkin's back a ways, probably still wading through that cursed swamp, but Lieutenant Brady's coming along with second squad." He turned back toward the jungle and pointed, "There he is now." He sneered and added, "Good luck."

Tarkington lifted his chin to Winkleman, "Stay with the men. I'll go introduce myself to Lieutenant Brady." Winkleman nodded but couldn't keep from staring at the bedraggled unit.

Lieutenant Brady strode into town with his rifle slung over his shoulder. He was tall and well built, but the days-long trudge through the jungle and swamps of the Musa River Valley looked to have sucked the energy from him. He looked better than most of his troops, but his cheeks were sallow, his face pale, and his uniform was black with sweat and dried mud. His blue eyes darted side to side and finally settled on Tarkington.

Tarkington stiffened and wondered if the lieutenant expected a salute. He knew from experience that Japanese snipers were excellent marksman and would like nothing more than to kill an officer. The problem was, none of these soldiers had probably engaged the Japanese in combat yet and hadn't learned the same hard lessons. "Sir. I'm Staff Sergeant Tarkington with the Alamo Scouts."

Lieutenant Brady looked him up and down much the same way Sgt. Ravel had. "Alamo Scout?" He looked at the unfamiliar insignia. "I don't know about any such unit."

Tarkington grimaced. Did this mean no one knew about their mission? "Sir, Colonel Bradshaw with the Sixth Army sent us here to reconnoiter and destroy any defenses the Japs had here before your arrival."

The officer looked even more confused, "Sixth Army? You mean back in Australia?"

Tarkington nodded, "They dispatched us from Milne Bay then to Wanigela. We met up with some Australians with a barge and went around Cape Nelson. Our mission was to take out any Jap installations here in Gobe." He looked around the pathetic little village, "But other than a few worn-out Japs, there was nothing here to worry about."

The mention of Japanese soldiers focused Brady's ice-blue eyes. "Japs? Here?"

Tarkington nodded, "A squad of looters. Yes, sir. We took care of them though. They're being held prisoner in a nearby village." He made a vague gesture south.

"From what I hear from the Aussies, Japs don't surrender."

Tarkington nodded, "I'd agree with that, but these men were half-starved skeletons without an officer. They didn't have much fight left in 'em. We didn't give 'em an option, although a few tried."

The lieutenant's focus shifted and he swayed slightly. The day was hot despite low cloud cover. The officer looked around the village and muttered, "We made it, finally."

Tarkington understood. This was hard country to move through. Even his small, highly-trained squad had a tough time and they were in peak physical condition, having trained specifically for it. Moving large numbers of men laden with heavy packs and weapons through this unmerciful terrain was nearly impossible. Yet here they were. Tarkington shook his head. *Look about ready to keel over, but they made it.*

"Yes, sir. I think you'll find the islanders eager and ready to help."

Lieutenant Brady seemed to remember he was in front of an enlisted man. His face hardened, "I know nothing about you or your mission, but perhaps Captain Grunkin does. I expect him in a few hours. He's hanging back with some slower platoons. Meantime, you and your squad will be under my command. Since you already know the locals, have them ready places for my men to rest and rack out."

Tarkington sighed, suddenly feeling the weight of General Krueger's letter in his pocket. He nodded. It was a battle best fought with Captain Grunkin rather than Lt. Brady. "Yes, sir. I'll inform the islanders of your wishes."

It took the rest of that day and most of the rest of the next day before the entire 3rd Battalion of the 128th Infantry finally arrived in Gobe. Like the leading platoons, the GIs looked dead on their feet. The trek down the Musa River Valley, which was only supposed to take a day or two, had taken five. Part of the delay came when they'd come to the town of Totore, halfway between Wanigela and Gobe. They'd been told they could cross the raging Musa River there, and the trail beyond was easily passable.

After sending scouting elements across, it was quickly determined the trail on the other side was under five feet of water and completely impassable. The river was rising and the scouting element barely made it back over the Musa in time. The delay had been costly, as the rains to the north swelled the river, making the already swampy ground even harder to slog their way through.

The GIs were exhausted and they hadn't even met the enemy yet. Fouled water made its way into canteens and men were already suffering from bouts of uncontrollable diarrhea. Dysentery was common in this part of the world, and Tarkington wondered how these men were expected to fight. Half of them should be in the hospital.

After settling into Gobe, the GIs of 3d Battalion quickly turned the sleepy village into a morass of foulness and rot. The hastily dug latrines quickly filled with shit and the effects of rising swamp water affected the area, overflowing the foulness into the town itself.

The only bright spot was Porlock Harbor. It was the prize for capturing

Gobe and was transformed into a workable harbor soon enough by a company of Australian engineers. They'd hauled tools overland despite the hardships, and after a brief rest, got to work updating the harbor facilities. Now all they needed was 2d Battalion to come sailing around the cape so they could take them away from this miserable little town. They were already three days late in coming.

They were disgusted with the conditions. The 128th had been through a lot of pain just getting here, but they made things worse with their unsanitary methods and the squad tried to steer clear of them whenever possible. They only ate the food they'd brought, never sharing and never asking to share the Australian-supplied bully beef the 3d Battalion soldiers subsisted on.

Captain Grunkin knew nothing of their mission either and had no orders for them from Colonel Bradshaw. Tarkington told Grunkin of their unique skill sets, but Grunkin was suffering just as bad as his men and waved Tarkington away, telling them he'd keep them in mind, but for now they should attach themselves to 3d Battalion.

There was nothing to be done for it, so he'd volunteered them to travel to the village and recover the Aussie sailors and Japanese prisoners. Captain Grunkin was ecstatic at the mention of prisoners and sent them on their way with orders to return as soon as possible.

Once out of the festering mess of Gobe, the squad felt better. The place was a cesspool of vermin and disease and the longer they stayed, the worse they felt about their chances of remaining in good health.

The rains started in earnest, moving down from the northeast in waves. Just like on Luzon, the roads became nearly impassable, and it took them all day to travel the three and a half miles to the village. Warriors carrying captured Japanese rifles greeted them when they were still half a mile from town and escorted them in. Some wore huge leaves suspended on their tall hair, keeping most of the rain off, but others simply ignored it as a fact of life.

By the time they ushered the squad into the village elder's hut, they were soaked to the skin and shivering despite the warm air. Tavist greeted them with a welcoming smile. "Welcome back, my friends," he said in Tagalog. He gestured for them to sit on the mats spread along the ground or draped over stout logs. The squad spread out and sat down, grateful to be off their feet and in a dry place.

"Oi, look who it is: Lonny!"

Tarkington noticed the two Australian sailors in the back of the longhouse and waved. "Looks like you two have managed well," he grinned.

Lonny looked as comfortable and confident in his own skin as always, and even Singlet looked relaxed. They'd shunned the rags of their uniforms for the airy, but much more comfortable, loins of the islanders. Both were bare on top and wore thin sandals made of animal hide. Although they'd only been there a little over a week, they looked like they'd been born there.

The Aussies went around the room, greeting each man as though they were long-lost brothers. Finally, with the chitchat over, Tarkington asked, "Where are the Jap prisoners?"

Lonny and Singlet exchanged glances, telling the tale without having to open their mouths. Singlet glanced at Tavist, the village elder, and uttered, "They're all dead. The village put them on," he raised his hands to mimic quotations, "trial. They found them guilty of theft, which is punishable by death." His voice caught in his throat as the image of them dying crossed his mind, "They didn't die well."

Lonny added, "To say the least."

Singlet brightened, "But after that nasty bit, things have gone swimmingly well here. You were right. These islanders are delightful people, as long as you're on their good side."

Tarkington shrugged, "Captain Grunkin was expecting prisoners. Doesn't sound like that's going to happen."

Stollman grumbled, "The way Colonel Donaldson runs his battalion, they'd die of disease in a day or two anyway."

The men weren't shivering anymore, and the smells of cooking meat wafted into the hut. Vick asked, "We don't have to go back there, do we, Tark?"

Tarkington shook his head, "Not today. Not tomorrow either, but the next day for sure. Maybe Second Battalion will be there by then and we can get the hell out of Gobe."

Henry drawled, "God Almighty, I hope so. That place'll be the death of us all."

They left the village a day later with no Japanese prisoners but with the Aussie sailors. The rain had stopped but the track back to Gobe was still muddy. By the time they made it back to Gobe, their baggy camouflage pants were hanging off them, weighed down with sticky mud.

Gobe was a mud-pit. The constant back and forth of combat soldiers churned up the ground, and in some spots the mud was knee deep. The good news was that the barges and converted fishing vessels, which the sailors called luggers, had arrived from Wanigela and were moored to the improved docks of Porlock Harbor or anchored offshore.

The 2d Battalion of the 128th Infantry were crammed onboard. Lieutenant Colonel Huntington was so appalled at the conditions in Gobe, that he opted to keep his battalion in the boats, continue their westward move, and offload at Pongani. He promised to send the boats and ships back to Gobe as soon as they were offloaded.

Tarkington gathered the squad together. They were in a shady spot overlooking Porlock Harbor, watching native islanders offloading supplies. Tarkington said, "We've gotta get ourselves onto one of those ships. We can't stay here in this quagmire. Bradshaw's orders weren't specific after the Gobe mission, but I think he'd want us to make ourselves useful to the war effort, not become casualties of disease." There were nods all around. "So here's what we're gonna do. Let's get as cleaned up as possible and just walk on. If anyone gives us any guff," he touched his pants pocket, "I'll pull out Krueger's letter."

Winkleman laughed, "That's it? That's your plan?"

Tarkington nodded, "Yep. You got anything better?" Winkleman shook his head and no one else offered anything either. "All right, those boats are leaving this evening, so we've gotta act quick."

Two hours later, they lined up on the docks in front of a skiff, which they'd observed shuttling back and forth to one of the larger lugger ships. There was constant activity and the mood was harried as the sailors and soldiers made ready for the last leg to Pongani. A second lieutenant holding a clipboard stood in front of the skiff, marking off supplies loaded and offloaded. He looked up at the squad. Although they'd cleaned off the camouflage face paint and scrubbed as much of the dirt and grime from their uniforms as they could, they still didn't look like your everyday regulation GIs.

"Who the hell are you?" asked the lieutenant.

Tarkington replied, "Staff Sergeant Tarkington and Alamo Scout Unit Alpha reporting, Lieutenant."

The lieutenant looked at his clipboard for guidance, then back at Tarkington. "Well I'm Lieutenant Unger." He shook his head, "There's no mention of you here. What the hell's an Alamo Scout?"

"Sir, we have orders to move to the front and that's at Pongani."

"Orders? From whom?" Tarkington presented the letter from General Krueger. The lieutenant stiffened as he read through it, then handed it back. He squinted, looking them up and down. "What kind of uniforms are those, Sergeant? They're not regulation. And what kind of rifles are those?"

"We're a reconnaissance unit, sir. The uniforms and carbines are for specialized troops—like us."

The officer guffawed and shook his head, "You think highly of yourselves, don't you?"

Tarkington's face reddened but he suppressed the urge to strangle him. "You read the order from General Krueger, sir."

"I've no idea who the hell General Krueger is, but I do know the Sixth Army ain't running this show. Hell, they're still not fully formed, in fact. Let me see your weapon, Sergeant." Tarkington unslung the carbine, wanting to crash the butt into the officer's face as he'd done to the Japanese soldier only days before, but instead, he handed it over. The officer hefted it and gave a low whistle. "It's light. Magazine fed. How many rounds?"

"Fifteen pistol-weight thirty caliber rounds, sir."

"Thirty cal? I'll be damned. How's it shoot?"

"Not as accurate as the Garand, but for close-in work it does fine."

He handed the carbine back and took a closer look at the men. "You've seen combat," he stated matter-of-factly.

Tarkington grinned, "Yes, sir. We were on Luzon when this whole thing kicked off."

He reared back, shocked. "Manila? How the hell'd you get out?"

Tarkington shook his head, "That's a long story, sir, and I'm not sure I'm supposed to talk about it."

The officer's demeanor switched from warm and curious to cold. "Well, without orders from Colonel Huntington, there's nothing I can do."

Tarkington's neck bristled and his face turned a new shade of red. He was about to threaten the second lieutenant with physical violence when PFC Stollman stepped forward, grinning. He snapped off a crisp salute, which the officer returned with some annoyance. Stollman pulled his pack off his shoulders, "Sir, can I speak with you privately?"

Unger looked from Tarkington to Stollman and sputtered, "What's this all about?"

Tarkington shrugged and Stollman stepped forward and draped his arm over the young lieutenant's shoulder, turning him away from prying eyes and ears, "You fancy a Jap souvenir, sir?"

"Souvenir? Like what, Private?"

Stollman reached into his pack, digging to the bottom. "You seem to know your weapons. Ever seen a Jap pistol? Pulled it off a Jap captain back on Bataan."

Unger licked his lips, clearly intrigued. "A Nambu?" Stollman nodded and pulled out the pistol. He'd traded a bottle of whiskey for it from an Australian soldier in Milne Bay. It had been rusted and abused, but he'd buffed it until it shone, knowing it would come in handy at some point. Again, the officer gave a low whistle as he held it and admired the craftsmanship. After a minute, he asked, "How much you want for it?"

Stollman shook his head, "I don't want money. It'll cost you a boat ride out to that lugger."

Unger aimed the pistol, squinting down the sight, and finally nodded. "Okay, it's a deal."

On the short boat ride to the lugger, Tarkington said, "I woulda gotten us on this boat one way or the other. You got screwed on that deal."

Stollman shrugged, "The firing pin's broken. It's a paperweight. And besides, I consider anything that gets us out of there a good deal."

13

The squad kept a low profile during the boat ride toward Pongani. It was late evening and as they passed the green jutting headlands of the New Guinea coastline, they were thankful to be on the boat. The terrain from Gobe to Pongani was thick roadless jungle. From here it looked impenetrable. The Musa River, which they'd observed from the cliff a week earlier, looked even more impossible to cross from sea level.

Nervous sailors manned guns mounted here and there almost haphazardly. The luggers weren't military vessels, so they bolted and welded weapon stands at various strategic points. Raker sidled up next to Tarkington and gestured at the nearest gunner manning a Browning .30 caliber machine gun. "That guy says they came around Cape Nelson at night to avoid Jap bombers and fighters. He's nervous as a cat, thinks this whole daylight thing's suicide."

Tarkington nodded, "I heard something similar from other sailors. It'll be dark soon, but we'd be a nice fat target if they come."

The flotilla approached Pongani as darkness descended, crawling forward and hoping to avoid the wholly uncharted reefs, which could extend out to sea for miles. It became blatantly clear that even if it were day, there was no way any of the boats could get close enough to shore for an easy offload. The problem solved itself when a long string of tiny lights approached. All guns swung toward the threat, but the lights were attached to native boats emerging from Pongani. As the canoes neared, their torches lit up native islanders who waved and shouted at the sailors and GIs standing along the deck.

A grungy sailor, chewing on a stogie, brushed his hat up his forehead and shook his head. "What the hell are they saying?"

Tarkington and the rest of the squad were nearby and he interpreted, "They say they'll help. Their boats are small but sturdy and can offload troops and supplies."

The sailor looked dumbstruck, "You can understand 'em?"

Tarkington grinned, "Yep." He extended his hand to the others, "We all can."

The sailor shook his head, but his grin spread and he hurried away, calling over his shoulder, "Stay here. I'll get the officer of the deck down here."

After Tarkington and the others helped with the language barrier, they put a process in place and soon the offloading became a smooth, albeit slow, endeavor. There was a constant stream of lit-up canoes circling back and forth from the ships and barges to the beach. It looked like a light parade.

Offloading the GIs was easier than offloading the supplies. Some gear was simply too big for the native canoes and skiffs and had to be broken down into smaller parts.

The squad took the first opportunity to get off the ship. They descended the treacherous nets and crammed themselves onto a large outrigger canoe along with another squad of GIs, and the natives took powerful strokes propelling them toward the dark outline of land. The ride was reminiscent of their outrigger canoe trip in the Philippines some months before.

Henry was the first to hear it. He held up a hand, "Shush." The gabbing GIs from the other squad glared back at him, their faces lit up by the torches. He hissed, "I hear a plane." The islanders continued paddling, but even over the hiss of the water passing by, the engine noise could be heard and soon everyone was looking skyward.

Tarkington yelled in Tagalog, "Ilabas and ilaw!" The paddlers closest to the torches pulled them from their stands and thrust them into the sea, immediately extinguishing them. The order was repeated up and down the line, and the light parade winked out one by one until there was only darkness. For a moment, everyone stopped and listened. Had they been seen? The answer came with the terrifying whine of a diving plane.

The islanders took up their paddles, stroking hard for shore. Tarkington didn't think anywhere would be safe; however, he'd rather die on dry land than sink into the crystalline waters of the Solomon Sea. He hardly had time to consider his options before the screeching of the plane surrounded him. From the front, there was a sudden flashing and streaks of red tracer fire erupted from the sky as though by magic. The ripping buzzsaw sound of enemy fire made him duck, though the attacking plane wasn't targeting the boats but the shoreline, and he realized there were still lights on in the town.

The squad riding along with them raised their rifles to their shoulders and Tarkington hissed, "Don't shoot. You've got no chance of hitting anything except friendlies and your muzzle flash'll just bring trouble."

The surly sergeant leading the squad agreed. "Keep a lid on it, boys," he uttered, and the GIs took their rifles from their shoulders.

The strafing run stopped after a few seconds and the pitch of the airplane's engine changed as the pilot pulled up and away. Lights extinguished onshore, but there was a small fire burning where the incendiary rounds had ignited something. The islanders were still paddling, pulling them ever closer to shore. Tarkington told them to stop paddling, and the canoe drifted and turned slightly as it glided to a stop.

The plane's engine noise was dimmer now, but it was still nearby. "He'll make another pass on the fire." Sure enough, the sound changed and once again the shrill screech of a diving aircraft filled the air. "Here he comes," uttered Tarkington. He instinctively ducked as low as the canoe would allow, even though it would give him little cover.

This time there wasn't tracer fire. The plane's noise peaked in a crescendo, then it was again pulling away. Three seconds later, there was a bright flash and an unbelievably loud blast of sound. A second later, the concussive wave passed over them, making its own wind and turning the canoe broadside. The residual echoes from the bomb seemed to last for minutes as it bounced around the bay.

The engine noise receded and Henry drawled, "Son of a bitch is leaving." The islander's wide eyes looked back at Tarkington and he thought they must be worried sick about their friends and family in the village. He nodded and they dug their paddles in with gusto, propelling them toward the beach.

Surprisingly, there wasn't much damage in Pongani. The strafing run had done more damage than the bomb, which had struck the beach away from where the offloading operation was taking place. Two islanders had been wounded in the strafing run, but their injuries were from flying debris, not actual bullets, which would've ripped them apart. Instead of being fearful, they exhibited their wounds with pride, smiling as a medic stitched them up.

The village of Pongani was small and off the beach a couple hundred yards. The number of islanders helping with the offloading operation couldn't have all come from there. Like in Gobe, the islanders flocked from all around to help the Allies oust the Japanese.

Tarkington had heard the audacious Japanese plan to unite all peoples of Asian descent under one flag—theirs. It was one of their excuses for this entire war, but he often wondered how they expected to do that by terrorizing them. He wondered what would have happened in places such as this if they'd treated the locals with respect and dignity instead of disgust and violence. Perhaps instead of welcoming and helping the GIs, the islanders would've attacked them. His war would have turned out far differently by now. If the Filipinos had turned against them in the Philippines, he and his men would be nothing more than picked-over skeletons.

The squad found a dry piece of ground and spread out their ponchos. They'd eaten on the lugger. The mess hall was overcrowded and underserved, but they'd gotten a decent hot meal of cooked Australian bully beef. The fishy taste the stuff was famous for was cooked out of it, and with the help of various spices, it wasn't half bad.

Sergeant Bulkort leaned over and farted long and loud, then settled back onto his back. Vick scrunched his nose and got to his feet, "Christ

Almighty, Bull. You're as rank as they come. There's something dead up there."

Bulkort smiled, "It's that beef, or whatever the hell that stuff was. Gives me gas."

Vick settled farther away, "Yeah, no shit."

The smell wafted over them. Tarkington smelled it and wondered if his olfactory senses were dulled from all the far nastier smells he'd been exposed to over the past year. It wasn't pleasant by any stretch of the imagination, but it didn't revile him the way he thought it should. It probably would have before December of '41.

Raker lifted a cheek and let one of equal power rip. Vick complained again, "You too, Raker? Hope you didn't do that in front of that girl in Gobe."

Raker shook his head, "I'd do no such thing in front of a lady. But you assholes deserve it." He leaned over and punched Winkleman's shoulder, "You get laid yet, Wink?"

"Fuck you, Raker." He lifted his shirt over his nose, "Damn, you're nasty."

From the beach, a familiar voice called out, "Hey, that you Sergeant Winkleman?"

The Australian accent was unmistakable, and Winkleman called out, "That you Lonny?"

Lonny hoisted himself up the little three-foot escarpment and stood over them. "Yep, it's me. Mind if I join you up here?"

Tarkington said, "What the hell're you doing here? Thought you woulda waited for a ride back to Wanigela."

Lonny sat down, "Singlet did, but I thought I could help out here."

"How'd he take that?" asked Winkleman.

"I didn't exactly ask his permission. He's probably still looking for me."

Tarkington shook his head, "You don't wanna get caught up in this, Lonny. Head back to Milne Bay. From what I hear, there's going to be a constant string of transports back and forth until there're enough men and supplies here to push into Buna. You won't have trouble finding a ride outta here."

Lonny looked up at the black sky dotted with stars and blew out a sigh. "I wanna see combat, Sergeant. I won't get that in Milne Bay."

Tarkington guffawed, "That's just stupid. Did you piss yourself when that Jap Zero bombed and strafed us?"

"No," he insisted.

"Scared you though, I'll bet. That's nothing. Wait till you're pinned down, bullets whipping inches over your head and the ground vibrating with explosions. Wait till your eardrums feel they'll burst as concussion waves sweep over you." He paused, "Wait till you kill a man."

"But that's what I want to do. Kill Japs."

Winkleman shook his head, "It's not what you think, Lonny. There's no glory in it. It's not like that."

Lonny pointed southwest, "You know what's that way a couple hundred miles?" No one answered. "My home. My country is threatened by these arseholes and I aim to kill as many as I can. You're from America, thousands of miles away. Your homeland's not threatened. Not like mine."

Tarkington's voice was low, "Then why don't you ask for a transfer to a line unit? There's plenty of Aussies fighting the Japs up the Kokoda Trail, I hear. Plenty for everybody from what I hear."

He looked at his boots and shook his head, "I have and they refused all three times. I'm needed as a damned engineer. They say I'm too valuable to be infantry."

Tarkington bristled, "You ever think they might be right, boy? For chrissakes, I know we've been getting our asses kicked six ways to Sunday by these sons of bitches and some of it's incompetence, but a lot of it's from lack of manpower. This thing is just getting started. Japan's a long way from here and we'll have to fight them every step of the way. Engineers aren't grown on trees. Your skills can save lives." The low murmuring of voices and the occasional bang of something being dropped or stacked drifted up to them from the beach. Men were struggling to offload supplies down there, hoping to finish before daylight when another air raid was a real possibility. Tarkington pointed that way, "Hell, I'll bet they'd kill to have your help right now."

Lonny took the hint, then stood and jumped back down the embankment. He waved, the motion lost in the darkness. "Good luck out there," he murmured.

No one responded, and when he was just a memory, Winkleman said, "He's just a kid."

Tarkington guffawed, "There ain't more'n a year's difference between us."

Winkleman nodded, "I know. Just seems that way."

The sounds of offloading continued throughout the night. Some men wanted to help, but Tarkington was insistent they stay put and get some rest.

As dawn broke in the east, they opened cans of rations, slurping the cold contents down their throats as quickly as possible in failed attempts to bypass their taste buds. The beach was unrecognizable from the day before. Nearly every square inch was covered with crates filled with food, ammunition, and other tools of war.

Tarkington looked up, hoping the Japanese air force didn't return. They draped camouflage netting over the exposed supplies. But he doubted it would fool anyone. Pongani was a fat target and may as well have had a bullseye painted on it.

The road leading from the beach to town was muddy, and as he watched, islanders struggled to push carts over it. They had hacked trees down and placed the logs at intervals for extra traction, but it still took a lot of time and manpower.

There were GIs everywhere. Most had discarded their shirts and sweat ran off their slick bodies in rivulets as they worked to move the gear into the jungle for better concealment. The sun wasn't quite up yet, but the clear skies promised to bring punishing heat.

Winkleman punched Tarkington's shoulder and pointed, "There's Lonny."

Tarkington nodded, seeing the lanky engineer helping to put together the final touches of an anti-aircraft gun. He noticed two others had already been completed and were spread to either side of the offloading operation, their long barrels pointed skyward. "I knew he'd be helpful."

A whistle being blown through a bullhorn made Tarkington flinch. He saw an officer down by the water taking the bullhorn from another GI. He yelled, "Incoming air raid! Man the guns and take cover!" For an instant, everyone stopped and glanced up. Exasperated, he yelled even louder, "Move!" Men dropped what they were holding and ran up the beach toward the jungle.

Tarkington yelled, "Get to the trenches." Out of habit, they'd found the dug-out trenches before going to sleep. Every man knew exactly where to go and took off double quick.

Soon they were shoulder to shoulder with other GIs. The stench from their sweaty bodies was overpowering in the tight confines. Tarkington had his back against the dirt wall and his knees touched the wall in front. They were packed in like sardines. Raker complained, "A direct hit'll take out half the battalion."

Vick added, "At least we won't have to pay for a burial."

An unfamiliar voice a few men down said, "Can it down there."

Tarkington leaned forward as much as he could and saw the officer with the bullhorn sitting a few yards away. Minutes passed and nothing happened. There were no engine noises, no screaming dive bombers, and no whistling bombs. The only men not under cover were the three-man crews manning the two operational AA guns and one or two men manning mounted .50 cals. He didn't envy them once the bombs started dropping.

More minutes passed and Tarkington leaned forward and addressed the officer, whose faded railroad track bars on his helmet told him he was a captain, "Sir, how far out's the raid?"

The officer leaned forward, and in the gloom of the slit trench answered, "Spotters saw 'em launching out of Buna. If we're the target, they'll be here in a few more minutes. Now stow it, Sergeant." The officer stared at him, obviously not recognizing him. "What's your name, Sergeant? I thought I knew all my staff sergeants."

Tarkington answered, "Staff Sergeant Clay Tarkington, sir. We're not in the 128th."

The officer looked annoyed. "Make room, men. Let him through. I'm sick of yelling." Tarkington looked at Winkleman and mouthed, "Fuck," then made his way over men until he hunched beside the captain. "Sit down, Sergeant, and tell me who the hell you are and how you got here."

While they sat sweating in the slit trench, Tarkington briefly outlined their training and their mission to Gobe. He told them they were supposed to get follow-on orders, but now that there weren't any, he was taking the initiative and advancing with the battalion.

The captain looked dubious. He inspected the Indian head on Tarkington's sleeve and shrugged. "Gotta admit, I've never heard of your unit, but I suppose there's going to be a lot of this kind of stuff as we try to adapt to the Japanese." He had a large wad of chewing tobacco in his cheek and he spat onto the wall in front of him. "So you're army commandos specializing in demolitions. Right?"

Tarkington shrugged, "Yes, sir. I guess that's correct."

"I'm assuming you still have demolitions 'cause you didn't get to blow anything up in Gobe. Correct?"

Tarkington nodded, "Yes, sir. We've got enough to blow up half the Nip army."

Just then the 40mm AA guns opened fire. The five round bursts came in quick succession. The officer, whose nameplate read Griffin, chanced a glance over the lip of the trench, straining his neck upward. Tarkington did the same and saw the black puffs of exploding flak from the guns, fouling the morning sky. The officer pointed, "There. See 'em? 11 o'clock high."

Tarkington nodded. There were three growing dots coming at them fast, weaving in and out of the flak bursts. "I see 'em," he growled.

The anti-aircraft guns continued barking but soon the whine of diving planes overpowered their thunder. Tarkington dropped to the bottom of the hole and wished he had a steel pot on his head rather than his floppy jungle hat. Neither was adequate protection from a bomb strike, but the steel pot would've made him feel less exposed. The .50 cals opened up, adding to the insanity outside. Tarkington covered his ears and opened his mouth trying to keep his sinuses intact. Any second now.

Even though he was expecting it, the concussive blast of the first bomb going off nearly made him lose his bowels. The ground shook and the dirt sides of the hole cascaded down upon him, filling the back of his shirt with loamy soil. The screeching hell outside continued and soon another explosion shook them to the bone. Someone was screaming somewhere and Tarkington wondered if they had hit part of the long slit trench. The last bomb exploded farther away. The effects were nowhere near as devastating as the first two.

It was over as quickly as it began. Sand, tree limbs, dirt clods, and seawater rained down upon them for a full minute after the attack. They remained in the hole until it finally stopped.

Captain Griffin looked out from beneath his dirt-covered helmet and had to yell to be heard over Tarkington's ringing ears. He pointed the way the Japanese planes had fled, "That's your target! Those fucking floatplanes are stationed in Buna."

14

The air raid had done damage but it wasn't as bad as it could've been. The two that hit the beach had buried themselves deep before exploding, evidenced by the deep craters. Despite the incredible noise and the ground shaking, most of their explosive power had been muffled. A few crates had been incinerated, but besides minor cuts and bruises, the men on the beach were relatively unscathed. The third bomb had exploded out to sea and whether it was on purpose or not, the results were catastrophic. A barge being used to shuttle supplies from the larger luggers took a direct hit, killing all ten of the men onboard. Bits and pieces of them washed up on shore for a week after the attack.

Captain Griffin told them to standby for orders. He was going to pass his idea up to Colonel Huntington, 2d Battalion's commander. He promised he'd get back to them before the end of the day.

In the meantime, Tarkington and the squad helped clean up the beach. Stacked crates had been thrown around, some wrenched open, spewing their contents everywhere. They went to work salvaging everything they could. One crate had spilled bully beef containers and some had opened, rotting and putrefying in the tropical heat. The overpowering smell of rotting fish wafted over the area, making men gag. The smell reaffirmed their commitment to steer clear of the Australian beef.

Vick saw Lonny staggering around and punched Tarkington's shoulder, pointing. Lonny had crusted blood trailing down his cheek from his left eardrum.

They approached him and Tarkington asked, "You all right? Are you hit?"

Lonny shook his head, looking despondent. "It didn't help."

"What didn't help?"

Lonny pointed at the AA guns he'd helped put together, "The guns. They didn't hit any of them. Might as well have been throwing wads of paper at 'em."

Tarkington shook his head, "Bullshit!" Lonny looked confused and Tarkington explained, "They only took one pass at us. Without the AA, they would've strafed us at least one or two more times. They'll head back to base and tell their buddies about the defenses. Your guns saved lives today."

Lonny pursed his lips and nodded. "Thanks, Sergeant."

He swayed and Tarkington steadied him, noticing his dilated irises for the first time. "You might have a concussion. Need to get yourself checked out at the aid station." Lonny was about to protest, but Tarkington barked, "Make sure he does it, Bull."

Sergeant Bulkort hooked his arm into Lonny's armpit, "You got it, Sergeant. Come on, Lonny. Maybe there's a nice-looking nurse there for you to ogle."

Lonny closed his eyes and shook his head. He looked at Bulkort as though seeing him for the first time, "Wh—what happened?"

Bulkort shook his head, "You hit your head during the air raid. Just relax and come with me."

Before Lonny was out of hearing, he asked Bulkort three more times what happened. Winkleman snorted, "He won't remember your words, Tark. He's concussed."

"Oh well. Maybe he'll lose his urge to get himself killed so quickly."

Captain Griffin didn't get back to them that day. The area was still bustling as 3d Battalion troops from Gobe arrived. The beachhead expanded even more. A couple of Jeeps were put back together and they helped expedite the process of hauling supplies into the jungle and out of sight from roving Japanese air patrols.

Another air raid occurred the following day, but was successfully turned back by the four operational AA guns. This time, only two planes descended upon them, and before it was over, one was a smoldering mess against the side of a mountain. They'd both dropped bombs, but their aim was off and the bombs exploded harmlessly out to sea.

"Think Captain Griffin's forgotten about us?" wondered Winkleman. "Maybe he thinks the Jap air raids ain't as much of an issue now."

Tarkington shrugged, "I dunno. Maybe he hasn't gotten a chance to bring it up yet. This place is busy as a hornet's nest."

Winkleman pointed, "Speak of the devil."

Lieutenant Trable, one of Captain Griffin's officers, approached. They both stiffened but didn't salute, not wanting to attract snipers. Trable was a big man. His gut pressed against the buttons of his sweaty shirt. Tarkington figured he must have lost weight since being in theater, since there was never quite enough food. Sweat poured off him in buckets.

He got right to the point, "Captain Griffin wants you and your squad at his tent as soon as possible."

Tarkington nodded, "Yes, sir. We'll be there in ten." The big man nodded and turned, shuffling through the mud and sand. When he was out of earshot, Tarkington turned to Winkleman, "You heard the man, Wink. We might finally have a mission."

Fifteen minutes later, they sat in the stifling tent set up in the jungle 100 yards from the hustle and bustle of the beachhead. Captain Griffin entered from the side. He was reading something an aid had just handed him. The aid hustled behind him, trying to keep up with his long strides. The squad made to get to their feet, but without looking, Griffin waved them off, "Remain seated, men. This won't take long." He signed the paper and handed it to the aid, who hustled out the way he'd come.

Griffin sat on the edge of a table at the front and looked the men over. Tarkington thought he looked tired; the dark circles under his eyes were obvious even from the back row. "I told Colonel Huntington about you and your special talents. He's old school and thinks units like yours are a waste of good men." The squad glanced nervously at one another. Griffin continued, "But he also wants that damned floatplane base dealt with before we kick off this shindig, so he's willing to give you a chance." Relieved grins before he continued, "You're not on his books, so he'd be spending someone else's dime." A long silence, "Those were his words, not mine. If you're as good as you say you are and accomplish the mission and return safely—well—you'll impress him. If you don't, it's a failed experiment and you'll prove his point, but it'll be no skin off his nose."

Tarkington lifted his hand and Griffin pointed at him, "Sir, we don't much care what anyone thinks of us. We just wanna do what we're trained to do and taking out a Jap floatplane base is right up our alley." There were nods all around.

Griffin nodded and stood, crossing his arms over his chest. "That's what I figured, but you need to know you won't have any backup. If you stir up a hornet's nest, don't expect any kind of rescue. The colonel will let you use one of the barges to get you close and that's it."

Tarkington grinned, "That's what we're used to, Captain."

"Good. You leave tonight." He checked his watch. "At 1930 hours, in fact."

Tarkington checked his own watch then asked, "If it's alright with you, sir, I'd like to tow one of the canoes behind us. We can swim in," he glanced at Henry then back to Griffin, "but these waters are full of all kinds of nasty things."

Griffin nodded, "I suppose those assets aren't really ours, so if you can convince the natives, go ahead. By the way, the barge won't linger past dawn. If you're not successful, they'll be sitting ducks in daylight. Hell, even if you are successful, the Jap Navy might spot you. They'll be taking a risk being out of range of our defenses here."

Tarkington smiled, "Even more reason to take along a canoe. We can always paddle home, sir."

Griffin nodded and clapped his hands, "Well—if that's all—I've got a million things to do before I sleep tonight and so do you, I suspect."

"Yes, sir. And thank you, sir. We'll get it done."

Griffin looked at each man, "Good luck, men. If you're successful, the colonel will have more missions for you." They saluted and he returned it before leaving the way he'd come in. His aid was waiting and flung another file into his hands.

The barge ride northwest was uneventful. The sailors were obviously nervous moving away from the perceived safety of the other vessels. Ensign Brunkauer was in command. He had drawn the short straw. He was a man of few words, but a master of navigation. Using the stars and the limited charts of the area, they churned their way at eight knots until he surmised they were a mile off the coast from Buna. The journey had only taken two hours. Low clouds blocked any light and the night was inky black.

Brunkauer whispered, "This is it. Remember, we lift anchor at 0500. If we don't see your signal before that, you'll have to paddle home."

Tarkington thanked him and moved to the canoe, which they'd pulled up alongside. He entered the middle and took up a paddle. Winkleman was in back as the rudder man. Everyone else would paddle. They pushed off and were soon out of sight from the sailors.

They steered directly toward shore. If Ensign Brunkauer was correct in his navigation, the floatplane base and the enemy stronghold of Buna should be directly in front of them. There was no light—not a surprise, as the battle for air supremacy in the area was still being contested by the Allies.

The only information they had about the base was from an overflight of the area by P-40s out of Milne Bay a few days before. There were no photographs, just a couple of Australian pilots who claimed they'd seen the planes tied up near Buna. Sketchy information at best, but no one was playing with all the cards just yet and those pontoon planes had to be coming from somewhere.

Tarkington wondered if perhaps one of them was responsible for wounding his friend Lt. Spaulding, the pilot from Milne Bay. If they found the planes, taking them out would be sweet revenge.

The darkness in front of them grew in depth, showing an outline of land. Buna was a Japanese strongpoint. Troops from Rabaul landed there months before kicking the Allies out and pushed overland to take Port Moresby. As far as Tarkington knew, the battle up the Kokoda Trail still raged, but the Japanese were being relentlessly pushed back and would eventually be forced into Buna for a final defense. In the meantime, command estimated a small force of sick and wounded Japanese soldiers held Buna Mission.

They had no intention of getting too close to the coastline. If they were heard or seen and spotlighted, there'd be no escape. He signaled for Winkleman to steer so they paralleled the shore. There were no signs of enemy or even human habitation. Perhaps Brunkauer's navigation wasn't as good as he thought it was. They slowed their cadence and watched the black shoreline. The boat hissed through the water, its delicate lines cutting through like a knife through velvet.

From shore, there was a sudden glow, which quickly extinguished. Tarkington keyed on it, knowing it was the flash of a match or lighter igniting a cigarette. Everyone saw it and stopped paddling. Winkleman kept the canoe steering straight as it slowed and finally stopped. The only sound was the gentle lapping of the sea against the sides of the canoe.

From the shore, the indistinct murmur of voices. Laughter and another flash of a cigarette being lit. The Japanese obviously felt safe. Planes had bombed and strafed them, but the waters near Buna were uncharted and full of shallow reefs, so they had nothing to fear from the Allied Navies. They weren't concerned with an Allied presence tonight.

"Buna," Tarkington whispered. "Let's find the planes."

Winkleman angled the canoe inland slightly and the men slowly paddled, watching and listening for more enemy troops. Tarkington stowed his paddle and held binoculars to his eyes, but they were nearly useless in the darkness. He was hoping to see the outline of a plane bobbing in the sea or pulled up onto the beach, but he only saw darkness.

"We've gotta get closer," he uttered. Winkleman steepened the angle toward shore. Henry and Raker—sitting at the front—stopped paddling and used the high gunwales to prop their carbines. Firing would be a last resort.

Tarkington held up a fist and the paddling stopped. Winkleman kept steering, and the canoe glided and finally stopped. In the gloom, a structure was sticking out from shore. An orange glow came from what Tarkington surmised was a shack at the end of a dock. A soldier was smoking—the cherry glow, the tip of a cigarette. There was something docked there, but it wasn't an airplane. Once again, the soft sounds of murmured conversation wafted over them.

Tarkington signaled and the paddlers stroked, creeping the canoe past the jutting dock only thirty yards away. They continued paralleling the shore. They were close enough to see other structures dotting the area. It was nearly midnight and Buna was mostly quiet, but he saw the occasional indistinct outline of a soldier on duty.

The shoreline slowly passed by and soon they left the village behind. They'd seen no aircraft. Had they left the area? It would be a simple thing to move the operation elsewhere; after all, they didn't need airfields.

Tarkington ordered them to stop paddling. He wondered if they should beach the canoe and take their mission onto land. Perhaps they'd missed the planes in the darkness. He discounted the idea as being too dangerous.

He whispered, "If we continue, we'll hit Gona. The intelligence was clear that the planes were south of Gona." He didn't expect anyone to chime in; he was speaking his mind. "Let's head back south and see if we missed something."

They turned 180 degrees and paddled slowly back the way they'd come. Once past Buna, they kept paddling, and Tarkington figured they were seeing fresh territory. The shoreline, relatively straight up to this point, suddenly expanded away. A dark inlet cut inland. It was either a river mouth or bay. Tarkington pointed and Winkleman steered the canoe into the cut. If nothing else, it would provide cover while they decided what to do.

There was a slight current fighting them as they entered the inlet, so Tarkington surmised it was a river mouth. It widened, forcing Winkleman to adjust the canoe's angle to remain in sight of the shoreline. The current was negligible near shore.

Henry held up a fist, then opened his palm for a full stop. The paddlers back-paddled, halting the canoe. Henry looked back at Tarkington and pointed. Tarkington strained to see. He used his peripheral vision and finally saw what Henry wanted him to see: the outline of a plane. It looked like a blob, much like the low buildings surrounding the docking area, but the long wings were unmistakable. They'd found at least one of the floatplanes.

Relief flooded Tarkington as he realized this mission would not be a waste of time and resources like Gobe. They paddled closer to the plane, and as they neared it, saw there was another one moored thirty yards from it. They scanned the thin line of white beach sand and jungle beyond, searching for guards. There was nothing obvious, although they could see what looked like stacked barrels nearby. They surmised it must be fuel.

They silently paddled to the next plane, and once they were close, saw another farther into the bay. They found four planes. As they neared the last plane, they saw a soft glow near the front. As they got closer, they could see Japanese mechanics standing on ladders beneath ponchos working on the engine. They heard sounds of tools hitting metal and the grunts and groans of men working. The ponchos did a good job of keeping the light from being seen by a passing aircraft, but did little to hide it from the squad.

They paddled the canoe until they were far enough away to talk freely. "Stolly, Bull. You saw what we're dealing with. How do you wanna place the explosives?" Tarkington asked.

Stolly could barely contain his excitement, "The middle two will be easy; they're unguarded. The first one's close to those fuel cans. We light that off and it'll burn the plane. The fourth one with the mechanics, we may have to leave. I don't think we can get close enough without being seen, which would mess up everything else."

Tarkington nodded his agreement. "We'll place explosives on the middle two first, then move to the first one. I expect there's at least one sentry around the fuel that we'll need to take out."

Vick raised his hand, "I'll do it, Tark."

"You and Henry. Take det cord and caps for the fuel. Raker, you'll go with Bull and Stolly to the middle two and deal with any sentries you find."

Raker nodded in the darkness. "We'll wait an hour before we go after the fuel. That enough time, Stolly?"

Stollman nodded, "Yes, that'll work."

"Wink and I will stay with the canoe and pick your asses up. Everyone have signal lights?" There were murmured affirmatives. "Flash us twice, we'll come to you. If it takes longer than five minutes, repeat the sequence but be swimming out toward the middle. You don't wanna be close when this shit blows." He could barely make out Bulkort's camouflaged face, "You've got the timers, right?"

Bulkort nodded, "Right. I've cut them to burn through just over an hour."

Winkleman asked, "What about the fourth plane? We could take out the mechanics and grenade it once the fireworks start."

Tarkington shook his head, "I wanna be outta this river mouth by then. The Japs in Buna will come running and they'll light this place up with spotlights. We've gotta be well away by then." There were nods all around. "Taking out seventy-five percent of the force'll be a good night's work."

While they were going over the plan, the men had their packs off and were putting explosives, fuses, and blasting caps into waterproof bags and sealing them tight. Their carbines went to the bottom of the canoe. They'd rely on their pistols if it came down to a firefight.

15

Once everyone was ready, they paddled the canoe back towards the middle two planes. They stopped thirty yards out, and Stollman, Bulkort, and Raker went over the side without a sound. Tarkington checked his watch.

Stollman and Bulkort pushed the waterproof bags in front of them as they sidestroked. Raker led the way, unencumbered. He looked back over his shoulder, seeing the canoe moving away. It disappeared into the gloom like a ghost ship. He angled toward the nearest plane, the one on his right. The plane wasn't his concern. His job was to check for sentries and kill them if they were too close.

When they were yards from the floating behemoth, he turned and caught Stollman's eye. Stollman nodded and treaded water alongside Bulkort while Raker silently swam to shallower water. When he could touch the ground, he stopped with only his head from the nose up exposed. The warm water lapped against his back in comforting undulations. He listened and scanned. The front of the plane was nudged up to the beach. The strip of sand extended ten yards to the jungle. There was a chair in the sand facing the aircraft. If it were for a guard, he wasn't in the immediate area.

He waited three minutes, then took a careful step forward. As the water shallowed, he crouched, limiting his exposure. He unclasped the holster but didn't draw his sidearm. He did, however, draw his K bar.

When the water was two feet deep, he laid down and floated. He pulled himself toward the plane using his one free hand. He passed beneath the massive engine cowling and propeller, then checked the beach to the right. There was no one there. He sheathed the knife and swam out to where Stollman and Bulkort were still treading water. Bulkort was doing all he could not to breathe too loudly, but the exertion was clearly affecting him.

Raker signaled it was all clear. Stollman wisely pushed Bulkort, and he swam toward the nearest metal pontoon. Raker and Stollman waited until he was safely attached before they swam toward the next plane thirty yards to their left.

Raker whispered in Stollman's ear, "He gonna be all right?" Stollman nodded and they continued swimming.

Raker repeated the process at the second plane and again found nothing. Stollman happily got to work. He pulled himself onto the pontoon as quietly as possible and opened his waterproof bag, like he was Santa Claus delivering presents from his magical bag of explosive toys.

Raker stayed in the shallows, floating and watching for sentries. The empty chair gnawed at him. Was it simply left there for the pilot to lounge upon, or was it for a guard who'd gone into the jungle to relieve himself? If he returned, he'd see Bulkort and this whole thing would blow up in their faces. He moved himself back that way. Stollman could take care of himself; Bulkort was still an unproven entity.

As he approached, he caught a movement from the plane. Bulkort was standing on the pontoon unscrewing an inspection port beneath the wing. The slight sound of metal on metal made Raker cringe. It sounded loud to him, but he realized it would be nothing to someone not listening for such things.

When he was yards away, he stopped and looked at the outline of the chair against the white sand. The light from the fourth plane was just a glimmer from here. He heard laughter and talking from that direction. Perhaps the guard was down there jawing with the mechanics.

The bang of metal on metal nearly made Raker jump from the water. He turned toward Bulkort. He was crouched and still as a stone. It was obvious what had happened; he'd dropped the screwdriver onto the metal pontoon. The sound reverberated up and down the beach. Raker froze and held his breath. Perhaps anyone close would assume it came from the mechanics down the beach. His hopes were dashed when a soldier emerged from the jungle. He held his rifle in one hand while his other held up his pants. Raker surmised the noise had interrupted a call of nature.

The soldier shuffled to the chair and called out, "Dare ga imasu?"

Bulkort was motionless on the pontoon. He looked like a black lump. Raker had little doubt the Japanese could see the lump and would investigate in a moment, but first he needed to deal with his sagging pants.

Raker pulled his feet beneath him, drawing the knife simultaneously. The Japanese soldier placed his rifle against the chair. It was what Raker was waiting for. He sprang from the sea only yards from the soldier and collided with him, burying his K-bar knife into his gut and slicing upward viciously.

The soldier called out an instant before Raker put his hand over his mouth. The soldier bit down and Raker grimaced, feeling his flesh tearing but refusing to let go. He plunged the knife into his soft belly over and over until he finally stopped struggling. Raker yanked his hand but it was stuck on the soldier's teeth. He lifted and twisted, and the teeth finally released from the meaty part of his hand.

The pain washed over him and he felt lightheaded. His own blood mixed with the dead soldier's and the scent of bowel and blood washed over him. He squirmed off him, dragging entrails along with him. He focused on the fourth plane. Had the mechanics heard the sentry call out?

Long seconds passed and he thought he'd gotten away with it, but then one of them called out. Raker couldn't make it out over the sound of blood rushing in his ears, but the tone was that of someone asking if another was all right.

He needed to do something fast or they'd come investigate. He wracked his memory for the phrase he was looking for, but his brain froze, caught in a loop of sensory overload. Another inquiry from the mechanics broke the spell. Raker got to his feet, the pain in his hand making him sway. He fought the urge to vomit and waved, finally remembering the phrase.

"Watashi wa koronda!" he answered, hoping he hadn't butchered it too badly.

A few agonizing seconds passed before he heard laughter from the mechanics. They were dim shapes against the light under the poncho and he doubted they could see him at all, but he waved again and sat down as though continuing guard duty. He saw Bulkort move on the pontoon. He wanted to throttle him, but kept his composure, willing the clumsy son of a bitch to hurry his ass up.

He stiffened when he heard another yell, this time from the opposite direction. *Now what?* he thought.

After dropping off Raker, Stollman, and Bulkort, they paddled silently until they were close to the first floatplane. Henry and Vick slipped over the side, Henry pushing the waterproof bag in front of him.

Henry glanced back at Tarkington, who was staring at him. Henry gave him a slight grin and began stroking quietly toward the dark shore. It galled him that Tarkington worried about him. He tried to push thoughts of sharks from his mind. He'd had a close call a few months ago and the incident had left him fearful of them. He wondered if they hunted in bays like this one or preferred the open ocean.

Fear. It was an unnatural feeling for him. He'd never been afraid of anything. Dangerous animals were a part of his everyday life growing up in the Bayou Region of Louisiana. He'd come across huge alligators and killed them in their own habitat. He hadn't done it out of spite, but simply to put food on the family dining table. He'd also spent a considerable amount of time offshore in the waters of the Gulf of Mexico and had a healthy respect for sea creatures, but never *feared* them. He pushed the feeling away. There was a more dangerous creature nearby—man. But he wasn't the point man this time. Vick, who had a natural affinity for knife work, would do the killing, unless there were more than one.

He followed Vick, keeping his head in sight through the gloom. The towering shape of the floatplane came into view. Henry had seen them diving from the sky during the air raid the other day, but they were much bigger than he thought they'd be up close.

Vick stopped at the back of the plane and reached out for the pontoon. They both listened and looked for anything that would tell them they weren't alone. Five minutes passed—nothing. Neither of them were as passionate about blowing things up as Stollman and Bulkort were, but they'd been through the training and could do the work. Rather than the plane, though, their target was the stack of fuel barrels on the beach.

They split up, each moving inland along the opposite pontoons. As he neared the front of the plane, Henry noticed it wasn't nudged up on the beach, but anchored. There was a short ten yards of water between shore and the pontoons. The white beach sand started a few yards to the right. The land directly in front was a rocky ledge.

Henry didn't hear or see anyone. He held onto the front of the pontoon, still unable to touch the ground. Vick pushed off after a minute and slid toward the rocky bank. Henry waited until he reached it, and when Vick dragged himself out of the water and lay dripping, he moved forward to join him. Vick was still as the night. The only sounds were insects and jungle animals calling in the distance. The other planes were out of sight. Even the glow from the mechanics wasn't visible from here, too many turns in the shoreline. The barrels of fuel were ten yards away. The fumes were the only thing he could smell, drowning out even the incessant rot of the jungle. Henry could see a hand pump sticking out the top of the nearest one, a long hose coiled at the base.

They listened for another five minutes. Vick slithered forward on his belly, dragging his wet body across the rock without a sound. Henry watched his progress. He'd wait until Vick signaled the all clear before leaving the water.

Vick disappeared around the barrels. Long minutes passed. Henry concentrated on his breathing, not allowing his imagination to get the best of him. Vick could take care of himself. He was the best knife-man in the unit. Henry had more experience wielding sharp weapons but Vick's close-in fighting instincts were second to none, as he showed repeatedly during hand-to-hand combat training.

Vick finally emerged, motioning him forward. Henry pulled himself from the water, careful not to splash. He allowed a minute for most of the water to drip off him, then slid in beside Vick, who whispered in his ear, "Enemy up the trail thirty yards."

Henry nodded his understanding. There must have been more than one or Vick would've taken care of it. It went without saying that Vick felt confident they could pull it off without alerting them.

Moving in slow motion, Henry opened the waterproof bag and gingerly pulled out detonation cord, three small magnetized blocks of explosives, and the accompanying pen-shaped timers. Vick moved off to watch in case the Japanese approached. Henry slid the pen timers into the plastic explosive blocks and crushed the tiny vial of acid, which would slowly eat away at the blocker material inside the pen. It would take seventy minutes to eat through the blocker. Once it did, the acid would ignite the small charge and the block of explosive would explode. He checked the watch he had stowed in the bag. The fireworks would go off at 0315. He wrapped detonation cord around the nearest barrel, cut it as quietly as he could, then attached the magnetized bomb over the cord, securing both ends. The plastic explosive alone might not ignite the fuel, but the detonation cord exploding an instant later would. It only took a couple of minutes to set the other two charges around two more barrels.

Once done, he tapped Vick's boot. Vick didn't react and Henry froze. He'd been so focused on setting the charges he hadn't picked up on the approaching danger. From the darkness, he heard the sounds of boots squishing through mud. Henry pulled himself behind a barrel and unsheathed his knife.

Vick was exposed but the darkness would hide him, unless they had flashlights or inspected the fuel barrels or floatplane. Henry couldn't see them from his position, but he heard them just fine.

The sounds of boots in mud changed to boots on rock. They'd left the jungle and were only feet away. A loud voice called out, and for a moment, Henry thought they'd seen the det-cord, but he relaxed, realizing the soldier was calling out someone's name. He hoped Vick didn't react.

They'd only been exposed to the Japanese language for six weeks, hardly enough time to scratch the surface, but they'd learned useful phrases and buzzwords, which would tell them if the soldiers were alarmed. Their tone wasn't one of alarm. A different voice said something in a lower tone and there was soft laughter. Vick decided there were four of them. Too many to take quietly.

They stopped and had a low conversation. A tense minute passed before they finally moved off. Henry was about to move when he heard a long deep sigh, followed by the clattering of what he supposed was a rifle butt touching rock. They'd left a guard here. They must've been relieving other guards. He wondered briefly how the others were faring.

The soldier was standing; Henry could hear him shifting from foot to foot. He heard him slap his skin, probably crushing a mosquito. Vick's prone body must be only feet away from him. Any movement from him would draw the soldier's attention immediately. Henry knew what he had to do; they'd covered this scenario countless times. He knew Vick was waiting for him to make his move, coiled like a spring. Henry would be the distraction.

He counted to thirty, forcing himself to keep it slow and even, then he simply stood up. The motion caught the soldier off guard and he startled but didn't call out. Henry could only see his dim outline in the darkness. He didn't react quickly, just stared, trying to puzzle out what he was seeing.

Vick launched from the ground driving the razor-sharp knife into the soft skin beneath his chin and into his brain. His momentum plowed the soldier backward and he rode him to the ground. The body twitched and spasmed beneath him as blood cascaded over his hand. He pulled the blade and wiped it across the soldier's tunic while watching for his comrades.

Henry strode to the body and grasped the man's boots, lifting his legs. Vick jumped up, sheathed the knife, and grasped the body beneath the armpits. They stowed him in the jungle a few yards back, hopefully hidden enough to give them a little time to escape.

They moved back toward the water. Henry grasped the fuel hose coiled beneath the barrel he rigged and pulled it toward the water. He punctured it with a quick slash of his knife and the smell of gas became even stronger as the fuel in the line ran over the rocks and dripped into the water. Before sealing the bag, he pulled out the flashlight and flashed twice while shielding the sides. Then they slipped into the bay and started swimming.

Sitting in the canoe out of sight of the shore and his men was maddening for Tarkington and Winkleman. The soft glow from the fourth plane being worked on by the enemy mechanics was the only light. The water was absolutely still, the undulations from the sea knocked down by the surrounding reefs and outgoing river water.

After dropping Henry and Vick off, they'd paddled back toward Raker's group. They'd been dropped first and would hopefully finish first. The waiting was agony. Winkleman kept checking his watch, the dull luminescence never seeming to move.

"Stop that, Wink," Tarkington hissed.

"They've been gone thirty minutes. What's taking so long?" Tarkington didn't respond, knowing he didn't expect an answer. He was wondering the same thing, but there was nothing to do but wait. There'd been no shots fired, so the worst hadn't happened, but something was holding them up.

Relief flooded through him when he saw two quick flashes. "There," he hissed.

Winkleman pointed toward the first floatplane, "I just saw the other one too."

Tarkington hadn't seen it, but he had the one he'd seen mentally marked. "Group one first. The others will signal again in five minutes."

Winkleman nodded and they took up their paddles and maneuvered the canoe toward shore. They kept their paddle strokes slow, even though they wanted nothing more than to go full tilt and get the hell out of there. From the darkness, the outlines of the planes loomed large. The light flashed twice only yards away but off to the left. Winkleman steered and soon Bulkort's camouflaged face was beside them. He hefted the waterproof bag up and Winkleman stowed it, then helped the big man in while Tarkington counterbalanced the canoe. Stollman and Raker followed, and soon they were moving back toward the first group. No one spoke. If there were imminent danger, they'd tell them; otherwise, silence was best.

The double flash again took them to Henry and Vick. They rendezvoused, and they slid in easily. The bottom of the canoe sloshed with water from their sodden, dripping clothes.

Each man took up paddles and soon they'd slipped out of the inlet and were in the open ocean. Tarkington deemed they were far enough away and said, "Report."

Stollman said, "Charges set." He checked the watch he'd pulled from the bag, "It'll go off in another ten minutes."

Bulkort's voice wasn't quite as enthusiastic, "I got mine set, same time frame."

Raker glared at him, "You nearly got us all killed with your clumsiness." Tarkington raised an eyebrow which went unnoticed in the darkness. Raker continued, "Dropped a screwdriver, alerted the sentry. I had to take him out. It wasn't clean."

Bulkort said something, but Tarkington shushed him and pointed at Henry. Henry nodded, "Charges set. They'll go off in twenty minutes. We had to take out a guard too. Vick did it."

Vick nodded grimly, "Thanks to you, it went well. We saw other soldiers heading toward your position though, Raker. Did you see 'em?"

"Yeah, we saw 'em coming and got the hell outta there in the knick of time. They'll find the dead sentry though. There was no time to hide him well. Hope they don't find the explosives." He glared at Bulkort again, then turned away in disgust.

After dropping Private Koji at the refueling area, Sergeant Kondo escorted Private Hoga along the narrow spit of beach. The private was due to relieve Private Ki and start his four-hour guard rotation. Normally, he would've left the privates to their own devices, but his lieutenant wanted an update from the mechanics working on the damaged Aichi floatplane.

He called out to the dim figure he could barely see, silhouetted against the light leaking from the mechanic's tarp. There was no reply from the seated guard and he wondered if he were asleep. If so, there'd be hell to pay. These planes were too important. He tripped and caught himself cursing the rock. When he looked up, the figure on the chair was gone. Odd, he'd been there a second ago. He must have heard his voice and stepped closer to the jungle.

They got to the solitary chair and looked around, but he wasn't there. Private Hoga spun in a full circle and shrugged. Sergeant Kondo raised his voice, "Private Ki. Your relief is here. Where are you?" Kondo knew many of his soldiers suffered from dysentery and often needed to dash into the jungle to relieve themselves, but surely he wouldn't have gone out of earshot. And he'd seen him only moments before. "Private Ki," he yelled again, this time with an edge of anger. One of the mechanics yelled something he couldn't decipher, but he ignored it. Surely, Ki couldn't have made it there so quickly. Concern creeped in and he pulled his rifle from his shoulder. Something wasn't right. "Search the area," he hissed.

Private Hoga unslung his rifle and looked around, suddenly nervous. He moved off into the nearby jungle after Kondo prompted him. Kondo looked at the plane. Nothing was out of place. He kneeled beside the chair. There was something there, but he couldn't quite make it out. He fumbled in his pants pocket for the red-lensed flashlight. He turned it on and it shone upon something long and glistening wet. He leaned closer and the smell of bowel hit his nose and he reeled back.

Private Hoga called out, his voice full of panic, "S—Sergeant! Come quick!"

Kondo sprinted to the voice and nearly tripped on Private Ki's body. He shone the light and the red lens made Ki look even bloodier than he already was. Private Hoga vomited what little rice he had in his belly. Kondo clutched his rifle and ran back to the beach. "The planes! Check the planes! Come on, you fool!"

He didn't wait for Hoga, but waded out to the pontoon and stepped onto it. It was grounded and solid. He shone his light along the fuselage, then the engine cowling. He yelled, "Go warn the others, Private Hoga. Now! Saboteurs!" Private Hoga sprinted back the way they'd come.

Kondo checked the right wing, stepping into the sea, moving quickly. He went to the back, the water coming up to his chest. Nothing looked out of place. He pulled himself back onto the pontoon, searching every inch until he got to the left wing. It looked different from the other: there was something hanging down. He shone his light. It was an open inspection hatch. He didn't know much about airplanes, but he knew it shouldn't be open.

The hatch was too high to reach, so he scrambled up the thick metal stanchion leading from the wing to the pontoon. His hands ached, but he pulled himself along until he was close enough to reach it. He put the flashlight in his mouth, and holding on with one hand, reached in with the other. There was something there, something boxy. He wondered if he were about to yank out some valuable piece of the airplane. He hesitated. He heard a sizzle and a pop. There was a bright flash—then nothing.

16

Ensign Brunkauer saw the terrific explosion as the refueling node went up and motored the barge in that direction. It wasn't long until they saw the signal light from the canoe and picked up the GIs. They pulled the canoe aboard quickly and found seats.

Not wanting to be caught on the open sea by a stirred-up Japanese Navy, Brunkauer maneuvered the barge back to Pongani by staying close to the dark, uncharted shore. He risked grounding, but at full speed the barge only drew a few feet of water and could pass over most shallow reefs.

The barge ride passed quickly, and they made it back to Pongani as the sun was coming up. As the GIs stepped off the barge, they were tired but exuberant. It was the first mission where they'd put their special talents to use, and it had been a smashing success. At least they assumed it was—based upon the explosions and robust secondary explosions.

They would have liked to have stuck around for a full damage assessment, but the area would be crawling with Japanese soldiers. The proof would be the cessation of air raids originating from Buna. They were still well within range of the sprawling airfields of Rabaul, but hopefully they ended the threat from the floatplane base.

Captain Griffin was waiting to debrief them. It felt odd since he wasn't officially in their chain of command and didn't really know their capabilities, but his own exuberance was evident. It didn't rub off on Colonel Huntington, however. He sat in on the debrief, his scowl growing deeper listening to the way the GIs callously talked about dispatching the Japanese sentries.

When the debrief was over, Huntington stood and faced the men. He scowled at their still-camouflaged faces. "There'll be no more raids in the foreseeable future." Tarkington squinted up at him and the men exchanged worried glances. "The Australians have taken the village of Kokoda. The Japanese are reeling and retreating towards the coast. We will push on Buna soon to keep them from linking up with their forces there. We'll need every man that can carry a rifle on the line." He sneered, "And none of you men are too good for that." He turned to the stunned Captain Griffin. "Fold them into whoever's short, Captain. And get 'em cleaned up for criminy sakes." He turned to leave and the squad got to their feet reluctantly. Huntington left the stifling tent, leaving a heavy pall of silence in his wake.

Captain Griffin shook his head, and when he thought Huntington was out of earshot, said, "Well, damn. I'll put you in Baker Company. We've suffered the most illness casualties and we're a good outfit. We'd be honored to have you men among us."

Tarkington nodded, "Yes, sir. If it's alright with you, I'd like to get the men squared away. It's been a long night."

Griffin nodded vigorously, "Of course. Of course." He paused, watching them stand to leave. He added, "If he won't say it, I will." Everyone stopped and looked. "Outstanding job." The men nodded their thanks and shuffled out of the tent into the blazing heat.

They collected their gear where they'd stowed it before pushing off for the mission and found their way to Baker Company's barracks, pushing through the front door. The long tent was mostly empty, but there were a few men lounging and sweating on their bunks. They found an empty corner and started wiping their faces and hands and stripping off their uniforms, which were surprisingly clean from all the swimming they'd done. The other men gave them furtive looks but mostly ignored them.

Before racking out, they opened K-ration cans with their can openers and K-bar knives. Thin metal spoons came from filthy pockets and they scooped and slurped the tepid food. One of the closest GIs piped up, "Mess hall's open, you know." He thumbed over his shoulder.

Bulkort answered when it was obvious no one else was going to, "Bully beef don't sit well with us."

The GI snorted his agreement, "Don't blame you. That's all we get though. Can't believe I'm sayin' it, but I miss *that* stuff." He pointed at the cans of K-rats.

Bulkort nodded, "We'll run out soon. Then we'll have to stomach the beef like the rest of you poor saps."

The soldier stood and stepped forward, extending his hand to the shirtless Sergeant Bulkort. "I'm Sean Biklin."

Bulkort shook the proffered hand, "I'm Sergeant Bulkort." The private's face blanched, not realizing he was addressing an NCO. "We're Baker Company's newest squad. Now shut the hell up so we can get some sleep."

Private Biklin nodded and backed away. "Sure thing, Sergeant. Sure thing." After a few seconds, he asked, "You guys just off a patrol or something?"

An empty can of K-rats flew at Biklin's head and he barely dodged it. "Shut up!" barked Stollman.

Biklin scurried back to his bunk. His curiosity was piqued though. He watched them sprawl on their cots and fall asleep within seconds. "Welcome to Baker Company," he whispered, but quickly clammed up, seeing a dirty hand extend him a middle finger salute.

Two days later, the squad was folded into Baker Company's Second Platoon Reconnaissance Squad. The original squad of twelve had been whittled down to five by illness. With their added ranks, the squad was back to near-full capacity. The squad leader, Staff Sergeant Clanson, wasn't pleased with the new situation. He'd been with Second Platoon for years and was a career NCO.

When they'd first met, Tarkington stretched out his hand, but Clanson kept his fists clenched against his waist and said, "I don't like cowboys in my outfit."

Tarkington withdrew his hand and stepped closer to the surly sergeant. They were face to face, their ranks equal. "I don't see any horses here, Sergeant. But I'd be happy to open a can of whoop-ass on you if it would make you feel better," Tarkington answered. They steered clear of one another, but the relationship remained icy.

Lieutenant Branson, Second Platoon's CO, was happy to have his Reconnaissance Squad back to its full complement, despite the obvious animosity between the two staff sergeants.

He called Winkleman and Tarkington into his tent. Tarkington poked his head into the tent and saw the officer sitting on a footlocker, lacing his boots. "Excuse me, sir. You wanted to see us?"

Lieutenant Branson nodded and waved them inside, "Yes, yes. Come on in." They took off their hats and entered. The canvas tent was hot inside, but the open sides allowed a breeze to pass through, making it tolerable. Branson finished lacing the boots, then stood and stomped, adjusting his feet. He was of average height, a little on the skinny side, but that was a recent change. His hair was jet black and thick, even though it was cut short. "New boots. The first pair rotted on my feet in the swamps around Gobe. Never seen anything like it."

Tarkington nodded, "Yes, sir. That's why you don't see the locals wearing 'em."

Branson nodded, "I guess it's just what you're used to." He glanced at their boots, which had seen better days. He pointed, "Looks like you two could use new ones too. When we're done here, get over to supply and get your whole team new boots."

Tarkington nodded, "Sure thing, Lieutenant."

Branson continued, "Supplies are coming in all the time. May be the last opportunity to replace gear before we move out tomorrow."

Tarkington glanced at Winkleman then back to Branson. "We'll be ready to move. No problem, sir."

Branson pursed his lips and lifted his chin. "I know you're trying to get word out to Colonel Bradshaw for new orders. As you know, our lines of communication aren't what they should be. Hell, our radios mostly don't work in this humidity, and until we get the airstrip in working order, all communiques have to go by boat. I doubt you'll get a reply before we shove off tomorrow. I want to know that your loyalties lie with us now. I need to know I can count on your team."

They both braced and Tarkington said, "I understand the communication problems, and we're not trying to weasel our way out of anything, sir. It's my duty to report back to my commanding officer. But we're ready to do whatever's necessary for the overall mission of winning the war. You can count on us, sir."

Branson nodded, "You and your men have seen a lot of combat. Your experience will be invaluable to the men." He paced in front of them and pinched his upper lip. "I've spoken with Staff Sergeant Clanson. It's an unusual situation having two squad leaders for one squad. I've let him know that he's in charge of Team One and you're in charge of Team Two. There shouldn't be any more problems."

Tarkington nodded, "Thank you, sir. Nothing I couldn't handle, but it was getting uncomfortable."

Branson grinned imagining the two sergeants squaring off, wondering who'd come out on top in a fair fight. His face turned serious, "We're tasked with moving up the coast to a village called Embago. It's just beyond Oro Bay but south of Cape Sudest where you hit the floatplane base." He grinned, "By the way—well done. We haven't had an air raid since. At least not from the floatplanes." Tarkington nodded his acknowledgment and Branson continued, "Once in place, we'll wait for orders to move on Buna. Intelligence suggests there's very few Japs left there—mostly a rear guard of sick, starving soldiers. We could take it tomorrow, but the overall plan has us waiting for all the supplies to be in place before attacking. You might find this operation boring after everything you men have been through." Winkleman exchanged a worried glance with Tarkington. Branson lifted his chin, "You don't agree, Sergeant?"

Winkleman stepped forward, "Begging your pardon, sir, but it's been our experience that until you've got boots on the ground, you really don't know what's waiting in Buna."

Tarkington added, "We've found that once they take an area they want to hold—and Buna seems like such a place—they defend it tooth and nail."

Branson fidgeted and finally nodded, "Well, we'll soon find out." He crossed his arms over his chest, "We'll move out at 0500 tomorrow. I'll have your team hold back while Team One takes point."

Tarkington nodded, "Yes, sir. We'll be ready to go."

The rain started at midnight and showed no signs of stopping. Despite the foul weather, 2d Battalion left Pongani right on time. Moving with a large force felt odd for Tarkington and his men. They moved along the beach when possible, but the trucks and Jeeps used the road, which was little more than a track. It was slow going and Tarkington was glad they weren't on the road dragging out stuck vehicles from the deep mud. The pace was maddeningly slow. Adjusting from being a light mobile unit to a cumbersome cog in a giant wheel was frustrating.

They would've preferred being on point but couldn't fault Lieutenant Branson's decision. They were the newbies, even though their combat experience was vast. No matter their experiences, Branson would not trust them until he'd worked with them awhile. Putting them out front wouldn't have gone over well with the other team either. Tarkington—though bored and frustrated—was glad Branson seemed to be a competent commander who made good decisions. He hoped that would hold true when the bullets started flying.

At 1500 hours, Team One of the Reconnaissance Squad reported that they'd made it to Oro Bay without encountering enemy soldiers. They reported that the terrain was similar to what they were seeing here, flat and swampy, but the road improved. They urged the company forward, wanting to get the vehicles over the precarious bridges before they were flooded by the countless rising creeks. It was exhausting, but Baker Company finally covered the nine miles with a couple hours of daylight remaining.

Oro Bay was beautiful even under the gray, wet skies. It was a natural bay, and the water looked deep enough for larger vessels, making Tarkington wonder why they hadn't been dropped off here, saving themselves the trouble of the overland march. He kept his mouth shut though; those decisions were made well over his pay grade, but it reinforced the feeling that this whole foray onto the north coast of New Guinea was being done by the seat of the pants. He only hoped the intelligence about enemy strength in Buna-Gona was accurate for once, but he wasn't holding his breath.

Soon after arriving, Tarkington was summoned by Lt. Branson. He returned an hour later and gathered the squad. "Branson wants us to move up to Embago tonight. It's five miles or so. He says the rest of the battalion won't be here until tomorrow, but once they arrive, Oro Bay will get crowded, so he wants us to check out Embago. We'll stay there tonight, sending word back in the morning."

Winkleman grinned, "The lieutenant finally trusts us?"

Tarkington shrugged, "He said we have more experience working at night than Team One."

Stollman piped up, "We've got more experience than this whole damned battalion in our pinky toes."

Tarkington ignored him, "Get some chow, we leave in fifteen."

Henry led the way from Oro Bay. The rain continued, and as they entered the low scrub and snaking vines beyond, the light of day faded quickly to darkness. It was eerily reminiscent of nights they'd spent in the rain-sodden jungles of Luzon. This time, though, they wore ponchos over their uniforms. They kept some rain out, but the GIs were soon wet anyway from the sauna-like conditions. They didn't carry much: ammo, rations for one day, and water. They left their explosives in a locked box hidden away in a corner of a supply depot.

Henry moved along at a good pace. The rain and heavy darkness concealed their movements—but that worked both ways. Baker Company hadn't run into any enemy resistance that day, but Henry knew better than to take anything for granted.

They kept mostly to the strip of land near the beach. It acted like a dike in spots and wasn't as muddy as it was inland or as difficult to walk on as the sloping sand. Countless coconuts in various conditions of rot littered the area, making each step difficult. Twisting an ankle out here wasn't a good idea but was a genuine possibility.

When they figured they were halfway to Embago, the rain died. There wasn't a gradual cessation; it simply stopped. There was a moment of clarity as the clouds parted overhead and revealed stars, now that the curtain of gray rain had cleared. Tarkington had seen this countless times in the Philippines and never tired of the fresh feeling it evoked. Henry stopped and they all crouched, taking it in. They knew it wouldn't last, and they were right. Five minutes later, the ground was thick with rising mist. They stowed their ponchos, drank water, and moved out.

Henry moved slower and Tarkington could tell his lead scout was sensing something. Tarkington moved forward until he was beside him. He matched his steps for a few minutes before Henry stopped and crouched, holding up a fist. Tarkington went to a knee slowly and searched the wispy fog all around him. It clung to the ground like stage smoke he'd seen at a play once back home. The night was still, the only sound the dripping of water off leaves. He felt his new boots sinking into the ground slowly, like he was being slowly consumed by the earth.

Henry was only a foot away, but it took Tarkington a moment to realize he was looking up and pointing at something in the trees. Tarkington followed his finger and searched the dark outline of large palm trees. There was a group of closely spaced trees, the tops of which leaned together as though they were a football team in a huddle. There was a denseness to them that looked unnatural.

It was where Henry was pointing. "Sniper," he hissed.

The word sent an icy shiver up Tarkington's spine. Henry had his M1 carbine at his shoulder. Tarkington didn't remember him doing it. He signaled the others to get down and waited a few seconds before he whispered, "Take him."

Henry took in a sip of air and let it out slow, then touched the trigger. Tarkington didn't flinch at the multiple pops, but brought his own carbine up and aimed into the treetops. Henry's three shots seemed to be absorbed by the trees, as though he had never fired them. After another few seconds, there was movement and Henry fired five more times in quick succession.

A few more seconds passed before Tarkington asked, "You get him?" Henry just nodded, keeping his eyes on target. Tarkington looked behind and pointed at Raker and Vick. He couldn't see them specifically, but knew their forms. He waved them forward and they bounded past. The rest of the squad spread out, keeping vigil on the surrounding jungle.

Tarkington watched Raker and Vick trot forward to the base of the nearest tree. They waved and Tarkington got to his feet and hustled forward. The rest of the squad moved out and they spread beneath the base of the palms. Henry stayed back a little, keeping a good angle on the tree-top, his carbine still aimed. Raker pointed and Tarkington saw cross pieces nailed into the palm, leading up like a ladder. Tarkington nodded and Raker slung his carbine and went up the tree fast.

A few tense minutes passed before something big crashed from the treetops and landed only feet from them. A body. Raker scampered back down the tree and jumped the last few yards, landing lightly on the balls of his feet. "Just one up there. He was on a platform—tied to it."

He handed a Type 98 rifle to Tarkington who took the familiar weapon. He worked the action, ejecting rounds. "Only four rounds," he stated.

Raker wondered, "Shoot and scoot?"

Tarkington shook his head, "Not their style. A couple well-placed shots would hold up the company for hours. Doubt this guy was planning on getting home." They all knew the score. They'd seen Japanese infiltrate the lines on the Bataan Peninsula with no regard for their own safety, sacrificing their lives to wreak havoc among the defenders. It worked. GIs lost sleep, never knowing if a Japanese soldier was sneaking up behind them to slit their throat. They never felt safe, even miles behind their own lines. It happened all the time, making every night a terror.

Winkleman came from the body and crouched, "Usual stuff. Letters and pictures. No extra ammo except a grenade."

Tarkington nodded, "All right. Let's rest here an hour, see if those shots bring anyone else."

They moved past the palms twenty yards and spread out in ambush. Their .30 caliber carbines weren't designed to put out large amounts of firepower, so if more than a team showed up, they'd let them pass if possible. As Tarkington settled into the mud, he wondered if he should bring a Thompson along next time. The carbine was lightweight and perfect for the tight confines of the jungle, but the light .30 caliber round lacked the punching power the .45 caliber Thompson brought to a fight. If their role switched from reconnaissance to line duty, it was something to consider. He'd grown fond of the little carbine. It only weighed five pounds and felt like a toy sometimes, but he'd been pleased to see what the high velocity round did to an enemy soldier at range.

They stayed in place for an hour and a half. When no one came to check on the sniper, they rose like apparitions from the steamy ground and continued their trek toward Embago.

17

The rest of Baker Company marched into Embago, following PFC Raker. Lieutenant Branson was ecstatic when Raker told him they'd dispatched an enemy sniper the night before and insisted he show him the body. Raker obliged and could barely keep from laughing as the young lieutenant gagged and threw up at the smell of the rotting flesh. Branson tucked his nose into his shirt and ordered the body buried.

Raker relayed the story to the others and they had a good laugh. "He's green as grass, Tark."

Tarkington shrugged, "He is, but if he survives another week or two, he'll be fine. He's no Lieutenant Smoker, but he has potential."

The mention of their CO back on Luzon made them all pause. Although barely a year had passed, it seemed like another lifetime ago.

Vick mused, "Reckon anyone's still alive back there?"

Stollman answered, "Probably wish they weren't by now. You saw them marching. Hell, if they survived that, they can survive anything."

Henry drawled, "Sooner we win this war, the better their chances."

Lieutenant Branson approached them. "Good job last night. I—I saw the Jap sniper you killed. He woulda caused trouble for us."

Tarkington nodded, "PFC Henry spotted him. Surprised there weren't more of 'em."

Branson gave Henry an appreciative nod. Henry spit out the reed he was chewing on and Branson finally turned away. "We're digging in here. Elements of the 126th are being flown to Pongani from Moresby. They'll move up to some place called Bofu. It's due west. Once they're in place, we'll advance on Buna as one and sweep 'em outta there."

Tarkington asked, "How long you figure we'll be here?"

"Depends, but probably a week." He pointed to the jungle beyond the tiny town of Embago. There were a few structures, mostly shacks on stilts with thatch roofs and no walls. There were few natives, although more were coming every hour as they carried most of the battalion's gear. "Our platoon will be dug in there. That thicket of palms is on the left flank. You and the rest of the Reconnaissance Squad will dig in there." Back in Pongani, they'd been in barracks and bunks, but now that they were on the front line with a known Japanese stronghold nearby, it was foxholes and trenches. "I want two men per hole with fifteen yards of separation."

Tarkington nodded then asked, "Where's the rest of the squad?"

"They'll be along soon. Get started on your holes, Sergeant."

"Yes, sir." He watched Branson stride away and when he was out of earshot, said, "We're a line unit again, men."

Winkleman shook his head, "Have to find entrenching tools. We weren't issued any of that stuff."

Tarkington grimaced, "See about getting more food and ammunition too." He unslung his carbine, "I'm gonna stow this and get myself a Thompson. Anyone else?"

Bulkort's hand shot up, "Hell's yes. I can't hit anything with this peashooter."

Vick guffawed, "Haven't fired a shot. How d'ya know?"

Bulkort glared, "We'll see if I can hit anything with it shoved up your ass."

Vick shook his head. "Perverted asshole," he murmured.

Tarkington barked, "Knock it off. We've got holes to dig."

They grumbled but dug their foxholes. The land was barely above sea level and the ground was heavy with water. Digging even a few feet down caused water to seep in. By the time they were four feet down, they were bailing as much water as digging mud.

Stollman was the first to complain, "This is horseshit. We really gonna sit in these all damned night?"

Tarkington struggled alongside him in the next hole over. He stopped digging and wiped the dirt and mud off his face. "Looks like three feet's about as deep as we can go. We'll follow his orders, but I ain't getting in mine unless I absolutely have to."

As the day gave way to night, it started raining again. They were dug in on the company's left flank. The rest of the Reconnaissance Squad was off to the right of their four foxholes. In the heavy darkness, they may as well have been a mile apart.

The rain was steady and came down hard enough that their already sodden foxholes were nearly brimming with water and mud. Tarkington and the others sat beside their holes, tucked beneath their ponchos. Henry, sitting a few yards away, murmured, "You think the other guys are sitting in their bathtubs?"

Tarkington shook his head, "I sure the hell hope not."

"Why the hell we have to dig in any way? We don't know if there are Japs within a mile of here."

Tarkington pulled the hood of his poncho to the side and looked at Henry. It wasn't like him to complain, particularly about something he knew there was no good answer to. "You all right?"

A long silence followed until he finally sighed and scooted a few feet closer. "Just feel like we're wasting time. Sitting here with our thumbs up our asses when we should be out there killing Japs." Tarkington didn't respond, knowing Henry would expound if he wanted to or simply clam up. He finally said, "Got a letter in Pongani."

Tarkington reared back in surprise. "You got mail? In Pongani? How the hell . . . ?" he stammered. "I mean, they can't give us new orders, but they can send you a letter? Good God above! How'd they even know where you were?"

Henry shook his head, "God only knows."

Another long silence and Tarkington asked, "From your folks?"

Henry nodded, "Two of my brothers joined up. One's in the army, the other's in the marines."

"Marines? God help him."

Tarkington could hear the smile in Henry's words, "He never was too smart." His tone turned serious, "The letter was months old. They're both nearly done with training by now and are probably being shipped out. I don't want 'em to see this shit, Tark."

Tarkington nodded, "I can understand that. Robert joined up too. He's probably on the same boat as your marine brother."

"Wouldn't that be something? I hope you're right." He sighed, "The point is, we were supposed to be out here kicking the Nips around, hitting them with surprise attacks, taking out their officers, but instead we're folded into a damned line unit with a green as grass company of GIs."

Tarkington sighed heavily, "You think I don't know that? I feel the exact same way. The more Japs we kill, the closer we get to ending this war and the better chances of protecting our kin. I've sent letters, radio messages— hell, I'd send smoke signals if I thought it would work—but the farther away from Australia we get, the less chance we've got of getting new orders from Bradshaw."

Henry spit, adding to the sopping ground. "I know you're doing all you can. I just feel like we're fruit rotting on an over-watered peach tree."

Tarkington guffawed, "Jesus, Henry. You a poet now?" Henry shook his head and Tarkington added, "Your brothers will be fine. If they're anything like you, they've been training for this crap since they were in diapers."

Henry guffawed, "Diapers? Mama didn't wrap us in linens, Tark. Babies around my parts stay naked and learn to do their business soon enough."

"Henry, you are one backwards son of a bitch, and I'm thankful for it every day."

The rain didn't stop, and soon they were soaked through despite the ponchos. It was nothing new for the veterans, but no matter how many times you get kicked in the crotch, it hurts every time.

The darkness finally gave up its grip, and in the east there was a glow of the coming sunrise. Just before full daylight, an anguished scream pierced the sodden morning. It subsided, then started with more fervor. Soon, nearly the entire platoon was standing near the center of the line, gazing down at the decapitated corpse of a GI from 2nd Squad. The head canted over the man's shoulder, floating in the bloody water which filled half the foxhole.

No one spoke; they simply stared at the grisly scene. The GI who'd found him was sitting on a fallen palm tree, shaking while a medic wrapped him in a wool blanket.

Lt. Branson approached him and asked, "What the hell happened, Wilson?"

The GI's eyes were red from crying, deep fatigue, and fear. "I—I had to take a crap. I've got the shits and last night was bad. I—I was gone for a half hour?" He shrugged, "I don't really know. Wh—when I came back, I found Phil like—like that."

Branson's jaw rippled, "While you were off shitting, your buddy—the man you're supposed to be looking out for—had his head sawed off."

The GI stammered, "Jesus, Lieutenant, I—I . . ."

"You fucked up and someone died!" The GI looked away. His shaking became uncontrollable, and a low keening came from his throat. It was full of anguish and sounded more like a wild animal than a human. Branson pulled his raging eyes from Wilson and found Tarkington staring at him. He took long strides toward him and squared up, "Sergeant Tarkington." He lifted his chin, "Your squad ready to exact some revenge?"

Tarkington's eyes narrowed. This wasn't how things were supposed to be done. It wasn't professional, but if it got him off this miserable line . . . "Yes, sir," he nodded.

It was obvious early on that finding the Japanese who'd killed Private Phillopson in the wee hours of the morning was highly unlikely. The rain had stopped but had washed away any obvious signs. Despite that, Henry and Raker moved through the area between jungle and beach, meticulously searching, while being careful not to lead them into an ambush.

No one had gotten any proper sleep the night before, but the prospect of patrolling versus being stuck in the line for another night far outweighed any desire for sleep.

By noon, with no sign of the enemy, Tarkington called a halt near a surprisingly clear-running creek. While they ate C-rats and drank from their canteens, he addressed them, "Since the lieutenant has given us an open-ended ticket, I say we move up to Cape Sudest. I had a look at Branson's map and I'm sure it's where we found the floatplanes. It's a big river inlet, the Samboga, and as you recall, we saw plenty of Japs there. Intelligence says Buna's gonna be a pushover, but you know how those guys are." Everyone nodded. "I'd like to get a better look."

Winkleman grinned, "That why our packs are so heavy?"

Tarkington nodded, "I had you pack heavy 'cause I'd rather be out here beyond the lines than festering in some piss-and-shit-filled foxhole waiting to have my head lopped off."

Winkleman put his hands out in surrender, "You won't find any complaints here, Tark. Less time we spend on the line, the better."

Tarkington continued, "I figure we'll do a detailed recon of the area up to and beyond the river—assuming we can find a crossing point."

They finished eating and were patrolling silently through the jungle ten minutes later. The heat was oppressive and wet. Mist clung to the ground, making the entire world look and feel like a giant sauna. Tarkington had stowed his carbine with their explosives and the Thompson felt heavy. He told himself he'd be glad for the extra firepower if it ever came down to it, but at this moment, it was just plain heavy.

They made it to within thirty yards of the Samboga River before the swampy edges stopped them from advancing. There was very little current, and the water was the color of chocolate milk. Immense trees drifted by, their dripping root wads scraping along the bottom in spots, making them jolt and stutter on their way to the sea.

"All this rain's swelling the rivers," muttered Winkleman. "No way we're crossing it here."

Tarkington agreed, "At least in the Philippines there were bridges. This area's more remote—if that's possible. Let's move upstream and see what we can find. That Jap got across somehow."

They found a trail which followed the river. It was muddy, and it was obvious by the large depressions here and there that something other than animals had used it recently. Tarkington felt the squad slip into a different gear. It was subtle, but knowing there were enemy nearby turned up the intensity level individually, making the entire squad focused. No one spoke, and although they slunk through the jungle alongside the trail, they moved in absolute silence.

They'd gone a little over a mile when Henry and Raker both stopped and crouched. Voices filtered through the foliage. Tarkington sniffed and could just discern the scent of something cooking—fishy smelling.

The trail ahead wound through a thick patch of brush. The sounds and smells were coming from behind it. Tarkington evaluated the terrain. To the right was the swampy edges of the river, to the left a slight incline and more jungle. He pointed left and Henry and Raker moved out slowly. Their mottled camouflage made them almost invisible. When they stopped, they blended perfectly—someone would have to step on them to find them.

The squad followed the point men and soon they were slightly above and to the left of whoever was cooking lunch. The jungle was still too thick to see through. They went to their bellies and with their weapons across their elbows, moved forward. The wet ground was writhing with worms. Tarkington had learned long ago to ignore them, but his subconscious was constantly searching for poisonous beasts. He'd seen the fabled and deadly giant centipedes more than once. He wondered how Sergeant Bulkort was handling things. New Guinea was a nightmarish place for anyone with even a mild aversion to snakes and large insects, and Bulkort had both in spades.

He pushed the thought aside when he parted the brambles and saw six Japanese soldiers huddled around a small cooking fire only yards away. Balanced over the top of the flame, a good-sized pot was frothing and spitting bubbles as rice boiled. He wondered if one of the soldiers was responsible for killing the hapless private that morning, but thought it unlikely.

The trail they'd been following led directly past this encampment. Anyone using it would certainly see them immediately, which told Tarkington they weren't overly concerned with the Allies being only a few miles down the coast. Perhaps they didn't know. They eagerly huddled around the fire, giving no thought to their surroundings. Tarkington wondered if he should take them prisoner but discounted it quickly. Unlike the soldiers in Gobe, these men weren't skinny and sickly. They looked fresh. Each man had a weapon slung over his shoulder, or propped nearby. Though lax, he doubted they'd go down without a fight, and he knew through experience they wouldn't surrender easily.

From the direction of the river, another soldier appeared. It was obvious he was a part of the group, as there wasn't a greeting, just a few nods. The soldier trudged through muck and mud, his boots sucking and slurping with each step until he got to solid ground. He carried a large bag of rice over his shoulder. He plopped it down beside the others with a grunt.

Tarkington tried to see where he'd come from. Was there a bridge? Or possibly a boat? He couldn't see anything beyond them, but his interest was piqued.

He glanced at Henry and Raker, who were staring at him. He held up three fingers, pointed at his Thompson, then slid his finger across his throat. Raker and Henry passed it along; they'd attack in three minutes with their firearms.

Tarkington counted down, bringing his Thompson to his shoulder in tiny increments of glacial movements. With sixty seconds to go, he had the stock pulled tight into his shoulder and his hand on the primer bolt. He thought about the motion; smoothly pull the primer, click off the safety, and fire a short burst at the nearest soldiers.

Three, two, one. He fired an instant after the others. The heavy sounds of the Thompson overwhelmed the pops of the carbines all around him. The enemy soldiers didn't have a chance. Their bodies writhed in place as holes erupted in their bodies, sending gouts of blood flying in all directions. The sudden and all-consuming roar of gunfire stopped as quickly as it started.

Through the thick gunpowder smoke, Tarkington saw they were all down—unmoving. He got to his knees, keeping his smoking muzzle trained on them. Raker and Henry got to their feet and moved closer, sweeping their weapons from side to side. "It's all clear," called Raker. The rest of the squad pushed forward, checking the dead carefully.

Tarkington stepped past the pile of smoking corpses. He sank in the same mud the soldier with the rice bag had. Keeping his muzzle up, he pushed through a layer of greenery and saw what he hoped he'd find: a boat.

He slogged his way forward and made sure it was empty. He called back to the others, "Found a boat." He looked across the wide expanse of water to the other side. It was at least 150 yards. The current was slow but steady. He noticed a small structure across the way. He ducked down behind the bow of the boat, realizing it was probably a dock. He wondered if their shots had been heard. He doubted it; the soaking jungle ate sound the same way it ate men.

He slogged his way back through the mud. The men were sifting through pockets, searching for useful intelligence and/or valuables. Winkleman came up with a handful of papers. "Don't have a clue what any of it says, but it looks more official than letters from home."

Tarkington nodded, "Stuff it in your pack. You never know, and it might appease our vengeful Lieutenant Branson." He moved to the bodies and looked them over. "These don't look like malnourished has-beens to me."

Winkleman nodded, "Their uniforms are new and their weapons too." He kneeled at a dead soldier's feet, "Look at the boots. No signs of rot. These guys haven't been here long."

Henry crouched over the fire. Miraculously, the boiling pot of rice had survived the firefight. "May as well not waste it," he muttered.

Stollman cringed, "I'm not eating Jap food. Besides, there's blood and stuff in it."

Henry grinned and used a nearby stick to pull the pot off the fire. He used the same stick to stir it, "Parts per million. Besides, a little protein's good for the brain, and God knows you need it."

Stollman backed away, "Shit, there are probably brains in it."

Henry pulled his spoon from his pocket and scooped out a steaming spoonful. He blew on it and stuffed it into his mouth. He quickly swallowed, "Those Nips know how to cook rice."

Stollman shook his head, "You're a crazy son of a bitch. You know that?" Henry answered by gobbling another spoonful.

They waited for nightfall to cross the river. The boat was sturdy and imported. Instead of paddles, there was a center seat, oarlocks, and two oars. Winkleman had the most experience with boats of this type, so he took the oars while the others piled in around him.

Before leaving, they dragged the dead soldiers to the river and pushed them into the churned-up, muddy water. The bodies drifted quickly out of sight and would undoubtedly make a meal for some lurking carnivore.

Winkleman rowed, pulling the oars expertly through the water while the others kept close watch for wayward trees and root wads. Since they'd need the boat to get back across the river, they opted to steer clear of the dock and drift downstream. Winkleman took them to the middle of the river and allowed the boat to drift slowly, taking occasional oar strokes to keep them moving steadily.

The river slowed even more, and soon Winkleman was having to row to keep them moving at all. Tarkington whispered, "Must be getting close to the sea. Start taking us toward shore, Wink."

Winkleman adjusted and rowed steadily toward the dark bank. When they were close, Tarkington stopped him and they searched the shoreline for anything hostile. They tried to land the boat, but each time they were stymied by the shallows and had to push themselves back into the river and move farther downstream. They finally found a stopping point where they could step onto dry land and also hide the boat.

After pulling the boat halfway out of the water and covering it with brush, they patrolled downstream. They needed to know how far they were from the coastline if they hoped to find the boat again.

It didn't take long before they found themselves on the edge of a beach. In the darkness, it was impossible to discern if they were on the true coast or just an inlet. Tarkington wished for the hundredth time that he had a map that was worth a shit. They'd make due; they didn't have any other choice.

Tarkington gathered them close and whispered, "We'll move along the coastline and see what we can see. This is a reconnaissance. No contact." There were nods all around.

Winkleman asked, "You think this is where the floatplane base was?"

Tarkington shook his head, "I don't know. This place is so full of bays and river mouths, there's no way to tell. If we get separated, meet back at the boat." When there were no more questions, "Move out."

Henry and Raker moved out first. They'd alternate taking point, as usual. They moved slowly at first, but the farther they went, the more they felt how utterly deserted the area was. They increased their pace and soon came to a small coastal village. There were outrigger canoes pulled up along the beach and a few thatch-roofed structures.

They moved like ghosts to the edge of the village, searching for any sign of Japanese. It was midnight and they worked their way around the village, not finding any sentries. Satisfied that there wasn't an enemy presence, Tarkington motioned them into the village and they converged on the largest of the buildings. They fanned out, and Tarkington and Winkleman hopped onto the deck. Tarkington's instinct was to bust in with his weapon ready, but instead, he knocked on the rickety door. He felt ridiculous standing there like a heavily armed mailman needing a signature from a client.

There was commotion from inside and the door opened inward. An islander stared back at him; his eyes wide at the unusual sight of an American soldier. Tarkington greeted him in Tagalog and could tell the man understood. He didn't move though—just stood staring in shock. Finally, as though a spell had been broken, he smiled and stepped back, allowing Tarkington and Winkleman to enter.

Light flared in the corner as another islander lit a candle. He saw swaying, sagging breasts and behind the woman they belonged to, many eyes staring at him. He repeated his greeting, waving at them and forcing a smile, trying to put them at ease. They didn't smile back but continued staring. The man finally answered the greeting with his own and more candles were lit. He directed them to sit, and the children and woman sat up in their beds and watched intently.

"Vick," Tarkington called. Vick's camouflage-painted face poked through the door and Tarkington said, "Your language skills are better than mine. Make sure I don't miss something."

Vick smiled as he entered, slinging his carbine. The family smiled back and uttered phrases of welcome.

They spent the next two hours talking in stilted phrases. It was frustrating, but by the end, Tarkington had increased his knowledge of the area tenfold and his concern for the coming Allied offensive grew exponentially.

In the wee hours of the morning, they took their leave of the family, leaving them portions of the rice bag they'd scrounged from the Japanese encampment. Tarkington tried to stress that their presence should remain a secret, but he doubted they'd be 100 yards away by the time the rest of the village knew.

At the outskirts of the village, Tarkington gathered the men and told them what they'd learned. "They've been working for the Nips for months. Forced labor. Mostly been building log bunkers with interconnecting tunnels and trenches throughout the peninsula. Hundreds of them. By the way he drew it up, they're built with overlapping fields of fire. He said they finished last week and he's only just returned to his family. He says many others weren't as lucky and had to stay on as slaves. He was wishy-washy on enemy numbers, but their concept of numbers differs from ours. He said there are many mouths to feed and not enough food, but plenty of weapons and ammo. He also said a large boat dropped off more troops the other day." He motioned the way they'd come, "I'd guess the patrol we attacked was a part of that group."

Bulkort gave a low whistle. "Fresh troops? Bunkers? Our guys are going into a meat grinder."

Tarkington nodded, "Looks that way. We've gotta get this information to Captain Griffin and Colonel Huntington."

18

That evening after recrossing the river and patrolling back to friendly lines without incident, they reported to Lieutenant Branson. In their absence, Baker Company had moved to the outskirts of Embago to allow for the burgeoning number of troops pouring into Oro Bay. The GIs from Second Platoon seemed on edge and Tarkington wondered if they were still thinking about the killing that had spurred their mission.

Baker Company's new position was far superior to their old one. They were spread out on a low hillock, which afforded them drier conditions. It was still a muddy mess, but there wasn't as much standing water. The foxholes he passed were only a quarter of the way filled.

Tarkington sent the men to clean up and get food and rest while he and Winkleman told Lt. Branson what they'd found. Branson was more interested in hearing about the Japanese patrol they'd successfully ambushed than the news of Buna's defenses, but understood the potential significance, so escorted them to Captain Griffin's tent.

A bored-looking GI wearing a uniform that hung off his thin frame like he was a human clothes hanger stood outside Griffin's tent and saluted Lt. Branson but scowled at the sergeants. His M1 Garand rifle looked too big for him, and Tarkington noticed the barrel was rusty. "We need to see Captain Griffin. Is he in?" asked Branson.

The soldier squinted at Tarkington and Winkleman, obviously not recognizing the mottled camouflage uniforms with the small Indian head on the shoulder. He nodded, but when Branson stepped past, he put a hand on Tarkington's chest, stopping him, "These two with you, sir?"

Branson nodded, "Yes, Private. This is Sergeant Tarkington and Sergeant Winkleman." The soldier stiffened, his eyes looking for some sign of rank. Once again, Tarkington realized they were covered in mud, but he didn't bother brushing them clean.

A voice from inside said, "That you, Lieutenant?"

Tarkington glowered at the private, pushed his way past him, and entered the tent behind Branson with Winkleman on his tail. Branson braced, "Yes, sir. With Sergeants Winkleman and Tarkington, sir."

Griffin was looking into a small mirror propped on a desk, making the final swipe of a razor across his chin. He placed the razor in the tin of water and used an olive drab towel to wipe the last vestiges of runny shaving cream off his face. "You're back. Branson told me about the mission." His eyes darkened for an instant and Branson fidgeted. The tension between the two officers was obvious. Griffin thought Branson had overstepped his boundaries by greenlighting the mission without his approval. "Frankly, I didn't expect you back so soon."

"We didn't expect to be back yet either, sir. But we stumbled upon vital information, so we hustled back."

"Vital information? Branson sent you out to kill the Jap that killed Private Phillopson."

Tarkington nodded. "We achieved that, sir. At least, we killed a Jap patrol up near the Samboga River. Not sure if they had anything to do with Phillopson or not. They were fresh troops, sir. New uniforms, well fed, and their weapons were still shiny."

Winkleman remembered the documents in his pack and rifled through it, then handed them to Griffin. "I found these on one of 'em. Can't read it, but looked like it might be important."

Griffin took the documents and quickly leafed through them. He raised his voice, "Private Black." The thin private at the front door stuck his head in. "Take these documents to G2. Utmost urgency." Private Black took them and glared at Tarkington and Winkleman as he hustled out the door while stuffing the documents into a filthy pants pocket. "Is that it then?" asked Griffin.

Tarkington glanced at Branson who gave him a nod to continue. "No, sir. After we encountered the patrol, we noticed a boat and used it to cross the Samboga once it was dark." Griffin's mouth tightened and Tarkington continued, "Figured while we were there, we may as well do some more poking around." Griffin nodded and Tarkington continued, "We came across a village about three miles from the river and had an informative conversation with a local who's been working for the Nips the past few months."

He told him everything he could remember from the conversation. Winkleman filled in bits he'd missed and by the end, Griffin's mouth was in a tight line and his eyes were dark. He paced, squeezing the bridge of his nose. He finally sighed, "So, you're telling me that all our intelligence about Buna, and presumably Gona, is wrong."

"Yes, sir. Dead wrong."

Griffin nodded and made his mind up. "Okay." He grabbed his soft cap and pulled it on smartly, the sewed-on captain's bars clean and white. "Good job. Get yourselves cleaned up and take tomorrow off." He looked at Lt. Branson who nodded. "The Lieutenant and I will report this to Colonel Huntington right away." Branson swallowed hard and stroked his hair nervously. Griffin slapped him on the shoulder, "Don't worry, Lieutenant. You look presentable enough." Branson's face reddened as he followed Griffin out the door.

They heard nothing more about their information for days. After their one day off, they were put back onto the line. The rain continued on and off and the squad longed to be out patrolling, but they didn't complain and did what was asked of them.

Lieutenant Branson had been avoiding their section, and Tarkington wondered if their information was being taken seriously. The area continued to grow with more and more GIs, and soon supply dumps and weapons depots were stacked high. There'd been the occasional air raid scares, but most of the raids struck farther south toward Porlock Harbor.

Three days after returning, Tarkington went looking for answers. He found Lt. Branson discussing something with an officer from another platoon and waited him out. As Branson was walking toward another section of the line, he walked up beside him. "Hello, Lieutenant."

Branson kept walking, "What is it, Sergeant?"

Tarkington adjusted his slung Thompson, "Sir, I was wondering how the briefing went with Colonel Huntington." He quickly added, "If you don't mind my asking." He hated kowtowing, but as his mother used to say, "You don't attract bees without honey," or something like that.

"It's none of your concern, Sergeant."

He tried a different tactic, "Did the papers Sergeant Winkleman handed over produce anything, sir?"

Branson halted and faced him. "Nothing much. It was a list. Like a grocery list or something. If anything, it refuted what your native told you."

Tarkington looked confused, "How so, sir?"

"Well, if there are . . ." he formed air quotes with his fingers, "*many* defenders, why are they making food lists with such low numbers? The amounts listed would barely be enough to feed a platoon, let alone a regiment or more."

"Perhaps it wasn't a list for the regiment but just his platoon?" he asked, trying to keep the condescension from his tone.

Branson shook his head, "It doesn't matter, Sergeant. The colonel wasn't convinced, even without the list. You know better than anyone how much the islanders skew numbers. Perhaps your native's working for the Japanese. You ever thought of that? Perhaps he's trying to stall an attack in order to give his buddies more time to prepare." His face reddened and he pointed at Tarkington's chest, stopping before actually touching him when he noticed the hint of danger in Tarkington's eyes. "The colonel even suggested your mission may well have tipped off the enemy to our proximity."

"That's ridiculous. The man was their slave. He hates them as much as you or I do, probably more."

"Drop it, Sergeant."

Tarkington wasn't ready to drop it, "So we're just gonna waltz into their trap?"

"I said, drop it," he seethed. "That's an order, *Sergeant*."

Tarkington glared and hissed, "Yes, sir." Branson took a step and Tarkington asked, "Will you be leading the company from the front when the time comes, sir?" It was too much, but he couldn't help himself. Branson's step faltered, but he didn't respond and kept walking.

Once back in the Reconnaissance Squad area, Winkleman approached Tarkington, noticing his long-time friend and leader's dark mood. "Uh oh. What's the scoop?"

"Command's ignoring the intelligence. They say the native's exaggerating or in cahoots with the Nips."

Winkleman was speechless, but he finally uttered, "Cahoots? Cahoots? He was a slave, for crying out loud. And what about the fresh troops?"

"You think I didn't tell him all that?"

Winkleman shook his head slowly, then sighed. "They haven't met them yet. The Japs, I mean. The other night when the private lost his head, that was their first real glimpse. We learned it back on Luzon, but these guys still think they're up against a second-rate military who just got lucky a few times. Sure, there've been first-hand accounts—like ours—but you can see it in their eyes—they don't quite believe us. They think we're exaggerating or shell-shocked."

Tarkington nodded, "You're right. I wrote countless reports back in Australia. It was as though they wanted more and more from me because they thought they'd catch me in a lie or something."

Winkleman squinted into the darkening clouds overhead, "They won't really know until we push off into Buna."

Tarkington sighed, "And they're green as grass. It's gonna be a meat grinder."

Days later, they were on the northern side of the coastal village of Boreo, close to the outskirts of Buna. They'd been transported from Oro Bay by boat, bypassing the Samboga River, and deposited at the village of Horiko

—the same village where they'd interviewed the native. From Horiko, they marched unopposed to Boreo and were now awaiting the order to attack along the coastal route to Buna. Their goal was Cape Endaiadere, two miles from their current position.

Countless overflights of the area showed that their first enemy obstacle would be two airstrips given the unoriginal names of the Old Strip and the New Strip. The closer New Strip ran east to west and was connected to the Old Strip, which ran north to south by a short bridge. Husks of burned-out aircraft dotted the airfields. Overflights showed no enemy troops or buildings that could be construed as serious obstacles.

As Lt. Branson briefed the platoon NCOs on the upcoming assault, the mood was jubilant. The men had been battling the elements for months now, but had yet to test their mettle against the true enemy. Tarkington watched the green troopers' excitement grow. They were sickly, and many had to leave intermittently to relieve their watery bowels. He kept his mouth shut. Good morale wasn't something to mess with, but he knew many of these men wouldn't survive the day.

It was midmorning, November 19th, 1942, when they got the order to move forward. A few 25-pounder shells streaked overhead, slamming into some unseen target. Tarkington listened for more as he waved the men forward, but that was the extent of the barrage.

Winkleman, at the other end of the squad, looked at him, "Is that it? Two shells?"

Tarkington shook his head but didn't answer. Second Platoon was spread out in a long line, moving up the coastline. The rest of the company was spread out to their left and the remainder of the battalion behind them. Tarkington's team was on the left flank of the rest of the Reconnaissance Squad. The going was tough for Staff Sergeant Clanson and Team One. There wasn't much of a beach to speak of, and the thick jungle undergrowth slowed them down.

Tarkington slowed his pace to match theirs, but they were lagging behind the rest of the platoon. Eventually, Team One moved inland to keep up, which pushed Tarkington's team farther inland. The thick, impenetrable jungle eventually forced the entire company onto a small track of land like a funnel.

Tarkington and the rest of the Reconnaissance Squad found themselves in the front quarter of the procession of GIs. The jungle overhead was thick and Tarkington felt exposed as hell moving in broad daylight in a snaking line of GIs. There were countless places a Japanese could hide, and they were moving much too fast to cover them all. He barked, "Raker and Henry, watch for snipers overhead. The rest scan for bunkers. I don't like this."

Stollman piped up, "I'm sure the artillery barrage sent them packing, Tark."

Tarkington shut him up, "Can it, Stolly! Pay attention."

Staff Sergeant Clanson was ahead of him. He turned to address Tarkington, "Relax, cowboy. Ain't no Japs gonna bite you." There was a smattering of guffaws from Team One and the other GIs close enough to hear.

Tarkington ignored him, continuing to scan the jungle. A sudden long burst of machine gun fire and the snapping of bullets passing close by sent him diving to the ground. The sickening sounds of bullets impacting men who weren't as quick to take cover reminded Tarkington of the early days on Luzon.

He hugged the ground as bullets whizzed inches over his head. More firing erupted, and it seemed it was coming from every direction at once. Men were screaming and Tarkington saw Sergeant Clanson curled in a ball with his hands over his steel pot. A GI beside him lifted his head, trying to see where the fire was coming from.

Tarkington yelled, "Stay down!" but it was too late. The distinctive gong of a bullet passing through the soldier's steel helmet ended his search. His head snapped back, then dropped forward, the helmet rolling into the jungle. "Sniper!" he yelled.

He aimed his Thompson at the trees overhead and let loose a long burst. He couldn't see anything but green, but perhaps he'd get lucky or at least keep the sniper's head down. The machine gun fire continued. The ground in front of his face was stitched with fire. Dirt and jungle plants covered his head. He tasted soil and blood and he spit. "We gotta get off this trail! Move left!" He was talking to anyone close, but the only GIs to respond were his own men.

Hugging the ground, they moved fast until they were pushing their way into the thick undergrowth off the track. Bullets continued slicing through the area, but they were out of the bullseye. The rest of the platoon was immobile, frozen in place. Gouts of dirt and blood erupted on the trail, and men were shredded in place. The air was tinged with a sickening pall of red mist and agonized screams of terror.

Henry was facing the other way, his carbine aimed toward the trees. "Sniper behind us," he said over the din of machine gun fire. A GI behind them and still on the trail suddenly lunged to his feet and ran toward the jungle. He only made it a few yards when his chest blossomed. He arched his back, dropped his rifle, and fell onto his face. Henry fired in quick succession, emptying his magazine. "Got you, you little piss-ant," he seethed.

A wide-eyed soldier close to the fallen GI made eye contact with Tarkington and yelled in a high screeching panicked voice, "They're behind us! They're everywhere!"

Tarkington bellowed, "Stay down! Move off the damned track!" He saw a soldier rise up with a grenade in hand. He'd already pulled the pin and was reaching back to throw it. "No!" Tarkington yelled, but it was too late. The grenade flew a few yards, hit the wall of jungle, and bounced back at the thrower. The grenade plopped onto the trail and rolled back, stopping beside the GI's head. The explosion tore the young man's head from his shoulders. Shrapnel bit into the soldier beside him and he yelled in agony, his back turned dark with blood.

The onslaught stopped all at once, as though a switch had been thrown. Smoke was heavy on the trail, wafting over the dead, wounded, and terrified. Moans and screams quickly filled the void. Calls for medics went unanswered. No one left alive wanted to move. Another shot and a soldier who'd been screaming and rolling side to side was silenced. "Snipers are everywhere. Stay down!" yelled Tarkington. "Move to the jungle. Get off the track!"

Men finally responded, crawling to the edges of the jungle and forcing their way into the undergrowth. Tarkington scanned the trees. The machine guns were either reloading or more likely moving to new positions. He'd seen it countless times on Luzon. They were masters of shifting fire. He yelled, "Lieutenant Branson! Branson, can you hear me?" A shot rang out and the tree Tarkington was behind shook with the impact. Raker fired five rounds. "Get him?" Tarkington asked.

Raker responded, "Doubt it. Can't see for shit. Just firing at the sound."

That was a low proposition. Sound, particularly at close quarters in the jungle, acted strange. Shots fired from behind sometimes sounded like they were coming from the front or to the side. It was confusing and terrifying, which didn't help these men any. A smattering of shots from other GIs grew in intensity. He doubted they were seeing any better than Raker was. "Vick. See if you can find Branson. We need to pull back, recover the dead and wounded."

Vick nodded and Tarkington was struck once again by his coolness under fire. He looked as though he'd just awoken from a nap. His rifle barrel smoked and he laid odds he'd found the mark. He watched him crawl away until he was out of sight.

Another machine gun opened fire. The bullets smacked through the trees and shrubs and Tarkington had to adjust his position to keep the tree between himself and the flying lead. "They shifted fire, dammit," he cursed.

This time there was return fire from the GIs. Tarkington figured they probably had a better chance of hitting one another than the well-concealed Japanese, but at least they weren't paralyzed with fear.

The thick jungle to their left suddenly parted and two Japanese soldiers burst through screaming with bayonets slashing. Sergeant Bulkort was closest. He rolled onto his side and pulled the semi-automatic carbine's trigger as fast as he could. Most of his .30 caliber rounds hit the first soldier. Some passed through him and hit the next man. They both fell onto Bulkort and he struggled to push them off.

Stollman put his carbine's barrel to each of their heads and fired, making sure, then fired the rest of his clip into the jungle where they'd emerged.

Bulkort finally pushed the dead soldiers off and scooted away from them on his butt. He crashed into Winkleman, who pushed him down, "Stay down, Bull."

Bulkort got control of his breathing and reloaded. "Jesus Christ," he blurted.

Another machine gun opened fire, this time from a different direction.

Tarkington shook his head, "We gotta get the hell outta here." Two GIs still on the trail got to their feet and ran as fast as they could. "Get down!" he yelled, but they kept running as though the devil himself were on their tails. They disappeared around the slight bend.

Others, seeing their success, rose and followed, and soon men were sprinting past. Some dropped, cut down by machine gun fire, but most made it. A screaming Japanese soldier burst onto the trail. Tarkington's Thompson was already aimed in his direction. He adjusted slightly and fired six rounds, starting low. The heavy .45 caliber bullets walked up his body, rising with the weapon's natural propensity to kick upwards.

The Japanese machine gun fire stopped and more Japanese soldiers burst from the sides of the trail, charging and firing. GIs still on the trail were too close to bring their weapons to bear. Tarkington and his men fired from their concealed, prone positions with practiced precision. The twelve Japanese soldiers dropped one by one, but not before burying their bayonets into three screaming GIs.

Vick crawled forward and yelled from ten yards back. "Fall back, Tark! Branson wants everyone to fall back!"

Tarkington gave him a thumbs up and yelled, "I'm throwing smoke. We need to get those men outta there! Sergeant Clanson! You alive?" He saw movement on the trail, the same spot he'd seen Clanson curled up and quaking. Clanson looked back at him, his face bloody against white skin. "We're coming for you. Covering fire! Now!" yelled Tarkington. He hurled the smoke grenade as far down the trail as possible. There was a smattering of shots as the GIs in front fired into the green abyss. The grenade sputtered and finally billowed green smoke. "Let's go!" he yelled.

The squad leaped up and ran forward. They left the dead but helped the wounded move back. A few sniper shots probed through the smoke, but no one was hit. Raker dropped to a knee and fired toward the top of a nearby tree. A dark shape spilled from the treetop and arrested suddenly as the rope tied to his ankle ran out of slack.

Tarkington went to Sergeant Clanson and kneeled beside him. "Come on, cowboy. Where you hit?" Clanson shook his head quickly, more like a tremor coursing through his body. Tarkington hoisted him upright with one hand, keeping the Thompson aimed into the jungle with the other, and pushed him toward the rear. "Get your ass outta here!" Clanson looked down at his soaked crotch and shame washed over him. Tarkington barked, "Forget that crap! Help your men. Hurry!"

Clanson seemed to snap out of his terror-induced fugue and helped Henry carry a GI with a seeping gut wound. They weaved their way through the bloody remains of GIs, and with the smoke dissipating quickly, got the wounded pulled back with no more casualties.

19

Second Battalion retreated back toward Boreo. The brief, violent clash was costly with fifteen GIs KIA and twenty-two wounded. Most had been from Baker and Easy Companies. Team One of the Reconnaissance Squad was down to two effectives: Staff Sergeant Clanson and Private Mohr. The rest were killed, missing, or wounded. They took the wounded back south to the under-manned medical facilities in Hariko.

Baker Company spread out around a clearing 500 yards from where they'd been ambushed. Shallow foxholes were dug. They couldn't dig deeper than three feet without water seeping in, so they were laying down in the shallow depressions, barely concealed.

Hours after the battle, Captain Griffin called the NCOs and officers to a briefing in Boreo. Tarkington sat on a downed palm tree alongside Winkleman. The morale, which had been so high hours before, had evaporated. The men were dirty, bloody, and shaken. Staff Sergeant Clanson's hands shook so badly he could barely get his cigarette to his mouth.

Captain Griffin had dark circles beneath his eyes, but his voice was strong as he addressed them. "The Japanese resistance is heavier than expected. We weren't the only ones to take a beating today. Third Battalion, moving on the airfields, ran into concealed bunkers and snipers too. The push toward Buna Mission along the Girua River met stiff resistance too.

They have stopped every thrust cold." He paused and scanned the bedraggled group of soldiers. He nodded, "We've had a setback. We've lost men." His mouth turned down and he paced with his hands clasped behind his back. "This will not be the pushover we thought it was going to be." He glanced at Tarkington who simply stared back. Griffin continued, "We're going to have to slug our way through. It will not be easy, but now we know what we're up against . . ." He shrugged, "We'll be better prepared." Tarkington exchanged a glance with Winkleman, wondering what change he had in mind. "Tomorrow," Griffin continued, "we attack again. But this time, we'll cut our way through along the coast. The jungle's as thick as it gets, and we'll need to hack our way through by hand. We won't get funneled into their guns this time."

Lieutenant Branson raised his hand and Griffin pointed at his platoon leader with some annoyance. Branson stood and said, "We don't have but a few machetes, sir. We've asked for them, but haven't seen them yet."

Griffin nodded, "I'm aware of the problem, Lieutenant. The colonel is lighting a fire under the logistics staff's asses, but for now we'll use shovels if we have to." Branson sat down and Griffin continued the briefing, pointing to an area on the woefully inadequate map. "This region here is the old Duropa Plantation. Once we're through the jungle and onto the plantation grounds, the terrain opens up and allows for some maneuvering room. The enemy won't be able to hide so easily. I want units hacking through as soon as we're finished here. We'll work through the night. We don't expect enemy contact since there are no passable trails for them to defend. Once through, we'll attack through the plantation, bypassing the airfields which are well defended. Our goal is still Buna mission and Cape Endaiadere. Once we take them, we'll coordinate with Third Battalion and hit the airfields from two directions."

Another platoon leader raised his hand and stood. He asked, "Are we getting any artillery support, sir?"

Griffin's lips thinned and he nodded, "Some. The Australians only have a couple of 25-pounders. More ammunition is being brought up for them and more guns are being offloaded in Horiko as we speak, but the guns won't be here for a few days at the earliest."

The same officer asked, "What about armor? Or excavators? They'd make quick work of the jungle *and* the Nips, sir."

Griffin looked annoyed, "Lieutenant Thorpe, we'll make do with what we have on hand. Armor has been deemed ineffective in this kind of jungle fighting." Thorpe sat down, chagrined. "If there are no more questions?" He looked around and when no one raised a hand, nodded. "Okay. Dismissed."

Small conversations broke out as the men stood and made to rejoin their men and tell them the happy news that they'd be working all night and attacking in the morning.

Winkleman shook his head as he followed Tarkington, "Should we tell command how effective those Stuart tanks were in the jungles of Luzon?"

Tarkington grumbled, "Lot of good that'd do coming from a couple of lowly sergeants. Besides—like you said—they've gotta learn how to fight the Japs all over again. Our experience means nothing to them."

Winkleman rubbed the back of his neck, "Sad but true."

The Reconnaissance Squad sat out that night's jungle-hacking mission. Winkleman figured it was either because they'd lost over half of Team One, or because they'd saved so many wounded GIs from certain death, but Tarkington was more cynical. "Probably saving us to lead the charge through the plantation," he grumbled.

They lay in their shallow foxholes and listened to the sounds of the jungle. Occasionally, the crackling of rifle and machine gun fire would cause the insects and night animals to pause for an instant.

Henry, laying a few yards away from Tarkington, stated, "Sure reminds me of Luzon."

Tarkington agreed, "It's like we've gone back in time." Faces of men he'd served with flashed through his head and he realized none of them were still alive. Or—if they were—probably wished they weren't.

Henry mused, "You think Duropa Plantation's as wide open as they say it is?"

Tarkington answered, "I think the Japs're sitting in their concealed bunkers looking over their cleared-out fields of fire just waiting for us."

Henry sighed and spit out the blade of grass he was chewing on, "Me too, Tark. Me too."

The whistling sound of an incoming mortar round made them turn onto their stomachs and bury their faces in the mud. Someone from Team One yelled, "Incoming!" but Tarkington was sure his men were already under cover. The shell landed behind them and exploded, making the ground quiver. The sound was muffled, more like a pop than a boom. Four more shells landed spewing debris, but the mud mostly absorbed the shrapnel.

Silence and smoke swept over them. Tarkington got onto his elbows, the top of his steel pot dripping with chunks of mud. "Well, at least the soft ground helps us with those things."

Henry nodded, "Sure be nice if we had some of those too."

Tarkington answered, "We do. I saw 'em being carried up by native porters. Sixty-millimeter tubes. Problem's this canopy doesn't allow for a lot of shooting. Japs have had time to clear their areas out."

A shot from a foxhole forty yards away made them look that direction. It came from the 4th Squad on their left flank. Another shot, followed with the distinctive pop of a grenade blast. The brief flash of light momentarily blinded Tarkington. He shook his head, "What the hell are they doing over there?"

Someone's distant voice yelled, "Take that, you cocksuckers!"

Henry drawled, "Shooting at shadows, no doubt."

"Normally I'd check it out, but I'm liable to get shot by friendlies with these uppity bastards."

Henry agreed, "Yeah. Let 4th Squad deal with 4th Squad."

"If the Nips didn't know where we were before, they sure as hell do now."

Henry's voice was low, "They know exactly where we are, Tark. Can't you feel 'em? They've got their eyes on us."

Tarkington looked sidelong at the dim silhouette of his lead scout. "That your sixth sense?"

Henry nodded, "Yep. They know exactly what we're up to. I expect they'll have a nice welcoming party for us in the morning."

They called the rest of Baker Company up at 0830. Able and remnants of Baker Company had rotated by squads all night and finally managed to cut a narrow path through the jungle and out onto the plantation. As the Reconnaissance Squad passed through their rear guard, the exhausted GIs scowled at them, upset that they hadn't been included in the night's fun and games.

Stollman muttered, "They look like shit."

Vick nodded, "I heard they hacked their way through with shovels, mostly."

Stollman shook his head, "Typical army horseshit. Hell, one big tractor would've done the job in an hour."

At the entrance to the narrow tunnel, Lt. Branson stopped them. A few GIs from less-damaged squads had transferred to Team One. Staff Sergeant Clanson looked about as happy to be leading them as a kid tasked with cleaning horse manure behind a ten-mile long parade of cavalry.

Branson ordered, "The way through is clear. I want your squad leading Second Platoon. Patrol 100 yards out and wait for the rest of us to fill in behind you." Staff Sergeant Clanson nodded and looked nervously at Tarkington. Clanson was in overall command of the twelve-man squad, but Tarkington was in command of his own men. At first it had rankled Clanson, and he'd complained mightily, but after yesterday his attitude had changed dramatically. "Go slow," Branson continued, "and be careful. I don't want anyone getting too far ahead and being cut off."

Clanson's voice cracked, "Yes, sir. Is—is there any artillery?"

"Not for us. They're going to shell the airfields, make them think we're pushing on them again. New radios are coming but we haven't seen 'em yet, so use runners." Clanson swallowed hard against a dry throat. Branson pushed him toward the hole in the wall of jungle, "Get going, and good luck."

Entering the tunnel was like entering a green worm's mouth. It was dark, with only pinpricks of light shining through. Shredded vines and creepers hung from the ceiling and pushed from the sides, brushing their shoulders and exposed necks like licking serpent tongues. The ground was soft, muddy, and littered with freshly cut branches and vines. In spots, it appeared that the jungle was already reclaiming the area, closing in, making them squeeze past by turning sideways.

Team One was in front. There was little danger while inside the tunnel, except from scraping thorns and angry bug bites. The tunnel seemed to go on forever, leading from one hellscape to the next.

When they finally neared the end, the tunnel widened. There were no longer as many hack marks, and the vines and creepers gave way to more widely spaced trees. The darkness inside the tunnel lightened as larger shafts of light penetrated the gloom. Tarkington couldn't help the lingering feeling of doom.

Team One slowed and spread out. Tarkington moved to Clanson's side and whispered in his ear, "We'll take point." Yesterday, Clanson would've fought the suggestion bitterly, but today he crouched and let Team Two pass silently by.

Henry and Raker took point and they moved through the towering palms slowly. The undergrowth was thick, but nothing like the jungle. They weaved between fallen palms. Some had been down for years, victims of age and wind, others were freshly cut. Off to the right, through a half-acre of leaning trees, the sea sparkled. Off to the left, the shrieking sounds of artillery pasting the airfields began. This time, the barrage continued for long minutes. The two 25-pounders were woefully inadequate for the job at hand, but at least it was better than the measly strike the day before.

Tarkington moved slowly, his eyes alternating between the treetops and the ground. Command had been correct, the terrain was much easier to move through, but he was sure it was going to be just as deadly as the close-in jungle. He didn't need Henry's sixth sense to warn him; he could sense the danger himself. The anticipation was palpable and sweat poured off him. His nerve endings sizzled.

Henry held up an open palm and went into a crouch at the same instant Raker did. Tarkington and the others immediately followed suit. It took Clanson and his men a few seconds to realize they'd stopped, and they nearly ran into them.

Tarkington glared back at Clanson's wide eyes. Tarkington pointed forward and signaled danger ahead, then signaled him to go prone.

Clanson passed it on and the team did so noisily. He recognized the soldier beside Clanson was the only other GI who'd come out unscathed from the fighting the day before, Private Mohr. They were dangerously close together. One grenade would take them all out, but there was nothing he could do about that now. Mohr's eyes were wide as plates and darted side to side, searching for the enemy. Tarkington heard a high-pitched moan escape his lips. Tarkington kicked him, getting the terrified soldier's attention. He put his finger over his mouth, signaling him to shut up. The soldier stared back—hyperventilating. *Green as grass,* Tarkington sighed.

Henry inched his way backwards and Tarkington pushed forward to meet him. Henry lifted his chin, "Bunker. 100 yards."

Tarkington nodded and looked past him. He saw what he was looking for. To anyone not familiar, the palm looked like any other fallen tree; however, there were no roots and no top. The thick trunk had been cut and put into place. They'd draped vines and branches over it, but the foliage was a slightly different color than the surrounding greenery. Either the cover was uprooted and dying or they were seeing the underside of the disturbed plants and leaves. There was no doubt to his trained eyes: it was a bunker. It was tucked a few yards into a thicket of jungle. The area leading to the bunker was cleared out.

They lay in the last decent cover. It was obvious to Tarkington that the 100-plus yards in front of them was a killing ground. He scanned the area surrounding the bunker, sure there must be more than one. It didn't take long before he spotted another anomaly off to the right. A low mound with a barely discernible corner. He pointed at it and whispered to Henry, "Something there."

Henry saw it immediately and nodded. "Probably more, and these palms are perfect for sniping. Hell, we've probably already passed a few. You know how they are."

Tarkington turned to Clanson, "Send word back. We see multiple bunkers. See if we can get some artillery on them. I'll adjust their fire from here."

Clanson tapped Private Mohr. He'd heard the entire conversation. "You get all that? Go!" The kid just stared back, glued to the safety of the ground. He shook his head slightly, refusing to move. Clanson's own fear evaporated in the face of outright disobedience. He seethed low, "Get off your ass and do what I tell you, boy." He still didn't move. Clanson's face reddened and he reached for his sidearm. That did it. The kid pushed backwards a few feet then got to his feet and started running.

Tarkington said, "Stay down," but the kid was off to the races, weaving and leaping downed trees like an Olympic steeple chaser. The adrenaline had taken over and the fight-or-flight instinct was heavily weighted toward flight.

A shot rang out and the tree beside Mohr's head shredded. The plume of smoke from the rifle shot was off to their left and behind them slightly. Raker saw it and swung his carbine, but before he could line up and fire, the sniper's rifle barked again and this time the bullet center-punched Private Mohr in the back and sent him sprawling headfirst into the base of a stout 125-foot palm. He crumpled. Raker emptied half his magazine and the sniper's body fell from a nearby treetop. They felt the body impact even from fifty yards away.

The brief exchange got the attention of the Japanese in the bunkers, and two Nambu machine guns opened fire. Bullets thunked into palm trees and sliced overhead. Tarkington rolled to the base of a palm that vibrated with impacts.

He leaned out and fired his Thompson toward the bunker he'd seen. He rolled back and a bullet from his right thunked into the palm an inch over his head. He spotted a flash of movement, a helmeted head ducking into the ground. He knew what it meant. "They've got spider holes!" he bellowed. He readjusted his aim and fired at the spot.

Henry, seeing where he was firing, pushed his way backwards to the front of an old fallen log. He lunged over it, scooted right, and came up with his carbine aimed. Tarkington spent the rest of his 20-round magazine and went to reload, all the while watching the hole.

Before he could reload, the head appeared again and the rifle barrel was leveling. Henry fired three rounds and the enemy soldier's head came apart and he dropped out of sight. The Nambus continued firing but the GIs were in good cover. After a few minutes, they stopped their incessant chatter and the jungle was quiet. Tarkington noticed the dull thumps of artillery from the airfield had stopped and the chatter of a firefight took its place.

From behind, he heard Lt. Branson hollering, "What's going on up there, dammit? Report!"

Tarkington's men weren't watching the distant bunkers but the treetops and surrounding jungle. There'd be more snipers and more spider holes. Winkleman called out, "No casualties except that stupid kid."

Tarkington got Clanson's attention, "Send another runner to Branson."

Clanson nodded and thumped the private to his right who was almost laying on top of him. He barked, "Tell Lieutenant Branson there're bunkers and snipers in the area. Tell him we need artillery support." The kid nodded and pushed his way backward. "And for God's sake, stay down!"

As they waited and watched, the sounds of battle from the New Strip intensified and became one constant stream of small arms fire. The Nambus to their front stayed quiet, unable to see their positions. There were no more surprises from dug-in or treetop snipers, but they had no illusions that they weren't still out there and close. Finally, word came forward for them to move back and join Baker and Able Company, who'd apparently made it through the tunnel successfully and had spread out.

It annoyed Tarkington. "Guess this means we won't be spotting artillery."

Stollman grinned, "I think they're trying to conserve. You know how much each one of those shells cost?"

Vick guffawed, "Do you?"

Stollman shrugged, "More'n you and I are worth, apparently."

They pushed back, keeping their intervals wide and their eyes peeled. Tarkington passed the base of the palm tree that Mohr had crashed into. It was stained dark red. The body had been removed, but the evidence of his passing would remain until the next rain.

Once they were fifty yards back, they saw the sallow cheeks and heavy eyes of exhausted GIs staring back at them. They looked about as ready to assault the Jap position as Winkleman was to tightrope over the Grand Canyon.

20

Baker and Able Companies pulled back as far as they could go without re-entering the tunnel. There was a smattering of shots, mostly soldiers shooting at shadows. The fire from the airfields continued, but not with the intensity from earlier.

Two hours had passed since the brief firefight with the bunkers and not much had happened. Lt. Branson came forward to their hastily dug positions and sat beside their shallow holes. The heat was oppressive, wet, and humid.

"We've been ordered to assault through the Jap positions," Branson's voice was low, almost apologetic.

Tarkington looked at the mud he sat in, "Any chance of artillery?" Branson shook his head. "Any word from the airfield? They've been going at it for a while now."

Branson sighed, "They've made no headway. They've run into bunkers, same as us. Command wants us to assault and take pressure off them."

Tarkington said, "We can sneak close, maybe close enough for grenades."

Branson shook his head, "They've ordered a general advance."

Winkleman shook his head, "Like the Great War? They want us to go over the top? Didn't we learn lessons there?" He added "Sir," as an afterthought.

Branson's face reddened, "Can it, Sergeant. We're not charging, for Christ's sake; we're advancing to contact. We'll maneuver once we know the situation better."

"Yes, sir," Winkleman muttered.

Branson looked at his watch and tapped the glass face, then put it to his ear, "Damned thing's stopped working. We shove off in fifteen minutes."

He moved off to relay the orders to the other squads. Staff Sergeant Clanson ran his hands through his dirty hair, which was well past regulation length. "We're just gonna walk into the teeth of the beast?"

Tarkington answered, "Move slow, keep your eyes on the treetops, and watch out for spider holes. Expect them to attack from any direction. They'll let you walk right on by then shoot you in the back."

Clanson shook his head, "But that's suicide. Surely the Nips won't make it back to their lines doing that."

Tarkington nodded sagely, "That's how they fight. That's why they're so damned tough to kill. They don't think the same way you and I do. Dying for the Emperor's an honor and a privilege."

"They sound like fanatics."

Henry chimed in, tilting his head and rubbing his chin, "It's more like an intensity. They fight with an intensity you've never seen before."

Tarkington nodded his agreement, "That's a good way of saying it. We've been fighting them for nearly a year and they're deadly, but they can be beat—you just have to match their intensity."

Clanson slapped a bloated mosquito off the back of his neck, "We were told they were just yellow monkeys—barely human."

Tarkington shook his head, "Well, those 'yellow monkeys' have taken over half the globe in less than a year. Don't underestimate them. It'll be the last mistake you ever make."

They moved forward slowly in a staggered line. Everyone knew where the bunkers were but the danger this far back was from snipers. This went against everything the squad knew about fighting the Japanese. They'd much rather have snuck in close under the cover of darkness and killed them in their bunkers, but that idea had been tabled without serious consideration—so here they were, marching into a known ambush.

Able Company was spread to their left. There was still sporadic firing from the airstrip region. Tarkington's head was on a swivel. Their only chance was to see the snipers before the snipers saw them, but they were at a tremendous disadvantage. The snipers would simply pick out the best target and whoever it happened to be would be hit. It was a game of chance and rubbed them the wrong way.

The squad stayed low and used the available cover, keeping trees between them and the bunker positions. Hopefully, it would be enough to keep them from being targeted. Tarkington seethed; this was a waste of good men.

The tension broke with a shot, followed instantly with an anguished scream off to the right. It sent them to the ground. Relief flooded Tarkington. It wasn't one of his men screaming. He felt shame at the thought, but there was no time to dwell on it. He tucked himself into the base of a palm and closed his eyes for a moment.

"Sniper!" Someone yelled. "McGunty's hit bad. Medic!"

Tarkington looked right, catching Henry's eye. Henry shook his head. He hadn't spotted the sniper. There was a smattering of fire from Third Squad as the medic raced forward, leaping and dodging. Another shot rang out and the ground behind the medic erupted in dirt. Tarkington shifted his search farther right, where he thought the shot came from. Henry had his carbine up and aimed but he didn't fire.

Tarkington leaned out from the tree and fired off a short burst with the Thompson, shredding a nearby treetop. Henry and Winkleman fired at different trees. Soon the entire platoon was firing. The medic slid in beside the wounded soldier. The screaming subsided to moaning.

Branson yelled, "Keep moving forward. Go!"

Tarkington cursed under his breath. He waved the others forward, "I'll cover you. Move up." He rolled away from the palm and hosed the treetops with .45 caliber lead. Tark's Ticks moved up, leapfrogging and staying low.

Tarkington spent his magazine. "Reloading!" He rolled back and quickly swapped out magazines.

Winkleman yelled, "We gotcha covered, Tark." A smattering of .30 caliber shots from the carbines and Tarkington got to his feet and ran toward the next bit of cover. Two strides and he leaped toward a fallen log. A bullet whizzed past his ear. A phantom pain in his head throbbed where he'd been shot months before. *That's new*, he noted. The long-healed scar across his temple throbbed. He hadn't thought about the wound in weeks. He'd often catch GIs from other units staring—then he'd remember the near miss. Was his subconscious trying to tell him something? The scar near his belly was far worse and it sometimes ached, too.

A flurry of M1 shots from the right followed by a triumphant yell, "I got him! I got him!"

Tarkington exchanged glances with his men and they shook their heads, reminded once again how green these soldiers were. In their jubilation, men got to their feet and moved forward quickly. Too quickly—too exposed. Another shot rang out and this time it wasn't from the treetops. The unmistakable sound of lead hitting meat was immediately followed with screaming. More yelling and firing. The ping of used-up M1 clips filled the air.

Vick fired from the left. Tarkington turned in time to see a Japanese soldier drop out of sight. They had spider holes on either side of them. Vick had kept watching his sector despite the action to the right, and it had saved his life. With threats coming from everywhere, they formed a loose perimeter.

The ground ten yards in front of him suddenly moved. A hatch opened, and peeking out was a rifle barrel and a helmeted Japanese soldier. Tarkington fired nearly point-blank. He could hardly see through the smoke, but knew he hadn't missed. He was too close. But were there more?

He lunged to his feet, took a step, and launched himself toward the hole. The hatch had fallen shut. He found the edge, lifted it with his left hand, put the barrel of the Thompson inside, and fired on full automatic, sweeping side to side. He flipped the trapdoor open all the way and waited for movement. The others pushed forward, matching his move. Inside, he saw the crumpled, bloody soldier. He left the lid open and yelled, "Only big enough for one." The others nodded and continued pushing forward.

Another ten yards and the machine guns opened fire from multiple directions. Tarkington and the others were already hugging the ground, pulling themselves into the narrow safety of palms and any slight depressions they found. The air over their heads was alive with pops, snaps, and thunks. Men from other sections yelled out, some hit.

"Move up!" yelled Branson, but no one was moving. Every attempt was met with near misses or men getting hit.

Tarkington hunkered as low as he could go. The palm tree near him was pulped and shredded with bullet scars. He looked for Branson and saw him ten yards back, waving men behind him forward. Some moved, but most acted as though they hadn't heard.

Tarkington pushed back, and when he was close enough, yelled, "If we're gonna do this, we need suppressing fire and smoke. Where's the damned Brownings and mortars?"

Branson crawled a few feet forward and they faced each other as bullets whizzed over their heads. Branson had to yell to be heard, "Radio's on the fritz again! I'll send a runner to the mortar crews."

Tarkington nodded, "Forget HE, make it smoke." He pointed back over his shoulder, "There's a bunker 150 yards over there. Smoke screen it out and we can advance and take it out. And get the damned Brownings going. We need their firepower."

Branson nodded; it was sound tactical advice. He sent one runner who crawled out of sight, then another in a different direction. Tarkington turned back toward his men. The wall of lead just overhead continued. He could hear occasional rifle cracks as GIs tried to find targets.

Branson yelled at his back, "When the smoke comes, I want you and Clanson's squad suppressing the bunker you saw." Tarkington glanced back and nodded. Branson yelled to men on his right, "First and Third Squads, get ready to bound. Wait for the smoke and the .30 cals to open up."

Tarkington tucked into the base of the palm and peered through a gap in the foliage. The bunker was barely visible. He couldn't see muzzle flashes, gun smoke, or tracer rounds, but he was sure one of the enemy machine guns was firing from there. He couldn't help but admire how well the Japanese had camouflaged their defenses. He was sure there were many more bunkers he couldn't see. The bunkers were configured to support one another, and once one was taken out, there'd be a whole new problem to contend with, but they had to start somewhere.

Minutes passed and finally the distinctive popping and whistling of mortar shells was overhead. The first few were high-explosive rounds. Tarkington shook his head as they landed well short and did nothing but stir up mud. He seethed inside, but the next few rounds landed and smoke slowly hissed out and blanketed the area in a thin layer of white smoke. It didn't look nearly thick enough, but it was better than nothing. The hammering of .30 caliber Browning machine guns from his right and left opened up.

Branson yelled, "Move up First and Third!"

Clanson yelled, "Covering fire!"

Tarkington rolled from cover and aimed through the smoke where he guessed the bunker was. The enemy machine gun fire slowed to short bursts. His Thompson wasn't good at this range, but perhaps—if nothing else—he'd draw their attention. Men bounded forward. The pops of carbines and M1s accompanied their movement. The bounding GIs stayed low but moved fast, using the cover of the palms. They'd made fifteen yards when there was more machine gun fire from a different section of jungle.

Men fell as bullets slammed into them from the left. Tarkington and the rest of the Reconnaissance Squad shifted their fire, pouring lead toward the new machine gun position. The smoke dissipated and the original two enemy machine guns joined in and the air was alive with bullets. They stopped the short advance cold.

Tarkington yelled, "Clanson! Do you see where that's coming from?"

Clanson was curled up, reloading his Thompson. His face was white and beads of clammy sweat sparkled on his nose. With shaking hands, he finally positioned the new magazine and slammed it into place. He shook his head, his eyes like saucers. The tree stump behind him splintered with bullet impacts and Clanson gritted his teeth, cringed, and shook.

Tarkington could tell he was about to lose his composure. "Get your men firing left!" he yelled. He looked behind him, "Branson, we need more smoke!"

Branson yelled something back that Tarkington didn't understand, but he could tell by his body language that that request would not happen. The Browning's staccato hammering died down to bursts and finally stopped. Over the din of incoming fire, someone yelled, "Gun's jammed!"

Tarkington shook his head in disgust. Large barrels of gun oil had been sent forward but there was no way to get the weapon-saving oil to the men who needed it in small containers, so the weapons weren't being cleaned and oiled, causing them to malfunction and jam frequently. He was thankful his men still had a good supply of personal gun oil stowed ingeniously in the stocks of their carbines. Unfortunately, they didn't have nearly enough to share.

The sound of incoming mortar shells combined with the din of machine gun fire. He glanced skyward through the swaying treetops of the palms and yelled, "Incoming! Flatten!"

His men were already as low as possible, but other GIs were still trying to get shots on the bunkers. The first explosion landed behind the main line. There was screaming and he glanced back, seeing a soldier getting to his feet and staggering. The left side of his face was smoldering and he stumbled aimlessly. His chest erupted as Japanese bullets ripped into him and he crumpled.

The mortars continued walking their way back and forth. Many exploded on the angled palm tree trunks, bringing many of them crashing down on the GIs' heads. Tarkington was tucked as close to the base of the palm tree as he could get, waiting for the shell that would shred him.

After long minutes, the bombardment finally stopped. The withering machine gun fire stopped too and Tarkington wondered if they'd attack. He rolled from cover and searched for the bunker he'd spotted earlier, but everything looked different. Trees were down and smoke wafted everywhere. He couldn't find the bunker again. He peered over the sights of his Thompson waiting for the attack, but it never came.

Winkleman, ten yards to Tarkington's right, took his eyes off his sights, "Guess they're content to sit back and cut us down from the bunkers."

Tarkington's ears rang, but he nodded, "No reason to come at us. They'll do a hell of a lot more damage this way."

Winkleman nodded, "We need artillery, air support, and armor."

Tarkington shook his head, "None of which we're likely to get."

A few bursts from the left machine gun kept their heads down. Wounded men moaned in agony. The only movement was medics crawling from man to man, trying to make a difference. A single shot rang out and someone yelled, "Sniper, ten o'clock." There was a smattering of fire, but no one called out triumphantly this time.

From behind, the call to pull back came. Some men were still forward, pinned down. Tarkington yelled to them, "Stay put. I've got one smoke grenade left." Tarkington pulled it off his belt, pulled the pin, and hurled it as far as he could. It sputtered and fizzed and failed to spew the covering smoke, but the GIs moved anyway and the MGs opened fire with gusto. The Reconnaissance Squad fired into the green abyss—it was enough to throw off the enemy gunner's aim, and the trapped GIs made it back to the main line unscathed.

They moved back fifteen yards, ceding the ground they'd gained with so much blood. Staying forward in the bullseye made little sense. Soon the order to dig in came and the GIs did the best they could to scrape out depressions in the mud while lying flat.

Tarkington left the men to dig and made his way back on his belly to the relative safety fifty yards back. He found Lt. Branson and the other officers of the platoon talking, looking as dejected and beaten as a winless football team having to play the best team in the league.

He saw a group of NCOs huddled behind a makeshift stack of palm logs and joined them. Earlier, they hadn't accepted Tarkington as being one of their own, thinking he held his combat experience over their heads too much, but now they'd been christened in fire and made room for him.

Clanson was among them. His hands still shook as he offered Tarkington his canteen. Tarkington took a long swig and handed it back. Clanson shook his head, "What now?"

Tarkington shook his head and sat down, propping his Thompson between his mud-caked boots and tipping his helmet back, exposing the puckered scar. "Hopefully something better than another frontal attack."

They had to cower as another three-round volley of mortar shells landed. Sergeant Collinsworth shook his head, "Artillery support would go a long way."

The crackle and fire from the airstrip region picked up in tempo and Clanson muttered, "Hear they're getting it even worse than we are. Japs sitting across the airfield, dug in tight with all the approaches covered. Least here, we've got these trees for cover."

Platoon Sergeant Donaldson made his way over to them. His bow-legged waddle from riding horses most of his life was unmistakable. "Spread out, you nut sacks. One damn grenade would take you all out and that'd be a shame." He squinted at Tarkington as though to say he should know better. He was right, but he wasn't going to move yet.

Donaldson crouched, adjusting the Thompson slung over his shoulder. He had a drawl which was hard to place, not quite southern. If Tarkington had to classify it, he'd say it was a cross between Texas and Hicksville. "We've taken a beating over the last few days." He picked at his boots, flicking mud off. "As of now, we're staying put until we can get replacements. We'll dig in here and attack again when we're ready. Expect more friendly artillery and air strikes. There's a few Mitchells that are gonna paste Buna along with this plantation tomorrow morning, so keep your heads down."

Tarkington said, "What we need's armor."

Donaldson tilted his head back, "That's one thing we don't have. Command thought the ground was too soft and the jungle too thick. Apparently, there was an entire platoon of Stuarts slated for this fight, but they got sent last minute over to some shithole called Guadalcanal." He spit a stream of black tobacco and continued, "I heard the Aussies are trying to get us a few of those armored Lewis gun trucks. But who the hell knows? For now, we'll dig in and wait for orders."

21

Two days later, Tarkington and his Ticks were well forward of their lines. The night before, after watching hopelessly off-target bombing runs and artillery barrages destroy vast swaths of empty jungle, Tarkington and Winkleman convinced Lt. Branson to let them move forward and adjust the fire onto the targets via radio.

Now they were a mere fifty yards from a line of bunkers connected by ingeniously disguised trench systems. They occasionally saw the tops of enemy troop's heads moving through them. They could see three distinct bunkers. The nearest trench was only twenty yards away. It snaked into the jungle, no doubt leading to another line of bunkers farther back and probably extending all the way to the airstrip.

Tarkington whispered into the handset of SCR-536. "This is Owl Six. Drop 40." They'd brought two radios and three batteries. Radios hadn't been reliable, but they had experience with them on Luzon and felt confident that with a few tricks, they could keep them operational.

There was an immediate tinny response, "Roger. Relaying drop 40." The GI would relay the correction to the Australian crew firing the 25-pounders from the rear. The low arc and quick fuses of the artillery shells were better suited for desert environs, but it was all they had. There were howitzers in the hills but the ammo for them was still stuck in Port Moresby.

The smoke from the first 25-pounder shell was still wafting through the trees when another shriek of incoming artillery made them duck. The explosion wasn't impressive, barely causing any damage to the ground or the bunkers. "Left 20," he hissed. Another minute passed before the next shell landed and this time it was right on top of the farthest bunker.

Tarkington squinted through his heavily shaded binoculars. One flash of sunlight off the lens would give away their position and they were too far out to make it back if they came under fire. The artillery crew had landed a perfect shot, but the only damage he could see was a scorch mark along the side. He whispered, "On target. Keep 'em coming."

Now both 25-pounders fired and every twenty seconds, shells landed on and near the bunker. Tarkington watched helmeted Japanese leaving the bunker. They used the trench to move to the middle bunker, which was bigger than the other two. He marked it on his map as a possible underground barracks or holding area. Perhaps it was an ammo dump.

The other team members were spread out in a loose perimeter. Tarkington knew where they were and still had trouble picking them out from their surroundings. If the Japanese got wise to their spotting, and he knew the suddenly accurate fire would tip them off soon enough, they'd have to trip over them to find them.

He watched two more shells land on top of the bunker before he called in another correction, "Shift left 15." There were still a few soldiers coming from the bunker and he hoped to score a hit on the trench and maybe get some payback. A minute later, a single shell landed and he smiled in grim satisfaction, hearing screams. "On target." Twenty seconds later, more shells bracketed the trench. The next two landed inside it and there were more agonized screams.

The radio crackled, "That's all they've got. They're asking how they did."

"Got 'em hollerin'. Good job. Out," he whispered.

They didn't move from their position, but watched the bunkers and trenches. The 25-pounders had clearly caused damage; there was a flurry of activity and Tarkington spied men helping wounded. The plan was to stay in position until dark, then crawl back to their lines. That was the only part of the mission that gave Tarkington the willies. Getting back to their own lines without being shot by an uppity sentry was a risky proposition.

As the day progressed, the heat and humidity intensified. Tarkington took a swallow from his canteen. He'd propped it near his head for easy access.

Since the shelling, the Japanese had filtered from the center bunker to the other two. He suspected they were preparing for a follow-on attack. When one didn't come, would they send soldiers out to find the mystery spotters?

The day slipped to evening. Tarkington flexed first one foot then the other, trying to maintain blood flow to his legs. His muscles felt tight and he desperately wanted to stand up and stretch. Just a few more hours until dark.

The communication line wrapped loosely around his ankle tugged and he looked left, seeing Raker staring into the greenery beyond their position. He'd sent the signal, but he'd gotten it from someone else. It wasn't a mistake; someone was coming. Tarkington felt the steel of the Thompson beneath his hand. Their best chance was to stay hidden and avoid contact. Using their weapons would be the last resort.

He didn't move his head, didn't search for the threat, but stayed perfectly still. He heard a stick crunch beneath a boot. They were coming from the left. More small sounds of soldiers trying to move with stealth marked their progress. They were getting closer. His chin rested on the soft ground. It had sunk into the mud, nearly to his mouth. Insects and worms inched their way across his half-buried body but he barely noticed them. They were simply a part of the job.

From the corner of his eye, he caught movement. He concentrated on his breathing—slow and steady. He was suddenly acutely aware of the need to blink. He shut his eyes, concentrating on the sounds of oncoming enemy soldiers. He opened his eyes slowly and caught the movement again. It was just a lighter green against the darker green. The soldier was only yards away, moving then stopping. Motion behind the Japanese soldier caught his attention. Was he the lead element or was there more coming from the right?

Tarkington rehearsed what he'd do if they discovered him. His knife was sheathed on the left side of his belt, buried beneath a foot of mud and soil. He'd roll right, freeing his hip, quickly draw it with his right hand, and drive it into the soldier. It would be loud and sudden and would probably alert the other soldiers, but it was better than firing and giving away their positions. This close to the bunkers, the machine guns would tear them up.

The Japanese soldier took a careful step and stopped. He was three feet away and directly in front of Tarkington. He could smell his body odor—it differed from his own stench, which he hoped was muted by the dirt covering most of his body. He stared at the soldier's muddy boots as they slowly sank into the mud. He didn't dare lift his head. He wondered if the soldier was about to lunge his bayonet into his back. Would he have enough time to stop it? How would it feel?

The soldier lifted his right foot and the sound of sucking mud seemed louder than normal. Tarkington's heightened senses were working overtime, exaggerating every little detail. His ears pounded with rushing blood and he worked to keep the adrenaline from making his body shake. The soldier took two more careful steps, then crouched. He was to Tarkington's right, only feet away. He wanted to hold his breath. But how long would he need to hold it? He forced slow breathing and fought the nearly overpowering urge to look up. *I am the jungle. I am the earth.* The phrase popped into his head and he remembered it was something Sgt. Clive, one of their Alamo trainers, told them to recite when an enemy was close.

The soldier stood and took another squelching step. Tarkington nearly erupted from concealment when he heard a sudden commotion. At first, he thought it was one of his men attacking, but when there were no follow-up sounds, he realized one of the Japanese soldiers had tripped. The nearest man rebuked the clumsy soldier who got to his feet with the help of the man behind him. A whispered back and forth and finally the Japanese continued their patrol.

The third and final soldier moved past Tarkington. Stollman and Vick were to his right, but he felt sure if the Japanese hadn't seen them by now, they never would. He let himself relax a little.

His blood froze when the radio in his pack suddenly squelched. He thought he had turned it off and stowed it, but either he hadn't turned it off, or he'd inadvertently turned it on again while shoving it—either way, the Japanese immediately froze in place.

He decided in a flash. He tried to turn onto his side, but the weight of the mud and soil was more than he'd bargained for and his movement was slow. By the time he got his knife out, the nearest Japanese soldier was bringing his rifle to bear upon the ground, which had suddenly come alive.

Stollman and Vick erupted from the right and tackled the two lead soldiers, driving their knives into them before they could react. Tarkington had his knife out but knew he wouldn't get there in time. He was a dead man. A sudden flash from the left slammed into the third soldier. Through the grit and grime, Tarkington recognized Sgt. Bulkort's stout arm driving his knife into the stunned soldier over and over. It was messy and the soldier screamed in agony before Bulkort's knife finally severed his aorta, spilling his lifeblood quickly and silencing him forever. Bulkort lay upon the quivering body, the funnel of arterial blood flowed over his face and ran down his broad shoulders, as though immersed in a gory park fountain.

He tried to push off but Tarkington hissed, "Freeze." He looked beyond the carnage to the bunker and trenches. A heavy mist clung to the ground, cutting visibility, but he could still easily see the trench. At first, there was no reaction and Tarkington thought they'd gotten away with it, but then someone called out. The soldiers in the trench had heard them. Tarkington hissed, "We need to go back. Now."

They kept facing the Japanese lines and pushed their way backwards slowly, leaving the dead bodies. Every foot helped as the mists enfolded them. More insistent calls from the Japanese and Tarkington knew it was only a matter of time before they'd open fire.

He turned away from the bunkers and crawled faster. He risked being seen, but figured once the Japanese determined they would not hit their own men, they'd either send out more soldiers or cover the area with lead. Either way, the farther into the mists and the more palm trees they put between themselves and the Japanese, the better.

They'd made another fifteen yards when the Nambus opened fire. The GIs rolled to cover, tucking themselves into any nook and cranny they could find. The Japanese swept the entire area, unsure of their position. Bullets popped and snapped overhead. Tarkington figured they had another two hours before nightfall, but doubted the Japanese would allow them to slip away.

After thirty seconds of heavy fire, they settled into occasional bursts, trying to flush them out. The mists thinned as a hot breeze blew in from the sea. With the Japanese alerted, moving now would give away their position. Henry whistled low, getting everyone's attention. He pointed. A six-man patrol was leaving the trench line and sweeping forward in a well-spaced line. The machine gun in the center bunker continued to probe the jungle with short bursts, well away from the patrol.

Tarkington pulled the radio from the bag and found it turned on. He gave himself a silent rebuke but keyed the transmit button on the side. "Pappy. This is Owl Six. You copy? Over."

A few seconds passed before a welcome, tinny voice answered, "Roger Owl Six. You kick a hornet's nest up there? Over."

"Affirmative. Can those Aussies repeat last shots? Over."

"Checking. Over."

Five long minutes passed. The Japanese patrol was closer. They were searching the area to the left of their current position. They moved cautiously but not as slowly as the first patrol. The machine gun kept firing short bursts but was concentrating on the area away from the patrol and away from them. The GIs had their carbines up and aimed toward the advancing soldiers.

Finally, the radio squawked, "This is Pappy. Affirmative on fire mission. But only three rounds. Over."

Tarkington cursed under his breath but nodded. "Understood. Let me know when it's on the way. Over." He didn't wait for a response but hissed to the others, "Three arty rounds coming our way. When we hear 'em, take out as many Japs as possible and take off."

They adjusted their carbines. The Japanese were angling toward their initial positions. Soon they'd come across their dead comrades. Tarkington put the radio back in the bag but kept it turned on. He brought the stubby barrel of his Thompson up. The muted radio voice finally said, "Shot out."

Fifteen seconds later, the first shrieking shell arced overhead. The Japanese froze and looked up. The GIs opened fire. Tarkington didn't have a target, but sprayed the area with hot lead. The artillery shell slammed into the trench line. "Go!" he yelled and emptied the rest of his twenty rounds.

He turned his back and took off as the next two shells shook the ground. He watched his camouflaged men darting through the trees, using the fallen palms to launch from one to the next like gazelles.

The machine guns stopped firing as they cowered beneath the 25-pounder's brief barrage. By the time they resumed their deadly work, the GIs were another forty yards back and almost out of sight. Bullets lanced after them and they threw themselves to the ground, crawling the rest of the way back to their lines.

Staff Sergeant Tarkington wasn't back from the spotter patrol more than an hour before Lieutenant Branson found his way to his foxhole. The remnants of daylight were receding quickly. Tarkington had laid down a thick layer of fallen palm fronds in an attempt to stay dry.

Branson commented, "This isn't half bad. Better than sitting in the mud." He peered over the stack of fallen palms into the gloom. "Didn't expect you back so soon."

"We ran into some trouble. Or more like it ran into us."

He kept his voice low, "Donaldson told me your mission was a success."

Tarkington nodded, "We got close enough to call in accurate fire. Donaldson give you the map I marked up?"

Branson nodded, "Yes. Very helpful. Your men okay?"

"Yes, sir. They're fine."

There was a long pause and Tarkington wondered what was on his mind. Branson finally said, "Look. I know everything you warned us about has come true. The Japs aren't weak, we're facing a hell of a lot more of 'em than we thought, and they're going to fight to the death for this godforsaken sliver of coastline. Our quick victory has turned into a slog and we've only just begun. Every front, including the Aussies west of the river, are running into the same defenses: bunkers with interlocking fields of fire and trenches."

Tarkington nodded grimly, "They won't surrender. These frontal attacks won't work. They're dug in too well."

"I think you're right, but command wants us to try again tomorrow afternoon. There's going to be a bombing run midmorning, which is going to run from the coastline to the airstrips along the line of bunkers you marked on the map."

Tarkington frowned, "We're awful close for that sort of thing, aren't we?"

Branson nodded, "We'll move back through the tunnel, then come back through afterwards."

Tarkington shrugged, "Okay. I'll tell the men." Branson didn't need to tell him this in person and his presence was making him uncomfortable. "Is there something else, sir?"

Branson tore himself away from staring into the gloom and looked at Tarkington's scarred temple in the dying light. He bit his lower lip as though weighing his next words. He tore a leaf in half, "You've fought these bastards before. Command has ignored your suggestions and insights. You must feel like you're reinventing the wheel."

Tarkington scowled, not sure where this was going. "A little, yes."

"How would you suggest fighting them? I mean, if you were in command, what would your strategy be?"

"Let 'em rot out here. Cordon them off from resupply and let 'em starve."

Branson shook his head, "That's not gonna happen. The Aussies caught too much hell up the Kokoda Trail. Everyone wants payback. Assuming that's off the table. What then?"

Tarkington didn't hesitate, "Guerrilla warfare. Sneak in close and cut their throats at night, same thing they do to us. Booby trap their bodies. Set timed charges and let 'em filter back in to the ground we took and watch 'em blow up. Keep 'em off balance all the time. Keep 'em awake and scared. After a week or more of that, these frontal attacks might just work."

Branson blew out a long breath, "That's brutal, Sergeant."

Tarkington nodded slowly, "Yep, and that's exactly what we need to be. If there's one lesson we've learned, it's not to underestimate their brutality."

He sighed then continued, his voice lower, "It's ugly but effective. They don't fight by any rules. Why should we?"

Branson was introspective, "Where did these people come from? How'd they get this way?"

"That's a question I'll never know the answer to, sir."

Branson clapped him on the shoulder as though they were old pals. In the darkness, Branson couldn't see his scowl deepen. Branson said, "I'll pass your suggestion to the captain. He's impressed with you men and he'll pass it up the line, but I don't think much'll come from it." He got to his feet and took a few steps toward the rear.

"No, sir. I don't either—not enough lives have been lost yet." Branson stopped and turned, ready to rebuke him, but thought better of it and disappeared into the gloom.

Henry's foxhole was only a few yards away. His outline was barely visible. Foxholes dotted the area every ten to fifteen yards. Normally, there were two men per hole, allowing one to sleep while the other stood watch. But, despite being reinforced, the company still wasn't at full strength, so tonight, everyone would need to stay awake.

Henry's Cajun drawl rolled across the couple of yards, "Lovely war we've got here, Tark."

22

They spent a sleepless night listening to a Japanese with terrible English language skills taunting them over a loudspeaker. *"You die, maline. You die."*

It was a new tactic which unnerved a few GIs, but Tarkington thought the mispronunciations were comical, and if he were going to be awake anyway, he may as well be entertained.

Someone answered the taunts, "We ain't marines, you asshole! We're soldiers!" The loudspeaker continued despite the correction.

Just before the sun rose, word came to leave a few soldiers forward at outposts while the rest of the company retreated through the tunnel. No one envied the men left behind, but they were assured they'd be relieved right after the bombing run.

All the traffic back and forth had widened the tunnel. It was wide enough to drive a truck through. *Or a tank,* Tarkington thought hopefully.

The company was glad to be off the line, but hoped the Japanese wouldn't notice and reinstall the snipers and infiltrators they'd paid so dearly to clear out. Branson assured them, "That's why we left the OPs. It's only for a few hours and we're staying in constant contact with them via land lines. If the Japs push, we'll move in again."

Winkleman whispered, "If they had confidence in the bombers hitting their target, they woulda left all of us up there. Glad I'm not one of those poor suckers on the OP watch."

They sat around for hours waiting to hear the bombers overhead. The weather wasn't perfect, but good enough for air operations. In fact, a Zero had already strafed the forward positions. Morning passed into afternoon and still no bombing run. Finally, just after 1400 hours, the low droning of bombers was overhead.

Branson stood peering through binoculars, scanning the partially cloudy sky. He finally pointed and shouted, "There they are!" He reminded Tarkington of a school-aged boy seeing a rocket ship.

Tarkington glanced up, squinting. He saw a formation passing in and out of cloud cover. They weren't very high—he figured 4,000 feet—and they seemed to be barely moving. Because of the clouds, he couldn't get an accurate count, but he saw at least six.

Branson kept up a rolling dialogue. "I—I can see their bomb bay doors opening." Seconds passed, "Here they come! I can see the bombs!"

Tarkington squinted; they seemed awful close, but perhaps it was an optical illusion. "Are they over the target?" he asked. The whistling of bombs falling through the air was loud. He'd been under many Japanese bombing runs and this sounded the same. He exchanged a glance with Henry and they both dove for cover. "Take cover! Take cover!" His men were already moving, diving for foxholes, trenches, and anything else they could find, but the rest just stood there staring upward.

The first bombs exploded in the ocean but marched closer and closer inland, shaking and rocking the ground. Everyone realized that the strike was much too far south. Everyone not already in cover scrambled as the bombs got marched ever closer.

Tarkington wished he had his steel pot instead of his soft cap, but realized if a 500-pound bomb exploded within thirty or forty yards of him, nothing much would help. The ground shook and the air sizzled with shrapnel and fire. Huge gouts of dirt and mud flew through the air and covered him and the hole he cowered inside under feet of debris. The weight on his back pushed him down and the sudden darkness was all-consuming. He fought to stay above it. He could feel the mud closing in around his mouth. Panic rose in his gut and he tried to push himself upward, desperately wanting to breathe, not caring about the deadly debris flying overhead like scythes.

The ground continued to shake and he felt himself rising through the mud. The weight forced his head down. He finally broke free, his head and shoulders erupting from the mud. He sucked in a desperate breath. His eyes wouldn't open, as they were sealed shut with dirt and mud. He struggled to free his arms and hands. He clawed gouts of mud from his eyes and squinted. The hole was brimmed with mud and dirt. More chunks of mud fell from his ears and the roar of bombs exploding was suddenly deafening, reminding him to keep his head down. He dropped back into the goo, as though it were a pond and there were a nearby fire. He waited for the ground to stop shaking before coming up for air.

He wiped the clots from his eyes and opened them cautiously. He desperately wanted to douse his head with water, but his canteen wasn't on his hip any longer.

He squinted: the blurry world was completely changed from only moments before. The bombing run had missed the Japanese by a large margin. The thick section of jungle they'd worked so hard to cut the tunnel through was now a jumble of burning, smoking ruin. There was no sign of the tunnel. Trees were uprooted, some cut in half, but none were intact. It was as though a giant, wielding a fiery sword, had cut his way through—or perhaps a meteor from outer space. Massive craters smoked and licking flames burned despite the massive chunks of wet mud, which continued to fall from the sky, blanketing the area.

Tarkington clawed the rest of the mud from his ears and eyes and pried himself out of the hole. He had to find his men. He tried to call out names, but he couldn't get his voice to work. One by one he saw heads poking up all around. Relief flooded through him as he recognized all his men. They were shaken, but like him, undamaged.

That wasn't the case for many others. Dazed men wandered the area, staggering like drunks on a Saturday night. One wandering soldier's arm was gone below the elbow as though cut off by a guillotine. Half his face was white, the rest mud-covered as though he wore a mask. He was looking around searching for something.

Tarkington swayed and croaked, "Dig 'em out. We've gotta dig 'em out."

His head pounded and he tasted mud and blood. He went to the nearest foxhole. He pulled downed limbs and huge clods of mud off and threw them to the side. The others joined him, gaining momentum as other men emerged and the shock of the nearby bomb strikes slowly wore off.

Hours later, after digging out countless men and moving tons of mud and debris, Lt. Branson told them that everyone was accounted for. Dead or alive. Some were simply gone. Bits of boots or scraps of smoking bone fragments were the only things left of men who'd been unable to find cover. None of the men manning the forward outposts had survived. The only evidence they'd ever been there was the frayed and severed ends of communication wire.

Three days passed before Baker Company was back on the line. In those three days, artillery pounded the Japanese defenses. More 25-pounders had come from Port Moresby and ammo for the American Howitzer crew arrived and they rained hell on the Japanese. The disastrous bombing run stopped bombing operations for the time being, but fighters from new airfields in the mountains strafed and bombed the airfields and plantation daily.

Lt. Branson called Tarkington to his log bunker HQ. Tarkington entered and was shocked to see Branson's vacant eyes. Dark circles beneath them showed a man under enormous stress who desperately needed sleep.

Branson looked up from the yellow lighting emanating from a single bare lightbulb. "Ah, Sergeant Tarkington. Come in." Tarkington hadn't seen the new HQ. It was stout. Made with thick, stacked palm trees. It was dug a few feet down to avoid the water table, but the roof was seven feet, allowing most men to stand upright easily. Sagging wires weaved throughout the space and Tarkington thought they looked like thin black snakes. "How are your men holding up?" Branson asked.

Tarkington joined him beside a makeshift table, "Fine, sir. Just like everyone else, we're low on food. But I'd say we're doing better than most. We've been in these jungles a long time and are more used to the climate than the others. It's a damned shitty place though, sir."

Branson nodded, "Yeah, I'd rather leave it for the Japs. Let them rot here, but that's not gonna happen." He pressed his hands into the base of his back, stretching. "Heard from your commander, Colonel Bradshaw." Tarkington's head snapped up. He'd been waiting for some word ever since the end of the Gobe mission. Branson gave him a tight smile. "Our communications are better now, and the new airfields allow for quick message traffic. I sent word yesterday and I got a response back today." He handed Tarkington a folded sheet of paper and while Tarkington read it, continued, "He sounds like a solid commander. Besides that," he pointed at the paper Tarkington held, "he sent me a personal letter, which he also sent to Colonel Huntington. He outlined your skill sets and suggested using you and your men as commandos rather than standard infantry." He scowled and continued, "Which is what you've been saying all along."

Tarkington finished reading the orders and stiffened. It wasn't what he was hoping for, but he couldn't say he didn't expect it. "Yes, sir. It seems they have released us to your command until further notice."

"Captain Griffin got the word too, and Colonel Huntington has directed him to use your men in any way he sees fit. The captain's had his hands tied till now, but the letter seems to have worked on Huntington. I heard through the grapevine that Bradshaw was an upperclassman to Huntington at West Point. Perhaps that has something to do with it." He shrugged, "Regardless, Captain Griffin ordered your men on a mission tonight. He wants you to infiltrate the Jap lines and create some chaos. Give back a little of what they've been serving us every night."

Tarkington couldn't keep the smile off his face, "That'll be our pleasure, sir."

Branson grinned, "Thought it might. To keep the Nips from being suspicious, the artillery will continue, but they'll target the airfields instead of the plantation. You've got thirty-six hours before the next push. You'll know you're late if the arty hits the plantation. They're planning an hour bombardment prior to the attack." Tarkington nodded and Branson continued, "The attack will happen whether or not you've returned, so make sure you're back."

"Yes, sir. We'll be back."

"Good luck, Sergeant." Tarkington turned to leave but Branson caught his arm, "One more thing. Griffin wants the Japs to fear for their lives out there. Wants them never to feel safe. You have any ideas on that?"

Tarkington considered, then nodded, "Yes, sir. I've got just the thing."

Sneaking forward was easier than it had been during the spotting mission a week before. Relentless artillery, daily strafing, and bombing runs had devastated the plantation. The once orderly stands of towering palms littered the ground. Very few remained undamaged.

They slithered beneath logs and wove between stumps, using smoking craters and natural cover to remain concealed. They wore their mottled camouflage and had every exposed piece of skin painted black. They carried light packs, mostly containing extra water, food, and explosives. Each soldier also carried six extra magazines and four fragmentation grenades. They didn't fool themselves that they could get out of trouble if discovered. A firefight would not end well, but they didn't plan on being seen. If all went well, the only sign they'd been there would be bodies and booby traps.

The stars shone down from a cloudless sky, helping them find their way. When they were close to the trench line, they crept at a snail's pace. They hadn't come across an outpost, although they supposed they must have passed by at least one during their stalk. If they had seen it, they would've bypassed it; their mission was in the Japanese rear area.

They stayed close to one another, Henry and Raker leading. Henry signaled when he found the first trench. Tarkington crept forward. He slithered over a fallen log and slid beneath another until he was beside Henry.

They'd planned on passing through the Japanese lines in the area between the New Strip and the plantation. As far as they knew, all segments were occupied, but this section—seen by aerial reconnaissance— was a longer communication trench and they hoped wouldn't have as many soldiers on guard. They could deal with one or two men, but not an entire bunker full.

Tarkington peered into the trench at the same time Henry did, each looking a different direction. Nothing. Tarkington gave Henry a nod, barely perceptible in the darkness.

Henry slithered forward until his body disappeared in the darkness at the bottom of the trench. No one moved for a few minutes as they listened. Satisfied, Henry crawled out the other side, while Tarkington covered him with his carbine. He'd left the heavier Thompson with Lt. Branson for safe-keeping. Raker followed, and soon Tarkington was the only man left. He rolled silently into the gloom and his skin crawled as it always did when he was this close to the enemy.

He pushed his way out the other side and saw Winkleman's eyes staring at him from the jungle. Tarkington nodded as he passed and barely heard the faint rustling as Winkleman slithered in behind him.

They continued crawling for another ten minutes. Henry led them to a dense section of jungle that was only penetrable by crawling. Even then it wasn't easy. They convened and relaxed a little, knowing they'd completed the hardest part of the mission: getting behind the Japanese lines.

Without a word, they pulled out canteens and drained each completely, erasing the possibility that sloshing water from half-filled canteens would give them away. They lingered for another twenty minutes, listening to the night sounds and readying themselves for the upcoming hours of stress and agonizingly slow movement.

Tarkington signaled. They formed up in the agreed upon patrol order: Henry and Raker, then Vick and Tarkington, followed by Stollman and Bulkort. Winkleman would take up the rear. The lead scouts would identify targets. Henry and Vick would do any knife work, and Stollman and Bulkort would place explosives. Each GI could perform any of the jobs, but this patrol sequence put the best men for each job in the proper position.

With many hours before daylight, they pushed out from the thick jungle, moving deeper into enemy lines, searching for likely and unlucky targets.

23

There were Japanese bunkers and connecting trenches everywhere. Each time they came across the well-camouflaged structures, Tarkington dutifully marked them on a map. He stopped doing so after the constant interruptions held them up too much. Originally, they'd planned to hit the Japanese that same night, but as it got later and later, they decided it would be best to do so the next night. All they had to do now was find a suitable target, get to cover, and wait out the daylight hours.

An hour before the sun rose, they returned to their jungle bivouac. They relieved themselves as best they could, then concealed themselves meticulously. They whiled away the daylight hours, listening to the nearly constant traffic moving through the trenches. Tarkington was amazed how many there were and knew he'd probably only seen a fraction of them. With each passing hour, his admiration for the defenses grew.

True to their word, no artillery fell upon the plantation defenses. From the sounds of it, the extra munitions were being fired on the airfields. The distant sound of rolling thunder was nearly constant, and he wondered if perhaps the trench traffic could be men being shifted that way to stem a perceived attack. He hoped so. It would make their job easier.

Evening passed to darkness and the men silently ate balls of sticky rice and dried meat. During the long day, they'd slugged down two more canteens, leaving them each with one more for the night ahead.

They left the cover of the deep jungle at 2000 hours and moved silently to their first objective—a lone bunker forty yards away. It was relatively remote, providing cover for another bunker to the east. All the other bunkers they'd seen had trenches coming into them from at least two directions—this one only had one coming from the north. Another advantage was that they'd seen very little back-and-forth traffic, and only two men manned the machine gun.

It didn't take long to get to the edge of the trench. Each of them slid in on their bellies, then got to their feet and crouched. Henry and Vick moved toward the target bunker, followed by Stollman and Bulkort. Winkleman took up the rear, watching for any stray infantrymen.

Henry approached the door leading into the back of the bunker. It was closed and no light emanated from the seams. It would be much easier to open the door, chuck in a grenade, and be done with it, but that would attract too much attention. They'd do it the hard way.

Henry inched his way forward until he crouched in front of the door. His knife was in his right hand. He wrapped his left around the steel door handle. It felt cool to the touch. He glanced back at Vick. The glint of his blade told him he was ready. He took in a breath and blew it out slowly, silently counting off the seconds. He pulled the door handle hard. It squeaked horribly.

Vick darted past him and Henry quickly followed, moving left. There was a startled grunt and slicing sounds as Vick closed with his man. Henry could only see commotion as two shadows became one. His target's head silhouetted against the firing port. He was frozen in place, watching the sudden and violent act playing out before him. Henry closed quickly, pressing his left hand over the soldier's mouth as he jammed the knife into the soft skin beneath his chin, cutting off his scream. Henry rode him to the ground, twisting and rotating the knife, cutting vital vessels and brain. There was a gurgling, then silence.

The sickening stench of death washed over them as they quickly searched for more soldiers. But there were only two, just how they'd planned. Henry sheathed his knife and gave a quick, low whistle. Stollman and Bulkort entered the small space while Vick and Henry dragged the dead soldiers out into the trench. Bulkort gagged at the smell, but swallowed the bile threatening to come up and got to work.

Henry saw Tarkington staring at him. He gave him a thumbs up and shoved the dead soldier to the side. Five long minutes passed before Bulkort and Stollman exited the bunker. Bulkort took a deep breath as though he'd been holding it the whole time.

Vick shook his head while he crouched on the man he'd killed and muttered, "Pathetic."

Stollman patted Vick on the back, signaling that they'd finished planting the explosives. He whispered in Vick's ear, "We sabotaged the gun. Don't put the bodies too close or you'll fuck it up." Vick nodded and dragged a corpse back into the bunker, propping him up against the wall beneath the gunport. Henry did the same, and they were back outside in under a minute. Henry shut the door slowly, avoiding the squeak.

They moved down the trench. Vick and Raker moved past Winkleman just the way they'd talked about. Vick was arguably the best knife man. He didn't relish killing—none of them did—but he had the best chance of killing a man with a knife before he could raise the alarm, so he was the lead man. Henry was glad to give his position to Raker, who'd insisted on being a part of the knife work. Henry slipped into third position.

Vick's carbine was slung over his shoulder, snugged up tightly. He walked in a low crouch along the trench, his knife leading the way. Tonight, there were no stars, but his eyes were accustomed to the darkness and Vick felt sure he'd see someone in time to silence them. Behind the lines, the Japanese felt comfortable and safe and probably wouldn't react to their dark shapes until it was too late.

The next target would be more difficult. Vick moved along the trench, the only noise the occasional scraping of his arm along the dirt wall. As he counted off 200 paces, he slowed, knowing the intersection with the main trench line was somewhere just ahead. He heard voices. They all froze. At least two black silhouettes walked past the trench junction the GIs were moving toward. They talked in normal tones, not worried this far behind their own lines.

Their voices faded as they rounded a corner and moved away. Vick moved to the junction. He looked both ways. The five feet he could see in the gloom were clear. He looked back at the others and signaled them forward.

He turned the corner, stepping into the main trench line. A jogging soldier crashed into him. They both went down hard. The Japanese soldier landed on Vick and pinned his arms beneath him.

Understanding he was on a person, the soldier said something that Vick didn't understand, but there was no fear in the words—in fact, he gave a startled laugh. His eyes quickly changed to fear when he saw the painted face and round eyes of a Caucasian.

He didn't have time to call out before Raker was on him. He thrust his knife through the back of his neck, severing his spine. His body stiffened and vibrated sickeningly against Vick. The man's tongue poked from his gaping mouth, then his teeth clenched down unnaturally hard, puncturing the fleshy muscle nearly in half.

The weight of the dead man was suddenly pulled off and Vick backed away from the still-convulsing body. He wanted to scream in revulsion but took a breath, closed his eyes, and regained his composure. His heartbeat slowly returned to normal. The body was quickly shuttled around the corner out of sight.

Tarkington was at his ear, "You okay?" Vick gave him a quick nod and Tarkington hissed, "We gotta get this done quick. Move out." Vick nodded, adjusted his rifle and pack, then took the lead position again. He trotted the direction the soldier had come from—his senses on overdrive.

Vick led them thirty yards along the trench. He moved quickly, not wanting to spend any more time than was necessary in the well-used trench. He came to another junction. Instead of a T intersection, this one was a Y. The night before, they'd seen more activity moving along the right side and relatively little from the left. They'd investigated as best as they could and found it led to a large bunker. It wasn't a machine gun bunker, and based on the lack of traffic, they figured it wasn't a barracks either.

With the way clear, they jogged down the left-hand path. It was eerie using the enemy trench system. Vick couldn't stop thinking about the enemy soldier quivering on top of him. He wished he could wipe it from his memory. He slowed his pace as the looming entry to the bunker came into view through the murkiness.

Raker touched his back, letting him know he was close and ready. Vick stepped closer, straining to see inside, but it was impossibly dark inside. He stopped at the edge of the entrance. Unlike the first bunker, there wasn't a door. He strained to hear breathing or some sign that there were soldiers inside. He heard nothing except night jungle sounds. The dank air wafting from inside smelled of wood and dirt. He thought he smelled body odor, but it was faint and he might have been imagining it.

Raker touched his back again and Vick moved into the inky blackness. As soon as he crossed the threshold, the ground changed from mud to hard-pack. After a few more steps, he noticed some kind of flooring, probably wood. He inched along, his senses taking in everything. He felt—rather than saw—the narrow entrance open into a wider room. He had the distinct feeling that the room was empty.

He continued moving, low and crouched, his knife at the ready. Raker was right behind him. He reached the back wall and stopped. Tarkington pulled the pack off his back and rifled inside. A red-lensed light bathed the space and everyone breathed a sigh of relief. The room was empty.

Tarkington shined the light all around and they marveled at the stout construction. The large room had benches along the walls, enough for half a platoon. It was sparse otherwise, and they assumed it was a bomb shelter.

Tarkington pointed at Stollman and Bulkort. They quickly got to work pulling explosives from their packs. They conferred briefly about placements and were soon stuffing explosives into the hidden nooks and crannies in the walls beneath the benches. Once they set timers, they covered the holes with dirt. The minimal sound from the acid eating away at the buffer separating the blasting cap would be difficult, if not impossible, to hear—especially during an artillery strike. When they finished, Henry added the final touch and they reversed course back to the open trench.

They slithered over the top, not wanting to press their luck in the trenches any longer than was necessary. They crawled slowly away, not moving toward their own lines, but laterally toward the New Strip airfield. The shelling had stopped and the night was loud with chirping and buzzing insects. The faint sound of distant Japanese voices reminded them of the danger.

Ideally, they wanted to return to their original point of departure, but it was obvious they wouldn't be able to find it reliably at night, so they continued moving west. They came across more bunkers, some empty, others manned. They eased their way around them.

An hour passed and they'd only moved 200 yards from the bomb shelter when the night suddenly rippled with an enormous explosion. They froze as the flash of light and concussion swept through the jungle, silencing the insects.

Tarkington hissed, "What the fuck was that? The first bunker?"

Stollman nodded, "Think so. Faulty fuse. The constant wet out here wreaks havoc on 'em."

Winkleman shook his head, "Shit, Stolly. What if they'd gone up while we were there?"

Stollman shrugged, "We wouldn't know about it. Just be dead."

Tarkington asked, "What about the others? They reliable?"

Stollman shook his head, "No telling. We've been keeping 'em as dry as possible, but you never know."

Henry's Cajun drawl, "Place'll be crawling with Nips soon. Can we jaw 'bout this later?"

Tarkington clenched his teeth, Henry was right. "We'll keep moving west. But we'll go to ground if they do a search."

Captain Nagato awoke from a fitful sleep, jolted by a sudden, ripping explosion. He blinked the sleep from his eyes—whatever dark dream he was having fled into the recesses of his mind. He swung his legs off the bunk and aligned his leather boots. His feet were swollen from some unknown jungle malady and the boots felt as though they were two sizes too small, even though they'd been handmade specifically for his feet by a cobbler on Rabaul.

"Sergeant Major," he barked, his voice raspy with sleep. A thin, bespectacled Sergeant Major burst into the room and stiffened. "What is going on? That didn't sound like artillery."

Sergeant Okamoto shut the door behind him, nodded, and turned on the light. Electric light was one of the few luxuries in this wet hell. "I don't know, sir. It sounded like it came from Bunker 12. I didn't hear any incoming artillery, sir."

Captain Nagato stood, slamming his aching feet into the boots. He stood tall and tucked his rumpled shirt into his pants. He cinched the leather belt around his waist and scowled; he'd had to cut new holes in the belt and he was due for another. He hoped his pants wouldn't fall down. As an officer, he had it better than his men, but there was only so much food to go around and he was on half rations.

He wondered if his wife would recognize him. She'd loved his powerful physique, often stroking his muscled arms and chest. He banished the thought. His chances of seeing her or his home again were zero. Since things weren't going well on Guadalcanal, there would be no respite from the relentless push by the Allies on Papua New Guinea. His orders were clear: hold Buna to the last man.

He adjusted the Nambu pistol in his belt, then placed his hat upon his thinning hair—another gift from the jungle. *Will I ever be rid of this place?* "Take me there, Sergeant."

"Hai, sir." He held the door for his officer, turned off the light, and followed him into the trench system.

Nagato saw the flickering of fire coming from the direction of the explosion. He knew the defenses like the back of his hand. He'd helped design them alongside Colonel Yamamoto and considered the meshwork of interlocking bunkers and trenches to be impenetrable. The only way the Allies could take them would be with armor, but even then, it would be a costly prospect. The bunker he pictured in his mind's eye came to him and he scowled. It wasn't one on the front line. Perhaps there'd been a mishap.

Sergeant Okamoto led the way, keeping low. Nagato did the same. Although he felt safe this far from the front line, he hadn't survived this long by being careless.

They wound their way through the labyrinthine trenches. Startled soldiers straightened and hurried out of the captain's way. His men respected him. He was a soldier's soldier—never shying away from combat or his duty. The men often saw him on the front lines and even watched him man a machine gun, staving off ill-fated Allied attacks. The explosion had brought the men from their bunkers. They were used to artillery and airstrikes, but this sounded different and they were all curious.

At the junction from the main trench line to the stricken bunker, they came to a glut of soldiers. Sergeant Okamoto barked, "Clear the way for Captain Nagato." Men quickly scattered, some climbing from the trench. The flickering flames lit the area where the machine gun bunker had been. Soldiers aimed rifles into the gloom beyond, but there were no targets.

Nagato saw one of his platoon leaders sifting through the wreckage. "Lieutenant Otake." Otake turned and snapped off a quick salute. "What happened here?"

Otake was impossibly young. The war had aged him considerably; however, his voice was still that of a boy. "Sir. It appears there was some kind of accident. An explosion. There are no survivors and as you can see, the bunker's destroyed."

Nagato's scowl grew, "An enemy rocket perhaps?"

Otake shook his head and pointed to a nearby soldier. "Private Hu saw it explode. There was no warning."

Nagato turned to the soldier, "Tell me what you saw, Private."

Hu stiffened, "Hai, sir. I was bringing rice to them. I'd just turned the corner from the main trench. I was looking directly at the bunker when it suddenly exploded."

Nagato nodded, "Were you injured?" Nagato could see the man's face was dark with soot and his eyelashes and hair were curled and singed.

Hu shook his head. "My ears ring. But I'm uninjured, sir."

Nagato nodded and turned back to the destroyed bunker. The roof was gone and the logs were charred and burnt. In the darkness, he could see the twisted machine gun pointing toward the sky. He strode into the smoldering crater. There were burnt body parts scattered throughout, and if he didn't know there were only two men, he wouldn't have been able to guess how many had been here.

He knelt in the center. The smell of burnt flesh mixing with burnt palm trees was nauseating, but he'd smelled it many times before. "There were no explosives here. Just machine gun ammunition. Correct?"

Lt. Otake came forward and nodded, "Yes, sir. I think so . . . sir." Nagato remained crouched and spun on his heels, glaring at him for clarification. Otake sputtered, "I—I mean, they must have had some kind of explosives for this to happen, sir."

Something caught Nagato's attention. Something small. He reached for it. It was a western-style playing card. His brow furrowed. It was wholly out of place. His men had no such things, or so he thought. He stood and took the card closer to the light coming off a burning log. The painted death's head skull was obviously added and the words scrawled beneath it left no doubt, *Tark's Ticks.*

He held the card out to Lt. Otake and hissed, "Sabotage! Search the area. I want them found and killed."

Otake didn't understand the significance of the playing card, but sprang into action. Soon he had squads organized and they began sweeping the area for saboteurs. They found more charred playing cards with the same macabre symbol and cryptic message.

Nagato returned to his fortified bunker HQ. Minutes later, Sergeant Okamoto burst in and stiffened. "Sir, another one of our soldiers was found. He was killed with a knife to the back of the neck. His body was in the jungle near Bunker 12. We found another playing card tucked in his shirt pocket." Nagato's jaw rippled as he gritted his teeth and Okamoto asked, "What are these Yankee playing cards, sir? Have you seen them before?"

Nagato shook his head. Normally, a noncom wouldn't speak to an officer unless spoken to first, but they'd been fighting side by side for years and had earned each other's respect. Nagato answered, "No. But I've heard of them. I thought it was an unfounded rumor. Something to keep the men vigilant. Much like a scary bedtime story for children. It seems I was wrong."

"It seems impossible they snuck this far behind our lines."

Nagato nodded his agreement, "Yes. Skilled soldiers. Dangerous soldiers. We must find them before they escape back to their lines."

Okamoto bowed slightly, "The lieutenant has his entire platoon out looking for them, sir. They'll find them."

24

The GIs continued crawling west until they heard the sounds of pursuit. The premature explosion wouldn't pass off as an accident, not with the playing cards and the other body they'd hidden in the jungle.

It wasn't long after the explosion that they heard Japanese voices calling out to one another. The area between the plantation and the nearest airfield wasn't large, but it would be difficult to search at night and the GIs were masters of camouflage.

They pushed themselves deep into the thickest, nastiest jungle they could find and hunkered down. Tarkington knew they were in a difficult situation. He wanted to be out of there before daylight. He figured they could remain hidden during the day even while the enemy vigorously searched for them, but the big artillery attack would come at dawn and the general attack soon after that. He didn't want to be here when that happened.

He checked the pale glowing hands of his wristwatch; it was ten minutes past midnight. They'd taken a risk starting their mission early, but he was glad they had. There was plenty of darkness left to wait out the patrols and get back to their own lines before daylight.

Pinpricks of light flashing through the jungle caught his attention.

Everyone hunkered. The lights were still a long way off but were moving their way steadily.

Retreating west was the obvious choice since it was the more sparsely defended area. Tarkington kicked himself for not going southeast toward the coast, but there were even more densely packed pockets of bunkers and trenches that way. They might not be pursued, but the likelihood of being spotted by an alerted enemy was greater. There was nothing to do about it now.

The lights advanced, cutting through the darkness. They came in a long line, as though beating the bushes for tigers. It wasn't a bad method, but Tarkington doubted they'd be able to push into this section of jungle unless they got on their hands and knees, the same way they had. Even then, it was full of thick, cutting thorns and bits of razor-sharp kunai grass. The GIs had a terrible time of it and had the cuts and scrapes to prove it. He doubted the Japanese would try it, but realized it depended on their commander.

Tarkington signaled and pulled his carbine off his back, placing it within easy reach. He considered a grenade, but it was too dense for grenade work. The others followed suit. Then they waited.

It seemed to take a lifetime before the Japanese were finally in front of their position. The jungle was still relatively open to the south and north, and the pinpricks of light went around them. The men directly in front of them couldn't go forward. Barked orders and powerful beams of light aimed in their direction. They were too far back and too well camouflaged to be discovered with light alone.

Another order and soon the sound of a hacking machete. That would also be a futile tactic. It had taken an entire company of GIs all night to hack through similar jungle. Some flashlights shone on the ground, and over the sound of hacking, soldiers tried pushing their way into the thicket on their bellies. Tarkington could see the flashlight holders illuminating the ground for their struggling comrades. The GIs had been forced to weave sideways to fit between thickets of thorns, vines, and creepers. They had to slither over and under rotting logs and through soft mud and dirty pools of water to get where they were. Would the Japanese do the same? He doubted it.

The lights to either side of the thicket stopped and reconvened toward the center. The GIs were still thirty yards back from where the Japanese stood, but they barely breathed. Voices conversed back and forth in clipped Japanese. They couldn't see anything except the beams of light. One by one, the lights went out. The unmistakable sounds of bolts on rifles being pulled sent a chill up Tarkington's spine, and in that instant, he knew what was about to happen. He hissed, "Stay down."

He drove his head as far into the muck as he could. He felt helpless knowing what was coming but being unable to do anything about it. The loud reports of rifles firing indiscriminately into the cover made him cringe. Bullets thumped into rotten wood and slapped into the muddy ground. It was a large area, and the soldiers fired where they thought their bullets would have the best chance of flushing someone out. Tarkington didn't dare look up, but thought for sure he'd catch a bullet at any moment. Would he be able to keep from calling out? He hoped it would be a quick, silent death. It seemed to go on forever. Bullets whizzed and smacked all around them. His breath came in quick gasps with each crashing shot.

The riflemen finally stopped firing. Tarkington couldn't believe he hadn't been hit. But what about the others? No one called out or took off through the brambles. Another order in Japanese and they turned the lights back on. The platoon spread out around the thicket, bypassing it.

Five minutes passed before he finally hissed, "Sound off." They went in order, and when it was Bulkort's turn, he uttered, "I'm hit. I—I'm hit, I think."

Stollman was nearby. He moved to him, having to claw his way through creepers that seemed to want to make a meal out of him. He finally got to his side and in the darkness asked, "Where you hit, Bull?"

"It's—it's not bad, Stolly."

"Where, goddammit?" Stollman couldn't see much, so he frantically ran his hands over Bulkort's back. When he got to his lower back, his hand came away wet with blood. Bulkort's breath caught in his throat at his touch. Stollman hissed, "He's hit in the lower back. He's losing blood."

"It's nothing. I'm okay," but his words were slurred with pain. Stollman rolled onto him, pressing his hand hard over the wound. Bulkort tensed and drew in another sharp breath. "Get—get off me."

"Shut up and lie still. I'm putting pressure on the wound, dammit."

By now Vick and Raker were there to help. Vick pulled his pack off his back and brought out bandages. He showed them to Stollman who lifted his bloody hands, allowing Vick to pull Bulkort's shirt up and place the bandages. Stollman pressed them into his back hard, and they turned from white to red. Vick wrapped a long strip of cloth around Bulkort, having to roll him slightly to get all the way around. Bulkort whimpered slightly at the movement, but bit his lip to keep from calling out. Vick secured the cloth as tightly as he could, keeping solid pressure.

He pushed Stollman's hands away and watched for seepage. The bandage held, although blood continued to soak through the bandage and cloth. "Keep pressure on a few more minutes." Stollman did as he was told, pressing hard, evincing another low whimper. Vick asked, "You okay to move, Bull?"

Stollman hissed, "Move? We can't move yet even if we wanted to. The Japs are all . . ."

"I mean when it comes time," interrupted Vick. He leaned down and looked into Bulkort's bloodshot eyes. "Can you move if we have to?" He held up a small vial of morphine, "Or do you need this?"

Bulkort knew the morphine would dull the pain and he desperately wanted that; however, it would make him even more of a burden. He licked his dry lips and shook his head, his voice low and sure despite the pain, "I don't need it. Not yet."

Tarkington finally pushed his way through to them. The flashlight beams were fading to the west. He wanted to move south while they could slip behind them, but Bulkort's wound would make that difficult. He'd heard the brief conversation. He was face to face with the big man, "Bull. Be honest with me. Our lives depend on it. Can you move?"

Bulkort saw the puckered scar on Tarkington's temple only inches from his face. This man whom he respected more than any other man he'd ever met, besides his father, needed his honest answer. He shut his eyes, evaluating his pain level. "Let—let me try." Stollman released the pressure and Bulkort pulled his knees slowly beneath his body and pushed himself forward in a crawling motion. It hurt worse than anything he'd ever felt in his life, but he gritted his teeth and swallowed the pain. "I can do it, Tarkington. I can hack it." Tarkington nodded and Bulkort grasped his arm, "I don't think I can run though. Crawling seems okay."

Tarkington growled low, "I don't want a repeat performance of fish in a barrel. We need to leave now while we've got the chance. They might throw grenades in next time. Get him ready to travel the best you can. We're leaving now."

They dispersed the gear from his pack, forcing him to drink the rest of his canteen. They buried his empty canteen and pack in the mud. Stollman took his rifle, snugging the sling along his left side. Vick applied another layer of thick bandages and was satisfied he'd done everything possible to keep him from bleeding out—at least for a while.

Once they were ready to move, Vick whispered in Tarkington's ear, "I've bandaged him up good, but crawling and moving will make him bleed. We'll have to do this quickly, before he passes out."

"Understood. You and Stolly stay with him."

Vick nodded and took his position beside Bulkort. "You ready for this, Bull?"

Bulkort looked at him through pain-glazed eyes, "As I'll ever be."

Getting out of the thicket proved to be the hardest part for Sergeant Bulkort. There was no easy way out. He had to bend, scrape, and turn onto his side just to get to the more open part of the plantation. Vick and Stollman did all they could for him, holding brambles back and sometimes cutting through areas with their knives, but Bulkort felt like he was going to pass out at any moment. He found himself overheated and sweating excessively, then cold and clammy to the touch a moment later.

They finally got out of the thicket. They'd moved thirty yards and Bulkort felt as though he'd run back-to-back marathons. He'd drank an entire canteen full of water only minutes before, but felt parched. His tongue was swollen and dry. They couldn't see the lights from the Japanese platoon, but even in the more wide-open plantation terrain, that didn't mean they weren't close. Vick placed his hand on Bulkort's shoulder. "Hold up, Bull. Lemme check it." Bulkort stopped moving, thankful for the respite from the incredible pain. Vick probed and felt his back. His hand came away bloody. "You're bleeding again."

Tarkington moved to them in a crouch while the others searched for enemy soldiers. They had their carbines ready. If they were discovered, they'd have to shoot their way out. "How's he doing?" he asked Vick.

Stollman answered, "He's fine. Right, Bull?"

Vick shook his head, "He's losing a lot of blood. I'm amazed he's still conscious at all."

Bulkort's words slurred, "I—I'm f—f—fine." His head dropped into the mud with a soft splash.

Vick turned Bulkort's head sideways to keep him from drowning in the puddle and hissed, "He's passed out, dammit."

Stollman slapped Bulkort's cheek trying to rouse him, "Bull. Bull. Wake up. Is—is he dead?"

Vick shook his head, "No. He's passed out. He's lost too much blood." He looked at Tarkington, "What d'you wanna do?"

Stollman seethed, "I'll carry him. I can hack it."

Tarkington felt the heaviness of the decision like a physical weight. The image of Atlas holding up the world crossed his mind. "Do it. We'll take turns. Swap out every couple of minutes."

Vick and Tarkington hefted the big man to his knees, struggling with his dead weight. Stollman offloaded his pack and the two carbines. They draped Bulkort over his shoulders. The movement elicited a low murmur from him. Stollman staggered to his feet, the extra weight pushing him deeper into the mud. Through a labored breath, he said, "Let's go."

The area was littered with downed palms from the incessant artillery and bombing runs, and every step was contested for Stollman, but he pushed forward relentlessly. Henry and Raker spread out, covering as much ground as possible as quickly as possible. It felt reckless and wrong, but if they wanted to save Bulkort's life, they had to move fast.

They'd gone forty agonizing yards before Raker and Henry both went to ground. Stollman stood on shaking legs, knowing he'd be unable to get down without collapsing under Bulkort's weight. Vick and Winkleman were beside him quickly, taking the weight, and they lowered themselves slowly.

Tarkington went forward and saw the low outline of a bunker only yards away. The low murmuring of voices told him it was occupied. He checked his watch, scraping the mud off the glass face. They still had four hours before the artillery turned this place into shrapnel hell. Plenty of time, if they didn't have to carry Bulkort.

A Japanese voice called out in a questioning tone, as though they'd heard something, but since it wasn't to their front, they thought it was a fellow soldier. There was no way they could move forward or backward without alerting them more. They had to take them out. They only had seconds to act or they'd turn their machine guns on them.

Tarkington hissed, "Henry—grenade."

Henry immediately snatched a grenade from his waist, pulled the pin, flicked the spoon, and counted to two before tossing it into the trench. The bunker doorway was only yards away and the grenade disappeared inside. There was a flash and a muffled blast, followed by screaming.

Raker was on his feet and running before the smoke cleared. Winkleman was right behind him. They slid into the blackness of the trench and charged through the smoking doorway. Raker saw movement and fired twice. The muzzle flashes lit up others and Winkleman unloaded into them. It was over in seconds. Five shredded Japanese lay smoldering on the floor.

The other GIs piled into the trench, ready to counter the inevitable response. Stollman dragged Bulkort inside and his big body slunk to the bottom. The sound and the movement pulled him to consciousness and he called out in slurred agony, but everyone was too busy to notice or help.

The bunker had two well-used trenches leading into it from two sides. Henry leaped into the trench coming from the right, his carbine ready to take on whatever came. Winkleman joined him while the others watched the left trench.

It didn't take long. A soldier came around the corner running straight for Henry and Winkleman. They crouched in the darkness, invisible to the enemy soldier. Henry fired twice into center mass and the stunned soldier's face lit up in the muzzle flash before he fell face first into the mud. A second soldier rounded the corner and Henry shot him in the face, dropping him instantly.

Raker and Stollman were in the other trench, staring into the gloom with their carbines raised. Tarkington's mind reeled. They had to get the hell out of there fast or they were dead men. He yelled, "Use grenades. Throw 'em all and move south. I'll carry Bull."

Raker and Stollman fired simultaneously as soldiers came running into sight. The first man dropped and the second tripped over his body. The third raised his rifle but didn't get his finger on the trigger before Raker and Stollman's .30 caliber rounds punctured his chest and head.

Tarkington hurled a grenade over the trench toward the plantation, hoping the explosion would distract them, then slung his carbine and hunched to put Bulkort over his shoulder. Bulkort pushed him away and Tarkington was amazed he was conscious. "Come on, Bull. We gotta get outta here now!"

Bulkort bellowed in pain and determination and got to his feet, swaying unsteadily. "You won't make it carrying me," he slurred. Tarkington ignored him and tried to sling Bulkort's arm over his shoulder again, but he pushed him away and stumbled toward the open bunker door. He pointed inside, "Get—get me the machine gun." With great effort, he hauled himself out of the trench. He stumbled his way around to the other side of the bunker and faced the enemy rear. Tarkington saw what he intended. From his position in front of the bunker, he'd have an excellent field of fire along both trench lines.

Grenades exploded as the GIs hurled them one after the other. Screams pierced the night. Tarkington went into the bunker and hefted the machine gun. It was heavy and awkward, but he finally lifted it from the tripod. He hurried out the door and met Stollman just coming in, "Take this to Bull. I'll get the ammo."

Stollman looked around, stunned. "Where is he?"

Tarkington pointed to the other side of the bunker, "Up there. Hurry." Stollman took the weapon and disappeared out of the trench. Tarkington yanked the tripod and grabbed all the sticks of ammo he could carry. Winkleman had thrown all his grenades and was firing into enemy soldiers as they attacked. More and more enemy were out of the trench and advancing along the edges. He fired steadily and as Tarkington hefted himself and the tripod from the trench, Winkleman yelled, "Reloading!"

Tarkington yelled, "Stolly! Here!" He threw the tripod and pulled his carbine from his shoulder, aimed and fired at a dark silhouette. Another was close behind and he fired into that one too. He didn't see more targets. He took the brief respite to pull another grenade. He threw it into the darkness. "Grenade out!" He turned to hoist the ammo and tripod, but they were gone. He saw Stollman placing the weapon on the tripod, which was splayed out on top of the bunker facing north.

Tarkington yelled, "Out of the trenches! Now!"

There was more firing as the GIs covered one another and lunged from the trench. They converged on Bulkort behind the bunker. The Japanese were no longer rushing headlong at them, but more and more muzzle flashes lit up the night and bullets whizzed and smacked into the wooden sides of the bunker. It was chaotic and confused. There was firing everywhere, even well away from their position. The Japanese were trying to piece together what was happening and had yet to pinpoint the threat.

A stick of ammunition poked from the right side of the machine gun. Bulkort leaned on the machine gun and pulled the trigger, but nothing happened. Stollman cursed, "You've gotta chamber a round first and click off the safety." He did it for him as Bulkort's glazed eyes took it all in. "Now!" yelled Stollman.

Bulkort looked over the open sights, his stance wide for stability. He pulled the trigger and let loose a short burst. The tripod bounced backwards and one leg fell off the top of the bunker. Stollman saw it coming and caught the weapon before it toppled all the way off. He gripped two of the tripod legs and held on tight. Bulkort let loose with another short burst, and when he was satisfied it wouldn't move, fired a longer burst. He swept the muzzle across the dark trench lines, sweeping both with equal vengeance. There were no tracers, which made aiming difficult. The three-foot-long muzzle flash took any remaining night sight, but he knew generally where to shoot and the enemy muzzle flashes were good aiming points. He fired until he'd chewed through the stick of ammo. Stollman jammed another full stick in and Bulkort chambered the first round.

He fired a short burst then let off the trigger and yelled to the others, "What are you waiting for? Get outta here!"

Raker and Henry arrived with pilfered enemy sandbags. They stacked them on the rear feet of the tripod as Stollman pulled his hands back. Stollman shook his head, "We ain't leaving you, Bull!"

A bullet zipped past his ear, making him duck. Bulkort depressed the trigger and sent another hail of lead into the night. His eyes were bloodshot and crazed in the wicked muzzle flash. His voice was raspy when he stopped firing and spoke again, "I've had it. I can feel it. Go! I'll cover you. Hurry!"

Tarkington grabbed Stollman's shoulder and pulled, "We've gotta go now, Stolly!"

Stollman shook him off and yelled, "No! I ain't leaving him!"

The incoming fire intensified but Bulkort never let up, sweeping the muzzle back and forth. He finished another brick of ammo and Stollman quickly reloaded for him. Bulkort's voice cracked with rage, seeing they hadn't left yet. "Go! You sons of bitches! Go!"

A bullet smacked into Bulkort's shoulder, momentarily taking his finger off the trigger. He looked at the fresh wound through glassy eyes, then looked Stollman in the eye, his voice losing some of its power, "I've had it. Please, go." Stollman finally relented and Bulkort adjusted his aim, seeing three soldiers sprinting straight at them. He pulled the trigger and the heavy caliber bullets nearly cut them in half.

Japanese soldiers converged on the massive tongue of fire leaping from the weapon's muzzle. They didn't immediately attack Bulkort, since it was their own machine gun firing—even though it was firing the wrong direction. The explosion earlier, along with the obviously foreign sounds of the MI carbines and grenade blasts, told them there were enemies nearby, but perhaps the machine gun was firing on them. The hesitation and uncertainty were enough to allow the GIs to slip away from the battle as Bulkort continued to cover them.

They moved fast, crouching when they saw soldiers moving toward the still-raging sounds of battle. The Japanese were concentrating on the situation to their rear and the GIs had little trouble getting past them. The machine gun stopped and the GIs hoped it was because Bulkort was reloading. Relief flooded them when the firing continued a few seconds later. A series of explosions put a stop to it suddenly and everyone paused and looked back the way they'd come. Muzzle flashes sparked everywhere and there was a flickering flame casting bizarre shadows.

Tarkington felt his soul ripping. Seconds passed. He gnashed his teeth and kept them moving. The heavy machine gun opened fire again, making them all look back again.

Stollman shook his head, "He's still in it. He's still hammering 'em."

Tarkington nodded, "Let's make it worth his while. Move out!"

25

Captain Nagato was furious over the loss of men during the frenzied and confusing night engagement. To make matters worse, they'd only found one dead enemy soldier. The body was shredded nearly beyond recognition, but Nagato assumed it was an American instead of an Australian since he wore strange mottled camouflage, which he hadn't encountered before.

The stalwart warrior never stopped firing the machine gun until grenades finally silenced him. He'd taken nearly twenty Imperial Army soldiers with him when it was all said and done. Until now, he wasn't impressed with the Americans. They'd had no trouble stopping their pathetic thrusts from the south. Some early reports even claimed they'd run away. But the shredded American soldier he'd watched being unceremoniously thrown into a shallow grave had fought with the valor and tenacity of a samurai. He hoped there weren't many more like him—these *Tark's Ticks.*

The rest of the saboteurs must have slipped away while this soldier sacrificed himself. This was another impressive and unexpected circumstance. Nagato wasn't as arrogant as some of his fellow officers when it came to respecting one's enemies. The west was weak; however, he'd seen incredible fighting spirit from the Australians, and now he'd seen something from the Americans too.

The night action had disrupted his men, but now they were back in the bunkers awaiting daylight. He wondered if the sabotage was meant to soften them up before an attack. Colonel Yamamoto felt the same way and ordered more men to the forward positions along with more ammunition. The newly arrived 81 mm mortars were standing by too, along with an influx of reinforcements from Rabaul.

If the Americans followed their usual tactics, they'd first shell them with their growing arsenal of big guns. They scored hits occasionally, but mostly the shelling did nothing except alert them that an attack was coming. At the first hint of artillery, the men would retreat to the safety of the bomb shelters and emerge unscathed in time to repulse whatever forces were arrayed against them.

Nagato was inside a forward machine gun bunker in proximity to where the night action occurred. The bunker the saboteurs had destroyed was behind him. In the grand scheme of things, losing it was of little consequence. Yes, men had died and the ensuing battle had been costly, but he figured they didn't intend to get into the firefight. They wanted to slip away unseen. Their intent was to keep them on edge. It was a tactic right out of his own playbook.

He'd ordered many men to certain death, having them hide as the Allies pushed past, then hit them from behind. They understood they were being sacrificed, but the psychological effect on the Americans was worth it. They never felt safe, no matter how far from the front lines they were. Now the Americans had done it to him.

He'd ordered silence concerning the macabre playing cards, but doubted it would work. Word of such things always got out, no matter how heavy-handed the orders were. Sensationalism was human nature, and soldiers were especially susceptible. He wondered how long it would be before he'd hear men whispering, *Tark's Ticks.*

The sky was just changing from dark to light when the familiar distant whomp and screech of incoming artillery filled the morning air. The enemy artillery fire had been directed toward the airfields over the past day and a half, but now they were arcing toward his lines. Yells of "Incoming," raced up and down the trench lines, and soldiers not occupying fortified bunkers scurried in orderly fashion to the many nearby bomb shelters.

Through the machine gun firing slits, Nagato scanned the shredded plantation trees to his front with binoculars. The ground shook but he wasn't concerned. Even a direct hit wouldn't destroy these bunkers. He'd seen firsthand proof of that fact.

The barrage lasted longer than normal, and by the time it lifted, it was full daylight. He listened to clods of mud and debris raining down upon the bunker roof, adding to their already superior camouflage. He reached for the radio handset, hoping the Allies hadn't gotten a lucky shot and shredded the phone line. He heard static and knew they hadn't. He was about to order the men back to the line when the ground shook with another, much larger explosion. It sounded and felt different from the artillery. It gave him pause.

The line clicked and went dead. The men manning the two machine guns looked over their shoulders at him. Nagato waved them off, "Watch for the enemy. I'll see what happened." They were veterans and had been fighting the Allies for months alongside Nagato. Without a word, they turned their emaciated faces back to the front, waiting for the inevitable.

Nagato pulled the steel door open and stepped into the trench. A soft breeze touched his cheek and he breathed in, relieved to be out of the stifling bunker, but concerned about the explosion. Bits of debris continued to rain down, but the dangerous chunks had long since landed.

Platoon Sergeant Okamoto was running toward him. He stopped in front of Nagato and straightened, speaking through heaving breaths, "A bomb hit Shelter Number 4. A direct hit. It's been completely destroyed. No survivors. Men from 4th Platoon, sir."

Nagato's temper flared and his jaw rippled as he gnashed his teeth. "I heard no more incoming artillery. The explosion happened after." Okamoto scowled, not understanding what his commander was getting at. Nagato seethed, "That was more of the saboteurs' work." He pointed, "Get word that we are short on men and need reinforcements. The explosion cut the phone line. Send a runner. Hurry!" Sergeant Okamoto took off and Nagato poked his head into the machine gun bunker he'd just left, "When you see the enemy, open fire."

"Hai!" the ranking man answered.

Nagato had his pistol out and was trotting along the trench line toward

Bomb Shelter Number 4. Men were streaming back into the lines, but not as many as normal. They gave him a wide berth, seeing his angry scowl. Nagato was a revered officer, but his temper—though rarely seen—was legendary, and it looked ready to explode.

It didn't take long to get to the bunker. It was obliterated. What had once been a secure, comfortable place to ride out a barrage was now a smoking crater. Massive segments of palm trees, which made up most of the basic construction, were pointing skyward as though a massive dragon had pushed its way through, scarring and searing them with fire as it passed. Bits of bloody cloth and dripping body parts were everywhere. It was impossible to know where one man began and another ended. They were intertwined like a goulash of carnage. There was no one alive.

The chattering of machine guns tore his eyes from the grisly sight. He turned to run back to the bunker but noticed something fluttering in the air, flitting down like an autumn leaf. He plucked it from the sky, noticing many more similar pieces of charred paper all around. The familiar crude death's head and the scrawled *Tark's Ticks* on the back left little doubt who was responsible. He crushed the card in his iron grip and ran toward the fighting, bent on killing every American he saw.

Upon their return, Tarkington reported to Captain Griffin, and although they'd lost a man, Griffin was happy with the results. He told them to take the next twenty-four hours off, and to get some food and a well-deserved rest. As Tarkington was turning to rejoin the men, Griffin said, "I'll need your after-action report, Sergeant. I'm putting Sergeant Bulkort in for a medal—Silver Star, at the least. Your words will go a long way for him."

They found an out-of-the-way section of jungle near the lapping ocean waves and tried to get some sleep. The constant din of gunfire, crashing mortars, and artillery was difficult to sleep through, not to mention the crushing guilt and sorrow that filled each of them. They didn't know for sure if Sergeant Bulkort were dead, but he hadn't returned, and just like the rest of them, he wouldn't let the Japanese take him alive. If by some miracle he *had* gotten away, he'd lost too much blood and wouldn't have been able to make it back without help.

The sounds of battle from the front were finally fading. The outcome of the attack was unclear from this far back. Yelling caught their attention. It sounded like Stollman. He'd wandered off an hour before and it sounded like he was arguing with someone. Winkleman stood and saw him holding a half empty bottle of whisky. An unfamiliar officer was haranguing him, his balled fists against his hips. Stollman stumbled along cursing unintelligibly.

Winkleman called, "Dammit. Stolly's mouthing off to an officer."

Tarkington didn't get up; he'd found a nice comfortable palm tree to lean against. "You and Vick go get him."

Vick got to his feet reluctantly and followed Winkleman, who bounded toward the confrontation. Winkleman got to Stollman just as he was slurring, "You listen to me. You little . . ."

Winkleman put his arm around him and interrupted, "That'll be all, Private." He yanked the bottle from his hand, "No more apple juice for you."

The officer, whose new uniform and relatively clean overall appearance marked him as a new arrival, shook his head, "Apple juice, my ass. That man's drunk and disorderly—in a combat zone, no less. I'm bringing him up on charges," he strained to see Winkleman's insignia through the caked mud, "Sergeant," he finished.

Winkleman pushed Stollman toward Vick who was just arriving. "Get him outta here," he whispered. Vick put his arm over Stollman's shoulder and guided him toward the others. Winkleman raised his voice, "No need for that, sir. We'll take care of him. He's fine, just needs some rest."

The officer shook his head—he would not let it go. "No, Sergeant. I want that man arrested. He's a poor example for the men."

Tarkington watched, wondering how Winkleman would handle things. Vick continued guiding Stollman toward the squad. Stollman tried to break away, reaching for the bottle, which Winkleman held behind his back. Vick easily kept him under wraps.

Winkleman brought the bottle from behind his back and held it up to the sun. The amber liquid sloshed and he nodded as he admired the label. "This is good stuff, Lieutenant. Care for a slug?"

The officer's expression turned from confusion to exasperation to anger, "No, I don't want a slug, Sergeant. Dammit, I want that man brought up on charges!"

Winkleman untwisted the lid, sniffed the liquor, then took a long pull, his Adam's apple gulping up and down. He brought the bottle down, gave an involuntary shiver, and wiped his mouth with the back of his hand. The alcohol burned as it scorched its way down his gullet and warmed his belly from the inside out. He shook his head and screwed the lid back on. "On second thought, you haven't earned a slug yet, sir."

The officer's mouth hung open, not knowing how to respond. He finally managed, "Wh—what did you say to me?"

"We lost a good man last night. Son of a bitch saved us all. We wouldn't be here if not for him." He pointed to the distant gunfire, "More men dying right now—good men. Men better'n you by a long shot." He took a few steps until he was in the officer's personal space. He breathed liquor onto him and pointed, "You're gonna be out there tomorrow, sir." He nodded grimly, "You're gonna be in the grinder—you may not make it. May lose a leg, an arm, an eye." He shrugged, "Who the hell knows?" The officer reeled back from the smell. "But until you've been there and *earned* a drink," he held up the bottle, sloshing the whisky, "don't you dare threaten my men with your penny-ante bullshit."

The officer hesitated for a moment, weighing his options. His eyes dropped and he took a step back. He was flustered, probably hadn't been spoken to that way his entire pampered life. He pointed toward Stollman who was still trying to break away from Vick's iron grip. In a much more subdued voice, he said, "You—you keep him under control." Now that he was ten paces away, he stiffened and faced Winkleman, who was still scowling like a tiger ready to pounce. "Understand, Sergeant?"

Winkleman grinned and saluted with the bottle, "Oh yes, sir. Understood." Sarcasm dripped with every word. When the officer was out of sight, Winkleman turned back toward the squad. They were grinning at him and he passed the bottle to Tarkington. "Asshat," Winkleman murmured, gesturing toward the officer.

Tarkington raised the bottle. "To Bull," he bellowed. "The only thing more lethal than his gas were his bombs!"

The men guffawed and Tarkington passed the bottle to Raker who raised it, "To Bull!" He grinned, "The snake charmer!" He took a drink and passed it to Henry.

He raised it, "To Bull! About as quiet as one too."

By the time the bottle got back around to Stollman, there was one slug left. He stared at the amber liquid. He swayed on his feet. The smile faded then returned and he raised the bottle overhead, "To Bull!" He grinned, "The man really loved to blow . . . " he let the pause linger before finally finishing, "shit up!" He poured the last gulp onto the mud and the men laughed in appreciation. As one, they raised their voices, "To Bull!"

The sabotage combined with the heavy artillery barrage gained the GIs a few more yards during the attack, but in the end, they were stopped cold. The overlapping withering machine gun fire combined with the unwelcome addition of the larger 81 mm mortars was deadly.

Three days passed since the attack, and Tarkington and Team Two were ordered forward and deployed in the middle ground separating the front from the rear. The sun beat down upon them mercilessly. The ground was still muddy, despite the heat, making the overall effect muggy.

Most of the overhead cover in Duropa Plantation had been knocked down, leaving no shade. The only respite from the heat was in the relatively untouched jungle, but it was 350 yards from the front line and no one wanted to abandon the ground they'd paid for so dearly. Men on the line withered in the sun. Many suffered from heat exhaustion and dehydration.

Time crept by. Tarkington tried to keep them busy, making sure they cleaned their weapons and shaved when possible. Many GIs in other units were scraggly messes. It wasn't something Tarkington felt passionate about, a scraggly-haired soldier could fire a weapon as well as a clean-cut soldier, but he felt better about himself when he was clean shaven, and if they had the time . . . why not?

He lay in a shallow hole beside Sergeant Winkleman getting the daily report, "We're doing okay, Tark. Our guys are used to this crap. Can't say that about the rest of the company though. I've seen at least six men carted out of here today with heat exhaustion. They're dehydrated—sick and hot at the same time. Can't keep the water down so they spiral out of control. I'd say they're at their wits' end."

Tarkington sighed and shook his head slowly, "I agree. If the Nips knew how thin we are, they'd push us outta here easily. But they won't attack. Least I don't think so. They're happy to sit back and kill us from the comfort of their bunkers."

"Think they'll send us out again? I mean on another raid?"

Tarkington shook his head, "There's scuttlebutt. A bunch of officers are being relieved and rotated out of here. Getting a new batch of top brass taking over—colonels and generals."

Winkleman wiped the sweat from his brow, "That's never good. They'll wanna prove themselves."

"Yep. With our blood."

"Least it's giving us a break."

Tarkington watched a puffy white cloud drift by, "They're promising to bring in armor. Real armor. Not those thin Bren Carriers that got obliterated the other day, but Stuarts."

Winkleman turned and looked at Tarkington, "We've heard that crap before on Luzon. You remember." He held up his hands as though illuminating a marquee outside a movie theater, "100-mile-long ship convoy bringing everything we need to stop the yellow tide." He shook his head and said bitterly, "I'll believe that when I see it."

"You've become quite the cynic, Wink."

Winkleman rubbed his chin, "You've told me that before." He let the silence linger, "Sometimes I wonder if my folks'll even recognize me. Assuming I make it outta here." He sighed, "Hard to imagine home. I mean, I can't even picture it. You know?"

Tarkington itched his crotch, "I think about the smells. The cut hay, how it smells after a rain—not like the rot here, but a summer rainstorm over the plains. That's how I see it—through the smells." He closed his eyes, "Mom's fresh bread. Steak on the grill after it's been soaking in her marinade all day."

Winkleman nodded and thought about it, "Fresh salmon just a mile from the sea. Bright as a new silver dollar. Not one of those inlanders, but fresh and clean—new. The sea smells different there. Here it smells like your nasty crotch, but out there? I dunno—just different. The trees after a rain. Pine trees—ponderosas and redwoods. You've gotta come out and see these trees, Tark. They're like nothing you've ever seen. I'm telling you, you wouldn't believe the *size* of these things."

Staff Sergeant Clanson poked his head over the edge of their hole. He looked as though he'd aged ten years since they'd first met him. "When you two are done holding hands and rubbing each other's crotches, Captain Griffin wants to meet with the NCOs in an hour."

Winkleman shook his head at the crass staff sergeant, "You're a real son of a bitch, you know that?"

Clanson smiled, showing off his chipped front teeth, compliments of a near-miss by a Japanese grenade. "You don't know the half of it, Sergeant."

Captain Griffin relayed the orders he'd received from the batch of new commanders. Tarkington was pleasantly surprised. Instead of the frontal assaults of the past, they were trying a new tactic, one in which he and his men were adept: sneaking in close and taking out individual bunkers one at a time.

More good news: the supply problem had ended. The rains stopped and new airfields had cropped up everywhere. Engineers quickly cut roads connecting the landed supplies to where they were needed. Food, ammunition, better radios and phones, along with fresh troops from Port Moresby and Australians from Milne Bay were pouring in daily.

At the end of the briefing, Griffin gave them the best news of all, "There're sacks of letters from stateside. Be sure to pick 'em up on your way out."

They hadn't seen consistent mail since leaving Australia. Each of the men got mail, including Henry, who'd insisted none of his kin could read, let alone write. He shared a letter from one of his sisters with Tarkington and they both laughed at the misspellings and cartoonish letters, but Tarkington hadn't seen his old friend this happy in a long time. Hearing from home reminded them why they were fighting in the first place.

There was a stack of letters addressed to Sergeant Bulkort. They were all from a woman bearing the same last name. It pained them knowing his wife would get the news of her husband's death any day now. Tarkington jotted down the return address and wrapped twine around the stack of letters. He'd send them back along with his own personal letter. He dreaded it, but she deserved to know what kind of man she'd married.

26

Along with the new equipment and supplies came an updated map of the Buna area. The maps combined with the newly arrived spotter planes, meant they didn't need to crawl forward to direct artillery strikes. The spotter planes would buzz lazily overhead, spot a target, and soon the shrieking of outgoing 105mm howitzer shells were slamming into enemy concentrations.

Long days passed and the Japanese lines were hit incessantly with artillery and air strikes. Sometimes the spotter planes were forced from the area as the skies overhead turned deadly and fighters tangled with one another.

The word finally came for another advance. But instead of a headlong rush, they moved cautiously, bounding forward while other units covered them. They were approaching the New Strip's eastern edge. More patrols were doing the same thing farther east toward the Duropa Plantation, but so far the day had been quiet.

Tarkington's squad was the farthest west and was approaching an area that was a known killing ground. Bunkers along the northern edge of the New Strip were a known entity and had been impervious to the artillery and air strikes. Tarkington wasn't interested in those. They were searching for a much closer bunker suspected to be somewhere nearby, tucked into the very southeastern corner of the strip.

The other two squads stopped while they continued forward. In their mottled camouflage and painted faces, they were nearly invisible as they slithered forward beneath the sweltering heat. When they were in position, Tarkington signaled Sergeant Clanson, crouched thirty yards away. He passed the word and two men got to their knees and unleashed quick bursts into the suspected area, then dropped onto their bellies.

Seconds later, the bunkers from across the strip opened fire, raking the area with lead. Tarkington and the others ignored it but watched the closer area, searching for the telltale wisp of smoke or sudden movement.

Raker saw it first, a thin strip of smoke emanating unnaturally from the jungle forty yards in front of them. "I see you," he seethed.

He pointed and the others saw it too. The proximity of the firing GIs was too much for the enemy gunners to resist and they'd given away their position. It surprised Tarkington how close they were, thinking they'd be farther back under the cover of the jungle. They were too close for heavy artillery, but the mortars should be able to knock them out or at least keep their heads down while they closed in and destroyed them. "Raker, put smoke on 'em," Tarkington ordered.

Raker nodded, pulling a smoke grenade from his pack. He had a good arm from his days playing high school baseball. He got to his knees and hurled it, then dove back down. The machine gun fire didn't shift, but continued hammering the other squad's position. White smoke billowed out, engulfing the small machine gun nest. A minute later, the sounds of mortar shells arcing through the air—called in by the circling spotter plane —exploded with bright flashes all around the nest.

Tarkington got into a crouch and moved forward. The others followed. They moved ten yards and dropped to their bellies. The agreed-upon six mortar shots had been accurate, but the stout bunker wasn't out of commission yet. They could hear the machine gun open fire and see the white smoke from inside mixing with the darker smoke from the mortars.

There was a slight defilade a few yards in front of them, which would give them cover from the bigger guns across the airstrip but also give them a lane to attack from. Tarkington signaled and they crawled forward until they were in the grassy depression.

Henry continued forward and poked his head over the top. He immediately dropped back down and pushed his way back into cover. He rolled to his side and signaled, "Enemy close." He tugged a grenade off his belt, pulled the pin, and tossed it over the low lip, then backed up farther. They all cringed when the grenade exploded. There was screaming, and Raker and Stollman ran past Henry and opened fire.

The rest of the team was up and following. Tarkington was stunned to see three dead Japanese infantrymen. They'd only been a few yards away and he hadn't seen them. If they had seen them first, they would've ruined their day. Their smoking bodies were full of holes from the grenade and the .30 caliber bullets—dead.

There was yelling from the bunker another fifteen yards away. No firing ports pointed their direction, so they advanced at their leisure, watching for anyone coming out the back door. The small door swung open suddenly and a soldier emerged. He didn't get two steps before they cut him down with multiple shots.

Raker reloaded and Stollman bounded forward, unharnessing a grenade. At the open back door, he calmly chucked the grenade inside and closed the door, as though putting the cat out for the night. He leaned away and held his hat. There was a "whump." The blast flung the door open and acrid smoke spilled out. No one emerged and Vick lunged past Stollman and unloaded his magazine into the dark interior, then took cover opposite of Stollman's position.

Stollman changed out magazines and went inside. Raker followed him in and he emerged a second later signaling there were no survivors. Stollman stayed inside and planted a timed-fuse bomb beneath the ammunition and came out a minute later. "We've got ten minutes," he growled.

Tarkington nodded and tossed another smoke grenade to Raker, "How's your arm feeling?"

Raker caught the smoke grenade and hefted it, "Never better, Tark."

"Hurl it toward the airstrip bunkers. You don't have to hit 'em, just signals our little friend overhead that we're leaving."

Raker nodded, "No problem." He put his carbine down, took a step back, and stepped into the throw. The grenade landed thirty yards in front of the bunkers and rolled another ten before erupting in red smoke.

"That'll do," Tarkington said. "Wait for the arty, then we hightail it outta here."

Two minutes passed. The bunkers shifted their fire toward them, but the proximity of their own bunker meant they fired too far left. The screeching sound of the 25-pounders firing from on high was the signal for them to leave. The shelling would do no damage; indeed, the 25-pounders weren't much more than a nuisance for the Japanese, but it kept their heads down, which is all they needed.

They low-crawled over the defilade and were soon back beside the other squads. They retreated together without drawing more enemy fire. When they were halfway home, there was an immense explosion. They turned to see the remains of the bunker blowing sky high.

Tarkington looked at Stollman, who was admiring his work with a broad smile. "Use enough TNT, Stolly?"

Stollman grinned, "That one was for Bull."

Nearly every day, squads probed all along the line from the Duropa Plantation all the way to the western edge of the New Strip. They'd identify a bunker or enemy position, call in artillery or mortars, then attack with grenades and rifles. They gained better positions as they moved up slowly.

Not every foray was successful, but they kept chipping away at the Japanese. Making their lives miserable for once. There were casualties, but nothing compared to the past month, and the men's morale skyrocketed. They finally felt like they were dishing out more than they were taking and it felt good.

During a rare break, Lt. Branson gathered the platoon 400 yards from the front and addressed them. It was night—concealing them from enemy aircraft.

"Men," he began, "things are looking up. You've probably noticed a contingent of fresh Australian troops filtering in on our right flank. They're taking over the 128th positions, which are shifting farther west. When it's all done, Baker will be on the battalion's right flank and on the Aussie's left flank. You've also no doubt noticed we're flush with food, ammunition, and men. There are fresh faces in the crowd and I hope you veterans will make them feel comfortable." Grumbling rippled through the ranks. The troops who'd seemed so green to Tarkington and the others were now veterans putting the newbies' feet to the fire.

Branson continued, "There have been breakthroughs north of us. As of yesterday, Buna Village is in Allied hands." There was a smattering of stunned voices and even some clapping. Buna Village wasn't Buna Mission —their initial objective—but it was an important stepping stone. Branson smiled and held up his hands for quiet, "Good news, yes. But it doesn't mean we're done here—far from it. The Japs still have formidable defenses all along our line, but capturing the village will keep them from being resupplied easily, which will make our jobs easier." He waited for the chatter to quiet down, then continued in a more serious tone. "A big operation's coming. I can't tell you the exact date, but know it's coming soon. Within days. It will be a massive combined push. We've been softening up the plantation, and command thinks they're ripe for the picking."

Tarkington scowled, having seen firsthand the array of well-built bunkers arrayed against them. He shook his head, leaned toward Henry, and whispered, "They expect us to take pillboxes with bayonets?"

Henry spit a stream of tobacco juice onto the ground, "Starting to strut like roosters."

Branson continued, "The fresh Australian troops combined with the howitzers, bombers, and armor will be enough to break through."

Winkleman leaned close, "Did he say armor? What armor? Haven't seen anything except those damned Bren Carriers rusting out there."

Tarkington shrugged, "Maybe that's why they're so confident. Armor'd go a long way in the terrain near the coast. Been saying it all along."

Winkleman agreed, "Been obvious for a while."

Henry nodded, "To us anyway."

Someone near the front stood up and asked, "Did you say armor, sir?" Tarkington saw it was Sergeant Clanson.

Branson lowered his voice as though he weren't supposed to have said that part. He nodded and grinned, "Yes. Australian armor has landed and it's heading our way, even as we speak. They offloaded two days ago and hid while their crews arrived and got oriented. They're moving at night so it's slow going, but they'll be here soon." He looked around, knowing he was giving away more than he was should to the rank and file, "They'll be leading the attack along the coast."

Tarkington slapped his knee, "I can't believe it. It's the first I've ever heard of an army rumor actually coming true."

Winkleman shook his head, "Well—like I said—I'll believe it when I *actually* see it."

Tarkington was woken from a fitful sleep by an unusual and unexpected mortar attack on the Japanese front line. The men had rotated to the rear, 400 yards from the farthest OP for the night. The big push was on for that morning, December 18th, but the artillery barrage wasn't supposed to start until 0600 hours and that was hours away. The Japanese hadn't tried anything for a while and Tarkington wondered if perhaps they were making a push and the mortars were trying to break it up. If that were the case, their timing couldn't have been worse. The Allied line was flush with troops ready to shove off for attack. The Japanese wouldn't get far.

A new sound from behind him made him sit up from his poncho. It was the unmistakable sound of churning motors and clanking tank treads. In the darkness, he couldn't see them, but the noise was overbearing as they clanked past. He yelled to Winkleman in the next hole, "There's your proof, Wink."

Winkleman yelled back, "I stand happily corrected. Hallelujah! Thought we were going to attack without them."

Raker yelled, "What's with the mortars? We going early?"

Tarkington shook his head, "I think they're covering the sound of the tanks moving into position."

Raker muttered to himself as he rolled over and pulled his poncho over his ears, "I'm going back to sleep then."

As the tanks continued churning up the ground, a few of the 25-pounders joined the mortars. The ground shook slightly and Tarkington didn't even try to sleep. It was too loud and the thought of attacking in a few hours had him keyed up. The Australians would push off at 0645, after the artillery barrage and after a bombing run by Army Air Corps A-20 bombers. The Air Corps had had no mis-drops since the initial disaster and their heavy 500-pound bombs wreaked havoc on the Japanese lines. Hopefully, it would stun the defenses long enough for the M3 Stuarts to get close and smash pillboxes and bunkers with their 37mm main guns.

Tarkington looked up at the stars. It was a beautiful night and promised to be a clear day for a successful bombing run. Normally, he didn't wander around at night for fear of a jumpy soldier firing on him, but there were soldiers wandering around everywhere, so he got up and walked through the Australian lines. He had his Thompson slung over his shoulder, having left his carbine in the foxhole.

The Australians were jovial and upbeat, eager for the coming combat in the way only green troops could be. Not everyone was excited though; there were many veterans among them who cleaned their rifles or slept.

As he passed a group of soldiers sitting around on discarded ammo boxes, one of them said, "Sergeant Tarkington. Is that you?"

Tarkington stopped and squinted into the low light. Lonny stepped forward smiling and Tarkington greeted him, "Lonny! Good to see you." He extended a hand and they shook. "What've you been up to? Figured you'd be back in Milne Bay by now."

Lonny shook his head, "I told you I wanted to fight. There's no fighting in Milne Bay. I helped with the port facilities at Porlock, did some road building too, even helped get the 25-pounders put together off the barges."

"You've been busy. Knew they'd find use for a talented engineer."

Lonny introduced him to the others sitting around staring at the American sergeant with the scar. "These are my blokes. The unit I was attached to before hitching along with you on the barge to Wanigela."

Tarkington nodded, "Seems like ages ago."

"It does. When they arrived in Oro, I couldn't believe it. It was fate. We're attacking in a few hours and I'll be in the thick of it."

Tarkington nodded but was scowling, "That you'll be. Surprised they'd risk an engineer in combat that way."

Lonny shrugged, "They're expecting the tanks might run into some of that marshy shit and may need us to put crossings together quickly." He beamed, "That'll be our job. But in the meantime, we'll get a shot at the Japs." There was a smattering of hurrahs and such.

Tarkington pointed over his shoulder, "The guys are that way a hundred yards or so. You should say hello if you get a chance."

Lonny beamed, "I've been telling these guys all about you fellas— driving 'em batty." He leaned in conspiratorially, "Don't think they believe most of it."

Tarkington sighed and looked the men over. They were staring at him as though he were straight off a movie screen. It made him feel uneasy. What if they did something stupid trying to live up to some false ideal? He wasn't one for lectures but couldn't help saying, "Look, fellas. Don't do anything stupid tomorrow. Keep your heads on a swivel, but keep 'em *down*."

It was Lonny's turn to scowl, "We're not children, Sergeant. We can fight."

Tarkington nodded, "Yeah, I know." He smiled and clapped Lonny on the shoulder, "Give 'em hell. We'll be on your left flank. Good luck."

At exactly 0600, the artillery barrage started. It was by far the largest strike to that point and the ground shook for a solid fifteen minutes as every available gun rained hell upon the Japanese front.

A flight of ten A20 bombers flying in low and fast followed a brief lull. They dropped their bombs in an east to west string of destruction. In the early morning light, the bomb flashes were brilliant and the massive upheaval of debris, dirt, and fire rivaled the beauty of the sunrise.

Right behind them, three waves of four Army Air Corps P-39 Airacobras strafed, and the sounds of their nose-mounted 37mm cannons combined with the two .50 caliber machine guns was like a buzz saw. Each group wheeled around twice more before flying off to their airbases carved from the jungles. It was an impressive show of power; it left the men in awe and Duropa Plantation a smoking ruin.

Four Stuart tank engines fired up, spewing white smoke from filthy tailpipes. There were three other Stuarts. Two would attack the west end of the New Strip, the third held in reserve. The tanks in front of the plantation lurched forward, supported by four companies of Australian infantry streaming behind.

Baker Company was the hinge point; they'd move a few hundred yards and hold the line, keeping the left flank free from Japanese counterattack. They moved forward slowly, keeping pace with the Australians. It felt good to be moving with armor support.

The first Japanese machine gun opened fire. The nearest Stuart lurched to a halt. The Australians and GIs alike dove for cover. The Stuart sparked as bullets zinged off it in every direction. The slow, inexorable top turret rotated slowly toward the spewing machine gun nest. The turret stopped and the barrel of the 37mm cannon lowered slightly, then fired. There was an unimpressive explosion, which jolted the bunker. The machine gun opened fire again. The Stuart gunner adjusted aim slightly higher and fired again. The shell entered the enemy gunner's firing slit and exploded inside. The machine gun chatter cut off. A cheer went up and the Stuart lurched forward, searching for a new target. The forward-facing .30 caliber machine guns spewed death as it slowly moved over fallen palms, crushing them beneath 30,000 pounds of steel.

They made steady progress. Each time a new pillbox came into range, the Stuarts methodically took them out one by one. The first smoldering pillbox was directly in front of Baker Company. GIs from First and Second Platoon stormed into the interconnecting trenches. The pops and pings from the M1s ended any resistance.

Tarkington's squad was back from the trenches a few yards, watching the GIs sweep through them with deadly efficiency. When it was their turn, they moved forward and slid into the trenches. Lieutenant Branson was there. He ordered men to move toward the New Strip using the trenches for cover. The large bunkers on the north side of the New Strip hadn't opened fire yet. They either were still reeling from the morning barrage or didn't know the bunkers across from them had been overrun. Either way, it allowed the GIs to make good, unimpeded progress.

GIs peeled off, exploring side trenches, and soon Tarkington's squad led the way north along the main trench line. The urgency from behind to keep moving made Tarkington nervous, but he continued moving, keeping his Thompson ready. He came to a turn and stopped. He heard voices— Japanese voices. He unclipped a grenade and hook-shot it around the corner, yelling, "Grenade out!"

There was a brief squawk of panic interrupted abruptly with a blast of shrapnel and fire. Tarkington remained crouched but lurched around the corner. He fired the Thompson point-blank into the writhing enemy soldiers at his feet, then walked the rounds into more soldiers standing stunned and reeling, knocking them backwards. "Reloading!" he yelled.

Stollman ran past him, careful to keep his balance as he weaved through the twisted bodies. His focus was on the trench unfolding in front of him. He wished he had his old BAR, but the quick-firing carbine was a nice lightweight alternative. It didn't have the stopping power of the Browning, but it was deadly enough.

The bunkers across the New Strip finally woke up, and the GIs dove into the bottom of the trench as a lethal buzz of bullets scythed overhead. Stollman kept his barrel aimed down the trench line. He was beyond the dead soldiers, but heard Vick and Raker cursing behind him, as they were forced to lie among the blood and gore.

Movement caught his eye and he watched a hissing grenade arcing toward him. He reacted instinctively, reaching up and catching it as though he were a shortstop making a play on a sharply hit line drive. For a sickening moment, he held the hissing bomb, then hurled it and ducked. The grenade blew a second later, sending shrapnel in every direction. He felt needles of fire lance into his back. He looked up in time to see the soldier who'd thrown it sitting down hard from the nearby blast. Their eyes met for an instant before Stollman emptied half his magazine into his chest. The Japanese remained sitting, but the life left his eyes and his head finally slumped forward.

The rest of the squad bounded past him. Vick stopped to look Stollman over. His back was wet with blood and smoked slightly. Vick placed a hand on his back, "Let me give it a look, buddy." Stollman tried to move but Vick held him down and yelled, "You're hit! Let me help, dammit!" He ripped the shirt the rest of the way off, exposing the wound to the dust and debris raining down.

Bits of smoldering, hissing shrapnel protruded from Stollman's fair skin. The adrenaline wore off enough for Stollman to feel the heat. He swatted desperately at his back, but Vick held him down, yanked the largest piece out, and flung it away. It burned his fingers and he cursed. Tarkington arrived and helped hold the bucking Stollman down. Vick used Stollman's torn shirt like an oven mitt to extract the next three burning chunks of metal.

Relief flooded through Stollman and he collapsed, suddenly exhausted. Vick dripped water over the wound, washing off most of the dirt, then spread sulfa powder generously and finally covered it with a bandage. Tarkington gave him a questioning look and Vick nodded, "He'll be alright. Probably won't be making catches like that one for a while though."

Tarkington shook his head, "Damndest thing I ever saw, Stolly. You play ball back home?"

Stollman shook his head and grimaced, "Nah. Got cut in the first round."

Tarkington guffawed, "They missed out on a true talent."

GIs flooded around the corner and soon the trench was overcrowded. The machine gun continued to hammer overhead. Sergeant Clanson scooted beside them and gave a concerned look at Stollman still lying on his stomach. Vick gave him a thumbs up and Clanson said, "Branson wants us to hold here. He's directing the howitzers onto those bunkers. If that doesn't work, he'll have one of the Stuarts veer off and pop their tops, but they're busy busting through so it might be up to us."

Tarkington asked, "Stuarts are busting through?"

Clanson grinned, "Yep. Armor was the key. They're hundreds of yards ahead of us now. Be through the plantation and probably all the way to the Cape by the end of the day."

Despite his protestations, stretcher bearers carted Stollman out of the area back along the trench line. The machine gun fire from across the New Strip tapered off to the occasional burst as the GIs waited for the artillery. To the northeast, the sounds of incessant battle, punctuated by the crash of the main tank guns, continued.

Finally, Branson yelled down the line, "Shots are on the way!"

They crouched lower and heard the freight train screeching of 105mm rounds overhead. The howitzers had been busy supplying covering fire all up and down the line and now it was their turn. The high angle and the longer fuses allowed for penetration before the shells exploded and the great geysers of dirt and flame were visible without having to look over the top of trench.

The enemy machine gun fire ceased as the Japanese cowered in their bunkers. Branson urged the GIs forward until they were at the end of the trench system where it butted up against the edge of the New Strip. The way was blocked with layered barbed wire. The only way through would be going over the top and across the open stretch of the airstrip.

One of the side trenches branching off from the main one ran horizontally west in front of the strip for fifty yards, and Branson had his heavy weapons .50 caliber machine gun crew set up there. Behind them, in another trench line, mortar crews were standing by to help cover the coming assault. They were flanked on either side by two .30 caliber machine guns.

The GIs were stacked up in the trench and Tarkington figured this must have been the way soldiers in the First World War felt—waiting to go over the top. The howitzers finally stopped their rain of fire and steel. The echoing booms only lasted seconds before the supporting machine guns opened fire, filling the void. The hollow thunks of smoke rounds joined them from the 60mm mortars.

Branson waited for the smoke, then yelled, "Go! Go! Go!"

GIs launched themselves out of the trench. Tarkington's squad was only a few rows back from the others, and when it was their turn, they sprinted over the top. The scene was chaotic. Smoke and debris drifted down and they could see the tops of Japanese soldiers' helmets across the strip in the trench line. The hammering of the .50 cal was comforting, and great chunks were splintering off the already beleaguered left bunker. It appeared the nearest bunker on the right had taken a direct hit from the howitzer. Through the wispy white smoke, it smoldered and burned.

They'd made it forty yards before the remaining bunker finally started firing on them. A swath of fire cut down three GIs. They skidded into the dirt on the airstrip. The smoke thickened, and soon the bunker was out of sight and the incoming fire lessened. The .50 cal and the accompanying .30 cals continued to rake the area, keeping enemy infantrymen pinned down.

The GIs sprinted, taking full advantage of the smoke and covering fire. Sooner than they thought possible, they were across the open ground and onto the northern edge of the airstrip. Tarkington slammed his back into the smoldering remains of the nearest bunker and the rest of the squad joined him, breathing hard. Other GIs dropped into the trenches connecting the two bunkers and small firefights erupted as they swept through the stunned Japanese. Within minutes, they were upon the second bunker. The supporting machine gun fire stopped and under cover from rifle fire, GIs moved along the blind side of the bunker and shoved grenades into the firing slits, making quick work of the men inside.

There was a moment of stunned silence as they realized they'd achieved what they'd been trying to achieve for the past month: taking the New Strip. It had happened so quickly and relatively easily that it didn't register as having happened.

Grins spread as men got their breath back, and soon they were laughing and slapping each other's backs. Their joy was short-lived when another set of bunkers fired on them from the western end of the Strip. They took cover in the trenches, but even that couldn't keep them from laughing.

27

Baker Company stayed on the line after taking the eastern edge of the New Strip. The bunkers on the western edge continued to harass them; however, the Japanese were being threatened from two sides now and couldn't cover the GIs from the east and the constant threat from the south.

Two of the eight M3 Stuarts had deployed with the 128th Battalion on the western edge and after the GIs took the eastern edge, they assaulted.

Tarkington and the squad watched the assault from their protected positions. The Stuarts fired on the bunkers, but they were dug too deep into the ditches and they couldn't seem to get their 37mm rounds on target. The Japanese rained 81mm mortar fire onto them and after twenty minutes, they forced the tanks to withdraw. One was smoking heavily from the engine compartment but made it out of harm's way.

Winkleman stated, "They shoulda waited till we pushed from here. Coulda put 'em in a pincer."

Tarkington said, "Need to hammer 'em with the howitzers again. Keep 'em up all night."

Henry nodded, "Doubt they'll get much sleep anyway after the beating they took today."

Vick poked his head over the lip and watched the dissipating smoke from the brief battle. "Reckon we'll be assaulting in the morning?" he asked.

Tarkington nodded and looked grim, "Probably. You hear anything about Stolly?"

Vick shook his head, "Nah. But he'll be fine. The wounds were superficial. That close to his spine I was worried, but all his parts worked when he left."

"That grenade woulda landed right in the middle of us," Raker said. "Helluva catch."

Lieutenant Branson came around the corner and hunkered beside Tarkington. His face was black with soot and mud, but his eyes were still shining blue with the high from their victory. He nodded at the cluster of soldiers. "We've got orders to hold here overnight." He pointed, "I've got the fifty cal over there and the Brownings over there in case the Nips try something." He pointed back over his shoulder, "The mortars are behind us. They'll be firing flares now and then to keep those bastards awake." He looked up at the sun blazing overhead. "Couple hours till dark. You men get some sleep while you can. Could be a long night."

Tarkington nodded and asked, "We assaulting them in the morning, sir?"

Branson shrugged, "Haven't heard anything yet but I doubt it." He grinned, "The Aussies broke through. They're past the plantation and pushing on Cape Endaiadere." The men shook their heads in disbelief. "Those tanks made all the difference. Casualties are light, although a Jap threw a Molotov cocktail onto one of them, but that's the only one they got. The other four are still pushing and reporting light resistance. Command's ecstatic. I expect they'll push all the way to Simemi Creek by tomorrow. Ground turns to marsh after that so they won't go any farther. Word is, they'll join us here and we'll roll over these assholes from two sides."

Winkleman grinned, "We've been saying 'armor' all along."

Branson nodded, "Better late than never, I guess." Before moving along to the next squad, he said, "Good job today. Get some food and rest. Like I said, gonna be a long night."

The night was black. No stars shone through the layer of clouds overhead. The night air was a few degrees cooler than the day; however, the mugginess factor was tenfold.

Beside the trenches, the GIs had dug shallow foxholes and spread out watching the western edge of the airstrip. Occasionally, the howitzers sent out a screaming 105mm shell and the 60mm mortars lit up the area with flares every hour. The Japanese were undoubtedly awake, but the constant harassment worked both ways. The GIs took turns on watch, but sleeping didn't come easily for the off-duty men and most were up and watching.

Henry was in the trench beside Tarkington peering over the edge. "They're coming tonight," he stated, his voice low and sure.

Tarkington looked him in the eye, "Your sixth sense?"

Henry spit out the long piece of grass he chewed on and nodded, "I'm sure of it."

Tarkington sighed, "I've got that feeling too. Sons a bitches love their damned counterattacks." He peered into the night, "Think they're trying to sneak on us?"

"Lot of ground to cover. I'd want to get close if I had to do it."

Tarkington got into a crouch, "I'm gonna find Branson." Henry just nodded and continued watching.

He found Branson with Third Squad's leader, Staff Sergeant Higgins. In the gloom, Tarkington could barely make out their faces, but he nodded in greeting. "I think the Nips are coming tonight, Lieutenant."

Branson sat up, "You've spotted them? Why didn't you use the radio?"

Tarkington held up a hand and shook his head. "I haven't seen them. It's just a feeling. Henry, my lead scout, is never wrong and I've never seen him so sure."

Branson's mouth twisted and he shrugged, "Well, we're ready. I can't fire on something that's not there, Sergeant."

"I'm not asking you to. We think they're gonna try to get close—sneak in on us. The flares have been going out like clockwork. Wouldn't hurt to alter the schedule a bit, see if we can catch them on the move."

Branson looked annoyed but finally nodded, "Guess it can't hurt." He looked at the glowing hands of his watch, "Top of the hour's coming in ten minutes. I'll tell 'em to send it on time, then send another fifteen minutes later."

Tarkington nodded, "That'll do. Thank you, sir."

The flare at the top of the hour lit up the airstrip with eerie shadows that moved as the flare drifted beneath the mini-parachute. The GIs strained to see anything that might be an enemy, but the area was clear. Word had passed that there'd be another flare in fifteen minutes and everyone was keyed up. Henry wasn't the only one with a feeling of approaching danger.

The darkness was complete and the time moved as slowly as quicksand. Finally, the flare went up. The field was doused with harsh white light. Enemy soldiers froze in their tracks in an instant of indecision. There looked to be hundreds of them only sixty yards away. Stunned GIs also froze trying to process what they were seeing. The Japanese reacted first. An inhuman yell went up and was joined with a hundred more crazed voices. They charged. Someone yelled, "Open fire!" and it broke the spell.

The .50 caliber's heavy thump was joined by the .30 caliber Brownings. The yellow tracer fire ripped into their ranks. GIs fired into the mass of humanity and the sound was one steady roar.

Henry fired twice into each target then moved calmly to the next. Japanese were falling in rows and the men behind them had to leap over their fallen comrades. Many got cut down mid-leap and were blown backwards, but more replaced them and they continued to push.

One mortar kept firing flares, but other tubes fired HE rounds and the blasts tore into them, leaving large swaths of carnage. Tarkington was on his knees, his Thompson tucked into his shoulder. He fired short bursts. He aimed low, walking the rounds up as the muzzle rose.

Some enemy soldiers fired from their hips but most simply charged, trying to close the gap and get in amongst the GIs. The .50 caliber stopped firing as they reloaded. The Brownings kept up their steady wall of lead and the Japanese continued to topple, but it was obvious they'd make it into their line.

Tarkington yelled, "Reloading!" His squad fired relentlessly and Japanese dropped like discarded rag dolls. He swapped magazines, letting the empty fall into the mud.

He rose up as Henry yelled, "Reloading!" A screaming enemy soldier charged only yards away, his gleaming bayonet aimed at Henry's back. Tarkington didn't aim; he squeezed the trigger and held onto the bucking Thompson. The heavy rounds slammed into the soldier, spinning his body away in a fountain of blood and shattered bone. Another was right behind him and Tarkington steadied his aim and shot him in the face.

Henry finished reloading and fired methodically, but his .30 caliber rounds didn't have the same effect, and the stricken enemies continued into the trench. He smacked the butt of his carbine into a mortally wounded soldier who continued to slash his bayonet. The sickening crunch of breaking skull was as loud as a rifle shot and the soldier fell at his feet, bleeding from his ears and eyes. Henry took a step back and stuck the barrel against the back of another soldier's head who'd stumbled on a comrade and was struggling to get up. The quick shot ended the struggle.

A Japanese officer launched himself at Henry, who didn't have time to use his carbine. It was knocked from his grip as the screaming officer slammed into him. Instinctively, he rolled with the momentum and the officer went flying off him and into the back wall. The enemy quickly righted himself and squared off with Henry, who was forced to turn his back on the front. The roar of Tarkington's Thompson, the incessant pings of M1 clips firing their last shots, and the popping of the carbines told him he was well covered.

The Japanese officer snarled, whipped a short sword from his belt, and lunged at Henry. Henry sidestepped and the overextended officer slipped on the blood and gore of his own soldier. Henry punched him in the face as he went by, knocking him senseless.

The officer fell on his face and Henry drew his hunting knife. The blade gleamed and he gripped the smooth leather handle. He dropped onto the enemy's back, using his own body weight to drive the blade into the officer's spine. He felt the sudden spasm and stiffness beneath him and he held on working the blade side to side.

The roar of the battle subsided. He withdrew the knife and got to his feet, searching for more enemy. But there were none. The flares lit up the grisly battlefield with white piercing light, which seemed to give the world a grayish, otherworldly hue. The machine guns raked back and forth one more time before falling into silence. The airstrip was littered with dead and wounded soldiers. Henry found his carbine wedged beneath the officer's body. He yanked, but the forward sights caught and he pulled, ripping the officer's sleeve and pulling torn flesh from the dead man's arm.

Tarkington put a hand on his shoulder, "You okay?" Henry couldn't hear the words through his ringing ears, but nodded at the concern in Tarkington's gaze. The shrieking of outgoing artillery fire cut through and he looked up, searching for the shells. Howitzer rounds lit up the far western field and great explosions erupted around the bunkers and walked forward across the airfield. The 60mm mortars methodically walked shells along the swath of prone enemy bodies back toward the bunkers. The lethal hail of 105mm shells and 60mm mortars met somewhere in the middle. It didn't last long, but when it was over, there was no one left alive on the airstrip.

Tarkington's voice was hoarse but he yelled, "Winkleman!"

Winkleman's voice came back low at first then with more gusto. "Sound off Tark's Ticks!"

It was slow coming but all of them checked in, their voices dry as desert sand. Tarkington collapsed into the bottom of the trench, clutching his smoking Thompson. Henry went to him quickly and kneeled beside him, "You—you okay, boss?"

Tarkington pushed his head against his weapon and nodded, then spoke low, "Yeah. I'm okay. I thought you'd had it, Henry. Thought you were dead for sure. I—I saw you go down but I couldn't help you, had too many still coming behind the one who tackled you."

Henry nodded. Then remembered something and held up a finger. He disappeared into the gloom and darkness of the trench and came up with the short sword. "He came at me with this."

He held it out and Tarkington took it. It was covered with blood and mud, but even in the low light he could see the fine craftsmanship. He nodded and held it out to Henry. "Looks like a good one."

Henry shook his head, "I've got my hunting knife. Swords are your thing."

Tarkington hefted it, feeling the weight and balance, "I have kinda missed having one on my hip."

Henry bent down and found the sheath still firmly attached to the officer's belt. He handed it to Tarkington, "He don't need it anymore."

Exhausted and stunned, the GIs got to work pushing the Japanese dead out of the trench. Soon there was a wall of bodies blocking their view of the airstrip. Flares continued overhead and there was rarely darkness. Harassing artillery fire along the attack route continued the rest of the night, discouraging any more attacks.

Winkleman put his back against the wall alongside the rest of the squad. Everyone was there except for Stollman. The clouds parted and the stars shone down upon them. No one spoke, far too exhausted. Shoulder to shoulder, they watched the stars.

Word came down the line—they were being relieved by Charlie Company. Two hours later, just as the sun was coming over the eastern horizon, they entered the rear. Instead of foxholes and sandbagged bunkers, there were canvas tents and Quonset huts. With the breakthrough, command felt secure and wasted no time getting comfortable.

Baker Company found their area upgraded as well. A barracks tent lined with cots greeted them. Soon the sounds of snoring men whose bodies had been pushed to their limits filled the space. The low din of artillery fire and the occasional burst of machine gun fire couldn't keep them from dropping into oblivion.

The heat eventually woke them. Tarkington sat on the side of the cot and rubbed the back of his neck. None of them had bothered cleaning up and there was dried blood and caked dirt covering every inch of his uniform. He imagined he must smell terrible, but his nose was incapable of noticing anymore. The rest of the squad was up too. A few other GIs from Baker were awake, but most of them were still asleep, sweat pouring off them in dirty rivulets.

The squad made their way out the door and headed for the medical tent. The large red cross gave it away. It looked like a bullseye for a Japanese Zero pilot.

Stollman was easy enough to find. They heard him before they saw him. His voice was raised as he berated a poor nurse as she tried to keep him in bed. She had dirty blonde hair that stuck out from beneath her sweat-streaked white nurse's hat. Stollman's unruly red hair was easy to spot.

Vick yelled, "Leave the poor girl alone, you old cad."

The nurse turned, startled at their unruly appearance. She quickly recovered, blew a piece of sweat-soaked hair out of her eyes, and asked, "You know this pain in the ass?"

They hadn't seen a white woman in months and they stared lustfully at her. Tarkington shook his head, snapping out of it first, "Matter of fact, we do, nurse. He giving you trouble?"

"From the get-go," she huffed.

Stollman couldn't keep the grin off his face, "See, I knew they'd come. These are the guys I was telling you about."

Winkleman's mouth hung open as he stared at the nurse. She walked straight up to him and pushed his mouth closed, "Drooling's not a good look for you, Sergeant."

Winkleman turned bright red, and the tips of his ears throbbed. They would've steamed if they were wet. She kept her eyes on him as she walked past and his eyes tracked her like a wild animal. The spot where she'd touched his chin still tingled.

The squad burst out laughing and Raker punched Winkleman's arm, "You might have a chance at that one, Wink." Winkleman tore his eyes off her backside and he couldn't form words.

Stollman shook his head, his face turning serious, "Jesus, you guys look like shit. That you I heard last night?"

Tarkington nodded, "Yeah. Japs charged us. Snuck in close and got in the trenches . . ." His voice faded as ugly images flashed by. "Lost six men from Baker." He pointed his thumb at Henry, "Thought we lost this jackass too."

Henry shrugged it off, "Not even close, really," he drawled.

Stollman's face hardened, "I knew it. I tried to get outta here last night. Just had a feeling they'd attack, but they strapped me to the damned bed. Took three of 'em." He lifted his chin toward two MPs standing near the entrance. One had a swollen nose and an ugly black eye.

Vick saw the unfortunate soldier, "Jesus, Stolly. You're wounded. I seem to remember you getting all over me about staying off my feet when I was wounded on Luzon."

"You were shot! I have a coupla scratches." Before anyone could respond, he pointed at the gurney next to his. A soldier lay wrapped nearly head to toe in white gauze. Bits of pink showed in spots as blood seeped through. "Not like him." Everyone stared at the unfortunate soldier. Stollman gulped hard, "It's—it's Lonny, Tark. That's Lonny." The air seemed to leave the room and Tarkington couldn't get a breath. "He came in yesterday, just after I did. I didn't know who it was till I saw the name on the chart. Asked around," he gulped again. "It's the same Lonny. Doc says he's burned bad. If he survives, he'll be . . . well, his own mother won't recognize him."

They released Stollman the next day. The doctor wanted him to stay longer, but he was such a pain in the ass; he thought it best to release him or the nurses would mutiny.

They carted Lonny off the same day in the back of a truck on his way to the airstrip at Oro Bay where a transport would take him and other critically wounded soldiers back to Australia. The squad was there to see him off, each man putting a hand on his unconscious body and wishing him well.

The ever-present sound of fighting continued, but Baker Company wasn't going back on the line for at least a week. The Australians had pushed all the way to Simemi Creek as expected. There was one bridge crossing the lazy, deep waters, and even if it could've supported the tank's weight, it was heavily defended. The tanks shifted back to the New Strip, and combined with the tanks from the west, made quick work of the faltering Japanese holding the western edge.

They called Tarkington to HQ. His men were fully rested and ready to get back into the fight. He wondered what Griffin had in store for them this time. Simemi Creek had stopped the Allied advance, and each time they tried to make a crossing, they were either stymied by the Japanese or the quicksand-laced swamps. He suspected they'd be involved somehow.

Captain Griffin welcomed him. Lieutenant Branson was there too and Tarkington acknowledged them both. Griffin got straight to the point, "Your squad's been ordered back to Port Moresby, Sergeant." Tarkington furrowed his brow and Griffin continued, "Just got word this morning. Now that we've broken through the plantation, Colonel Bradshaw wants you back."

Tarkington was conflicted, "But this fight's far from over, sir. I mean, aside from Buna Village and the plantation, there's a lot left to do."

Griffin glanced at Branson who had a slight grin on his face. Griffin said, "I thought you'd be pleased getting back to your home unit."

Tarkington looked at the floor then back up, "I don't like leaving things undone, sir."

Griffin nodded, "I can understand that. You're right. There's a lot of fighting left to do here, but Bradshaw wants you back and he got that straight from General Krueger. You'll leave in the morning. A truck'll take you to Popondetta Airfield and you'll be in Moresby for lunch."

Tarkington nodded, "Yes, sir." He looked at Branson then back to Griffin, "Is that all, sirs?"

Griffin lifted his chin, "You and your men have been a great asset to us here. I want you to pass that along to them. You've chewed the same ground as the 128th, and as far as we're concerned, you're a part of us and always will be. Baker Company especially." His voice lowered, "I've sent off the paperwork for Sergeant Bulkort's accommodation. He was a good man." Tarkington nodded his thanks and Griffin looked at Lt. Branson expectantly.

Branson nodded grimly, "They found his body, Sergeant. I mean Bulkort's body. He'll be sent back to the states along with his medal. He was buried close to where the action happened that night." He swallowed, "Just thought you'd like to know. So there's no lingering doubt—he's gone."

The squad surrounded the drab wooden box holding the remains of Sergeant Dwayne Bulkort. No one spoke, just lowered their heads and silently wished him well on whatever the next phase held. Tarkington put his calloused, deeply tanned hand on the box. The others did the same. The truck idled behind them, waiting to take the squad to the airfield. The driver was antsy to leave before it got too hot. He leaned against the driver's side door and looked away, feeling he was eavesdropping on something he had no business watching. Their gear was already loaded and ready to go.

Stollman had his shirt loosely draped over his shoulders, keeping it from scraping the bandages clinging to his back. He nodded and uttered, "Goodbye, big fella. You'll be missed, but at least your suffering's over." He looked at the others, his gaze softening, "You were one of us, Bull and always will be." There were nods and murmurs all around.

Tarkington looked at the men he'd been through so much with. He owed each of them his life—many times over. Any one of them could've ended up in that box. The thought was sobering, and he silently hoped he'd pass before he had to watch any of them die.

He growled, "Let's get on with it, Ticks." They helped one another into the back of the truck and Winkleman thumped the side. The truck lurched into gear and bounced along the jungle road. No one looked back.

AFTERWORD

The Alamo Scouts were a highly effective reconnaissance force that performed more than 150 combat missions during WWII. They are the true precursors to Special Forces but didn't get that recognition until the 1980s.

They didn't start out the way I have depicted in the book. As far as I know, there weren't any "direct action" Alamo Scout units, nor were there any early test units. I also have them forming in 1942, but in reality they formed in 1943. What can I say? It's fiction.

I hope you enjoyed the book and if you're so inclined, leave a review.

DARK VALLEY
Tark's Ticks #5

Some missions are FUBAR from the very beginning.

Tarkington and his men are tasked with a long-range reconnaissance mission deep behind enemy lines. But when their C-47 is shot down, Tark's team must make the perilous trek through the jungle to a besieged Wau airfield. The airfield is vital to both the Allies and the Japanese, and soon Tarkington and his men are embroiled in its defense. To make matters worse, an American airman has been captured by the nearby Japanese forces.

Can Tark's Ticks defend the airfield and rescue the downed aviator? Or will a hostile jungle and determined enemy prove to be too much?

Get your copy today at
severnriverbooks.com/series/tarks-ticks-wwii-novels

ABOUT THE AUTHOR

Chris Glatte graduated from the University of Oregon with a BA in English Literature and worked as a river guide/kayak instructor for a decade before training as an Echocardiographer. He worked in the medical field for over 20 years, and now writes full time. Chris is the author of multiple historical fiction thriller series, including A Time to Serve and Tark's Ticks, a set of popular WWII novels. He lives in Southern Oregon with his wife, two boys, and ever-present Labrador, Hoover. When he's not writing or reading, Chris can be found playing in the outdoors—usually on a river or mountain.

From Chris:

I respond to all email correspondence.
Drop me a line, I'd love to hear from you!
chrisglatte@severnriverbooks.com

Sign up for Chris Glatte's reader list at
severnriverbooks.com/authors/chris-glatte